WONDERFUL

First published in Great Britain in 2025 by
Archetype Books.

A CIP record of this book is available from the British Library.

ISBN 978-1-7395593-1-1

Set in Baskerville, 8.5/13pt
Cover photography GM Paniz, Unsplash

Archetype Books

archetypebooks.net
info@archetypebooks.net
f: @ArchetypeBooksLtd
I: archetypebooks

PEACHY WONDERFUL

Sophie Holland

Archetype Books

For Mat

And to the memory of my dad, Barry
I could not have chosen better

PART ONE

This actually happened
2004

The satnav says twelve minutes. Bea pulls up at a T-junction. In the field ahead, a clump of sheep stares at her over the hedge. She adjusts the mirror and a breeze through the open window flutters the dark trim of her pale yellow sleeve. Clem, beside her in the passenger seat, has given this outfit the thumbs up. But does she look like a daffodil, or – worse – a bee?

The Devon hills roll past. Countryside is not her natural habitat and, cresting another blind bend, she slows to a crawl, pulling her sunglasses down against the bright cloud.

'Are you *sure* Frisbee will be alright?' Clem asks, badges clicking on her T-shirt. They almost brought the ancient guinea pig with them, since every parting could be the last. Bea had finally convinced Clem that Gavin would stroke and fuss over it when he went to the house to do the feeding.

'Your dad will tell him jokes,' Bea says. Though now she's wondering if they should have brought Frisbee along after all. She hasn't seen her parents or Lonnie or Andrew in the two years since she and Gavin separated, and suddenly she and Clem, just the two of them, seem flimsy out in the open.

Is this family weekend another attempt by her father to win Bea over? *Can* she be won over? Her face feels hot. She catches her reflection: round sunglasses, windblown hair – the adult version. *Good.* Surely she and Dad can get through two days.

She grips the wheel. The bones in her hands stand up, knuckle to wrist. A picture flashes through her mind of her own skeleton, like the one that hangs in the back of her science class. Its thigh bones kick up a can-can when the year nines flick them with a ruler. The thought makes Bea smile. She loosens her hold and her hands return to the living.

Eight minutes.

'Is the pool *just for us*?' Clem asks. 'Is there a diving board?'

'Yep, just for us.' Bea took the online tour. The house is palatial: brass bedsteads, cream rugs all over, dark wood floorboards. A holiday home for a glossy, carefree family. Not this one.

Moira checks the map on her lap. They really are far from home now, and the Friday traffic's not so bad after all. She's just not sure about all this *fuss*. They've never made a thing of anniversaries before; a card and a kiss suited them both fine. It was Ted who insisted on this ruby wedding weekend, and he expects too much. His humming says so.

A lorry hurtles past in the oncoming lane and the car shudders. The roads are narrowing, the hedges getting higher. Clem will be taller. What is she now, eight? And Andrew's son, lovely Tom, the first grandchild, is ten. It will be nice for the cousins to see each other. Moira thinks of her grandchildren as a bonus – a marvellous going-home present at the end of a tiring party.

Birds flit across the windscreen between hedges.

'Slow down,' she says, and Ted does. Up high, Moira spots a hunter against the brightening sky, wings quivering to keep still. Ted follows her gaze, swerves, straightens up.

'Sparrowhawk,' she says accusingly. 'Or kestrel. Watch out small birds and voles.'

'A lot of effort,' Ted says, 'just to hold still.'

'It's a good skill,' Moira muses, 'my mother used to do it.'

'Dylis? Flap?'

'I mean hold still. At key moments.'

'I'm better in motion,' Ted says.

Moira turns the map over and traces her finger along the black vein of a road that will lead to the house. What will they all *do*? Not swimming, not her anyway, it's not warm enough. And not Ted either, water's not his strong suit. She should have brought some packs of cards. With luck, there'll be some, or games, or a big puzzle. Ted won't have thought beyond the fancy place. She should have talked him out of it and got him to book a little cottage, just the two of them.

'Gavin won't be there you know,' she says.

'I know,' he says, throwing her a confused look. 'They're getting a divorce. I know that.' They drive on in silence for a while. Ahead, a camper van rises and dips like peek-a-boo, cows graze in peppered sunlight. Ted glances at the map on her lap.

'Wait till they all see it,' he says in a dreamy voice. He pats Moira's knee and the map crackles.

Ted stands on the timber deck with his hands on his hips, surveying the sky – widening stretches of blue – lucky, for September. It matches his sweatshirt, new for the trip, upon which a badge was pinned by Clem on arrival: "Oldie but Goodie" with a winking smiley face. Tom shoots past on the grass peeling off his T-shirt, ribs jutting from his milky torso.

'Coming in, Grandpa?'

'In a while,' Ted says. He won't. With his own children he stuck to shallow ends of pools, in the sea only up to his knees. Clem follows Tom in a flash of flesh and swimsuit. They jump in and smash the glistening blue pane, white spray fizzes around them. How cracking to be young! Though Ted isn't one to wish himself back in time. In fact, he might just be coming into his own. Some days he feels something like ease, if he dares to call it that. While his knees and hips grow creakier, at the top end there's a lifting away.

Through the French doors, he watches Moira and the girls move around in the kitchen. His daughters: unfathomable Bea and big-hearted Lonnie. Ted pats the badge from Clem on his chest. Lonnie had read it out loud, laughing, as she planted a kiss on his cheek. Bea just stood there, even after he complimented her blouse. Her greeting was a stiff hug. But Ted will fix this – the weekend will fix it.

He has a good fists-in-the-air stretch. What a place! The

showstopper he had hoped for, and a great deal, just out of season. Crunchy gravel drive, pillared entrance, sash windows, classy slate roof – pristine, not a chip. A recent refurb, he'd guess. Modern but not gimmicky, rooms intact, none of this open-plan nonsense. A smooth lawn sweeps around the front of the deck. Ted lets out a long sigh. From the pool there's a loud shout. He turns to give his grandchildren a wave, that they don't see. Forty years of marriage, three children, two grandchildren and here they all are. Champion.

The three Starling women gape at the kitchen. Bea notices the half-open mouths of her mother and sister, and closes her own.

'Wow,' they all say, uneasily, from where they stand at one end of the table – a huge slab of dark oak flanked with high-backed chairs. At the other end is a gleaming, cavernous sink. Behind them is a vast bay with a window seat and fat peach cushions. Double doors open out onto a wooden deck.

'Well,' Moira says, half-question, half-statement.

'In case we forget where we are,' Lonnie nods at a wide, framed painting of sand, sea, and sky above the steps to the entrance hall.

'I've got the same in my room,' Bea says, 'a bit later in the day, the sky's more pink.'

'*And* in the front room.' Lonnie rolls her eyes. 'Jeez, we're at the coast, we get it.' Then she looks tentatively at Bea. 'Did Gavin mind not coming?'

Bea sighs. She could tell them Gavin's fine, only not living with her anymore, but they would want details, which Bea doesn't intend to spill. Her resentment has petered out. He's proving to be an OK dad, good with money to spoil Clem with. In the early days, Lonnie had got along well with Gavin, but then Lonnie gets along well with everyone. She's got that bit of Bea's favourite poem licked: *As far as possible, without surrender, be on good terms with all persons.*

It's a wonder to Bea they share all the same genes.

'It's been two years, Lon,' she says.

'You can see the actual sea from the top bathroom,' their mother says brightly.

'I can't,' Lonnie says with a grin, on her tiptoes, craning her neck. Lonnie's smallness and curviness always take Bea by surprise – she's the odd one out next to Bea and Moira. It should be Bea who's the odd one out; it's how she feels.

'I could give you a piggy-back,' Bea says. Lonnie puts out her tongue and, to Bea's surprise, a tiny silver stud is balanced on the pink flesh. That wasn't there last time (though when was that?). Lonnie's hair is new too, auburn this time. With her green eyes, it might be her best combo yet. As a teenager, Lonnie dyed her hair bright pink, like a sweet. Sweet Lonnie, twelve years younger; Bea can never get over her sister being a woman. Where did Lonnie the girl go?

'What about this, eh?' Ted flings open the double doors and stands there with his arms wide, as though welcoming them, sleeves rolled up, his freckly forearms catching the light. He hesitates, and Bea watches some flicker of doubt cross his face; his open arms seem to plead, and his smile becomes fixed. In his uncertainty he looks younger, then suddenly older, his thinning hair is almost completely grey. Then he's in motion again. He claps his hands and rubs them together as he walks around the table, nodding eagerly.

'Smashing, Dad,' Lonnie says. At this, Ted relaxes, beams at her, skips lopsided up the steps and off for another tour.

'He's been really looking forward to this,' Moira says, looking between Bea and Lonnie, then back to Bea, who widens her eyes as Clem might do. *Not my problem.*

Lonnie and Moira open cupboards, unpack food bags. Moira just passed her first test in Beginners' French, Lonnie's working on the set for a modern remake of *The Crucible*. Bea sits on a peach cushion at the window and watches Clem fling herself into the water, doubtful about the remake of her life:

no longer married, teaching biology instead of chasing a cure for cancer. There should be a word for a family thrown together at long intervals, like shedding your skin then trying to squeeze back into it, but it's too loose or too tight, no longer a fit. There's definitely a word for the shedding. Bea can't remember it.

Tom skids through the double doors, dripping. Bea thinks of a pale daddy-long-legs; he's less sturdy than his cousin.

'Clem's gonna teach me to backflip!'

'You be careful,' Moira says.

'You be reckless,' Bea says and cuts off her mother's protest. 'Flick of the legs, right?' she says to Tom.

'Can *you* do one?' he asks, incredulous.

'The younger version of me could,' Bea says. She would love to reinhabit the version of ten years ago: single, working in the biotech lab, planning for a Masters, not a child. Her current life is the one she'd like to shed. That's it. 'Desquamation,' she announces. They all stare at her blankly. 'Shedding the outmost layer of skin.'

'Thanks, Miss,' Lonnie says.

Tom shivers – at the thought of this perhaps, or with actual cold – and gets an idea. 'If I do it – if I make the flip, then *you* have to do one.' His wet face is so serious Bea almost laughs.

'You're on,' she says. She offers her hand and finds herself looking at her own reflection. How had she forgotten she and her nephew share the same eyes? They grin like conspirators and shake on it.

Doigdoigdoigdoig-domp. The sound of the diving board as Tom jumps and jumps, his back to the pool, then stops the board with bended knees. Moira watches from the kitchen, and hears Andrew shout 'Go for it!' and Tom say something back. She's not seen her son and his wife yet, Ted took them both, Andrew and Lisa, straight off for a walkabout. Moira hurries up the steps, but stops still in the wide entrance hall as she did when they first arrived. She turns a slow circle. A great long sofa in the sitting room, the staircase with thick curved bannister, solid kitchen table: *space*, all around you, in every room. It brings back the farmhouse.

Moira was seven during the final wave of evacuations; a late, snap decision by their mother, Dilys, to get her and David away from London and the buzz bombs. Dilys was supposed to join them and never did. Moira wants to phone David and describe this place to him.

From outside, Andrew and Ted are giving a countdown. None of this would be happening if Moira and her brother had not gone to Duckworth Farm so long ago. The dark hallway, Buffalo the dog, the long kitchen with cold tiles – all of these open up in her mind. *All of you* she thinks, and it brings rare tears to her eyes. When Moira opens the front door she almost runs into Andrew and Lisa. She pulls them to her, both at once.

Later that evening, with lit candles, the kitchen glows red and gold like Christmas, and smells of Italy where none of them have been.

Bea presses at the annoying dimmer switch. The room flares bright and she twists and lets go just above dim. Lonnie and Moira serve up bolognese and garlic bread, the kids are pool-weary, the men have put on shirts, Bea pours the wine. From throne-like chairs, they all compare rooms. In their ensuite, Andrew and Lisa have a bath with curly legs *and* a shower. Lonnie's four-poster bed has slim velvet curtains down the sides.

'Like bars, or ropes,' she says, wrinkling her nose, 'it's kind of kinky.' Bea almost launches into who her sister might tie up, then thinks better of it. The kids wolf their food and disappear to the TV room, leaving a gap at the table. Bea has the urge to call them back; she'd like Clem on her lap as a shield, even though she's too big. Head of the table, Ted talks loft conversions while Andrew listens, patient, attentive. Growing up, Bea found her brother wet, lacking in opinions; as an adult this turned out to be generosity. Ted is justifying his costs; Andrew does the accounts.

'The extra beams are non-negotiable,' Ted holds up a finger to make his point. 'I'm taking no chances,' he says gravely.

'Everyone's safe, Dad,' Andrew pats his father's shoulder. 'It's not going to fall down.'

Ted winces, then nods like Eeyore. 'That's the idea.' When he looks up he tries to catch her eye, and Bea pretends not to notice. She talks about school to Lisa, who laughs at her impression of Miss Chowdra. Opposite her, Lonnie describes the play with a lot of hand movements.

'It's a witch hunt, everyone guilty until proven innocent.' She double-taps her heart. 'It's intense.'

'How does it end?' Moira asks. A typical Mum question, but a good one. Lonnie has to think.

'John Proctor dies, it's pretty sad,' she waves a hand. 'The set is more about the beginning, setting the mood.'

'Oh, well.' Moira says. Bea can see her mother isn't satisfied. 'And what's the mood?'

'Stripping back,' Lonnie leans forward, 'right to the emotional bones.'

'Oh, well,' Moira says again. Bea wants to laugh, then a familiar squirming starts in her belly. She read the play at school – doesn't some illicit sex get revealed? *Christ*. Dad will go weird. *Your family remind you who you are*, she read it somewhere recently. No, they remind you who *they think* you are, and you get stuck there. The candles flicker and the walls appear to twitch. She takes a gulp of wine, watches her sister and envies her being twelve years younger.

Ting ting. Andrew taps his glass and gets to his feet. Is he going to perform a magic trick? No, that's Bea getting him stuck as a teenager. Touché, she thinks grimly. Long face, thick eyebrows, ironed shirt, Andrew looks to Bea like a proper grown-up. She needs to go easy on the wine – no repeats of Andrew's wedding.

Bea shudders at the memory and sinks down in her chair. Tom and Clem appear at the top of the steps. Bea waves Clem over, but she shakes her head and stays with her cousin.

'Um. To Mum and Dad,' Andrew says. 'Congratulations!' He sits down quickly, red-faced. Bea feels a rush of affection for him. They all reach for their glasses. Ted stands. He's shorter, and stocky compared to Andrew, his jaw square. Bea feels her own jaw tighten. *Be a grown-up.*

'Forty years ago, I was at the edge of the dance floor, and with the best luck—'

'Mum flew into your arms,' Lonnie and Andrew say together.

Lonnie groans. 'Dad, we know this! Someone called Bert barged her—'

He shushes her with a hand. 'But it's *true*,' he looks at each of his children in turn as he continues. 'Some stories are just stories, but this one actually *happened*.' He meets Bea's eyes. Before she can decide what look to give him, he moves on to Lonnie, winks. 'And it's a good one – the best. There I stood, Duke Ellington swinging the band, and Moira literally flew into my arms.' He smiles at the memory, and closes his arms in front of him, catching her again. 'And somehow, through better and worse,' he pauses, and for a horrible moment Bea thinks he's going to list the details, 'I've held onto her these forty years.' Ted looks at his wife with such tenderness that Bea finds she has to look away. The feeling is growing inside her as she sits here among them. It's not the usual defiant fire and energy, tonight it's a germ: a solid microbe, malignant.

'To family,' Ted says with a thick voice, 'and to the *future*.' He sweeps his glass in a circle to include them all. Moira smiles at him and lifts her glass bashfully to the group.

'To all of you,' she says, 'thank you for coming.'

'To the Rubies,' Lonnie says.

'To backflips,' Bea says with effort. The kids laugh loudly from the steps, Tom claps. Around the table, they raise their glasses and tip them back.

*

Day two, and the four women have the sun loungers arranged on the far side of the pool. Bea took an early, unsatisfying swim, five strokes to a length, stymied just as she gathered momentum. It's not quite sun lounger weather, gusty but bright, tipping towards autumn. Bea squints at the whitewash, she left her sunglasses upstairs. The deck, tagged onto the end of the house, has the look of a lolling tongue.

'Ted's been working on a big house like this,' Moira says, 'they took out all the walls.' Her dusky pink polo neck peeks out from her coat. Always neat, Bea thinks. They're all fully clothed apart from Lisa, who has on a chiffony robe over bare, crossed ankles, her fuchsia toenails like delicate fruit.

Bea shivers. 'Will we do a cliff walk?' she says. 'Will we leave here at all?' When no one answers, she asks, 'Is Dad still planning a refurb of Granny Dil's house?' The little house is in Lower Ashton village, where Moira grew up. Where Uncle David still lives.

'I don't think David would appreciate any bashing around,' Moira says. 'It's not really a house, is it,' she looks around for agreement, 'without *rooms*.'

'Definitions,' Lonnie says, twirling her hair around her finger in a way that makes Bea think of Clem. 'Is a play only a play if it has acts?'

'If I had a wetsuit I'd go in the sea,' Bea says.

'I've never been to a real play,' Moira says, 'only a pantomime.'

'Easily fixed,' Lonnie says, smiling. 'We'll go. I'll get us some VIP tickets. We'll dress up.'

'A house is just a building,' Lisa says, hugging her knees, 'it's the *people* that make it a home.'

'We might have a funeral when we get home,' Bea says, and the other three look at her. 'Frisbee,' she shrugs. 'You never know.' Her dissension is like a switch that flicks to sabotage. What's alarming to Bea is that she can't seem to control it. She could try harder to stay in her adult self, but with her family it seems impossible. She should have stayed away.

'What was Granny Dil like?'

'And how did she *die*?' Clem and Tom have come to find Bea, alone on the deck, for a straight answer. 'She's an angel in heaven' Moira will have told them, or similar. Goofy Tom, with Bea's own eyes, Clem all innocence and freckles, hungry for gory details. If Granny Dil were here, all would be well. Bea knows this as surely as she knows the stratum corneum is the outermost layer of the epidermis. If only she had lived a few more years, three or four. Ten, fifteen.

'Lung cancer,' Bea says. 'There was a lot of coughing.' Then she adds, 'I wish you'd both known her.' The words are so true they choke her.

'Dad gave me a pack of cards that used to be hers,' Tom says, 'with one missing. Eight of hearts. She drew on the hearts, around the joker, but she started too big and they get smaller at the bottom.' Bea pictures the shrinking hearts, Granny inking them onto the card in her bony hand with all the rings. She clears her throat.

'She was really funny,' Bea says, 'you two would have liked her a lot.' She feels an overwhelming need to make this crystal clear. 'And she would have got a big kick out of both of you.' It's an outrage she left Bea alone with the rest of them. Preposterous.

'What does cancer *do*?' Clem asks. Maybe her daughter will be the scientist.

'The cells keep on dividing,' Bea says. 'They don't know when to stop. They grow into a big lump. It comes down to faulty molecules. A protein, p53 for example.' Bea sighs. 'Bigger and bigger. And did she stop smoking?' She shakes her head, her resentment growing. 'Nope.' *How could she not have tried harder to stay a bit longer*? 'A lot of coughing. Phlegm for breakfast, lunch and dinner.'

'OK, OK,' Tom says, unsure now.

'She became thin as a skeleton,' Bea says. 'She was in a coma at the end. I talked to her but I can't be sure she heard.'

'Were you with her when she *died*?' Clem asks, half-appalled, half-thrilled.

Bea had been with her. She had sat at the bedside and poured herself out. She told Granny Dil everything, because it was the last chance. Never before or since has she spilled herself in such a way.

She looks into her daughter's face, death nowhere near either of them.

'I was,' she says.

From the sidelines, Ted watches Tom and Clem chortle and wriggle on the rug in the sitting room. The afternoon game of charades was their idea. Above their heads, the chandelier glints slender daggers. Wind-blasted from the cliff walk, the adults loll in the furniture: Andrew and Moira on the small sofa, Bea and Lonnie on the big one with space for the kids, Lisa on the fat leather beanbag. Ted was last into the room, so he's got the stiff-backed armchair. Bolt upright, he feels like a judge. A large painting fills the wall opposite – strips of primary colours make a beach scene. One of the kids could have done it, and better. The house seems to have changed overnight: the rooms are too big, sofas stranded in the middle of the floor instead of nestled against walls. But look at his grandchildren: golden, bursting with promise.

'Do the faces, Tom,' Ted says with a wink.

'Yeah, do the faces,' Lonnie joins, 'which one was first?'

'Worry,' Andrew and Lisa say together, smiling at their son. They all begin what Ted likes to think of as a family tradition. Each with their own interpretation, they pull their mouths, their eyebrows into the four expressions, in order. One: wrinkled confusion; two: knitted brow fury; three: wide-eyed terror; four: beaming joy. Except Bea, whose face doesn't move, and Tom, who tries to scowl at them all but ends up grinning, his teeth too big for his mouth. He can be teased now. For years no one was allowed to mention his star status as a pin-up toddler, advertising vitamins. 'Head-hunted from the sandpit,' the story goes.

'Grandpa's turn!' Clem pulls Ted from the armchair, blocking his view of Bea's strained smile. Tom cups his hand and whispers hot breath in Ted's ear. He needs two repetitions. Tom must have got *Dances with Wolves* from Andrew, he used to love big hero films. So does Ted.

'Let the dog see the rabbit,' he says under his breath.

'You can't talk!' his grandchildren cry, falling back on the sofa.

Ted mimes the camera, holds up three fingers and feels tremendously pleased with himself. He starts jiving.

'*High School Musical*?' Lisa puts in, '*Grease*?'

'Oh well done,' Moira says. Ted shakes his head, and gallops round the rug, baring his teeth.

'*Incredible Hulk*,' Andrew shouts.

'That's two words,' Ted says.

'You *can't talk*!' Clem shrieks, beside herself.

'*Frankenstein*.' That's Bea, she looks impassive. He now understands Moira's warning on the way here – getting along with Gavin these last eight years had convinced Ted he was getting along with Bea. Ted stands up straight; this is harder than it looks. Then he gets an idea and rubs his hands: they'll like this. He leans back and draws an imaginary bow, closes one eye, and aims at the chandelier. He sees Bea's eyes widen but he's caught in the drama.

'*Robin Hood Prince of Thieves*?' Moira says. 'Too many words.'

'Is it that caravan holiday?' Lisa says with a cheeky smile.

What? Ted lowers his bow, loosely keeping the pose. *Not that*.

'It's Bea!' Tom shouts before Ted can think of another mime. 'She shot Grandpa!' A slither of ice slides straight through the centre of Ted. This is exactly what he wanted to avoid.

'No way!' Clem looks from her mum back to Tom, exhilarated.

Bea stares into her lap. Andrew's face is trained on Bea for her reaction. Lisa chews her lip. Lonnie rolls her eyes. Moira looks to the chandelier for help. If Ted could still make it into a joke, he would.

'She did,' Tom says, looking around, hesitant. 'She shot him with an arrow.'

Bea's head remains lowered.

'It wasn't a film though,' Moira says in a thin voice.

When Bea raises her head, it looks to Ted as though she's in pain. Then her face hardens and she glares at him, her blue eyes blazing.

'Yeah,' she says to him, her voice barely controlled, 'like *I* was the loose cannon.'

Good god. Ted feels the blood drain from him. His hands drop to his sides. All the adults in the room turn to wood. No one moves or speaks for what seems like an age.

'People do evolve, Bea,' Moira says quietly, into the silence. 'In case you hadn't noticed.' Bea stares on, bitter, or pleading? Ted can't read the look. Just as he couldn't read her face on that day.

'Clem, come here,' Bea says in a low voice, but Clem is whispering with Tom.

'Let it go, Bea,' Andrew says gently.

'What's *wrong* with her?' Lonnie mutters to Andrew. She means Bea.

'Nothing's wrong with her,' Ted says, louder than he intends, just as Clem bumps into his legs.

'It was *Dances with Wolves*!'

'Move on, people,' Andrew says.

'I'll do one,' Clem shouts. Ted steps gingerly back to his chair and sits down like a sack, but the chair won't allow him to slump. Now he feels like he's in the dock.

When will this end?

On the rug in the centre, Clem raises her arms and opens her mouth wide, miming song. To Ted, his granddaughter looks like an angel: chin raised, eyes closed, her mouth a perfect 'O'. It makes him want to weep.

Doigdoigdoigdoig-domp. From the deck, Bea wills Tom to be brave. *This one – now*! He bounces and bounces facing the bushes, the pool at his back, the sky a deep pink. He's running out of time. The stubby board waggles to a stop, again. Above the bushes, the crimson horizon thins and disappears. Bea steps silently back into the kitchen.

The rest of them mill around the table.

'He'll come in for tea,' Lisa says to no one in particular.

'Awareness of one's own dignity; group of lions. Five letters,' Moira says, pencil in hand.

'She's a whizz at these now,' Ted says to Andrew.

'I know.' Andrew was the one who started his mother off on crosswords, years ago.

'The sister of one of Mum's French *lovers*.' Clem's clutching Lonnie's arm and explaining where her name came from. 'When she was at *school*.' Bea catches Ted grimace and lean over Moira's newspaper.

'Gavin must have told her that,' Bea murmurs.

'It's true,' Clem says. Bea likes the story, and it is true, sort of, but not for discussion here.

Doigdoigdoigdoi-oi-oi-oi-oi

At the splash, everyone turns to the window. A high-pitched whoop follows and they all pile through the double doors onto the deck. Outside it's almost dark.

'I did it, I did it! Yeeeah!' Tom clambers out of the pool and flaps across the grass, dripping and pointing. His face is all grin, his finger points at Bea.

'Your turn!'

Her heart plummets her insides until it hits the bottom, while Tom's grin might split his face in two. They all look from Bea to Tom and back to Bea.

'Aw Tom, I'm not sure I—'

'We *shook*,' he whines. Bea feels the least springy she's ever felt.

'Tomorrow, I promise.'

'I believed you,' his smile disappears.

Ted steps forward. 'I'll do it,' he says.

'What?' Bea's mouth drops open.

'Bea *said* she would,' Tom wails.

'So now you've got me instead,' Ted says, forcing a grin. The others have eyes on Tom for his reaction, but Bea catches her father's glance at the pool, his wince of fear.

Yes, she thinks, *you do it*. Now he looks at her and she gives him a quick nod.

'Yes, I'll do it,' he says again.

'Don't be daft,' Moira says.

Andrew shakes his head, 'You've got to be kidding.' Bea watches her father turn and walk with lopsided gait back into the kitchen, around the table, and up the steps on the other side. Her mother follows him in.

Ted thumps up the stairs. He'll jump off that board, flip backwards if that's what it takes – a sort of penance. He'll make it to the shallow end, won't he? Anyway, someone will fish him out. He swallows his fright. He'll do it for Bea. She'll see what he's prepared to do and it will open things up.

'Ted?' Moira's on the stairs. 'Ted, you're not serious.'

But he is. He's never been more serious. He must keep in motion now or he'll bottle it. In a matter of minutes, he's stomping back down. There are voices in the kitchen – consoling Tom – and Moira's in the hall, still protesting. His walloping heart drowns her out. He gives her a look to say *Let me do this*, and he's out the door into the semi-dark. One person follows him, and without looking he knows it is Bea.

The cool air smells of pool chemicals and grass. Should Andrew be out here? In a way, this is for him too. Bea stands barefoot on the edge of the lawn where it meets the poolside.

Tiny lights give the water an eerie glow, like a cauldron.

Ted's at the board now, pale-legged, his green swim shorts flapping above the knee, his hips and stomach a thick trunk, his arms not quite thick enough to match. He's smaller than Bea remembers; when she thinks of her father she thinks of a big man. As he steps onto the board a dart of sorrow, or guilt, shoots through her. She almost says 'Dad, don't', but when he glances over she stays silent.

He reaches the end of the board in three small paces, chest puffed, chin up, not looking down. A bat flits across the pool, and another. Bea watches him slow-step around, placing his feet carefully like an Olympic diver. Now he's facing the bushes, his right arm towards her with the swirling red pattern on his bicep. The 'M' and the love heart come into focus. Bea had forgotten this, so fascinating to her when she was small: 'M' for Moira, his heart on his sleeve.

Before she even existed.

And if she was closer, she would see the raised pink scar – of her making – at the curve of the heart.

What does she really know about her father? About anyone?

He flexes his knees without leaving the board, bony elbows out at right angles. The effect is comical.

'Backflip,' he says under his breath.

'For me.' She means it to sound breezy, but it comes out flat, like a demand.

Ted knee-bends again, the board wobbles.

Holy crackers. His insides carry on bouncing. What was he thinking? *Look straight ahead.* His fear allows him only small sips of breath. From the hedge, a dark twig-finger points at the sky. Night will soon swallow them up. Then day, then night. *Move on, people.* He has moved on; too late.

Doigdoigdoig. A rushing in his ears and a stabbing from his knees. The breeze teases his chest hair, his nipples, he feels naked before her.

Will this do? Will it?

He has done things he would never dream of doing. Their small wrists in his hands, their soft heads: his own children.

'Gram-pa! Gram-pa!' The kids chant from the kitchen window.

He is a grandfather.

But first, he was a father.

With an almighty wrench of the shoulders, a roar, a foot booted at the sky, he hurls himself backwards.

Don't be sorry for that

Her father's roar rips the air, limbs splay at outrageous angles: whirling arms, a heel kicked up.

Bea gasps. Her heart stops.

The splash is huge. Her T-shirt, her legs, are soaked.

An elbow, fingers, a gasp-gulp—

Fuck, he can't—

Andrew flies past and launches himself into the pool, fully clothed. Andrew! She runs to the edge, Clem and Tom are behind her.

'Grandpa can't swim!'

'Grandpa!'

'He can just not very— Stay there!' Moira shouts. The children stop dead at the edge, as if tasered. Lonnie and Lisa appear beside them. Two flailing bodies churn the water halfway down the pool. Should Bea jump in? Andrew's head emerges.

'Dad!' Andrew yells. 'Stand up!' Ted, in a headlock, continues to thrash. Andrew ducks underwater, his shirt balloons, and the thrashing moves to the shallow end. Ted's head and shoulders appear, eyes squeezed shut, mouth opening and closing like a dying carp. The sisters haul him onto the edge, Bea treads on Lonnie's bare foot and she squeals.

'Sorry,' Bea says, hunkering down beside her father.

'Not clever, not clever,' Ted mutters between coughs.

'Don't be sorry for that,' Moira says. Bea takes in her mother's stern face as Moira drapes a towel around Ted's shaking shoulders, then passes one to Andrew who's squatting the other side.

'Alright, Dad?' Andrew puts a sopping arm around him. 'You gave us a fright.' The pool glow lights their faces in wavy flickers; they could all be in the cinema. Behind them, Clem and Tom hop silently from foot to foot.

'Go and put the kettle on,' Bea snaps. She and Lonnie get Ted to his feet and the towel slides off. The sight of his bare sloped shoulders fills Bea with dismay. Mention of the kettle sends Moira back across the dark lawn, Lisa with her. Ted searches the sky, mutters 'Dog star', and as if this has helped him find his bearings, lets himself be led away. Bea watches them go. Andrew appears to tower over Ted. Even Lonnie seems to be looking down at him on the way back to the house: the pool has shrunk their father.

Bea stays on the sandpapery pool edge.

'Easy now,' she hears Andrew say. When did her brother become this lifesaver, protector? *People evolve, if you hadn't noticed.* Except Bea, except *her.*

The pool's sickly yellow adds to her growing unease; she'd prefer total darkness. She leans back on her elbows, finds one or two faint stars between the clouds, and closes her eyes. Once upon a time, she could name the stars. Lyra? And there might have been a swan. Before she can steer her thoughts elsewhere, her hazy recurring vision swims into focus: herself as a baby, possibly a memory – her first? – staring up at the stars and her father. He breathes quiet words, then jerks his head, agitated. He wants something or he doesn't know what to do. There might be some threat, but she never sees what it is. That's all. The night, the sky, his voice, all of it disappears and she's left with the feeling that all is not well between them. Most people don't have memories from babyhood but it can happen, she's read about it.

Bea shivers and sits up. Her left sleeve and half her top are stuck to her. Behind her, the kitchen voices rise and fall with the rescue story, there's a spatter of clapping, no doubt led by Clem. And then a towel drops into her lap and Andrew sits down beside her in a dry shirt. She didn't hear him approach.

'Thanks.' She arranges the towel around her shoulders. 'Nice work saving Dad's life by the way.'

'He put up quite a fight,' Andrew says, 'considering you can stand up in there.' They both watch the flickering water. 'The kids are loving this,' he says. 'It'll become a well-told story. Probably end up as a double somersault with a pike.' He checks her reaction. Bea doesn't want to think about her father's well-told stories.

Their mother's voice reaches them. From the tone, Bea can guess she's saying something like 'Stop it' or 'That's enough.'

'She's such a control freak,' Bea mutters.

'Better a control freak than a total nutcase,' Andrew says. 'Lisa's mum.' Bea didn't know this, though it explains the timidity, the way her sister-in-law clings to Andrew. Bats flit across the pool, snatching insects from the night.

'I'm just saying it, you know...' Andrew falters, 'to keep ours in perspective.' He flicks his head in the direction of the house. 'Our parents.' He keeps going in this unusual candour. 'She still needs some help to keep it together. Lisa. She tried a few ways.' He tells Bea that for years his wife has been taking medication. Does Andrew think this is what *she* needs?

'And does it work?' Bea asks.

'It saved her life,' he says in a beat. 'Mine too.' He smiles. 'That and our pin-up boy,' he shakes his head like he still can't believe it. 'He made us a mint, right when we needed it.'

Bea marvels at this conversation – if she and Andrew can talk like this, surely anything is possible. She thinks about the lives she would have saved if she could.

'I wish Granny Dil was here,' she says. 'I wish it a lot, but especially here.'

'So do I,' Andrew says, with a wistfulness that surprises Bea.

'Do you?'

'Of course,' he says, irritated. 'She wasn't *yours*, Bea.'

'She sort of was though,' Bea says, almost pleading. Andrew

scratches at the pool edge with his fingernail – a rhythmic, crispy sound – while he thinks about this.

'OK,' he says finally, 'I know what you mean.' Bea feels like he's given her something, and she'd like to give something back. She pulls the towel tighter, but she can't think of the right nice thing.

'How do you do it?' she asks instead. He looks puzzled. 'How do you stay so ... *yourself*?' It's a huge relief to hit on exactly what she means. Her brother gives it proper consideration, his eyebrows furrow and meet in the middle.

'I don't know,' he says after a time. 'Maybe I just don't try so hard not to.' He gives her a tentative sideways look. 'D'you think...' he pauses.

'I won't bite you,' she says, then adds darkly, 'or shoot you.'

'Sometimes you even *like* being angry?'

No! She doesn't. Does she? Yes, she used to. Bea doesn't answer; she doesn't know the answer. They stare at the water in silence. This day is taking an impossibly long time to end.

Andrew gets to his feet. She looks up into his face against the dull night sky, he gives her a sheepish smile.

'Are you coming?'

From where she's sitting, he's extremely tall. 'In a minute.'

The jaundiced water has sealed itself to stillness. Andrew's voice comes faintly from the kitchen, then Lonnie's. Bea wonders if they're watching her from the window but she doesn't turn around. She hugs her knees while grey cloud pillows drift slowly above her. Whatever it was Bea hoped to feel is not emerging. Defeat weighs heavy in her chest – it's how Tom must have felt standing on that board all weekend, fighting back tears. She could get up now and do a backflip, but she won't. That version of her, if it ever existed, is gone. And now her father has made his grand gesture, and she feels precisely the same as she did before he almost drowned: stuck in her own skin. Did she imagine that her dad jumping backwards into a pool would release her from herself?

Beyond a wholesome discipline, be gentle with yourself. But *how?* Bea has never got the hang of gentle. She lies back on the stone, too quickly, her head thumps down and she feels a sharp pain. She stretches her arms out and stares up at the sky. Lyra, the swan, all the stars are hidden. A heavy yearning occupies her whole body: out along her arms, pulling through her thighs, pinning her skull to the ground. And what did Mum say? *Don't be sorry for that.* What did she mean? Bea didn't *ask* him to jump.

Or maybe she did.

Maybe she has been asking him her whole life.

Something biochemical

It's always the same teachers in early. Bea sometimes wonders if they've slept here, in the ancient armchairs of the shabby staff room, trapped under their piles of exercise books. She only comes in at this time on Thursdays, when Clem stays with Gavin.

'What did Keats say about autumn? Mellow and fruity?' says Paul Gadds from the deepest chair. 'And what about winter? It's brass monkeys out there.'

'Who's got F-9 this morning?' says Mrs Khan, still in her coat, 'I just saw Stephen Boyne with a bloody nose, top of the hill.' They all talk to the room as a whole. The staff room is like the set of a play: a large seventies lounge with faded green carpet; assorted non-matching armchairs, hulking and dainty and tilting; a long sinking sofa against the wall by the window; jars of coffee, mugs, teabags crammed on an actual trolley on wheels in the corner. Bea heads there now. The room is east-facing, handy for early November mornings. A hopeful yellow-grey light washes into the room.

'Fighting, at this time of day? Where do they find the energy?' says Mandy Packet, PE teacher, from the sofa. She's always in heels when not in pumps on the netball court.

'Try Vivaldi's *Winter*. Best one. Scratchy, needling,' says Miss Palmer without looking up from her marking.

'It was probably a love battle, they've all become amorous, don't you think?' Paul says. 'Change of season.'

'Next term, let's put what we're *listening* to on the white-boards,' says Mandy.

The door opens and three more teachers bundle in, pink-cheeked, as though from the Arctic.

'Morning!'

'Morning.' Bags are dumped en route to the kettle.

'Morning,' Bea says. 'I've got F-9.' Then she adds, 'I wish I was *amorous*.' All the romance that flies around the school reminds Bea of her own best days. To stop herself reminiscing, she bounces on the balls of her feet, fists clenched, a boxer warming up. 'Boyne's no match for me,' she says.

'Is that how you stay so thin?' someone asks, resentful.

'How's the Dickens going?' Mr Coots, Head of English, evading retirement, same tweed jacket through the seasons, calls from his chair. This term has seen the installation of little whiteboards outside the classrooms where the form tutors write what they're 'currently reading'. The board outside Room 114 says Miss Starling is currently reading *Hard Times* by Charles Dickens.

'Racing through,' Bea says with a lopsided smile.

'I'm going to change mine to *American Psycho*,' Coots says, 'see if it gets a reaction.'

'Is anyone actually *reading* the book?' says Alicia Chowdra, Chemistry and Pastoral, loud and peeved. A few mumble that they are.

'If we move to sounds,' Miss Palmer says, looking up with a grin, 'I'll go with Jay-Z, that'll impress them.' Miss Chowdra clicks her tongue, unimpressed. Bea raises her eyebrows at Mandy who raises hers back. Then she picks up her bag and exits with her steaming mug, wishing her colleagues a productive morning.

A gaggle of girls block the far end of the corridor (a flutter? a coven?). Unusual they're in so early, Bea should probably check if they're due in detention. Their squeaks and whispers rise and fall like music, and quieten as she approaches. The girls straighten, smile, flick their hair. Bea gets metal flashes from train-track braces and non-regulation jewellery.

'Morning Miss.'

'Hi, Miss Starling.'

Bea enters her empty classroom, the door swishes shut

on its heavy hinge. Giggles follow her in a ripple. She feels a brief ache of longing, as she does increasingly in the mornings, before noise and paper and strip lighting dull her senses. It's the girls who ignite this in her: they're choosing who to be with their syrupy smiles, a cold shoulder, a feigned confusion. The boys are less adept at switching selves, though they do a good oblivious: *Swear down Miss, you never set that last lesson.* Dejection, outrage, charm; they too are choosing.

At her desk, she tweaks her lesson plan on bioenergetics, cradles her mug, and the day fades in. Her classroom at the front of the school looks out onto the wide stretch of grass and, beyond that, the car park. A steady stream of staff now hurries towards the entrance, heads down against the cold.

Her tutor group, year eleven, will soon scuff in, bringing stale smoke from the bus, fruity hair, minty lips, angst, fatigue, hilarity. The first to arrive will flick the lights on. But for now, the space remains colourless and still, smelling faintly of disinfectant, chairs tucked obediently under tables. It is her favourite place and time: sitting here before everyone, at her desk, in her classroom. She could feel sorry for herself for feeling that she belongs in a bleached, empty classroom, but today, at least, she does not.

With her finger, Bea traces the curly orange letters on her mug. 'Clementine, meaning: Mild and Merciful'. Moira gave it to Clem years ago to mark the end of plastic cups. When Gavin moved out, before Clem spent her first night at his flat, she came solemnly to Bea with this badly wrapped gift and watched closely as Bea opened it and tried to hide her confusion.

'It's for when I'm not here,' Clem had said, serious, her wide eyes still clear in Bea's memory. It had been a comfort on the days she missed her daughter. Even a six-year-old understood Bea's needs better than she did. She takes a sip – real coffee, good and strong, not the granules some of them drink – and tries to recall the meaning of her own name, on her mug on its hook at Uncle David's house, that was Granny Dil's house.

She can't remember; something overblown and undeserved.

There's a loud rapping at the door. It's only ten past eight – too early for the mob, and they don't knock.

A squat boy with a head of black curls stands in the doorway in his white shirt and maroon tie, no jumper.

'Good morning, Magnus,' Bea says.

'Morning Miss,' he says, blinking rapidly. 'If your glycoproteins could break down a pathogen and de-activate it, it would be more effective than antibiotics.' She waves him in and indicates the desk in front of her. Magnus won't sit down, he never does. On his regular visits, he stands close to her desk and talks intently, his eyes pointing just over her right shoulder. 'The implications are massive,' he says.

'They are,' Bea agrees. 'Aren't you cold? It's six degrees, leaves falling, people in *coats*?'

'Not all of them are deciduous, some are evergreen,' he says, reasonably, 'and I'm fine because of homeostasis.' He gives a sweep of the hand, head to toe, unusually theatrical. Magnus is always himself, though what he will say is anyone's guess. 'Maintenance of a constant internal state in a changing environment.' His voice has recently stopped squeaking and settled into a deep boom.

'Thank you, Magnus,' she smiles, 'I taught you that.'

'A nerve impulse to speed up vasoconstriction would be useful,' he muses.

'It would.' Bea holds fast-growing hope that, once he's got his A levels out the way, Magnus will find cures for all diseases, a solution to the ecological crises, to global warming. 'I'm glad you're on cell structures,' she says, 'I've got a new theory for you.'

When Bea got back from the family weekend, she had dug out the picture of toddler Tom in his Andy Warhol squares: bewildered, furious, terrified, joyful. Each box, like its own cell, containing one pure emotion. It seems to Bea that when she is with her family her own receptors work in a special way, fixing her in one state. It's biochemical, triggered by her parents, mainly her father. She gets stuck in the child version, unable to access her adult self; stuck in the boxes like toddler Tom, though hers are only the bad ones. Has she ever been an adult with her family?

'I'm proposing that cell surface receptors can act in response to specific individuals,' Bea says to Magnus, 'and fix a state of being.' Right away she can tell she's picked the wrong audience. He narrows his eyes and moves his lips a fraction as he repeats her words in his head. He pats his hair in a worried gesture.

'But cell receptors—'

'It's a bit out-of-the-box, I know,' she interrupts. 'But could you suspend your disbelief, Magnus? Just this once?' He gives it a moment's thought and adopts his 'breaking bad news' face.

'Belief isn't something you can *suspend*, Miss.'

After school, pounding the water, Bea swims fast lengths – up and down, up and down – rotating her body just the right amount for each breath. She thinks of nothing. The goggles pinch the bridge of her nose, they'll leave dark indented circles around her eyes long after she leaves the pool. Ten front crawl, ten breaststroke, ten backstroke, her arms pulling hard against her ears. Up, down, up, down. This is a thing she's good at.

Back home, at the computer, she types in 'Magnus'. 'The great one; excels above all others.' She must remember to tell him. Pleased, she takes a glass of wine up to the bathroom and soaks in bubbles that spill over the tub. Downstairs again, on the sofa, she ignores the pile of books to mark on the table. She lies back with her feet up on the arm, facing the aubergine end of the knocked-through room. It had felt like a bold statement, that bruise of a wall. She might paint it all white again, though she probably won't.

She picks up *Hard Times* from the rug. 'Go for a classic,' Lonnie said. Bea and Lonnie speak more frequently since the weekend away. Bea's not making much headway with Dickens, but she loves the characters' names, and it makes her look clever. The best name in her classes this year is Sandy Pie, and the girl doesn't suit it, being spindly and pale. What had Clem told Lonnie about the provenance of her name? *Mum's French lover* – Bea's sure that's what she heard. She'll ask Lonnie next time they speak. The need to verify these details of the past is making her uneasy. She'll go round the corner to the Anchor, with the book and *New Scientist*. While she's never really missed Gavin these last two years, she misses distraction. It's the new Thursday routine: swim, bath, pub. Another recent change since the weekend away is her inability to be alone.

She orders chips and sits in the snug. The Anchor is a proper pub: dimly lit, wooden beams, faded pictures of ships, the smell of old fires and beer and stale carpet. She opens the magazine on the table but doesn't read it. Instead, she people-watches. One couple sip and smooch, the woman's older than Bea, mid-forties? The man's too big for his stool – not fat, just a slab of a man like some men are; not Bea's type. Though what *is* her type? Hard to say. Gavin was alpha, hunky, and look where that went. At the next table, a couple of grey-haired men sit neatly next to each other on the bench, facing out. Regulars. The smaller one now rests his head for a moment on the other's shoulder; an intimate gesture that stirs Bea's longing. On the round table at the end, a group of twenty-somethings shout and jeer, and one in a beanie hat with big lips and broad shoulders covers his face, laughing.

Bea and the two men would talk about food; and how to season a curry. To the round table, she would offer her hand, and the boy with the beanie would stand up and take it. He's taller than she expects, with long fingers. She leads him home; he's nervous. She pushes him onto the sofa and climbs astride him, he fumbles with her shirt buttons as she holds his gaze and grinds her hips; between her legs, he's hardening up nicely—

'Can I take this?'

Bea jolts, and knocks her book off the table. A woman with bobbed hair in right-angles smiles brightly, holding up a stool.

'Sure,' Bea mumbles, leaning down for *Hard Times*.

Sex is another thing she used to be good at.

Bea swings her legs up on the bench and leans back. She sees her reflection in the thick, gold-framed mirror. Her face is all dark angles, her eyes still faintly outlined with owl-like circles from the goggles. She tilts her head to catch the light and give her eyes back their blue. She's all straight lines: sharp nose, thin lips, straight hair, sweatshirt flat at her collar bone. She thinks of Granny Dil's Pomegranate Passion lipstick. 'Pearls for every day, always look the best you can.' Bea has never minded looking mannish, it has been a trademark of sorts, but right now she would like to see a curve, something soft, some colour. She might take Mandy Packer up on the makeover. Another wave of unease comes at her: these fantasy exchanges, this self-appraisal and memory searching, are not like her.

Her chips arrive, she turns the pages of *New Scientist* and scans an article on carbon capture. *Still want to be a real scientist?* asks the voice in her head. Maybe she's having a midlife crisis. She tries a page of the Dickens but nothing sinks in. The two men give her little finger-waggle waves as they leave. In the next snug, the women shout out song titles. Are they playing charades? Two go to the bar, one to the loo, and the pub quietens. Bea's thoughts drift to Ted's bow-and-arrow pose on the white rug under the chandelier. She closes her eyes and presses her back into the cushioned upholstery.

Now it's Bea holding the bow – her child self – back bent, aiming the arrow up into the clouds, in shorts and a T-shirt, in a field with grass tickling her ankles. There's a line of targets at the far end: circles of colour against the woods in the background. Behind her, jagged walls of an old castle chomp at the sky. A voice makes her turn around. Now the arrow points directly at her father, a younger version, though not far off his current self. This could be the story she's heard or the memory she invented from the story. What Bea can't see is why she did it, and if it's some kind of proof she really is *bad*. And where her rage came from in the first place.

Bea blames Andrew for all this queasy introspection. She repeats her favourite line from the only poem she knows by heart. *You are a child of the universe no less than the trees and the stars; you have a right to be here.* It doesn't comfort her.

Must be a mid-life crisis. Though she's not even forty.

She snatches up the magazine and book. She'll go home and call Sarah, her oldest friend.

The night air prickles her cheeks as she jogs along the pavement, her heart thumping harder than it needs to. Sarah will translate for Bea the reminiscences, the doubts. Then Bea will pull herself together and get to bed.

The phone rings and rings. Pick up *pick up*. Sarah's always home.

Tonight isn't always: the ringing rings itself into a continuous tone. No answerphone. Call me back, *Je suis dans une crise.* Bea slams the handset back on its stand, thumps the sofa arm hard, and lets out a low growl.

Sometimes you even like *being angry*. It was true once: the heat and the energy had felt like her superpower; her anger was like a second skin. *You came out fighting*, her mother once said. Thing is, anger ossifies like bone – calcium phosphate into brittle skeleton. If Bea sheds her rage she might turn into a crumbling pile of ash.

Present and past and future
1958

Fern Ashton town hall on a Saturday night: swishy skirts, chicken elbows, swinging hips, finger clicks, shoe-shuffles on the boards. Ted stands by the makeshift bar, brightly lit, next to the entrance. Long trestle tables strain under kegs of beer, a line of lemonade bottles and various-sized glasses. What these tables need is a batten in each corner, plus a couple of extra slats in the middle. He hands over his ticket and takes his glass of beer from one of the Church Committee ladies in a stiff brown tunic. She doesn't return his smile. On site, they laugh about these disapproving barmaids. Why not give the job to the flirty, lipsticked crowd from the factory?

Ted turns to the dancers in the hall and his toe starts tapping as he takes a sip. He gets wafts of shampoo, beer, wood polish. The hall is lit only from the bar; darker over on the far side for canoodling later on. On stage, the band strikes up a Duke Ellington number – great tune. Ted rolls his shoulders in his suit to loosen it up. His jacket feels like cardboard. He can't shake the feeling that dressing up is pretending; especially at the beginning, when he walks in alone.

For a good while he came with Brenda. Organised Brenda, with her shrill laugh, bookkeeper at the Tower and a good dancer. And before that with Louisa, small and shy, her back curved to conceal her large breasts, which Ted was lucky enough to squeeze, in the dark, on more than one occasion. Nice enough girls who drifted away. Brenda's going out with Greg from the Crown now, so Ted's heard. She might be here tonight. And Michael and Alf and the others should be here somewhere, though he's not yet seen them. He scans the floor and spots a figure lurching between the dancers. It's

Bert Tallis, who's become something of a liability in the town: sacked from all the building crews, and now also from his job as a dustman. Poor sod.

Ted nods to the beat – you can't help smiling with this music. A loose-limbed pair twirl in front of him, then another two, stiff and angular. Ankle flicks, shoulder shrugs, hair falling every which way. Ted has always admired the silky perfection of women's hair. His gaze settles on a pair of women dancing together, precise but fluid; the taller one looks serious and then flashes a quick smile at her friend as they swish past each other and catch hold again by the fingertips. She has on a pale blue sleeveless dress with little buttons all the way down the back. Ted pictures the curve of her spine beneath the dress. He keeps looking.

The trumpeter steps to the edge of the stage, his burgundy arms catch the light as he blasts out his solo, darting frantic notes over the low twang of the double bass. It's a tricksy motif, up and up, all the way to an impossibly high note, which he holds, cheeks turning the colour of his suit. The audience whoops, brays, whistles. The girl in the pale blue dress laughs with her friend, applauds, tucks her shiny dark hair behind her ears with both hands, then claps on, her fingers straight, like a prayer. Ted puts down his glass and heads towards her. At the same moment, Bert Tallis staggers in their direction, knocking into her with his back. Ted opens his arms, and the girl falls into them. He holds her briefly and inhales the faint smell of lavender from her hair. She is ever so slightly taller than him, so he takes up every inch of his height, almost rising on tiptoes. She smiles, embarrassed, and turns around to see what happened. Bert stumbles away, and her friend arches her eyebrows and leaves the dance floor.

Then Ted and the girl in the blue dress dance together. She has soft hands and perfect poise. He loses his step, admiring her elegant neck, her lips, her arms. He twirls her and she spins like a ballerina, dark hair fanning out. The music slows, and

Ted puts one hand around her back, giving a gentle press on the buttons just above her bottom. His other arm is around her shoulders, his fingers touching smooth skin. They sway. Ted pulls away a fraction, catching her shy smile. He imagines opening the buttons one by one as he presses his chest ever so gently into the small softness of her breasts.

They sit at a table on the dimly lit side, he takes sneaky glances at her knees, curved and held to one side. His own are scratched and knobbly. He's never seen such perfect knees! Her name is Moira, she lives a few miles up the road in Lower Ashton village, and she is the loveliest thing Ted has ever seen.

*

On a chilly, dark afternoon in late November, a few months into their courtship, Ted sits opposite Moira in Doilies on Fern Ashton High Street. A date fitted in between their shifts. Elvis croons quietly from the radio on the counter; only one other table is occupied; both of them have kept their coats on and a strip of Moira's knitted mustard-yellow cardigan shows below the crisp white collar of her uniform. Her dark hair flicks out at her shoulders. *Curled for me,* Ted thinks with pleasure. He wants to be next to her, not sitting against the wall across this flimsy tabletop, paper doilies as placemats. With his fingertips, he tamps down his own hair, not thick enough for a quiff, pasted to one side with pomade. He wonders what they will talk about. He puts his hands on the table, then in his lap. They smile at each other.

Their tea is brought to them in chunky white cups and saucers by a woman in a checked apron over wide hips. Moira has chosen a slice of sponge cake, Ted an iced bun that fills the whole plate. With a finger and thumb, Moira breaks off a bit of cake and eats it tidily.

'Blackberry filling,' she nods with approval. 'We picked blackberries on the farm, Mrs Alice had shelves full of jams and pickles.' Duckworth Farm is where Moira and her brother David stayed at the end of the war, evacuated from London way – Surrey? – in the final wave, fleeing those vicious doodlebugs. The farm's only the other side of Fern Ashton, next to the village where Moira now lives with her mother and brother. Ted likes to think it was Fate that brought her here. She makes a fine Land Girl in Ted's mind, striding across the fields on her long legs, in the pale blue dress with the buttons—

'She gave me a little patch of the kitchen garden. You should have seen all the things she grew.' Moira would have had Mrs Alice for a mother if she could, the way she speaks of her. 'We ate like kings and queens.' She's in a happy reverie, shaking her head as though she still can't believe it, then lowers her voice. 'I think it pushed the boundaries of what was strictly allowed. At Christmas there was whipped cream, brandy sauce, *more than one bird*.' She widens her lovely green eyes, then takes another mouthful. She's given herself an appetite. It's rare to hear Moira talk this much.

'I got my first taste of strawberries,' she says, turning coy. The music has stopped, and the woman at the counter fiddles with the radio dial. 'They say smell is the most powerful sense,' Moira continues, 'but I think it's taste.' Ted looks at her perfect lips, curled upwards. *He* should have been there on the farm with her, feeding her strawberries. 'When we first got there, I was scared of cows,' Moira says with a little laugh, her hand to her chest. 'Scared half to death.'

'Bet you didn't want to leave,' Ted says, then he smiles, teasing. 'Did you hide in the hen house when your mother came for you?' Moira changes instantly, flinches. She sits back in her chair as though pushed. In his alarm, Ted holds up both hands, but Moira is miles away, with a grave look on her face. Ted searches for something soothing to say, and finds nothing. Moira gathers herself and looks up, blank-faced.

'My mother came for us, yes,' she says. And then he remembers.

'I'm sorry,' he says. 'Your father. Moira, I'm so sorry.' She smiles weakly. He's an idiot. Her father had died while Moira and her brother were at Duckworth. The mother was supposed to join them at the farm and then the father was killed. Moira has given only these scant details, and Ted senses it is off limits. And doesn't everyone have something off-limits from that time? They chew in silence, the sweet icing sticks to the roof of Ted's mouth. Buddy Holly sings out cheerfully *Well that'll be the day when you say goodbye, yes that'll be the day when you make me cry—*

'My brother still works there,' Moira says in a flat voice.

'He's not scared of cows then?' Ted'll get this back on track.

'No,' she says slowly, 'David's not scared of things.'

'What about lightning?' A man from Stroud was struck by lightning just recently, up a ladder, almost died – it was all over the local papers.

'I doubt it,' Moira says, sounding sad.

'There must be *something*,' Ted says, annoyed at this brother, this super-being without fear who turns Moira misty or vague when he comes up in conversation. Why is he such a secret? Why does Ted always feel he's treading around private things? He wishes for some family of his own to make legends of.

The other couple leave the tea shop, calling their thanks, a rush of cold air sweeps in as the door closes behind them. Moira sits up, her face brightens.

'What about you?' She knits her hands together and rests her chin on them over her plate. 'What are you scared of?' Should he say 'Nothing' to match the brother? This might actually be true – right now he can't think of anything that frightens him. Except being ditched by Moira, a terrifying thought, but he can't very well say that.

'Your mother,' he says with a grin, 'if she catches me kissing you.' He taps her foot with his, and strokes her knee under the table, though his fingers only just reach. She blushes and looks away. He could get up right now and take her in his arms, they could dance together around the empty tables. Instead, he picks up the remains of his bun and takes a bite.

'I'll tell you who's really scary,' Moira leans forward.

'Who?' Ted says through his mouthful, leaning too so that their heads almost touch.

'Sister Hodge,' Moira whispers loudly and giggles. They're on safe ground now: the wards, her patients and their stories; his building site. Moira likes to hear about the men, their girlfriends, and their plans. And they can sit in silence too. Ted doesn't mind the pauses but he never has a clue what she's thinking. The time before the war maybe; the things she hides.

'I was sleepwalking before I met you,' he blurts, gripping the table edge. And he knows it sounds like a line, but it's God's-honest truth, cross his heart.

*

On a drab ward at the cottage hospital, Moira holds the bony hand of whimpering Mrs Taverner as Sister administers her injection. It is not a two-person job, but the patient was belly-aching for Moira, and it gives Sister an excuse to scoot straight back to her office. Moira allows her fingers to be clenched, and with her free hand she strokes the old lady's wispy hair.

Sister Hodge recruited Moira herself, from the shop, or 'poached' her, as Moira's mother Dilys tells it. Sister is not the sort of woman you say no to, and anyway there isn't regular work at Billington's. Moira only helped out when the other shop girl was poorly. Whenever Moira bumps into her school friend Pat, training at Gloucester Royal to be a proper nurse, Pat urges Moira to join her. But it would mean living away from home, and Moira can't imagine being away from David. So, Nurse's aide will have to suffice. Though even these curtained-off bays give more space and privacy than Moira has at home. In the room she still shares with her mother, her elbows knock against the makeshift partition when she gets dressed. But it's one of the few things her mother never complains about, and so Moira too keeps quiet. Ted has offered his services, but the thought of him inside her house hammering at walls is too alarming, and she tells him no, no thank you.

Away from her mother and David, when she is with Ted, or at work, Moira side-steps her usual self. The feelings that bump up against each other unsettle her: excited rushes, sadness, a strange ungratefulness, hope; a baffling and constant nostalgia for the present, and the past and the future.

In an ideal world (her mother's phrase), Moira would work at the farm. She would hoe and plant and pot chutneys with Mrs Alice, sit at the big table with David and Mister for lunch. The thought makes her weak with longing. Not that there is a job for her, not that her mother would allow it. When David had started there, as soon as he finished school, Moira thought Dilys would be pleased. David was safe in the fields, out of harm's way. But their mother had prowled around like a wounded dog. She has always been spiky about the farm, or rather Mister Jem the farmer, right from when she came from Morden at the end of the war. That was when the three of them moved to the little house on Bluebell Lane, which, Moira doesn't point out, Mister arranged for them. It's not Moira or David's fault Mister and Missus are so nice. Moira suspects jealousy, though she would never dare to say it. 'Over my dead body,' Dilys had said, when there was talk of David moving back into the farmhouse. Moira also doesn't point out the provenance of their ready supply of fresh vegetables, fruit, meat.

Mrs Taverner has fallen soundlessly asleep, Moira slips her hand away and creeps out. She has the dinner trays to collect, the linen to fold, and the balcony to sweep before her shift finishes. The pace of work here makes the shop look like a playground – another thing she keeps quiet about. And anyway, she loves it.

'You'll have to go back to your bed, Roger,' Moira says firmly to Roger Mason. He's the obstacle on the balcony, and the only person in the hospital known by his first name. 'Call me Roger' is his mantra. Moira starts sweeping leaves and cigarette ends from the near corner. The balcony stretches right down to Ivan Norris Ward. Only the convalescents are allowed out here, but the evening air has turned chilly, and it's her job to herd any loiterers indoors. Halfway down, on a bench in the dimness, Roger doesn't move. His big shoulders hunch over in a dark curve, and is that his coat over his dressing gown? Now his shoulders shake a fraction, and Moira sees the man is crying. She stands still and watches him.

'Never let a patient see your apprehension' is the overstated refrain in *On the Ward: Life in a Nurse's Shoes*, lent to her by Sister. Only the introduction and first three chapters apply to Moira, but she's read the whole book. It has been Moira's observation that, among the junior nurses, many are wary and sometimes fearful of patients. In particular the men; in particular the men who leak out their emotions. Moira realised early on that she is not apprehensive of the patients, whatever they are in for and whatever their emotional state.

Unlike at home with her mother, at the hospital she doesn't worry about what to say, and she doesn't say the wrong thing. The nurses get her to do the listening they don't have time for. Some of the patients are greedy for her listening. They want sympathy, company, reassurance; an *audience*. Moira can give them any and all of these. Her own voice sounds different here, sometimes soft, sometimes firm: tones that someone else might use, though it's definitely her speaking. Moira's apprehension is saved for the staff, whom she defers to and obeys. Her auxiliary role suits everyone just fine.

She props the broom against the wall and walks slowly over to the bench, rubbing her arms in the cold. Roger turns his head a fraction but stays facing forward, elbows on his knees, chin in his hands. He breathes heavily. His crying, if that's what it was, has stopped. Roger is a convalescent neck of femur fracture, but he's on Men's Medical as there are no free beds in Cons. No one has been able to get the real details of the fracture, he tells a different story to every questioner. He sighs deeply, his breath blowing a slim cloud into the dark.

'My girl's beyond help,' he says. 'They're going to put her away.' Moira sits down beside him and looks out at the statue in the courtyard: a shadowy figure with a top hat. 'It's been on the cards, and now I'm in here my Missus can't cope.' He sits up. 'I don't blame her. Our Emily's a handful, always has been. Brain damage.' He glances at Moira, checking her reaction. 'But she's a cracker, you know? She loves a bit of slapstick. You could fall over yourself all day just to make her laugh.' He smiles, mournful. 'She looks normal when she laughs – the full shilling.' Moira tenses, pats Roger's leg, then clasps her hands in her lap. *The full shilling. Not the full shilling.* The scar above David's eye is now a vanishing white thread.

'She'll still be your girl,' Moira says with determination, 'wherever she goes.'

'But I want her with me.'

'I know.' They sit in silence and stare at the statue of the founder of the workhouse, as this building used to be. His hat's a solid square of black against the cloudy night. Moira would have put up a statue of Florence Nightingale. She shivers. 'It's alright for you, you've got your coat.' Roger Mason doesn't appear to have heard her.

'Emily's not like anyone else,' he turns to Moira with a pleading look. 'It's not such a bad thing.'

'No,' she says, 'it isn't.' She helps him up, takes his arm, and they shuffle towards the door. It's an advantage being tall in this work. Her father was tall, she's fairly sure of this. She's gone from David to her father – must be Roger made her think of him – though Moira's father, Raymond, would be younger if he had lived. Her instinct is to shut out these thoughts using blocks of colour, a strategy that started as a child. She closes her eyes for a second: gold, orange, turquoise. Her patient stops to get his balance, leans his weight on her. The colours don't work. Moira badly wants to see her father's face, just a quick glimpse, and a giddy panic takes her when she can't picture him. She wobbles sideways, almost toppling the patient, and has to plant her feet apart and catch him with an arm around his back.

'You alright, girl?' he says.

The pair of them are standing still at the end of the balcony, but Moira still feels like she's falling.

'Alright,' she says, instructing herself. 'Alright.' She draws herself up. 'Now Roger,' she says in her work voice, kind but firm, 'let's get you inside.'

A fat red heart

The Victoria sponge sits like a trophy on a cake stand borrowed from Gina at the shop. Around the base, Dilys arranges two plates of scones, a small tray of almond biscuits, ham, cheese and meat paste sandwiches cut in triangular halves, with tomatoes dotted among them for pleasing spots of colour. Her shortbread's ready to go in the oven. The rickety dining table has never supported such a feast. Fingers crossed everyone's hungry – there are only four of them.

Dilys moves the cups around, puts the paper serviettes under the knives, then back on the plates, then under the knives again. She smooths her hair – a nice wave from the curlers – and casts her eyes over the shabby grey dining room, so poorly lit even today when the sun's out. She could fetch the corner lamp from the lounge, but David will be home soon and he doesn't like things moved around.

At the back door off the kitchen, she lights a ciggie. Moira has never brought a boyfriend home. Ted Starling, as far as Dilys knows, is the first, though her daughter is not generous with life's details. She squirrels them away or tells them to David when Dilys is out. Like their farm chatter: the two of them in cahoots and Dilys unable to join in. Moira's new romance pinballs Dilys from envy to intrigue, worry, terror. These last two days, in between cigarettes, her nervous energy has been ploughed into baking.

Courting is one thing, but anything past that Dilys finds hard to contemplate. Though at twenty-one, Dilys can't deny her daughter is readying for the next phase. The curtain 'wall' in the room she and Moira share has been replaced with a tasteful screen. The nights Moira spends at the hospital, Dilys folds it away and the room becomes vast and empty, though it's barely big enough for the two single beds. With nobody in it, Dilys can't help thinking of the cold, lifeless bed the other side as a coffin. Sleep is hard to come by when Moira isn't home.

The boyfriend is a builder. If he likes the spread, perhaps he will take a look at the upstairs window. Infuriatingly, Dilys can count the pieces of gathered information on one hand: Ted Starling is working on the new council flats; his mother died when he was young (there must be other family, but either they're shady, or Moira doesn't know herself, or she knows but won't tell Dilys); he likes scones and cake; his fair hair has the smallest hint of red; he doesn't like dressing up in a suit. After their dates, Moira will say what they had to eat; at a push what they danced to. Dilys feels starved.

Ted takes a sandwich from his piled plate and two sets of eyes watch him bite into it: Moira's fretful, her mother's keen. They watch him chew and swallow. David is the one Ted wants to talk to, but since they all sat down the brother's eyes haven't left his plate. He has thick dark hair with a fringe almost down to his eyebrows (the mother probably cuts it), the same guarded expression as Moira, and he's tall and thin, also like Moira. Though his shoulders have a slight stoop that keep his head down. He's the same age as Ted – twenty-three – but he seems to Ted somehow like an old man in his thick-knit brown jumper, threads poking out here and there.

'Champion,' Ted says, grinning at the women. 'Delicious. What a spread!' Walking in here he'd felt his prayers had been answered. *Pleasure to meet you, Mrs Brown*. Finally, after months of courting, he's made it into the house to find a table stacked in his honour. It's a poky little room, with a faint smell of damp, Ted might suggest a knock-through, some decent heating. But not yet. *Hold your horses*. Four of them around the table; he won't dare to think of them as family. Not yet.

'The council has money to burn, doesn't it?' Moira's mother

says. 'New flats, new library plans.' She knows more than Ted does about what's due to be built. For a Lower Ashtoner, she's impressively well informed.

'It's the shop,' Moira explains, 'you hear everything about everything at Billington's.' The pale green of her blouse matches her eyes.

'And every*one*,' Mrs Brown says proudly, through bright pink lips. 'Mrs Kitchener's husband had a stroke and his right arm just dangles. I worry he'll topple things. And Mrs Foot has ordered two dozen eggs for Ann's wedding cake. Two *dozen*.' Ted wonders if the lipstick is for him. He knows from Moira her mother is forty-four. She seems both older and younger.

'Ted doesn't know these people,' Moira reminds her. But her mother ignores her, she's talking only to Ted, visibly excited to have him here. He hides his smile – the woman's amusing without meaning to be. She still has on her apron over her dress. And how did Moira get to be so tall, with her mother so compact? He looks around for pictures of the father, to get some clues, and of the house where Moira came from in Morden, south of London. It's still the only thing she has told him. The walls give nothing away. Only a square, tacked-up piece of embroidery, and a single shelf with a few trinkets and dried flowers.

'Mr Worcester can't play any more football, with his leg,' Mrs Brown carries on, 'he was county level.' Ted seizes his opening.

'We've got two men down at the moment,' he says. 'You play any football, David?'

David looks up. His eyes are dark, with thick lashes, and fixed now on Ted. 'I know the rules of football,' he says.

'More than I can say for me,' Ted says, smiling. 'D'you fancy joining us for a game? Got openings anywhere on the pitch, spare boots if you need them.'

'I haven't ever played football,' David says. 'Two people at the farm play in a team on Sundays.'

'Right.'

'Last Sunday the score was four-one,' David says.

'To them?' Ted asks. David looks blank. Ted prompts, 'Did your mates' team win?'

'They lost,' David says. 'Their one goal was an own goal, scored by the other team.'

'Sounds like us,' Ted chuckles. He needs to get David on side, he's been planning this. 'How about a spot of refereeing then?' David's expression doesn't change, but their mother's face brightens.

'You'd make a good referee, David,' she says. Moira gives her a sharp look. 'He's very *fair*,' Mrs Brown says to Moira.

'Matches at North Road pitch, any Sunday you like,' Ted says, opening his hands to David, 'or just come and watch.'

'I don't ever go to Fern Ashton,' David says, blinking rapidly.

'You'll be alright now,' Mrs Brown says. 'That was years ago. And Ted will be there.' She pats the table next to David's hand. 'You'll look after him, won't you Ted?' He can't tell if this is a joke. It's not delivered like a joke. Ted feels himself slipping. He changes tactics: he'll go in man to man. He leans towards David and speaks out of the side of his mouth.

'What did you do to get barred from the whole town?' He's about to wink, when he catches Moira's face, not angry exactly, more like in pain. Ted sits up straight like a schoolboy.

'Thugs,' Mrs Brown announces, and turns to him, her pink lips thinned. 'I would have taken them on myself if I didn't have the flu.'

Moira narrows her eyes. 'I'm not sure you would have,' she says quietly.

Mrs Brown fixes Ted with a grim look. 'Boys who should have been born a little earlier and sent off to Hitler.' Ted doesn't know how to answer this. He considers asking David who they are, offer to avenge him. Now there's a thought: *hero to the brother*. But their mother starts in again.

'Are your family from here originally, Ted?' Ted tells her

they were, and watches Moira touch her brother's arm.

'Is Parker in the team?' Moira asks David, 'I bet he's the captain.' She speaks softly, just between the two of them.

'He's a defender, but not the goalkeeper,' David says. 'The goalkeeper is six foot five. He doesn't work on the farm.' There's something odd about the way he talks, Ted can't put his finger on it. Moira says something else but Mrs Brown is after more information about his parents. Ted tells her his mother died when he was barely out of short trousers, and his father before that. Moira's mother looks mightily disappointed. He could tell her it's been disappointing for him, Ted, being alone in the world, his frail mother trying to hide her pain when he was too young and too stupid to help her. How he's had to live with that, wishing it could have been different. *God knows, it hasn't been easy, Mrs Brown, but your daughter is the light of my life*. The fat red heart on his right bicep prickles under his shirt, as though beating of its own accord. He has to stop himself from pressing it: curling ferns, tiny rosebuds and a fat red love heart with an arrow, the letter M in the centre. He got the tattoo on Thursday, Michael's design, and he's told no one. Written on his body, she is *his*. Though right now Moira won't meet his eye.

With other girlfriends it was easy. After roast chicken at Brenda's, Ted teased her sisters and joked with her father. Around this table he can't get a foothold.

From the window in the tiny kitchen off the dining room, Moira pulls her cardigan tight around her and stares out at a clump of snowdrops in the flowerbed, their frail heads white and droopy. The crocuses, almost out, still hide their colours for the moment. She'd have a cigarette now, if she smoked. She can't remember why she came into the kitchen. Having given up on Ted's family, Moira hears her mother asking after his landlady. Is she local? Does she have other lodgers? Dilys should work for a newspaper, Moira thinks, or a detective agency.

The kettle, of course. Moira takes it to the sink, runs the water and sets it on the cooker, then she stands very still. The day outside is bright, only a few torn clouds in the clear blue sky. Moira wills the spring to lift her. She feels as though she's a thin piece of cloth, stretched and threadbare. She hasn't told Ted about the times she found David, more than once, curled and bloodied, in the long grass on the edge of the field opposite their school, the change gone from his pockets. How she knelt beside him, swallowing her dread, and dabbed at his wounds with a handkerchief while he twitched like an animal. And like an animal he would remain silent for days after, sometimes weeks. Moira doesn't know how she could ever speak of this to Ted. Time and again life has shown her that she and her brother are separate from others; it's up to her to keep it that way.

Over the rumble of water coming to the boil, Ted's voice cuts in, still hopeful.

'How about the White Horse? A pint?'

'The White Horse serves Best and Courage on tap,' David says, 'and Guinness in bottles.'

'Right,' Ted says. At the window, Moira watches a pair of magpies argue on the back fence.

'Where's the tea lady?' her mother calls, shrill and insistent. 'The tea *girl*. We need the tea girl.' There's a brief pause before Dilys says, a little breathless, 'It's how she used to announce herself when she brought me tea, when she was little.'

'What was Moira like in those days?' Ted asks. 'Was she a smasher even then?' Moira can almost hear him wink. So many *questions*. In the kitchen, she holds her breath.

'There's another White Horse, in Bristol,' David says, 'Lots of pubs are called the same name.'

Moira fills the pot, takes it through and sits back down. Ted gives her a helpless smile and refills his plate with another sandwich, a slice of cake, and a scone. Her mother beams approval. Moira herself has no appetite. Ted turns to David with a determined look.

'I'd call my pub something new,' he says, and looks to Moira, whose mind is completely blank for pub names. 'Cheer and Beer,' Ted says loudly.

'Raise a Glass,' Dilys says, laughing, 'The Queen's Knickers!'

'The Finishing Post,' Ted says, pleased.

David looks puzzled. 'Do you own a pub?' he asks, and the room descends again into quiet.

Time is a trick
1963

The remains of the harvest festival flank the altar in tall, wilting arrangements. The vicar speaks of bounty and charity. He sounds tired. Dilys closes her eyes, and before long David taps her leg with the hymn book. She nods to let him know she's not falling asleep. She's falling apart is what she's doing. Her insides have sunk, as though she's been swallowing pebbles on the quiet. Dilys is forty-seven and she feels double that. She opens her eyes and senses David's shoulders relax. No knee to pat on her other side. Moira and Ted married last month, and still Moira's absence calls Dilys into rooms, dances around the table. Dilys is beginning to understand that her daughter's absence will be larger than her presence. It is a small comfort to have all these real people here, in close proximity. The organ blast makes her jump. She stands for the hymn but doesn't join in.

At the end of the service, David leaves and she stays in the pew. She'll be along in a minute. She desperately wants a cigarette, but for now her stony burden anchors her in place. High up, the stained glass glints deep reds and blues, and specks of yellow. She stares at two figures with a goat or a sheep. The smaller one has its arm outstretched, offering, coaxing. There's nothing in the hand, as far as Dilys can see. All these made-up stories of sacrifice and helping. If Dilys had written the Bible she would have put some jokes in it: one of the disciples slipping on a banana skin, or *Knock knock, who's there?* Something to lift the spirits, for heaven's sake.

Outside, she stops on the top step and lights up, savours the first sweet rush while the congregation mills about on the sloped paving in front of the church. Dilys's gaze settles on a circle of women around her age as they chat and smile and tap each other's arms. She knows most of them from the shop, but not to tap and chat with.

She spots David, next to a man with his back to her, and gets a flutter of panic – an irrational vision of David going off too. She takes a long pull on her cigarette. The man turns. Of course, it's Mister *Duck*worth, the farmer. Dilys draws herself up. What sweeps through her, along with the nicotine, is a blaze of alertness, an almost audible rush of blood. *Here I am,* it says to the man who stole her children from her; took them, cast some spell on her son, and never really gave them back. Now David is the only one left.

Well.

She descends the steps on the balls of her feet like a dancer, in another body from the one she just hauled out of the church. She approaches her son and her rival.

'David and I were just talking—' the farmer stops. He reaches out a hand and is about to place it on her arm. Dilys steps away from him, closer to David. 'Are you alright?' the man says. The absence of Moira hovers around like a noiseless bird.

'I am, yes,' she says, with what she hopes is a glad smile. 'David and *I* were just talking about—' She'll need to start again, obviously, since they weren't just talking. 'It's been very busy, with Moira—' she drops the butt on the ground and stamps on it.

The farmer nods as though he understands. 'Wonderful she got married.'

Dilys might kick the man's legs from under him. 'We're going to my sister's.' Dilys's voice is high and loud, as surprising to her as the words; she's not seen her sister in years.

'London?' Mr Duckworth says, pleasantly. He's wearing green corduroy trousers, which make Dilys think of a slimy pond.

'When are we?' David says with his nervous blink.

'Soon.' She's not even sure she'll make it back to the house. She hasn't been back to Morden since she left in forty-five. Her sister moved to the south coast, and they seldom speak.

'Well, when you get back, David and I were just talking about a canine friend of mine.'

'I'm sorry?' In her fury, the meaning of 'canine' escapes her.

'A new litter. A while ago now actually,' the farmer waves his hand. 'It was a thought. Another time.' The man's face is like a pumpkin, and he clearly doesn't own a hairbrush. Dilys crosses her arms over her bosom. He's really no match for her – she will keep hold of her son.

'You didn't have my war,' she says. It comes from nowhere.

He looks confused. 'No,' he agrees, 'we were lucky here—'

'Getting a dog is a good idea,' David says.

'A *dog*?'

'Our house is less full now,' David says, looking directly at her in a way that makes her want to shield her face. Dilys looks around. The women have all gone. She looks up at the sky: grey and clueless. She needs another cigarette but her hands are shaking. *Our house is less full now.*

'It was just an idea,' the farmer says, patting his pockets, closing the conversation.

'My son and I,' Dilys says slowly, each word searching for the next, 'have things to do.' She's sorely disappointed in how the sentence turns out. The man takes a step back.

'We can put him in the sitting room,' David says. The farmer pats him three times on the arm. In order not to strike the man, Dilys grips her own arms around her so tightly her ribs hurt. This interloper. This *man* who shows affection to her son, when he will take none from her.

'When you get back from London,' he says to David, glancing at Dilys, 'we'll talk then.'

'I'm not going to London,' David says, matter of fact. But Mister Duckworth has turned and is walking off, back to his life.

Dilys curses herself for her war comment – a long-buried tic. Why the hell did she say it? She's beginning to make herself sick with her dishonesty, her mistakes. The truth is, her early war days were some of her happiest – the cheek-by-jowl life (and cheek-by-cheek, thigh-by-thigh, secrets) – open houses, noise, smoke, lending and borrowing: everyone held together with the same thread.

At home, Dilys can't remember how things move along. She and David sit opposite each other at the table; soft chewing sounds and the wind against the small windows. How can she stay in the present? Didn't she demand this once of her children, at this very table when they first came here? The future stretches out, each day the same. There is only the past. Dilys suspects that for a great many people time is a trick, like a reel of tape: you loop around and around, and when you slip out, if your life is static, you loop back around. Surely she can't be the only one? Fear presses on her like a heavy coat, in the evenings and in the night. Fear that she will get stuck in a past she can't be sure is even real. After all this time she starts to miss Ray, her gentle, nervous husband, brought out of his shell by his children. She had not loved him well, is the truth. Dilys had been disappointed in her marriage. It happened in a rush, and she always wished she had picked someone bolder, more showy. But now thoughts of Ray are like weak, warm sunshine – more tricks played by time – tinkering with her memories. He has been visiting her dreams.

David gets up, takes the plates to the kitchen and puts the kettle on. David will keep her in the present. But what to *say* to him? What would Moira say? Moira, now in her flat, in the town, with her new husband who builds and fixes and adores. Moira asked the right questions, acted as translator and facilitator; like those people on the radio who tell you what's next: a *continuity announcer*. Though Moira doesn't announce herself, she only nudges it all along. How funny, Dilys thinks bitterly, that it is only now she is gone that she begins to understand her daughter.

David comes back and places a mug of tea in front of her.

'Thank you,' she says. 'I'm afraid I'm all of a dither.'

'You are genuine steadfast and true,' he says.

Welcome
1968

Ted could beat his chest, turn a cartwheel, sing! Standing in the hallway – in *his* hallway – he taps his toe on the lino. He'll lay a new floor, parquet? Not easy, but it would be a stunner of an entrance hall criss-crossed underfoot. It's a dream come true – a *house*! They moved in yesterday and just in time. Moira's getting bigger, she's two months off. A corridor leads to the kitchen with the front room off it on the right. On the left is a recess under the stairs with coat hooks – nice use of space. The kitchen is dark, he'll put in a skylight. Skylights give a lot of answers, biblical in their way. And he'll knock through. He could get cracking with a sledgehammer right now – his arms, his fingers, twitch at the thought. Oh, he's like a kid in a sweet shop!

Ted had puffed up like a peacock when Andrew finally came along (after three years they had begun to wonder), and now he's giving the boy a house: number twelve, semi-detached. And it'll give Moira plenty to do so she won't have time to miss her job. With two kids, she surely won't miss it, though he'd thought that when Andrew came along. Then, Moira had pined for her work as she pined for her old home and her family after they got married and moved into the flat. Ted rubs his hands and comes back to his house. *Stairs*. Turning right on the landing. After the flat, stairs are a novelty. These two bottom steps in front of him widen out. *Welcome*, they say, *come on up*. It's the details.

Tacked on the end of the dining room is the quirky bit: a glass 'extension', a poor man's conservatory. Someone, in their wisdom (or lack of it), has tacked on a flimsy half-room, glass panels on a wooden frame. This sort of thing is popular, but Ted doesn't get it. Eating your tea with the dark looming at the end of the table? No, thank you. He stands under the panels, which are piled with leaves. Glass shouldn't act as roof and wall, it's all wrong. Luckily the downstairs loo, at the end of the extension, has a real roof and plastered walls. With his knuckles, he knocks top to bottom, as he has many times: still solid.

'Glory be,' his mother might say. It occurs to him that his mother would have liked very much to see Ted move into this house, and he would very much have liked to show it to her. He'll find the box where Moira wrapped and stacked their few photos, and he will put his mother on a shelf in the front room. He heads there now, back through the dim kitchen. He'll need to prioritise that skylight.

Lying in bed, Ted reaches for Moira's hand in the dark and squeezes it.

We've made it, he wants to say *This is for you*. He wants to ask *Are you happy? Will you be happy here*? He's trying not to think about when they moved into the flat after they married, how all of a sudden Moira was not the same. Her smiles became strained and she would look around in an odd, distracted way. He had busted a gut to get that flat ready for Moira, and when they got there she went into a state of mourning. She was homesick. It had killed him – after all, she *was* home.

This is different. This is the one.

'What do you think?' he says. Then to be clear he adds, shyly, 'of our house?'

'I like our house,' Moira says. 'Maybe not as much as you, but still a lot. And remember you promised me extra storage.' The smile in her voice makes his heart sing. This house is not so far from their flat, which is not so far from where Moira lived before, where Dilys and David still live. But it seems to Ted they have travelled a great distance – he feels like an explorer, his flag waving at the summit.

*

Four plus three plus six plus four. Seventeen hours. Ted is walking the streets near their house, one Sunday in late summer, at one o'clock in the morning, with nine-month-old Bea in the pram. Adding up his sleep has become a habit, like rubbing his chin or clearing his throat. If he averages five hours a night he's doing well. Tonight, he sang her to sleep, and he half expects someone to appear from the shadows with his cash prize. In the face of Moira's exhaustion, Ted's picking up some slack at the weekend. He carries Bea around the place squalling, and just when his panic rises to the point of shoving a sock in her mouth, she conks out like a snuffed candle. Then Ted is left panting, ears ringing, bamboozled.

A little girl! His desire to protect, to guard, was even stronger when a baby girl popped out. He almost felt bad for Andrew. Finally, someone who will need *looking after*, since Moira doesn't need much of that from him. But so far, this daughter has only got him riled and uncertain. So far, she's a different species to her brother. Andrew had been a doddle – he respected the night, more or less. This one's got a pair of lungs you wouldn't believe, and she'll stare you out until you can't stand the scrutiny. Asleep though, she's a beauty.

'Bee bop-a-loula, she's my baby,' he croons as they stroll in the balmy air, under a velvet black sky spattered with stars. The haze of the Milky Way stretches out over them. *Billions* of stars. When the dusty strip shows itself as clearly as this, it feels to Ted like seeing a secret. Night walks with Bea have rekindled his old hobby. When they were courting, he would prattle on to Moira about the stars as he walked her home. He forgot to tuck into the pram tonight Moira's first-ever gift to him: a small, ring-bound book, *The Night Sky*, with laminated pages. It had touched him deeply. He looks for the stars he can name. *Follow the curve of the Plough handle around to locate the bright Arcturus.* He glances down and gives a start: Bea's eyes are wide open like saucers, like planets, looking straight at him. She blinks – one clean movement.

She could be made of glass, or china. He's never seen her this still while awake.

'This here is a rare treat, Bea-bop,' he says, strangely flustered. He tries to get her gaze to follow his up to the sky, not wanting her to miss it. But she will only look at him. The night glow gives her cheeks a pearly glaze, her lips are a thin dark line, her eyes big knowing circles. He half holds his breath, waiting for something, while they gaze at each other in the starlight.

'My darling.' He has never before called her this. The surprise of the words makes his throat thick, his ears tingle. He gropes around for something else but nothing comes, and under Bea's constant gaze he starts to feel a kind of helplessness. As if in response, her lips suddenly part a fraction and she lets out a tiny sigh. Her eyelids drop, in slow motion, and she falls back to sleep with a half-open mouth.

An ideal world

David takes his cup from the hook. It is cream-coloured with a blue stripe around the top and says 'David, meaning: Beloved or Uncle' in blue letters. This is true. It is twice true now that Moira his sister has two children. 'Andrew, meaning: Manly and Brave', and 'Beatrice, meaning: Bringer of Joy'. He had to order the one for Beatrice as they didn't have it on the shelf. She's not yet two and doesn't use the mug in case she breaks it.

All the mugs are on the kitchen hooks. Moira's is back here now. She took it with her when she moved to Fern Ashton, and then she brought it back and hung it up again. His mother had put another mug there in the meantime, but it's better now all five are in a line. They had to order one for her as well – it wasn't in the shop. 'Dilys, meaning: Genuine Steadfast and True', in Welsh. David takes this mug down too and puts a teabag in both.

David is keen on origins. He still carries *Easy Tree Recognition* with him in his coat pocket. His favourite is weeping willow. Also copper beech, because a purple tree is very unusual and quite funny. Mister Jem gave him the book in 1962. Question one: 'Are all its leaves needle-like?' Yes: Page 2. No: Page 43. Question two: 'Are its leaves in the form of scales?' Yes: Page 52. No: Page 57. In the end, you have identified the tree.

In an ideal world, you would do this with everything. His mother says 'in an ideal world' quite a lot. Her ideal world has in it mainly cigarettes and tea, and Moira living here again (her mug back on the mug hook isn't the same). There are eight hooks under the cabinet, and currently, the mugs on the end three are plain white ones from Woolworth's. David has thought about getting one for Willow, but it would be a waste as she has her bowl. And there's no official meaning for her name, though a close match is Winola which means 'gracious friend' which is extremely apt. The library has an excellent book on the origins of names.

Raymond, his father's name, has a German origin and means 'protecting hands'. David can clearly remember his father's hands with their long fingers, holding and shaking a bright handkerchief before he made it disappear. David would get him to do the trick over and over, staring so hard at the fingers his eyes hurt, and only at the end, when his father shook out the yellow piece of silk, did David look up into his father's face. 'I'll tell you when you're old enough to keep a secret,' he would say when David begged for the reveal. '*I am*,' David insisted. And Raymond would wink and say 'I know', but still not tell him. And then he disappeared himself.

David once saw a 'Ray' mug in the new gift shop in Fern Ashton and wanted so badly to buy it that he got a stomach ache like he does when he's really hungry. The shop didn't last long. 'Good riddance,' his mother said. 'Full of tit-tat.' David still wishes he'd bought it; he could have kept it with the other things, away from his mother. He still thinks about that mug.

Moira moved out properly a long time ago, but his mother's ideal world would still have her here. David's too. According to his mother, David's ideal world would be full of dogs. She's right, but not all at once, because you need to train them individually. They have personalities, a bit like people but with fewer possibilities. You could look them up in the same way as leaves. Buffalo was big, curious and lively, and then turned slow. If you had a dog identification book you would need to re-reference when the dog was old. At Buffalo's burial, where there was only Mister Jem and Alice and David, Mister had put his arm around David's shoulders (the only time) and said, 'He was your dog too.' This wasn't true, but if he said it then it was what he meant. Perhaps in Mister Jem's ideal world, Buffalo belonged to them both.

Willow is medium-sized, soft and jumpy, and does belong to David. He got her when he was twenty-five and Moira was twenty-three. With ages, he always thinks about Moira's as well as his own. His mother does the same. She'll say 'We moved here when you were eight and ten.' Even things that don't involve David. She said, 'Andrew was born when you were twenty-eight and thirty, just when I'd given up.' (What she had given up, David isn't sure. Not smoking, she'll never give that up.) If they were leaves, would Moira and David be found on the same page? It's an interesting question, and one to which there is no answer. An *Easy Human Recognition* book would be impossible.

There are moments that David remembers very clearly. His father's handkerchief trick is one, the moment he met Willow is another. It was a Sunday in 1963. A Moira Sunday, but Moira couldn't get away from the hospital which meant his mother left her hair sticking out, smoked at the table, and didn't talk. She made David jump when, before he'd even finished his crumble, she pushed her chair away so hard it crashed to the floor and said 'We're going to the farm to see your friend.'

Everything about that evening was extraordinary. They had never been to the farm together; his mother may not have been there at all since the end of the war. David has been there six days a week ever since the end of school. They walked from the bus stop in the almost dark, his mother swatting at the overgrown hedge tendrils like flies. In an ideal world, she would live in the city, not the countryside. David pointed out the bats, which made his mother walk faster, almost run.

Mister Jem was waiting for them on the drive and when they went inside his mother stood back, and almost pushed David into the kitchen. A small dog hurtled across the floor and launched itself onto David's legs, tumbled back, then did it again. David sat straight down on the tiles. The dog was black and white, with lots of hair, floppy ears and big brown eyes, glassy like marbles. It clambered on him and licked his face and David let it. It was softer than anything David could remember, and more wriggly.

David stayed on the floor with the puppy for a long time while his mother talked to Mister Jem. The tiles made his legs cold, but the puppy sat on top of him and warmed his middle, chewing at the arm of his coat. David watched its teeth and stroked it. The fur was long and soft, like hair, not like Buffalo's. Mister came and squatted beside him.

'David,' he said in a serious voice, 'this is your dog now.' David felt dizzy, but a different dizzy than usual – a gaspy kind where he wanted to laugh. The dog slid off his leg, wagging its tail, wagging its whole self.

'You'll have to think of a name,' Mister Jem said. 'It's a girl.' The dog settled to chewing his sleeve again and David stroked her and thought, *I am in my ideal world.*

David and Dilys sit in the small front room sipping their tea. David on the old sofa, Dilys in the armchair by the window and Willow on the rug between them. Willow is eight now, and an asset to the household, David's mother says so. She trips over her sometimes and says things like, 'Bloody hell fire, are you trying to kill me?' But she always makes amends, particularly if David clears his throat. Then she says, 'My fault, my fault.' Or she says, 'Sorry Will, you're an asset to the household.' If David could choose name meanings he might have 'Willow, meaning: Filler of Silence' stencilled on a mug. Silence can have different meanings, and in their house silence is mostly sad. When it is just David and Willow in the front room, the silence is normal, but when his mother is there it's different. She isn't sad when she's moving around, or when Moira and her children are here, only when she sits down and her shoulders go droopy, like now. David scrapes his fingers on the sofa for Willow to get up, and he pushes her firmly towards his mother.

The dog puts her head on his mother's lap, and her shoulders un-droop while she strokes. She sings 'Love Me Tender' by Elvis Presley.

English cocker spaniels have an average lifespan of around eleven years and, while he doesn't want to, David occasionally thinks about her burial. When his mother has finished the song, and before she starts the next, David says 'She's your dog, too.' His mother looks pleased and sad at the same time, which is how she often looks.

'Thank you, David,' she says. Then she sings 'Hound Dog' and he joins in with 'You ain't never gonna rabbit and you ain't no friend of mine.'

Go placidly
1982

'*Mesdemoiselles.*' In front of the blackboard, Madame McFarlane pushes her thick glasses up her nose. '*Avez-vous une idée pour vos projets*?' She fixes her magnified gaze around the stuffy classroom. One by one, from their desks, the girls stir and utter barely audible responses.

'*Oui*,' they say. Or '*non*'. Languorous, nasal, grudging, elbows on desks, faces squashed on fists. Only '*oui*' or '*non*' up to Sarah, the new girl with frizzy hair and army-style boots, who holds her chin in a thoughtful way.

'*Peut-être*,' Sarah says. The class scowl, and shift in their uncomfortable chairs, all except Bea who laughs a quacking laugh. After the bell, Bea and the new girl are the last two in the classroom, sun streaming through the murky windows.

'Are you doing yours on *Les Liaisons*?' Sarah asks while they pack up. She has her back to the light, and the tips of the frizz glow in a halo.

'*Peut-être*,' Bea says with a slanting smile. They agree to work on it together sometime, after school. 'I'll come to yours,' Bea says.

Sarah's house is full of old things: pots and wooden chests and tall brass lamps with dangling tassels. Things that don't work: the grandfather clock in the hall, the giant food mixer to which Sarah's mother has sellotaped a note saying 'Mend me, please!' Fluffy circles in dark corners turn out on closer inspection to be balls of dust.

At the edge of the dining room sits a piano with its lid open, like endless rows of teeth. The whole place reminds Bea of a house in *How We Used To Live*, which she saw in primary school on the wheeled-in telly. This includes Sarah's parents. Her dad's a lecturer in philosophy or history or something, her mum's a social worker. Books are everywhere, and piles of paper; lots of things in piles, all important-looking. Bea thinks of her own house where nothing is important.

Go placidly amid the noise and the haste— The poem is bang in front of her in the boxy downstairs loo. She scans it, distracted, then reads greedily. *Many fears are born of fatigue and loneliness.* Oh! It's for her! The whole thing is for her. By the end, she has tears in her eyes. *Be cheerful. Strive to be happy*. Good advice.

She comes out wanting to hug Sarah, or anyone, but she keeps her arms to herself and sits at the dinner table with Sarah and her parents, 'Call us Morris and Eleanor,' where she's offered a taste of wine (wine!) because it's Friday. She has to concentrate to keep up. Once, the dad leans over and *kisses the mum*. Bea tries not to stare. Sarah's parents say things like 'if it wasn't for the government losing its critical faculties', and 'a nebulous point of view'.

Later, on the fluffy rug upstairs in Sarah's room, Bea has landed in heaven. Duran Duran plays from the stereo in the corner, next to a groovy lava lamp.

'I didn't understand half what they were saying,' she giggles (is she drunk?).

Sarah rolls her eyes. 'Tell me about it,' she says. Sarah's bedroom is like a grown-up's room: posh velvet curtains, patchwork bedspread, more books. Spandau Ballet on one wall *in a frame*, a seriously cool Picasso on the other. A giant globe, like a big blue head, sits on a dark wood table by the bed.

'*La monde*,' Bea says happily.

'Le *monde*,' Sarah corrects. 'Spin it.' Bea reaches a tentative hand and pushes the globe's surface, it wobbles on its axis and Sarah lunges across to stop it with a finger.

'Hey babe, take a walk on the wild side,' Sarah says in an American accent. Bea laughs along. 'United States,' Sarah explains. 'Wherever it lands, you talk the lingo, the *vernacular*.'

‘Right,’ Bea says. Sarah sounds like her parents.

‘Spin again.’

Bea does, and stops the globe with a finger in the Pacific Ocean. It strikes her that most of the world is ocean; that the pink and green and brown patches are stuck on as an afterthought, reaching out to each other across the blue. Her friend is doing a vigorous front crawl on the rug beside her, her big hair bouncing. Bea starts up a slow breaststroke. *Every breath you take* The Police sing from the speakers. Sarah turns it down and fixes Bea with an ultra-serious face.

‘Every game you play, every night you stay—’ she holds out an imaginary microphone to Bea.

‘I’ll be watching you,’ Bea finishes, and rolls onto her back, happy without striving.

*

Sarah comes to Bea’s house only once, by accident, just before Christmas. Bea swears it will never happen again. They start off in her room. It’s cramped, the carpet’s scratchy and there’s no beanbag, let alone lava lamp, bookcase, globe that twirls around. Her hedgehogs gawp at her, lined up on the shelf in descending size order, starting with a lumpy soft toy strangled with swim medals, and ending with a thumb-sized piece of moulding clay skewered with toothpicks. Who collects *hedgehogs*? David Bowie stares at them creepily from the wall with his funny eyes and ripped, sellotaped arm. Sarah looks around with interest. *Stop!* Bea wants to shout.

‘What are the medals for?’ Sarah asks in a polite voice she might use for a shopkeeper.

‘Swimming.’

‘Yep, thought I saw the technique—’

‘I gave up,’ Bea cuts in. ‘Didn’t get into County.’ She tries to say it casually, though the reality had been devastating: her secret dreams of County stardom, then Nationals, snatched away, with no one to comfort her. It's still unbelievable that this won't be her life.

Sarah's still looking at the medals. Bea winces. 'It's crap here, sorry.'

'*Où sont les toilettes*?' Sarah asks loudly.

'On the landing,' she mumbles. They get up and bang knees. Bea looks around desperately for something to inspire, something to bring back the friends who sit on Sarah's floor, cracking each other up. There's a thud and clatter from the next room. Dad's fixing up a bed for Lonnie, who's busting out of her cot. Lonnie! Why didn't Bea think of her?

They find Lonnie in the kitchen with Mum and haul her into the freezing Annexe. Bea flicks on the little heater and flops into the recliner. Sarah plays with Lonnie on the rug, then heaves her onto her lap in the big wicker chair and bounces her. They're all facing the back garden – almost *in* the back garden. Outside, it's getting dark. From the edge of the patio, the bare apple tree reaches out spooky, beckoning branches.

Sarah looks up and around, impressed. 'This place is so *cool*.' Her words form small speech-bubble clouds. 'It's a kind of greenhouse-sitting room hybrid,' Sarah says. Almost on cue, Dad starts hammering upstairs. Bea agrees with her friend about the Annexe. It *is* cool. Dad converted it for Granny Dil a few years ago, after he got fired and went mental (she doesn't say this), then Granny got better and never came to live with them after all.

Ted will always remember the Annexe as the turning point. Being hung out to dry by Alan bleeding Turner was enough for anyone to lose the plot; accused of causing a building to collapse, right here in town for all to see. It still makes Ted feel sick. But finally, three years ago, it was the Annexe that saved him. He had a stud wall up inside a week, sectioning off the kitchen diner; he'd got an electrician to run a cable under the floor for Dilys to control her own lighting. He then draught-proofed the panels as best he could. The utility room became a bathroom without too much alteration. From the dining room, you wouldn't know the glass room was there, on the other side of the curtain Moira hung to conceal the stud wall. Mealtimes at first felt squeezed and dark, though thank god for the skylight. After a while, they stopped noticing.

From the garden, the renovated glass room looked like someone had left it there by accident: a stranded bed and chair and rug on the outside of a house; the set of a school play. Not quite what Ted had planned – if he'd had longer, he would have tiled the roof – though a tidy enough job, given the time. Moira didn't like 'granny annexe', so they simply called it 'the Annexe'. And it was a good distraction.

The whole thing got Ted thinking. About space. *Rooms*, and how they can slip around easily. He'd never given much thought to domestic jobs. But when he had stood on the patio, surveying his work, he thought *I could scale this up*. And if he worked alone, Ted would be in charge of safety: no one, ever, would come to harm, he'd make damn sure of that. People had their Olds come to live with them all the time, all over. And even if they didn't, they might want a workshop, a cubby hole, a who-knows-what. He, Ted, could build it for them. Why had he not thought of this before?

Bea sleeps here sometimes, in the recliner meant for Granny with the lever that shoots out the footrest. Just her and the night, halfway to camping. She gets a thrill of exposure when she wakes, lying here in full view of the day. It makes her feel restless; excited in a vague, stomach-flipping way.

'My Granny was supposed to come and die here,' she explains to Sarah, 'but she got better.' Bea winces again. Why did she say it like that?

'That's good,' Sarah says. Lonnie thwacks her striped octopus on Sarah's leg, then stuffs it in her mouth. They hear Mum singing 'Love Me Do' over the boiling kettle through the wall. Bea wants to yell at her to *Shut your fat gob.* Lonnie reads her mind and lets out a loud squeal.

Moira puts her head around the door. 'Shall I take her?'

'No thanks,' Bea says and glares. *She's keeping this show on the road.* 'She's fine.'

'Tea in ten minutes,' Moira smiles.

Tea lasts for what seems like a week, everyone staring at Sarah as though she's an exhibit in a museum. Bea struggles to swallow her chicken pie. She notices only today how poky and dingy their dining room is. Dad comes in halfway through the meal and, seeing an extra person, he gives a sort of bow and says 'Evening all' in a voice Bea has never heard in her life. Andrew smirks in his seat, his spots glowing.

'Ted, this is Bea's friend Sarah.'

'Pleased to meet you,' Sarah says, in the shopkeeper voice.

Has everyone gone totally off their nut? Lonnie, who usually splashes and sings at mealtimes, has turned mute to amplify the rest of the family's total retard-ness.

'Are you off on the French Trip too?' Dad says to Sarah, with an unnecessary wink. It had been yesterday's topic, when Bea brought the letter home. The trip's not till next year but you can pay in instalments.

'Yes, it's for the whole set,' Sarah says. Bea grips her knife and fork so hard she gets cramp.

'Andrew went to Berlin, didn't you?' Dad says. He's gone all pally with Andrew just lately now he's teaching him to drive. Bea's envious of the driving – she literally can't wait to rev an engine and wheel spin away from this place.

'Bovenden. It's the twin town,' Andrew says, in his normal voice at least. 'No one's heard of it.' Bea's agony is diverted for a moment while she tries to picture her brother in a German city with German shops and German people. She can't imagine him anywhere. Or any of them. But it's a fact – he went. She clearly remembers him leaving. He survived and came back and must have done a bunch of German things. Hopefully she'll get to do French things, with French boys.

'Did you do German O level?' Sarah asks Andrew across the table.

What the—? Bea has got to put a stop to this. She kicks out under the table, aiming for Lonnie, to get her to make some noise, but misses and slides down in her chair.

'I got a 'B',' Andrew is saying, 'I'd have picked French, but my school doesn't give a choice.' His spotty cheeks turn slowly pink. 'My grandpa was killed by the Germans.' Is he actually trying to *show off*? Bea forks in a mouthful of pie, chews endlessly.

'I'm not sure that's true Andrew,' Mum says. 'Did Granny tell you that?'

'He was killed in the war,' Andrew says. 'His name was Raymond.' His face is now a deep red, it's sort of amazing to watch. Bea glances at Sarah who's also staring at Andrew's face. *Christ.* Why can't she have a normal family? Why can't they talk about the government and important things? What they all need is some *wine*.

'War war warmmm,' Lonnie interjects suddenly. Sarah laughs, delighted, while everyone else ignores Lonnie.

'He died *during* the war,' Mum says, and looks suddenly tragic, like she's only just remembered her dad is dead.

'Well, that's all in the past,' Dad says with his new voice and personality. 'We're all in the Common Market now. Peace on earth and goodwill to all men,' here he grins in Bea and Sarah's direction, 'and women.' Bea gives him a *You're tragic* look, then turns pointedly away. Since that fucked-up time three years ago when he didn't go to work, when he literally turned into a nut-job, when he actually *broke her leg*, she has tried to blank him completely. But lately, she keeps forgetting. Her father thumps his hand flat on his chest, over his heart, mimicking a blow received: a dig at her.

'Oof! Bullseye.' He winks at Sarah. 'If looks could kill.' Silently Bea wills him not to tell the story of her shooting him. Sarah might think *she's* the nutcase. Inside her chest, Bea's breath starts swirling about. Dad gets up, walks around the table and pulls Lonnie out of her chair, easing her wedged legs with repeated jiggles.

'Hello Pixie,' he says and rubs noses with her, not minding a smear of mashed potato on his cheek. It occurs to Bea that this is a pattern: when she won't look at him, he'll pick up Lonnie. She sits on his hip, pats his face, and dribbles a string of saliva. Has this been happening for a year and a half?

'Away for four days.' Mum's still on about the German trip. And suddenly Bea's head is full of memories of Andrew leaving.

From her bedroom window she had watched the car pull away. She'd been calling to him from her room, but her voice got lost in the general panic. None of them had been abroad before; Andrew was their very own Christopher Columbus, and everyone shared in the excitement. In the run-up, Bea had become increasingly jumpy about him going, strangely bound to each other as they were at that horrible time. She was desperate to get her message to him – she'd been practising the phrase – but she couldn't get down the stairs. Dad banged the car roof, 'We're leaving now!' She hopped to her window as the old suitcase was shut in the boot and they drove off. She couldn't get downstairs in time because of her broken leg. Because of *Dad* breaking her leg. And now he's all 'Peace on earth', wink wink. *He doesn't fool me.*

'In France, won't you?' Mum's asking her a question. And now they're all looking at her, Sarah included. And it's all she can do to keep her breath steady.

'Peace on *earth*'? she spits the question to the side of Dad's head. Lonnie's chunky legs kick out around his middle. A familiar thrill of fury burns in Bea's throat, brought up from nowhere; from everyone being so fucking weird tonight, from the time she was stuck and couldn't shout her wishes to her brother, from lying on the soggy ice with pain stabbing her ankle, from the crack of her head against her bedroom wall the day her County swimming dreams died. All of this has brought on her burning outrage.

Around the table, they stare at her. She's got their attention and she is suddenly victorious, like she's won something, her rage a bright flame lighting her whole being. It is her superpower. She's *right*, she's in *charge*. It's *Dad* who's the bad guy here. She can feel Sarah looking from her to Dad and back. Andrew's face has drained from red to white, quick as litmus paper. Bea stands up suddenly, her chair smacks the floor, she takes a noisy breath.

'*Auf Wiedersehen*,' she says loudly, to all of them, her fists are tense but she holds back from punching the air. Then a line from the poem pops into her head, why not throw that in? '*The world is full of trickery, but let this not blind you*!' she shouts. They all look at her like she's gone mental. And if she has, who's fault is *that*? She motions jerkily to Sarah to come. Her friend, hunched and cringing, gets up to follow.

'*Auf Wiedersehen*,' Bea says once more, to Andrew, giving the phrase as much drama and hurt and *meaning* as she can. And with her chin high, her friend trailing behind her, she marches out of the room.

Peachy wonderful

One day in the spring when Bea comes home from school, the air in the Annexe has changed: a delicate sweet-sour smell enters her nostrils. And there, tucked up in the recliner, is Granny Dil, shrunken and silent. Bea had almost forgotten this was all for her in the first place. She's come straight from the hospital. Bea squeezes around the front of the bed and curls up in the big wicker chair. She peers in and finds Granny's sleeping face, her papery skin flickering around the eyes. She's only about sixty-five but she looks a hundred-and-fifty, and she's smaller than when Bea last saw her: when they watched the Royal Wedding video, again. But that was ages ago. A pang of guilt pricks her chest.

Granny would put the video on whenever Bea went round, of Lady Di in the huge puffy dress that Granny loves, and tell Bea about her own wedding: the Harris tweed suit that sounds totally gross, and her pearl earrings and Pomegranate Passion lipstick. Always the clothes and jewellery, nothing much about the grandpa Bea never met. Granny calls Lady Di's story a 'real-life fairy tale'. Bea begs to differ. Lady Di is off-the-scale pretty, and if Bea was her, she would have got someone a lot better looking.

Granny wakes up and startles when she sees the garden right in front of her. She pats the blankets as though to check she's on solid ground. Bea leans out from her chair, and Granny's face crinkles into a smile.

'Hello, Beetle.' Then her face clouds over. 'What about David?' she says.

'David's fine,' Mum says, coming in with two mugs of tea. 'He'll be fine.' But her face is as worried as Granny's. Bea looks from one to the other, not sure what the fuss is about. Anyone would think Uncle David's a child – he's older than Mum.

'He's got Bear,' Bea offers.

'Yes, of course.' Mum seems relieved at the reminder of the dog.

'Bear,' Granny repeats. Mum puts the tea down and goes round the back of the recliner to sit Granny up.

'Arm under the axilla,' Mum says, to no one. Granny does a sharp intake of breath as she is straightened, and lets it out slowly.

'She's showing off,' Granny says to Bea, still wincing, 'now she's back at school.'

'I'll leave you to it,' Moira says and returns to the kitchen.

Today Moira's revising IV fluids. Her books are spread out on the table. She has to make the most of Lonnie's nap times. And she's determined that Dilys moving in won't put a stop to her plan. When Pauline suggested she train for her Registered Nurse diploma, Moira had been speechless. 'Don't be so grateful, Moy,' Pauline said. 'We win in the end, we get to keep you.' Pauline is the manager at Valentine's. Not only is she allowing Moira to do this in work time, she's not reducing her pay.

Pauline and Ang had been round again yesterday to get their weekly fix of Lonnie, whom they both claim to be in love with. They sat on the sofa and Lonnie clambered between them.

'Everyone asks for you when you're not in, Moy,' Ang said. It made Moira think of her first job at the cottage hospital.

'Bonny Lonnie,' Pauline sang, bouncing her.

'Her real name's Lorna, you know,' Andrew said, appearing with Bea at the door. They always come out of their rooms for Pauline, she brings them both a Mars bar.

'But Lonnie sounds nicer,' Bea said, 'though Debbie or Stevie were better.'

'Bea had a list of names for her sister,' Moira explained.

'But they went for Lorna *Mary*,' Bea rolled her eyes.

'Mary, for Ted's mother,' Moira said.

'*Dead* mother,' Bea said, 'not like she'll know.'

'No dead. You dead?' Lonnie parroted, and everyone laughed, even Bea. And then Ted had come in and the kids had disappeared. Ted made straight for Lonnie, as always; spun her around until she squealed, then whisked her away for a change. Moira may have closed her eyes and dozed off momentarily; the thought of her mother's arrival made her weary beyond measure.

'Well!' Pauline had said, and the two guests exchanged a look. 'They don't make them like that anymore.' Then for clarity, '*Husbands*.'

In the kitchen, Moira looks at her open textbook: labelled pictures of various-sized needles. A loud hoot of Bea's laughter comes through the wall, then another sound, a cackle and a long glide down the scale, followed by a lot of coughing. It takes Moira a few moments to understand her mother is laughing. Of course – with Bea she laughs. Moira wonders how this is going to work. How will her mother take to being looked after by her? How will she herself take to it? 'Dilys is the lucky one Moy,' Pauline had said. 'Not everyone gets a professional.' Moira didn't say Dilys has never and will never see herself as lucky. Another peel of laughter comes from the Annexe, and this time the cough sounds more strangled. Moira gets to her feet and puts her head around the door. Bea has her head on the covers, Dilys is patting Bea's hair with one hand and wiping her eyes with the other. The scene is hard to make sense of.

'Everything alright?' Moira says. Bea sits up, her hair tousled. Dilys turns to Moira, all innocence, as though she cries with laughter every day of the week.

'Fine,' Bea says, waving a hand. '*Ne t'inquiète pas*,' and she gives a little snort.

'We could draw the curtains,' Moira says, coming towards the glass, 'I velcroed—'

'I said don't worry about it, Mum,' Bea interrupts, loud and dismissive. Stung, Moira lingers for an instant in the middle of the room, she looks from her mother to her daughter and sees they are waiting for her to go. She turns on her heels and closes the door behind her.

'I won't need a clock, will I?' Granny says, staring out.

'It's really cool,' Bea says, 'like you're not really inside.'

'And that's a *good* thing?'

'Go with the flow,' Bea says, smiling. 'I love it here. You will too.' The low half-moon, out early, balances above the rooftops at the end of the garden. Granny reaches for Bea with a knuckly hand.

'You're an adventurer, like me,' she squeezes Bea's fingers. 'A romantic.' And right then a wave of gratitude, of *relief* passes through Bea like a current. Granny will be here *every day*. Before she can ask about adventure, romance, Granny leans forward with her secretive look.

'Show me something,' she nods at Bea's schoolbag on the floor. Bea had forgotten how, even before she was poorly, Granny liked to see and touch things from Bea's life: magazines, schoolbooks, a new scarf. Sort of like she wants to live Bea's life with her. Which is fine by Bea. She hoiks her bag onto her lap and empties the contents onto the blanket: maths exercise book, strawberry-tinted lip balm, string of multicoloured paperclips, crushed Tampax box, *Les Liaisons Dangereuses*, ironic pink lunchbox, half of a Rubik's cube. Granny scrutinises all of it.

'Is it peachy?' she asks while she looks.

'Peachy?'

'Peachy. Wonderful. Being young.'

Bea will tell her another day about the sham and drudgery, the waiting for something, anything, to actually *happen*. She now knows the poem in Sarah's loo by heart and chants the verses to herself in bed. She remembers the dream she had last night. Her dreams have been extra vivid lately. She tells Granny about being stuck halfway up a mountain. The Wellstone boys were left at the bottom and it started to snow and she couldn't see anything, only hear her teacher shouting '*Montez*!' Granny leans right into her, hungry for every word.

'What did you have on your feet?' she asks.

'My *feet*?'

'For climbing in the snow. Your footwear.'

Bea grins, and the current passes through her again: even her dreams Granny takes seriously.

'Alright in here ladies?' Dad's head pokes round the door, then the whole of him. Bea stops grinning. Dad rubs his hands and looks around, as though it's the first time he's been in here.

'Welcome to your new home, Dilys,' he says, opening his arms like an estate agent giving a tour. Except there's nowhere to go. He takes three steps in and arrives at the bed.

'Got everything you need?' he asks.

'She just got here,' Bea says.

'Thank you, Ted,' Dilys says, wheezing slightly. 'It's very comfortable.'

He beams at her. 'I'll bring some water.'

'We had tea, we're fine,' Dilys says.

'We're peachy,' Bea says. 'Peachy wonderful.'

Finally, something does happen, later that spring, on Hardelot Plage, worth reporting in the Annexe, though maybe not all of it. The aim of the trip is to snog a French boy, and Bea sniffs some out on the afternoon of Day One at the end of the beach: one fat, one tall, one ratty-looking, and Laurent. Laurent has floppy hair and a tight T-shirt with *Mon Plaisir* across the front.

'*Je m'appelle Béatrice*,' Bea says, grinding the 'r' at the back of her throat. She flicks her hair, pulls back her shoulders to display her small tits, moistens her lips. With Sarah's help, they arrange to meet there the following evening, in front of the old-fashioned merry-go-round with blue-and-gold skewered horses.

The date is arranged in bright sunshine, but the next evening is overcast. Bea and Sarah slip away after *mousse au chocolat*, both a bit pink from the day, Sarah's hair bigger than usual and her shorts clinging unflatteringly to her thighs. It occurs to Bea that her friend may not help her cause. But Bea needs a backup, and Sarah's green top is pretty with fluttery sleeves above the elbows. And she can speak French. Bea's wearing jeans and an off-the-shoulder top showing her peach bra straps. They find the four boys by the merry-go-round, smoking.

'I'm not staying with them,' Sarah mutters, as Laurent peels away and comes towards them in tight jeans, barefoot in the sand. He throws a tennis ball to Bea.

'*Bonsoir Béatrice*,' he says. Bea catches it as her stomach does a flip: *adventure, romance.* Generously, Bea passes the ball to Sarah who throws it back to Laurent. Tonight's T-shirt says 'Everything She Wants'.

'Wham!' Bea goes right up to him and pats his chest, it's surprisingly solid. Sarah starts humming 'Club Tropicana'. His slicked-back hair leaves a large amount of forehead. Without a sunset, the staked horses look dejected and abandoned.

The three of them form a triangle in front of the carousel and throw and catch. Sarah keeps her eyes on the boys by the wall. The sea's closer tonight, lapping towards them. Bea runs to intercept the ball, collides with Laurent and they fall onto the sand. He smells of cigarettes and hair gel. Laurent pulls himself close beside her, takes the ball and lobs it up: *crack*, it hits the carousel roof. He puts an arm around her waist. Just behind them, Sarah catches the ball when it comes down. Laurent gets up and holds out a hand to Bea, raising his eyebrows. '*Viens*.' He leads her around the back of the carousel. The other boys move away from the wall, they kick up sand and eye Sarah.

Once they're out of sight, Laurent wraps himself around Bea.

Crack.

'Come straight away if I stop throwing,' Sarah shouts. Before Bea answers, Laurent pushes himself against her, his hands are between her shoulder blades, then on her buttocks, then travelling up her back. *Crack*. She puts her arms around him as his jaw scrapes her cheek. Now his wide lips are on hers, his tongue huge in her mouth, waggling. He tastes of stale smoke, meat, tongue. *Crack*. She tilts her head to breathe better. His fingers are at the top of her jeans. The arm around her back tightens while he fumbles; he's strong. *Crack*. They wobble and stumble backwards, losing the mouth seal. Close-up, he has tiny craters in his cheeks from old spots, one with a freckle dropping into it. *Crack*. His chest swells and drops with his fast breathing. He says something Bea doesn't understand, plants two hard kisses on her lips and pulls her down onto the sand. She's pretty disappointed in her French lessons right now.

'*Quel âge as-tu*?' she breathes into his face. She'd quite like to talk for a bit. He laughs and strokes her cheek, loosening his grip. *Crack*. He runs his fingers down the side of her neck, curls one under her bra strap and tugs gently, then he circles her breasts one at a time. It tickles. Should she take her top off? *Crack*.

'*Dix-neuf ans*.'

'Nineteen,' she says. He grins – he likes her talking.

'Nine-teen,' he echoes. His accent is really *French*. She can't believe she's actually lying here in the cool sand pressed into Laurent. Peachy. *Pêcheuse*?

'*Moi quinze*,' she says, then he rolls on top of her and her breath goes right out of her. She gasps, and practically swallows his tongue as it re-enters her mouth. She can't breathe. She tries to tell him and it comes out like a moan.

'*Béatrice*,' he says, throatily, pulling away to unbutton himself.

'*As-tu des frères ou des soeurs*?' she asks, and she does actually want to know. He breaks into a broad grin. He really likes her.

'Seester,' he says, and they both find this funny. She has a bunch of other questions but he slides his hand into her jeans.

'*Comment elle s'appelle*?' Bea squeaks.

'*Clémentine*,' he murmurs, 'shhhh.' His fingers are crawling into her pants. She can't remember which ones she's wearing.

She wants to stop now, and just talk. Maybe talk and kiss.

And there's no sound from the roof.

'Sarah!' She jerks away and jumps up, zips up her jeans and leaves him sprawled on the sand, flies undone. She darts around the side and looks down the beach.

No one.

She starts running, away from the road. Further up there's a dark-coated figure with a dog – not one of the boys.

'Sarah!' she screams. Where would they have taken her? The tide's right in. She runs fast along the thin stretch, yelling Sarah's name. Her left ankle sparks a pain with each push against the sand; she hasn't run like this since she broke it. Way ahead, a shape appears, dark against the sky. A pier? A hut? *Fuck. Fuck.* They've taken her in there. Three of them. Her breath comes in gasps, she holds off a sob. *Please.* The roof is pointy and uneven. A shack, a wreck. *Please don't let anything happen to her.*

'Sarah!'

A hand grabs her arm. She whirls around ready to punch. It's Laurent, panting, pointing back at where they were.

'They've taken her,' Bea cries and thumps his solid chest. He takes her by both wrists. He talks fast, jerking his head in the direction of the merry-go-round.

And now she can see them: a tiny line of figures on the sand right by the water's edge, almost at the road. How could she have missed them? She throws her arms around Laurent who hugs her tightly back, saying a string of delicious French words in her ear, and they set off back up the beach with their arms around each other.

They run the last bit hand in hand. As they get close to the line of four on the hard sand, their toes almost in the water, Bea hears Sarah singing 'Club Tropicana'.

'There's enough for everyone—'

Astoundingly, like backing singers, the boys respond. 'All zat's meesing eez ze seeeee!' It goes up in a shout, followed by whoops and cries. Tall lies back in the sand, in hysterics,

Fat doubles over, slapping his legs, and Ratty grins his head off. And Sarah, sitting in between, throws her head back and laughs, punching the air with a green fluttering arm.

'*Enfin*!' she shouts. 'Oh, hello.'

Bea stands beside them, gaping. She drops Laurent's hand.

'*Ça va*?' Sarah says, smiling hugely. It's a smile Bea has never seen before. It is the best thing about the day – about the whole trip – it gives Bea a full-to-bursting feeling.

Je t'aime, she almost says. She smiles hugely back. '*Oui*,' she says, thinking, How weird, for *this* to be the best moment. '*Ça va bien*.'

Don't sing

'Foot on the clutch, into second,' Ted says in his best driving instructor voice, 'and on we go, checking the mirrors.' Bea leans forward and squints at his feet. 'Nice and easy.' They've driven around the car park twice now. It's her first lesson.

'What's the point of *telling* me,' she says, 'when I can't *see*?'

'No. Right.' The air in the Fiesta is thick. 'Shall we swap?' This might be a mistake. It was Moira's idea. An almost-sixteenth birthday present. 'Build some bridges,' Moira said. Ted winds his window down and pulls to a halt. The retail park looks out over the town and the hills beyond. It's where he started with Andrew.

They both get out and cross over at the bonnet. Ted stops to watch the sun, at that moment a bright, gold disc, dropping into the horizon. Bea stops beside him.

'Wow,' she says.

Wow indeed. The dazzling sun, his beautiful daughter. They are so rarely alone. And the long stretch of her ignoring him seems to have passed. They stand side by side as the hills swallow the sun in a long, slow gulp.

Bea has on her usual jeans and T-shirt, her eyes are lined in black. She's an inch or so taller than him, tall and slim like Moira, and now driving a car! The speed of it all – it's crackers.

'Right then.' He walks round to the passenger side. Bea gets settled, puts her hands on the wheel. Her face, tinged pink in this light, with her jaw set, still looks like the face of a stubborn child. He has an urge to stroke her hair.

'Right then!' he slaps his thighs.

'Tell me what to *do*.'

This isn't going to be like teaching Andrew.

Ted talks her through the pedals, and she presses left and right, biting down on her lip in concentration. Her thin fingers clasp the gearstick and slam it forward and back. She may be slight, but she means business. When she turns the key they lurch forward, and Bea lets out a laugh of surprise. This happens several times, and she stops laughing. Calmly, Ted explains how to release the handbrake. They jerk and stall, jerk and stall. Her mouth tightens, her face takes on a fierce expression.

'Ease it off,' he says, 'squeeze with your feet.'

'I'm *trying*,' she growls, as they shoot off. A wedge of unease lodges in his chest.

The car park is long and empty. They've worked their way past Boots, and now they shudder to a halt in front of Mothercare. A fluffy bunny sits in the window on a giant green swing set, the whole thing plastic and shoddy. Ted's shoulders tighten, in a minute he'll get the ache up his neck.

'Who taught you?' She shoots the question at him while they're stationary.

'To drive?' Ted has to think. 'A mate, on a building site.'

'Ever crash?'

'No.' Ted says. 'Yeah. Once. Into a fence. The van was all scratched.'

'Did you own up?'

If I did, would that be alright? 'Can't remember. I think I had to pay for it.'

'Is that the worst thing?' Bea says, eyeing him sideways.

'How do you mean?' *Nothing like teaching Andrew.*

Bea clamps both hands around the steering wheel, facing front. 'What's the worst thing you ever did?' She's half-smiling, but it's not a mean smile.

Christ. 'A woman died, but it wasn't my fault,' Ted hears himself say, looking at the dashboard. 'It was an accident. Remember Turner's, where I used to work? A balcony came down, cantilevered beams. They tried to pin it on me.' No, it's the other thing he needs to sort out. She has to know he didn't harm her on purpose that day. He glances at her and starts again. 'An accident, like the ice rink. Your leg?' He speeds up. 'I swear Bea, I was trying to help. You might not remember, but you'd already fallen when I came to pick you up.' He turns now, and Bea's looking at him like she's just swallowed a lemon.

'I mean the worst thing you did when you were *fifteen*.'

'Right. Yeah.' *Balls.* He draws a blank. Some slapstick from a building site? Paint spills, boots in cement mixers. Fifteen is when Ted's mother died and he did nothing to save her. How can he have done nothing at all?

'Never mind,' Bea sighs.

'A bonfire got right out of hand,' he says quickly, catching a memory. Bea nods. 'Four or five of us, middle of the night.'

'What happened?'

'We ran around like idiots, with silly little buckets. And cried for help like schoolgirls,' Ted chuckles. 'Not sure why we were there, s'pose we must have broken in.' Bea looks mildly impressed. 'In the end, they sent a whole fleet of fire engines. I think it made the papers.' *So did the flats, the dead woman.*

She turns the key and they start off again, and after a few seconds jolt to a stop.

'Crap,' Bea says quietly. She's got her chin on her chest, her hair falls across her cheek. Oh boy, does he know how she feels.

'I bet Andrew got it straight away,' Bea says, not looking up.

'Course not,' Ted says, 'we've only just started.'

What was he thinking? He looks down at his useless hands, crusted and cut, in his lap. A lifetime of lifting and shifting and mixing has not taught him anything he can use here. He had even fantasised that while driving along in the Fiesta, side by side, he might acknowledge to her his mistakes. *Did you own up?* He would try and explain how he lost himself completely after Alan Turner screwed him over – get her to see it wasn't really *him*. They would establish, casually but definitely, a clean slate between them. Bygones, yeah? *I'm sorry about back then. I wasn't myself after Turner's*. Well, he had half a chance just now, and she didn't want to hear it.

Bea blows her breath out loudly, flapping her lips. Ted thinks of a young horse. The light's fading. What would Moira do now? Sit and wait patiently, no doubt. His wife's evenness can tire him out, like moving around under a thick blanket, though where would they all be without it?

Bea tucks her hair behind her ears with both hands, then she leans forward and turns the key. Ted sits up straight.

'Another go?' he says. The engine revs and revs and then she rams it into first and they creep forward. This time, they keep going. Bea steers them around the car park, a whole lap in first gear. A smile nudges into her lips. Ted watches her profile and the smile grows. He should get her to change to second, but why risk it? A warmth spreads out in his chest, his shoulders relax.

'Bee-bop-a-loula—'

'Don't sing,' she says. They're still moving. As they inch past Mothercare for the second time, Ted expects to see the bunny swinging high on its green plastic. Outside, little puffs of cloud form pink quiffs in the sky. He rests his elbow on the open window. They could stay right here and drive round and round, all night.

Other angel

'That's a big sigh, Beetle.'

'Sarah's house is better,' Bea mumbles, curled in the wicker chair.

'Is there a night-time observatory at Sarah's house?' Granny says. The fan heater hums. Something flutters outside the glass, probably a bat. Bea was amazed to discover from Mum that the dusk birds weren't birds at all. She loves surprises.

'There's a massive grandfather clock,' Bea says, 'tall like a person, it makes me jump.' Andrew's tragic guitar twangs away upstairs. 'The bass is the soul of the song' he says. Someone else must have said it. He's such a *parrot*. She comes back to her friend's brilliant house. 'Sarah's got a bookcase in her room, and there's old things everywhere. It's sort of like a museum.' Bea tells Granny about the lamps, the shiny wooden table, the piano, all the things that don't work, Sarah's parents with their clever jobs, wine. 'Cabernet Sauvignon,' she says, '*c'est très bon*.' Though in truth, she's only had it twice and it's like dry vinegar. She has to gulp it.

'Oo, lah-di-dah,' Granny says, flapping her hands in a mocking gesture.

'They're really nice *actually*.' Bea wishes she'd not said anything in the first place.

'No brothers or sisters?' Granny says.

'Nope. Another bonus.' Though as she says it, she feels bad for Lonnie. Granny shakes her head. Bea can't see her face properly.

'It's not a bonus Toots, really it isn't.'

'That's a nebulous point of view,' Bea says, and Granny gives her a look she can't read.

'Is it? Oh well then.' Granny's mouth droops suddenly, all the skin on her face seems to sag down with it. 'I know all about wanting to be somewhere else, Beetle.' She almost whispers it, like a confession. Bea starts to feel uneasy. Then she considers what Granny just said, and feels indignant.

'Where else do you want to be?'

Granny cackles, forgetting whatever was drooping her. 'Not *now*, petal,' she wrinkles her nose and flashes her yellow teeth. 'Now, I'm in heaven.' She looks into the darkness and it seems to amuse her. 'My little greenhouse heaven.' She clears the phlegm in her throat, it takes her several goes. 'And talking of somewhere else, I want to go *shopping*.'

Pushing uphill, Bea's body is almost flat to the concrete. She had no idea it was a wheelchair in the side alley. Mum whipped off the blue tarp and there it was. Up front, Her Highness hums little tunes, and half turns her head now and then to ask 'Alright, Beetle?' There's a sharp wind. Bea would be freezing were it not for the pushing being such bastard hard work. Granny can walk, but not this far, and not up hills.

Wide and flat, the High Street's a relief. Bea's arms ache when they reach A Piece of Cake, the tiny pink café with steamed-up windows. Granny puts her veiny hands on the table with a little clatter. She has put on all her rings. Bea feels suddenly, inexplicably sad at the sight of them. Now they're facing each other, Bea startles at the dark pink lips. 'Pomegranate Passion,' Granny tells her. A string of pearls peeks out from under her scarf. Bea had already forgotten the old Granny, pre-Annexe.

'Always look the best you can,' Granny says. 'A bit of effort costs nothing.' Bea holds out her arms with a grin, in her sweatshirt and jeans. 'We all have our own style, Toots. You'll do it your way.' She's gone a bit over the edge with the lipstick.

They have a pot of tea for two. Bea has an éclair, Granny a shortbread half dipped in chocolate, which she snaps in half and gives Bea the chocolate side. They laugh behind their hands at the ginormous-bummed waitress; Granny tells Bea stories about the shop in Lower Ashton village; about someone called Gina who married a train driver, had twins and got divorced. She studies the cheesy sunflower pictures lining the walls, and her crinkly face lights up with another memory.

'This place used to be called Doilies,' Granny says, dabbing her mouth with her pink serviette. 'I have a feeling Ted and Moira used to come here when they were courting.' Bea pulls a face at the thought of her parents on a date. She's getting bored.

Back outside in the cold, they trudge along the High Street, Granny still chatting on. Bea recognises a group of sixth-formers with candyfloss hair. She'd like to nip over to check out the arcade for boys – the only thing missing at Sarah's – but now the commentary from the chair has stopped abruptly. They're outside a new shop, Maybe Baby, bang in front of a giant pregnant mannequin with a fluorescent jumper-dress stretched over its swollen belly. It reminds Bea of Mum a few years ago. The main bonus of her actually giving birth (apart from Lonnie) was her mother's stomach returning to normal size. The embarrassment of that great stomach to her twelve-year-old self had almost killed her.

'They shouldn't be allowed to put that there.' Bea shudders, and steps around the wheelchair. Under the blanket, Granny's very still, her gaze off to the side. Through the window, Bea scans the long shelf. Fluffy hats and gloves, stupid plastic rattles, stupid little shoes when babies can't even walk. She tracks Granny's gaze to the shoes, more like slippers when you look properly, or ballet shoes with silk ribbons. Old-fashioned things now trendy.

'D'you want to get something for Lonnie?' Bea asks, though the slippers are for teensy babies, not big blundering toddlers. Granny has her ringed hands up to her cheek. When her head drops to her chest, Bea squats down and tries to look at her, but she covers her face.

'I want to go home,' Granny says in a wobbly voice. Without

asking more, Bea turns the chair in a wide, clumsy circle, slicing in half a couple walking arm in arm, and they head back down the hill.

In the living room, Granny revives a little in front of the *Paul Daniels Magic Show*. Bea leaves her with Debbie McGee being chopped up, and goes to the kitchen to tell Mum what happened. She describes Granny slumped over, staring at the old-fashioned baby clothes, and Mum's face freezes in the expression she has on. Her 'interested listening' face: eyebrows raised, mouth halfway to a smile. Still with the expression, she starts making tea. Usually, Bea would say something like *Have you had plastic surgery while I was out?* But she doesn't say this.

'Go and sit with her,' Mum says, her voice firm and urgent. And Bea does as she's asked.

Granny has turned the telly off.

'Is she dead?' Bea asks. And Granny reacts in horror, her eyes wide, her mouth trembling. Bea sits in the armchair. Just her luck to miss it. 'Did something go wrong?' Bea's always hoping Paul Daniels will fuck it up and blood will spurt into the camera live on telly. Except according to Andrew, it's pre-recorded.

Granny doesn't seem to hear. Her face is glazed, miles away, not thinking about Debbie McGee, dead or alive. Mum brings in two mugs of tea and puts them on the table, then hovers beside the sofa while some discomfort works its way across her face. Something is going on here that Bea doesn't understand, and it makes her jumpy, impatient. Granny won't look up, Mum's balancing from foot to foot like she's on hot concrete. Mum should either say something or leave, and it's clear she's not got the balls for either.

'Mum?' Bea says, but Mum keeps looking at Granny. 'What? Bea says loudly. 'What is it?'

Moira opens her mouth, then closes it. Bea feels suddenly scared. Why won't Mum speak? She does the fish mouth again.

'It's alright, Mum,' Moira says finally. Bea can't recall her mother ever calling Granny 'Mum'. It sounds really weird. Her face becomes hard then, and she says it to Granny again, but this time she's harsh. 'You're alright now.' It's like an order. She doesn't sound like Mum at all. Now she looks at Bea, and she tries to smile, but it doesn't work. She says what she always says to Bea and Granny, 'I'll leave you to it.' And she turns and goes back to the kitchen.

Granny stays silent. With a knot in her stomach, Bea moves to sit beside her on the sofa and puts her hand on her grandmother's lap.

'What is it?' she asks quietly. Granny looks at Bea and her whole face starts to wobble – all her extra skin and her lips. She gives a little squeak and swallows.

'There was another one,' she crackles, a glob of saliva forming at the corner of her mouth.

'Another one,' Bea repeats.

'Another life,' her voice is a tiny creak. 'Another baby, in another life.'

'Another *baby*?' Bea's stomach slides around as she understands the meaning, no longer wanting to know. Granny nods, and in slow motion, large tears form in her baggy eyelids and slide down her sunken cheeks. It is the worst thing Bea has ever seen. She almost shouts for Mum, then remembers Mum's face and decides not to. Now she feels her own cheeks are wet, and she's got a panicky feeling where the knot was. Granny gulps, and lets out a quiet cry, then folds over and her shoulders shake in small movements.

'Oh no, oh no,' Bea hears herself say. She rocks Granny in her arms, and the rocking calms them both. Her grandmother almost disappears in the embrace. Bea feels like a powerful giant and loosens the hug. Granny's curled-up body slackens, as though she has somehow given up, and Bea keeps her arms there, not sure what will happen if she lets go. When she finally pulls away, Granny's face is back to non-wobbly. Her eyes, still pink, stare right into Bea's. Bea doesn't want to hear any more, but where can she go?

Dilys looks into the face of her angel. No turning back now. She has not spoken this aloud in decades, and assumed she would take it to her grave. Not a secret so much as her past left in the past. Those little shoes. Beautiful ivory booties. She has the very same pair in a box, still, at home with David, or maybe here. She never did ask Moira about the sorting. And now that her other angel has been brought to the surface, she will tell Bea, as she was surely meant to do.

Dilys can feel the word travel up through her, inside her chest, pressing briefly on her heart: *hello!* Then up and along the passage of her throat, around her mouth and now on her lips. Bea's head is close, almost touching, as Dilys utters the name of her dear lost daughter.

'Eliza.'

Long after the whole house is asleep, Dilys lies awake staring into the gloom. On other nights she likes to think of Bea and Andrew sleeping upstairs, safe and sound in their rooms full of their many things, of their good fortune. Tonight, she is not thinking of them.

No more tears are waiting, and yet her sadness has joined her, again and after all this time; an ache, deep and wide and dark. It was a time of so much suffering. Dilys wondered, back then, how the world did not sink with the weight of it.

Eliza. A dear little thing with a button nose and dimpled cheeks. Bonny and bouncy one day, feverish and rattling the next, then gasping, then no more.

In bed, just the two of them, Wilmot Street, Morden.

After the frantic patting and shaking and crying out, Dilys holds the rubbery, heavy form to her, in the sudden, crushing silence. They lie for a long time on the crumpled sheets.

Dilys needs a cigarette, but she dares not move. The baby is on her chest. The baby is still here.

A cigarette. She must have a cigarette.

She lays the baby down, slowly, slowly, avoiding the slack mouth, the rolling eyes. They will go out to the shop to buy cigarettes. Dilys's thoughts leap and trip. A walk together, just the two of them. Eliza will wear the gift Dilys has been saving. She moves quickly now, rummages under the bed where she retrieves her shawl and the roll of cloth. She places it on the covers and unfolds it. *There*. Pearly booties with shining ribbons, fit for a princess. She has opened this parcel several times to feast her eyes and run her fingers along the silky strips. Now, Eliza will wear them.

Dilys cups the baby's feet into the slippers, like Cinderella. A perfect fit! With trembling hands, she loops the ribbons around the ankles and ties a bow, first one leg then the other. Then she gathers up the floppy bundle and swaddles her to her chest in the shawl, her silky feet dangling out of the bottom.

Along the street, left at the post box. It's a bright, late autumn day with quite a wind. Dilys hugs the shawl to her bosom as they pass a cluster of women on the corner. She catches Peggy O'Brien's stare. *Look! Eliza has new shoes!* Dilys should have put a scarf around her hair, it's blowing across her face. The woman's eyes follow her. Dilys passes with a quick stride.

The little shop is dark. Dilys snatches up the packet from the counter.

'The baby's sleeping, yes. Beautiful shoes? Yes, a gift.'

'What's the occasion?'

'An afternoon walk, just the two of us. Good to get out.'

Up and down the cracked pavements. Perhaps they will go as far as the park, the sun might show itself proper. The sky rushes clouds along. Dilys quickens her pace to keep up. Her arms ache around and under the flaccid, heavy cargo. The ribbons have loosened and fallen down; pearly curls around the ankles. Dilys can't reach down to re-tie them without dropping the baby. And now they have come away. Streamers, ribboning behind. Ripples of silk, like slim flags, waving, chasing her as she starts to run.

Pebbledashed
1945

Dilys can't get over her two children on the stones against the blue sky, in front of the enormous farmhouse. How happy they look! Sun-baked and freckled. Happy strangers. It has been over a year. Through the lens of her grief, even Dilys can see they are thriving. Her little Moira, the girl she knew, the girl she had *raised* – placid, tidy, sweet-natured – now a long-limbed stick of a grinning, grubby girl, still loyal as a knight to her brother. David, her funny scrap of a boy whom Dilys had wrung herself out over. He looks almost a man, at ten, with his dog and his cap. Standing in the sunlight, one either side, she knows she will have to re-think everything. In the city Dilys has only ghosts; what would she be bringing them home to anyway?

The farmer arranges the rental of a small terraced house with pebbledash walls, on the end of a strip of identical houses behind the village hall. Six Bluebell Lane, Lower Ashton Village. Two up, two down, divided by the staircase, a tiny kitchen off the dining room, and a square of high grass out the back. The house is more familiar to Dilys than it is to the children, who squeeze into the bedroom upstairs like their own private chicken coop.

Lower Ashton village lies stranded in a dip between deep countryside and the puny town of Fern Ashton. Blink, and you could miss it. The village has two shops, a squat pub, The White Horse, with a sign almost as big as the building itself, a school, a village green and a village hall. Roads snake up and away from the centre, and at the top of the steepest hill stands the church with its thin spire, Saint Stephen's, surrounded by an overgrown graveyard.

They move in in November, just before the first frost.

The night-time silence in Bluebell Lane strikes alarm in Dilys at first. In the quiet, the 'what-ifs' ping around her head. What if she had left Morden with the children, and not waited for the baby to see the doctor – all the bloody good that did; what if Ray had made the deliveries the week earlier; what if Pete had left Barbara and asked Dilys to stay? She lies awake listening to Moira's stop-start sobbing, unable to offer comfort, before the girl seals herself off. David is a blank, she can't know his thoughts. Holding her gaze like an interrogator, he had asked questions about his father, and the baby.

'Pneumonia,' Dilys had said, in the steady, practised tone. 'Eliza's an angel watching over us all, think of it like that.' Of their father, she was equally honest and brief. 'Poor Raymond, hit by a motor car. Sepsis. Unlucky.' David had looked around him, as though it might not be true. Dilys had watched her son – this new one, tall and strong – walk into rooms, and tilt his head, listening, waiting. As though if he was patient, his missing family would return to him. It took all of Dilys's resolve not to break down. But she did not. Numbed by the baby's death, she was strangely untouched by her husband's passing. And then of course there was Pete, not even hers in the first place. Another flicker of happiness now snuffed out.

They sit around the table on the third evening at Bluebell Lane, their few boxes all unpacked.

'I'm at the end of my wick,' Dilys says to them in the chill grey dining room with its faint smell of mould, and its small windows. Moira and David blow on her as if she really were a candle, and she collapses on the small dining table in a heap. Then she sits herself up, smiles weakly and reaches for her Woodbines. They have just finished a dinner of corned beef and potatoes. It's their first time around this table, delivered today, and with a wobbly leg Dilys will need to fix.

'Three people,' David says, unblinking. A statement of fact, and David's way of announcing their new situation – their reduction. Dilys takes in a sharp breath and becomes very still, holding her cigarettes in her lap. Three sets of breath are the only sounds in the room. David's summary of their shrunken state feels like an accusation, and it fills Dilys with a quick, dark anger. Do they think she mislaid the baby, their father, out of *carelessness*? She grips the packet and keeps her eyes down. Here she is, making a life for them. When she looks up, they are both staring at her, David unblinking, Moira's light, greeny-brown eyes swimming and fearful. She has Eliza's eyes. *Sweet Jesus.* For a moment, Dilys can't speak.

Damn you both, she thinks, and shakes her head to rattle the thought away. *Please God he can't see inside my head.* It is her suspicion that her son has powers none of them know of. Very slowly, Dilys puts the packet of cigarettes on the table and places her hands flat either side. Trembling slightly, she speaks to her fingers, red and peeling.

'It would help me,' she says in an odd, low tone, her voice calling up from the deep well of her loss, 'It would help me if we all stay in the present.' Without meaning to she lifts her head and glares at them, one at a time. Moira instantly lowers her eyes, but David keeps his dark stare steady on her. After a long moment, it is Dilys who has to look away.

In their bedroom that night Moira lies awake in the dark, the blanket scratching her chin. She has a mattress next to David's bed, and from here she looks up at the gap in the sheet hung as a curtain. She spies a triangle of stars, one bright, the others faint. Downstairs, the door bangs shut as her mother comes in from the loo. She wants to call out to her to go outside again and look at the stars. A kindness to make up for Moira's private dismay at being here. She could get up, right now, and run all the way along the lanes back to Missus. But would David come? Moira knows she should be pleased and happy – Missus Alice kept saying so while she helped Moira gather her things. 'You'll be so happy to be with your mother again.'

It will come soon, Moira tells herself. The first night here, after her mother told them about the pneumonia that killed the baby, Moira thought she might never sleep again. The tears came from her whole body. Every inch of her weeping for Eliza. And then they stopped. That might be it for her entire life. Could it be she has used up all her tears?

She pulls the blanket over her cold nose and holds herself absolutely still, as her mother did earlier, at the table. Moira will try it and see if it works. What comes into her mind is a sound. The high, keening sound David had made when forced to leave his collections at their first home more than a year ago. The sound has found its way inside her, now pressing behind her nose. It escapes her as a whimper. She squeezes her eyes shut, and with great effort she fills her head with blocks of colour. Sunshine gold, deep blackcurrant purple— But still the pictures creep in. The kitchen in their old house, arms and legs dangling over the stove. 'Stop them!' their father would jokingly shout, 'they're diving in the soup!'

She puts her arm up on David's bed.

'Hello,' he says, in a normal voice, not even a whisper.

'I thought you were asleep,' she whispers. He doesn't say anything. 'What are you thinking about?'

'Buffalo,' he says in a quiet voice. Moira closes her eyes, and there, behind her eyelids, on his mat under the huge table, is Buffalo the dog, his ears cocked in dreams.

'Me too,' she whispers, calm for a second. But only moments pass and here again are the checked arms of her father's shirt, the pot of stew.

'Do you remember the sleeves diving in the soup?' she breathes, barely a whisper. David's breathing becomes quicker but he doesn't answer. The bright star twinkles. She waits in the dark, for ages. 'David?' She pushes up on her elbow, enough to see the outline of her brother's face against the pillow, the gleam of his eyes staring upwards, the movement of his mouth.

'We mustn't,' he says.

So many people
1951

The shop front has 'K. Billington' in painted blue letters over the doorway, and beside it in smaller letters 'Family Grocer Est. 1922'. When the shop's quiet, Dilys goes out onto the pavement and waves her hands like a cinema attendant, left a little, right a little, for Gina to get the display basket centre-stage. They could be mother and daughter: forty-one and eighteen. Billington's is always well stocked. Several sorts of tea, chicken-and-ham paste, packets of biscuits and jams in squat jars in the wooden cabinets on the wall, fresh batch loaves and fruit bread in baskets on the counter, tins of pears and fruit salad. Cooked ham and corned beef that Dilys wraps in brown paper, folded carefully into points at the ends, like a gift. On one end of the thick wood counter are bags of toffees and sherberts, and behind it, cigarettes in packets and singles. It's one of the perks. At work, Dilys smokes for free, from the singles. She doesn't pinch them, Mr Billington invites her to help herself. He calls her 'Mrs Brown' in an overly fussy way that makes Dilys feel old. And it doesn't feel right. In this life, she should be a Miss, though of course she will never be a Miss again.

Dilys knows there has been talk in the village of her and Mr Billington. People here have nothing to talk about, and so they make things up. Dilys knows all about this, but she finds it distasteful, pairing her with her boss simply because they are both widowers. And really, can't they see the skinny, balding man is too old and nowhere near handsome enough for her? Mostly, he's in the office doing the ordering and accounts, or out on errands. Dilys imagines calling him 'Keith', knowing she never will. It makes her snigger inwardly. Mr Billington is a cousin of Mr Duckworth; it's how she got the job. But she won't give that farmer her gratitude. It's enough that David disappears to the farm on Saturdays and holidays, on the old bicycle, and that Dilys has to watch Moira's face as she waves him off, pained with all she's missing.

In her brown shop coat, Dilys arranges the loaves in a neat line. When she first stood behind this counter, she overdid her London voice to show people she wasn't one of them. She squared her shoulders and told the customers, 'You didn't have my war.' It had become her motto. Though aren't mottos supposed to be helpful, rallying things? Her trump cards: a dead husband and a dead baby. Dilys wishes she had a more heroic story to tell. Others have war heroes for husbands, she has a motor car accident and sepsis.

'It might be today,' Gina says, pulling on her cigarette with smiling lips. They're out the back sitting on crates, smoking, while the shop's quiet. It's dingy, and smells of bread, old fruit and stale ciggies. Thick-necked Gina is referring to her future husband, who will come in one day, place his hat on the counter, and swoon at the sight of her. An unlikely scenario, to Dilys's mind. The shop coat turns the girl into a solid brick, while somehow flattering her own shapely bosom and small waist.

'Describe him,' Dilys says. And Gina takes an enormous breath and says he will be tall, very tall, with wide shoulders, nice clothes especially coats, lapels and big brass buttons, and smile a lot, though not so much as to be annoying.

'He's got blue eyes and a nice moustache,' she looks coyly at Dilys. 'Or would that be scratchy?' and she giggles into her hand. Dilys blows out a slow line of smoke. It's obvious the girl hasn't the faintest idea how this future husband looks or smells or tastes. How he will pull her into a corner and press himself to her, so hard she will be crushed; *want* to be crushed. How she will feel herself ablaze, run her teeth along his stubble. Like her secret Pete. Not hers at all, and left in Morden. He has been on the tip of Dilys' tongue many times in this back room. To keep from spilling today she starts to hum and then fills in the words.

'"I was foolish too, cos I never thought that you, would sing my love song, to somebody else."'

'You're giving me goosebumps!' Gina does a fake shiver. Tickled, Dilys keeps singing. She rises to her feet, crushes her cigarette end, and shimmies her shoulders. She hums the bits she can't remember, closing her eyes.

'"I may not be smart, but I never have the heart—"' Dilys drops down an octave and croons under half-closed lids. Gina's face is lit. With an arm around the back of her imaginary lover, Dilys dances herself around a crate of tinned pears, rocking her hips. She does two final sweeping turns '"You sang my love song, to somebody else."' She throws out her arms, Sinatra-style, on the last note. Gina claps and gives a little whoop.

'In an ideal world,' Dilys says, pouting, 'I'd have been a cocktail singer.'

'You're *funny*!' Gina says. Dilys looks at the girl with her whole life ahead and feels her smile fade.

'I was,' she says. She's been taken out to pubs, to the races, by local men, but none of them 'took'. Dilys had prepared with care and no small excitement for these dates, yet each one ended in disappointment. Too keen, too small, too awkward. Not Pete. Or even Ray. The dates only made her sadder, and without really meaning to Dilys has allowed something inside her to fold up. Her heart a thin sheet of paper folded over and over, shrinking to nothing; widowing herself all over again.

*

Moira's satchel bounces on her hip as she runs to keep up. It's a warm Friday afternoon in May, billowing clouds crowd the sun. David is fifteen, he has finished his School Certificate, and they're walking home together from the bus stop for the last time against these high hedges. Once they get this far Moira can relax. The Town boys don't come out here. It's been a while since the last trouble, but out of habit she still darts out of her classroom and pulls David away.

Up ahead, he's staring at the sky. A faint screeching careens above them, as though from the cloud.

'Swifts,' David says, 'from Africa.' Moira can't remember where Africa is. Much further than London, and that's the furthest she's been. 'They sleep while they fly,' he says, as the black specks scream softly away. He must be teasing her, but then David never teases. She will miss him next term after he starts at the farm every day.

They take a shortcut through the field. This weekend David will be couching.

'Couch grass is an unstoppable weed,' he tells her. 'It's the enemy.' Mister, or one of the farm hands, must have said this, since David wouldn't describe grass, or anything, as 'the enemy'. Not even the boys who kick and punch him. Neither Moira nor her mother ever got the full story. The wound above his left eye has shrunk to a thin red line. It was her fault for not being there. In her presence, David has never come to harm.

As they walk, David explains patiently how you chain-harrow the couch grass, pull it up, build a rick and then burn it. Moira can picture the small fires in the fields because she has seen them. Little beacons. Her time on the farm is almost a dream now. Sometimes, if she thinks about it too long, her whole body turns as heavy as stone and a small pebble comes into her throat. Did she pick blackcurrants and gooseberries that clawed her arms? Pluck warm eggs from the straw? Her mother only snaps if she suggests going there, so she no longer brings it up. She makes do with miniature daydreams – fire beacons, bobbing hens, strawberries – and diverts herself before the heaviness comes.

Their mother calls David 'The man of the house', his wages are a 'godsend.' She has bought herself a wireless: a brown box with twiddly black dials that she carts from room to room. Moira loves the music but not all the talking, though it's all better than silence, and it keeps their mother happy, or at least distracted. When the radio goes off it's Moira's cue to step in with the sewing box, or the baking trays, or dream up a story about the girls at school.

Halfway through the field, without warning, the world turns suddenly dark. A large raindrop taps her head, another hits her cheek, and then the heavens open. They run the last half mile home, Moira with her satchel over her head. They burst into the house dripping rain and mud and gasping with laughter. She's relieved the house is empty – keep it just the two of them for a little longer. David empties his pockets onto the low table in the lounge and sifts through the contents, ignoring the drips from his hair and nose.

'Look.' He holds out something small and green. Moira recognises a clover, and this one has four leaves. The rain has given way to sun, it dives in from the window and shines a pool on the rug.

'It's rare,' he says, 'but we've already got one, from 1945.' Now there's the scrape of a key in the lock, and their mother appears. 'It's in the press,' David continues, 'I'll get it.' Moira pulls his arm and shakes her head.

'Later,' she says quietly. The flower press, a Christmas present from the Duckworths, will send their mother into a black mood.

'Whisper whisper,' Dilys says in the doorway, annoyed. Moira thinks of the enemy couch grass and can't find her smile.

David opens his fist to display the four-leafed clover. 'It means good luck,' he says.

'We'll need it,' their mother says, 'Gina's poorly.' She looks at Moira. 'You'll have to help out tomorrow, Saturdays are busy.'

Moira ties and re-ties her apron behind her back. She's been in the shop many times, but not with an apron and a *purpose*. Almost fourteen, and a shop girl! It will be Moira's job to wrap the bread and add it to the bill. Currant scones are a ha'penny more than plain. She mutters the prices over and over.

'How do you remember them all?' Moira asks, gazing around. There are six different packets of tea, for starters.

'You get used to it,' her mother says, looking pleased. 'Mostly I add them in my head,' she nods to the counter. 'You can use the pad.'

'I might need a practice.'

To her surprise, her mother goes out of the door, waits a minute and comes back in with an exaggerated limp: a pretend customer!

'May I help you?' Dilys prompts out of the side of her mouth as she laughingly hobbles around.

'May I help you?' Moira says, biting her lip. Her stomach does a little leap; the day feels so full of promise.

The bell tinkles non-stop. Moira runs around, wraps bread, and fetches eggs from the back. Her mother smiles broadly, coos over a baby, does a squeaky laugh with her head back, booms 'How's the day out there?'

'Don't gawp,' her mother hisses in between customers. And Moira busies herself with an open box or dusts the shelves. She gets her hand patted *Thank you, Treasure,* and her mother gives a quick, approving smile. Moira might be a shopgirl forever.

An old, bent-over lady comes in, and Dilys swoops over to take her basket. She puts her arm around the lady's back, says in a soft voice, 'We'll get you sorted out,' and sends Moira off for her tea and her crackers.

It's hard *not* to gawp. Her mother is so many people, and not one of them familiar.

There's a lull around lunchtime, and Dilys disappears into the back room for a smoke. Moira stands at the counter and welcomes imaginary customers, nodding warmly and saying under her breath, 'How's the day out there?' Then the bell tinkles and she stands up straight. In walks a man with a cap, he looks surprised to see her.

'May I help you?' Moira says. This seems to amuse him.

'Younger and younger, Mrs Brown,' he says and winks. Should she tell him it's 'Miss'?

'Let me see now,' he says. He sounds just like Mister at the farm. He might be the same age. Thick black hair pokes out from under his cap when he turns sideways.

'Got any pork pies?' Moira can't tell if he's teasing her. His eyes sparkle and his grin is off-centre. 'And a plum pudding.'

'We have scones?' she says and indicates the end of the counter. 'Currants or plain.'

'And which do you recommend?' he says, leaning on the wood and looking into her eyes in a way that makes Moira feel uncomfortable. He's younger than Mister.

'Currants,' she says. He nods seriously. She feels herself blush. Dilys comes in from the back then and looks from one to the other.

'Mrs Brown,' the man says with a slow smile, 'I was getting some advice from your new assistant.'

'My daughter,' Dilys says in an even tone. 'This is my daughter Moira.' She steps in front of Moira who has the familiar knowledge she's done something wrong, but not what it is. 'Woodbines, Mr Rush?' Her mother holds out the packet of cigarettes and the man takes them.

'Moira,' he says, looking from Moira to her mother. 'Yes, I can see it now.'

'What can you see?' her mother says, tilting her head, her voice turned husky.

'The resemblance,' he says, 'around the mouth.' Moira has always been told she and David look like their father, tall and dark, compared with their small, curvy mother. Dilys is about to say something but the bell rings and in comes the vicar.

'Good morning, Reverend,' her mother says loudly with a false smile.

'It's afternoon,' the man whispers, winking again at Moira.

'Do you know Mr Rush?' Moira asks in the next lull, after a nice customer leaves and while her mother's still humming. She had spent the last three customers planning how to ask it. 'Friend' didn't sound right.

'He took me to a dance,' her mother says carefully, 'a long while ago.'

'Did you like him?' At home, Moira would never ask this. At home, she's not sure her mother would have answered. But here in the shop, it's different. Instead of getting irritated, she thinks about it. And then she shrugs.

'No more or less than anyone else,' her mother says, returning completely to the person Moira knows: weary, pinched, sorry for herself. Moira searches around, but there's nothing at hand to stand in for the sewing box or the wireless. She's about to suggest a scone, with currants, when her mother heads out the back for another ciggy.

Alone in the empty shop, Moira waits behind the counter and looks out over the bags of toffees at people passing the window. A white-haired couple make steady progress up the street, him with a walking stick, her with a hat that looks more like a hairnet. A mother and a young girl stop and look at the jams in the display basket. The little girl has on a chunky necklace of big blue beads almost reaching her middle. It must belong to the mother. All of a sudden and for the first time, Moira wonders what will happen in her own life. *What might it be*? A thought so astonishing it makes her sway on the spot. She has to hold on to the counter to keep her balance.

Ready
1984

'Are we going to the Disco for Dicks?' Sarah asks.

'Toss a coin?' Bea says.

'Spin the globe.' Sarah pushes it lazily. 'Land we stay, sea we go.' The tip of her finger touches the Indian Ocean, but neither of them can be bothered to swim. The school disco alternates between the Girls' and Boys' Grammars. Lower sixth is their last eligible year, and word in the hut is that the College will be invited for the first time. And there's a smoke machine.

'Dani said Oli Marks is coming. She slept with him in the Christmas holidays,' Sarah grimaces. 'She gave some pretty graphic detail.'

'Dani Bush? She's a *connasse*. She's full of shit.' Dani was the only other girl to snog a French boy last year. A few copies of *Lace* have been circulating the sixth form hut – a thick book with a woman in black lingerie on the cover – and reported exploits have become more explicit.

'Have you replied to your French letter?' Sarah says, smirking. Bea pulls the crumpled page of loopy, girlish writing from her bag. Out of the blue, another letter from Laurent.

At the end of the best of all evenings on Hardelot Plage just over a year ago, as two advancing figures in the distance were confirmed as teachers, Sarah had found a scrap of paper in her shorts, and with a stubby pencil end from someone's pocket, Bea had scribbled her address. When an airmail letter arrived only a week later, she couldn't believe her eyes. She would have stowed away on a boat to be held again by Laurent on the sand. She wrote back, and he wrote again. Short love letters, a mixture of biography and amateur bilingual porn. And then it stopped. But a year later, here's another. They translated it together (Sarah's going to be an interpreter for the United Nations). The news: Laurent wants to come to England and find a job. Bea gives it all her attention – the beach, the carousel, his tongue in her mouth – but she can't properly see his face, just a wide expanse of forehead and some freckles. She badly wants to bring back his touch, but the only thing she remembers clearly is the sound of his sister's gorgeous name, and Sarah singing and punching the air. She has re-read his old letters, with the words '*amour*', and '*chérie*', and while she's tempted, she can't see it going well, him coming over and moving in with her. She's not ready for that. Though she's ready for *something*.

*

The faint smell of sweat and sandwiches in the atrium of Wellstone Boys stirs something in Bea. She gets a stomach flutter stepping down into the darkened school hall, ringed with coloured lights, and yes, a smoke machine. 'Cruel Summer' blasts from the two huge speakers on the front of the stage. As carelessly as they can, Bea and Sarah saunter across the floor past clusters of girls shuffling in unison and stand in the dark along the far edge. From here they scout the whole place. Chairs line the walls with twos and threes from both schools. They compare brief notes, shouting over the music. No College boys, Dani's group not here yet, Carla Owens and her 'fiancé' stuck to each other already in the corner. Bea and Sarah stick their fingers into their mouths and mime being sick. Then they stroll along the back wall, coolly, to the drinks table, and get a Coke.

'Should have brought a bottle of wine,' Bea shouts. They sit on the side and drink their Cokes, then dance to 'Electric Avenue', 'Too Shy' and 'The Reflex'. They sing every word to every song, get drowned in smoke, get another Coke, and sit again. The smoke machine is switched off.

Bea starts to feel restless. The small gangs of Wellstone boys are slim pickings; some of them in jeans, a couple in leather jackets, some in school uniform. A whole bunch of them dance like demented spiders to 'Too Rye Ay'. Bea's heart slowly sinks. Maybe Laurent could come over and they could find a flat? Sarah seems equally bored, and they cheer each other up taking the piss out of the ones who have turned up in uniform. Dani's group arrive all in pastels and swinging multicoloured earrings, hair crimped into electric shocks. Bea and Sarah dance with them, and they all fake-smile at each other. With the first stutters of Chaka Khan, Bea and Sarah peel off to perform their own intense robotics, and then pogo ironically, hilariously to 'Wake Me Up Before You Go-Go'. Bea dares Sarah to dance with a chunky boy in a denim jacket and jeans. She gives the thumbs down.

'Double denim,' Sarah shouts, her cheeks pink, a sheen of sweat on her forehead. One of her shoulder pads has slipped and she looks dislocated. They slump back into the plastic chairs and get lost in their private fantasies while the smoke machine chokes out another go.

At almost kicking-out time, Bea spots what might be a College boy sitting alone, in school trousers and shirt, a slim black tie, his arms folded. He seems bored. He catches Bea looking at him and raises his eyebrows. Sarah pokes her in the side; Bea keeps looking. 'Careless Whisper' comes on and the dance floor clears, leaving only clinging couples. The boy comes over and offers his hand. Bea follows him onto the floor and he puts both arms around her back. She clasps her hands around his neck. He rests his chin against her head, and they sway.

Should have known better than to dance again—

She opens her eyes to see Sarah swaying with the denim. Bea closes her eyes again just as the boy leans down and kisses her neck. Her stomach does a big lurch. By the end of the song, they are kissing, Bea on tiptoe. His tongue probes gently her mouth, he tastes of Polos. He chews lightly on her bottom lip.

With his hands, he smooths her back and presses her into him. When the lights go up, she can barely stand.

Sarah gives her a thumbs-up and motions for them to leave. Her dad will be waiting. The boy steps away from Bea and nods towards the doors. He takes her hand and they leave the hall like this, moving quickly across the floor and up the steps. Sarah will cover for her.

They walk fast in thrilling silence along the park and stop for another beautiful kiss. He's got a muscly back. Remembering *Lace*, Bea starts tugging at his clothes and gets her hand jammed in his belt while trying to free his shirt. They pull apart and Bea laughs breathily. He keeps his arms loosely around her waist.

'Wait,' he says. He's almost a head taller than her. He's got messy hair, and thick eyebrows. His straight teeth shine in the streetlight. He doesn't seem at all nervous.

'What's your name?' His tone is gravelly.

It's hard to get her voice working. 'Bea.'

He smiles. 'I'm Simon.' She looks up at him, her heart clubbing in her chest. Very slowly, not taking his eyes from hers, he leans down, and runs his fingers up the inside of her jeans, fluttering his fingers *there*. Then he carries carefully on up, across her breasts, brushing her nipples with his fingertips. She arcs herself to him, her belly alive with butterflies.

'We can go to my brother's flat,' he says.

All too brief

Dilys blows out smoke through the open window and watches it float away like a steam train.

'Woo woo,' she says quietly and coughs into her hanky. Ted brings her a pack every so often. It's their secret.

Bea tumbles into the room and thumps a large black tape recorder onto the footstool.

'It's freezing,' she says, 'shut the window.'

'A little puff,' Dilys says, 'don't tell your mother.'

'I've got a new tune for you.' Bea punches a button and a tinny voice emerges from the black mesh. Dilys grimaces. So far, she is unimpressed with modern music, all flitty and fast, manufactured, no *heart*.

'Not that one.' Bea holds the button down, and the machine does a squiggly squeak. 'You have to keep an open mind,' she warns. Dilys isn't sure she's ever had one of those. Bea presses again, and now a man's voice sings breathily of guilty feelings. Dilys listens, and Bea's lovely blue eyes go into a reverie. That *face*. Dilys could still eat her up, her darling Beetle.

'Better than the rest,' Dilys says when it stops, 'but too much breath and waffle.'

Bea groans.

'It's not *mine*, Toots, I need *my* music.'

'What music?' Bea asks.

Dilys squeezes her eyes shut. 'Bing Crosby. Frank Sinatra.' She lights up another, 'I won't have one tomorrow or the next day,' she says, and puffs away. 'I loved to dance.'

Bea tilts her head to one side. 'Who with?' she asks with a lopsided smile, a *knowing* smile that eats into her cheek.

Good lord. Bea's eyes are ringed with black now, her breasts pert and ready, small like Moira's, not swollen like her own were. At sixteen, Dilys had been terribly conscious of her curves. But the world is a new place, where sixteen is a woman. What was the question? Dancing. Pete whirls by in the back of her head. She's not seen him in a while.

'Who are *you* dancing with Beetle?' she asks, and Bea swells up in her chair and cocks her chin.

'Simon,' Bea says, the word rising as though Simon is a question. Then Bea leans over and plucks the cigarette from her hand, takes a dainty puff, and another, through round lips, and slots it back between Dilys's bony fingers.

'Miss Beatrice!' Dilys goes for shocked, but gets thrilled by accident, sparking the sharp pain in her chest. She takes another draw, then leans forward. 'Tell me.' Ripples of pleasure pass across Bea's face. For an instant, she looks just like Moira. It takes Dilys by surprise. Her own daughter must have had these rushes when she first met Ted. Had Dilys noticed?

'Simon?' Bea says, chewing her smile. 'He's someone I met.' A pout, a blush.

'And where did you meet this Simon?' Dilys asks, carefully.

'School disco.' Bea's eyes flick around. Dilys senses that might be all.

'And is this Simon a gentleman, Beetle?'

'Depends,' the panda eyes widen, 'on your definition of *gentleman*.' Then she bursts into a fit of giggles, and the woman is gone.

It's all too brief! Dilys thinks with sudden panic. *So pitifully brief.* As hard as she is able, she squeezes Bea's hand.

She thinks *This has been my dance.*

*

The engine roars.

'Change *down*,' Ted says. What's come over her? Bea lifts her arm to rub the window with her silly gloves missing the fingertips, and sets off the windscreen wipers.

'Whoops!'

'Two hands on the wheel,' Ted says loudly.

'Keep your pants on!' But she's not cross, she's all sing-song. They're on a private road. Soon she'll be seventeen and they can put the 'L' plates on and get out and about proper. Usually she's a good driver, but today she's giddy as a kipper.

'You might be better with those mittens off.' He tries not to sound impatient.

'Fingerless gloves,' she says, 'get with it.' And to his surprise she peels them off, shoves them in the side of the door, then stalls.

Ted has come to love their infrequent drives. They're on number six or seven. If it wasn't for the lessons, he'd hardly see her – him at work and Bea always at Sarah's, thick as thieves. Ted dares to hope she's given him the benefit of the doubt. She no longer blanks him, like in those awful months after the ice rink, when Ted feared they would never speak again. And before that. It still sickens him, how he treated Bea and Andrew after he lost his job. He tries not to think about it. But she's growing up, maybe she understands that people make mistakes. Maybe the fire she was born with is burning out.

The clouds are bulking up in dark clumps. He needs to get back to site and do some covering up.

'Call it a day?'

'Whatever you say, boss,' Bea says in an American accent and laughs at her private joke. 'I might get a Spitfire,' she says breezily as they swap sides for the drive home.

'Oh, might you?' It's not what Ted expected. What does she know about Spitfires? She's doolally, he thinks happily, she's all over the shop.

Two days later, Ted finishes early. A warm breeze brushes his arm resting on the van's open window. The fields on either side are a lush green. He's ready to invoice for this job. Another satisfied customer. He could up his profits if he cut the new RIDDOR site safety checks. 'No one else does it,' the lads moan. But Ted holds firm. Nothing will stop him from implementing the recommended best practice regime. Even Michael tells him he's over the top. But Michael hasn't been held responsible for a balcony falling off the side of a block of flats. 'It wasn't your fault,' Moira still reminds him quietly, at intervals. He can't explain to her that culpability has nothing to do with fairness. What Ted has come to accept is that if you're accused, and you were there, then you carry a share of the guilt. He no longer expects anyone else to understand. He doesn't understand it himself.

Saint Stephen's steeple appears on the hill, pale in the sunlight. Ted steers his thoughts back to the day, the happy customer, the greenery.

He leaves his boots in the hall and goes into the kitchen. There's a thumping from upstairs. Andrew and his music. The kettle boils. He takes down his 'Edward, meaning: Prosperous Guardian' mug, a thoughtful gift from Moira, and one he seems at last to be fulfilling. The skylight right now is a square of pure, bright blue. He's got a bit of bonus time. After this cuppa, he'll fix the fence panel Moira asked about weeks ago.

A high-pitched, donkey-like braying comes through the ceiling and another thud. Sarah must be up there with Bea, the pair of them dancing. It's unusual, normally they go to Sarah's. Maybe he should take Moira dancing again. When was the last time they took a turn on the boards? It makes him smile. Moira in her blue dress with the buttons. Bea's voice cuts into his dance hall daydream. She cries out something like 'Yeehaw, baby!' like a cowgirl.

Then another voice.

A male voice.

Not Andrew's.

For a split second, Ted freezes.

Then he climbs the stairs two at a time and bursts into Bea's room.

Curtains drawn, limbs in the dark. There's a leg, an arm, another leg. And a bare back and buttocks, facing him. And the face of a stranger twisting round. On Bea's bed. Then the limbs come into horrifying focus. Bea's legs. Bea's legs are curled around the neck of this stranger with bare buttocks, who's now whipping himself off the bed, grabbing at sheets, leaving Bea, his baby, for a second with her legs splayed. Ted turns his head and covers his face with a hand. Before he knows he's doing it, he lunges at the boy. The grubby, filthy pervert. He's bellowing the words.

'Filthy pervert! Raaaah!' He lets out a cry as he lifts the creature off the ground, by his shoulders, the sheet, his neck? Only then does he hear his daughter screaming. She slams her body against his. He is rigid with rage and she bounces off him. She falls backwards to the floor, and scrambles onto her knees, scraping the carpet for covers. He takes in her bare shoulder, like milk, her hair falling across it, a thin arm curled to shield herself. He throws the boy down and heads for the door. Bea's screams follow him out of the room.

A week later she is gone.

A second-hand emotion

Bea's things pile up in the corner. A pair of jeans, hairbrush, stack of books, medium-sized hedgehog, makeup; a drawerful. Then a roomful. Her own room at Sarah's house, with a little chest and a mirror on curvy wooden legs. Sarah's parents are much cleverer than hers. They help with her UCCA form and tell her to take her 'scientific ambitions' more seriously. Bea feels herself growing taller as they talk. In the kitchen, with his arm around his wife, Morris Rosefoot tells her about admission requirements, interview panels. 'Bea will charm any panel,' Eleanor says, giving her an indulgent smile.

She applies for Biological Sciences. She pretends they are her parents.

Bea watches telly in the den, a snug room off the living room with a sink-in sofa, hoping Sarah will join her after she's finished on the piano. The stuff she plays goes on forever. Bea turns the sound up. Sarah needs three A's and is mostly in her room, but Bea has spent the last two nights at Simon's, which often draws her friend out. A crashing finale drowns out the telly, then she comes in, flops down beside Bea, and they both stare at items trundling past on the *Generation Game* conveyor belt. Sarah always remembers more than Bea. She turns the sound down.

'How's lover-boy?' Sarah asks.

'OK. He's working with his brother this weekend.' Bea tries to think what to ask back. She no longer asks what Sarah's been up to since the reply is always, 'What do you think?'

'Did you ever write to the other one?' Sarah says. 'The French one?' It takes a minute for Bea to understand she's talking about Laurent.

'Yeah, ages ago,' she tells Sarah. 'I told him I was no longer available.' She'd actually told him she was engaged, or she hopes that's what she told him. She didn't use a dictionary.

'Does Simon live with his brother?' Sarah asks.

'On and off. You should come over. They've got a ping-pong table in the lounge.'

'I don't play,' Sarah says.

'It's dead easy, you'll be good,' Bea rubs her elbow. 'Except there's not much room around the edge. Look.' She rolls her sleeve up to reveal her elbow, blooming purple, tinged with yellow.

'Wow,' Sarah says. They both admire the bruise. 'Only you could get an injury playing ping-pong.'

'I know,' Bea holds up her hands, 'me and extreme sports.' When she first did it, the pain was so intense she almost puked, but sharing the bruise here with Sarah, it seems worth it.

'It looks like a mineral,' Sarah says and taps her temples. 'Might be a tourmaline.'

Bea shakes her head, impressed. 'I swear you should go on *University Challenge*.'

'I'll go for an ITV one,' Sarah says. 'Better prizes.' On the screen, a couple embrace then punch the air. 'They've probably won the toaster.'

'What about *Bullseye*? Ow!' Bea's arm catches the edge of the sofa. Carefully, she rolls her sleeve down. 'They've got a dartboard too.'

'Who?'

'Simon and Dougie. His brother's doing up a Spitfire. He'll take you for a drive.' She tells Sarah how Simon took her out; how she tied a scarf and wore sunglasses, like a film star.

'You're good at pretending,' Sarah says.

'I went to see my Granny,' Bea tries, 'but I couldn't stay long cos Dad was due home.'

'I never got what's so *bad* about your dad,' Sarah says, sounding genuinely confused. Bea's humiliation had prevented her from giving all the details of their latest falling out.

'Where to start,' she mutters.

'At the beginning?' Sarah says.

Hard to know exactly where that is. She'll tell her the early stuff. She's never told Sarah this, and now more than ever she needs her friend on her side. Bea's heart quickens. She inhales deeply and explains how her father went mental after he was fired.

'Some building fell down. It wasn't his fault. Or it was. And he got the sack. I was, like, eleven?' She drops her voice and widens her eyes. 'He literally went crazy.' She leaves a pause but Sarah doesn't fill it. 'Total schizo. Me and Andrew were frightened of him.' Heat rises in her face as she talks, her outrage coursing through her like an electric charge.

'You? Frightened?' Sarah says.

Yes, me. Bea needs to raise the stakes. She sits forward, blocking Sarah's view of the silent, trundling fountain pen, fondue set, teddy bear.

'One time, he *smashed our heads*,' she mimes with the heels of her hands. 'Mine and Andrew's. Andrew had to go to *hospital*.' This last bit isn't true, though there had been talk of it. Andrew's headache had lasted for hours. Did Bea have one too? Was there blood? In the end, Mum decided everyone was fine and they all went to bed with an aspirin.

Sarah looks sceptical. Bea's pitch rises.

'Remember my broken leg? In plaster?' she shoots her leg out straight, to remind her friend. 'He *dropped* me.' But Sarah doesn't remember, because she hadn't started at the school. And now, from nowhere, Bea's got an image of *that fucking story*. Her shooting *him*, where *she's* the crazy one. Bea smacks the back of one hand against her open palm, desperate to pull up more evidence. But she doesn't have words for how she felt sitting in her room with the door shut, praying he wouldn't come in. Her mind races on. Her naked self, just a few months ago, flung against him. Falling to the floor, catching his red face; murderous, repulsed. She might cry.

'I won't go back,' she says in a small voice. *Please be on my side*. Sarah keeps on looking at her for ages, then she turns slowly away, pulls a curl from her frizz and twirls it around her finger while Bea holds her breath.

'My dad says we choose our parents,' Sarah says airily.

Bea slumps back. Sarah doesn't care about anything she just said, her indifference is shocking. Though Bea's a tiny bit relieved not to be cross-examined.

'Someone else probably said it,' Sarah says. 'Aristotle or Shakespeare,' she rolls her eyes, 'you know how he's always quoting.' She puts on a deep voice, '"We choose our parents."'

Bea grunts her acknowledgement. Her breathing slows, and the heat leaves her. She feels like a popped balloon while she repeats the quote in her head *We choose our parents*. She stares at the ceiling, a light shade of terracotta, then closes her eyes and conjures up a line of couples behind her eyelids. Mothers with wavy hair and long coats, tall fathers in suits. And she could have had *any* of them?

'You made a good choice,' she says truthfully, to the ceiling. Sarah doesn't say anything, she gets up and goes upstairs to revise. On the screen the credits roll, over the wavy arms and wide-open smiles of the winners.

Bea misses Lonnie, and weirdly Andrew, all smug with his new job and suit (suit!). Apprentice accountant. Impossible to picture. She sneaks back to see Granny Dil in the Annexe, going in around the back. When Mum's there, she tries to make it all OK in her pathetic Mum way. Humming, asking in a bright voice, 'How's life at Sarah's?', and, 'What would you like for tea?' *A new fucking life, with chips and peas*. As soon as Dad comes in, Bea leaves. She can't look at him.

Once, Andrew was in the Annexe, reading from a book. Bea was so surprised she just stood on the patio and stared through the glass. Andrew in the wicker chair, leaning back with his legs crossed at the ankles, and Granny peaceful, her eyes closed. Bea had felt a scream rise in her throat. She was about to turn around and leave when Andrew looked up, saw her, and shut the book. Granny said something but didn't open her eyes, and Andrew's mouth moved with his reply, still fixed on Bea through the glass. Granny opened her eyes then, smiled, and gave a limp wave like the Queen Mother.

'You weren't here,' Andrew mumbled, brushing past her – an explanation, not an accusation.

'I'm not anywhere,' she mumbled back, wanting to grab his sleeve, either to thump him or to cling on.

She gets an Unconditional Offer.

On Saturdays, she still takes Lonnie swimming, strawberry hair floating around her like Ophelia. Moira brings her to the pool, and Bea and her mother exchange nods and tight smiles while Lonnie looks from one to the other, her bright eyes questioning the new arrangement.

'How's school?' Moira asks.

'Sitting around, talking bollocks,' she says. 'It's fine'

'Not long now.'

Bea turns this over afterwards. Not long for what? Until the exams? The end of school? Until they can be rid of her for good? She revs up her defiance. *I didn't choose them* she says to herself. *They want me gone and I don't care.*

*

The oval dining table is cold against Bea's cheek. Through her half-closed eyes, a swirl pattern in the dark wood beside her nose looks like a giant comma. It's the last week of exams and she just did a crap Chemistry Paper 2. Her arms are spread wide. Shadow dots of wind-blown blossom rain across the table, across her fingers, from the giant cherry tree outside the French windows. Snow from the blue sky, weird and surreal. According to Sarah's mum the blossom's late this year.

Bea could fall asleep right here. Night-time sleep is getting harder. Uncle David knows about trees, he can name them from his little book, just from a leaf. She'll get up in a minute and make a cup of tea. She used to love getting her name mug at Granny Dil's house, now David's house. 'Beatrice, meaning: Bringer of Joy', in gold letters. A sob heaves up from deep inside her. A long rising then falling note echoes around the empty room. She wipes her nose with her sleeve. She'll go to Bluebell Lane and see Uncle David after the exams. They'll drink tea and play Scrabble and he won't ask her questions.

'Bea?' The soft voice of Eleanor Rosefoot. 'Bea? What's up?'

Bea gulps but she can't talk. Eleanor helps her up to the bedroom and brings her two slices of toast and honey.

Speak your truth quietly and clearly.

They sit on the bed. Eleanor picks out a few things about her day, then says, 'And how about you, hmm?'

Bea starts talking and can't stop. She tells Eleanor she won't go home because she and Dad can't look at each other. This is the truth. She says he might lash out again. He's dangerous, she hates him, he hates her, she'll never go back. And here it is: the hot, agitated feeling in her core.

What *is* her truth? Why is she even crying?

'You could write him a letter?' Eleanor suggests. 'Sometimes it's easier to write things than to say them.' And she starts on about an old woman, estranged from her family. Sarah's mum has examples of every eventuality. But Bea isn't listening. She tries to calm herself. She fixes on Eleanor's red dangly earrings, the wrong colour against her orange shirt. Mum would never wear a clash like that. Eleanor gets to the bit about the letter of reconciliation. Bravo old woman.

'It'll be OK,' Eleanor says.

How?

'In time it will, you'll see.'

'What's time got to do with it?' Bea says, wiping her eyes, roughly, with her sleeve.

'It's a second-hand emotion.' Sarah stands in the doorway, blank-faced.

'That's love,' Bea says in a beat. *How long has she been there*?

'I know,' Sarah says. Eleanor looks from one to the other. No one says anything. Eleanor gives Bea's arm a final squeeze and leaves the room. She strokes Sarah's shoulder as she passes.

'How was French Literature, sweetie?'

'*Pas mal*,' Sarah says, and her mum disappears downstairs. 'What's the matter?' Sarah asks Bea from the doorway, unblinking.

'Oh, nothing. I dunno, I kind of lost the plot,' Bea's voice is tight. She looks around, up at the ceiling, and points upwards, 'There it is!'

Sarah doesn't smile. 'What were you saying to Mum?'

'About my dad,' Bea says. 'My sorry-arse life, *le catastrophe*,' she peters out. Why doesn't Sarah come and sit on the bed? She stands in the doorway for ages. Bea can't think of anything else to say. Nada, nicht, noots, nul, rien. Nothing.

'Why don't you tell your mum?' Sarah says, then turns her back, goes off to her room and shuts the door.

*

When Bea does leave, it couldn't be further from how she pictured it. No Spitfire or even Mini Metro. No punching the air out of the window, sunglasses on against the bright glare of her future. Her university is taking on admin staff for the summer. After her last exam, Bea stays a week at Simon's and then gets on a train with her big rucksack. She waves at Lonnie on the platform for two whole minutes. Mum clasps her hands, waves, then clasps again, as though the other hand might fly away. Lonnie waves rhythmically, like a windscreen wiper, smiling her wide smile. She has on a pink tracksuit, a bit short in the leg. It looks like skin and clashes horribly with her hair. Lonnie must have insisted on it. Mum would have pushed alternatives. She stops only to ask Mum a question, probably 'When will the train leave?' After the answer, she carries on waving and smiling. And Bea waves back, with what feels like her whole body stuck in her throat.

When the train finally hisses away, she slumps back in the seat, her arm aching. With great effort, she swallows the boulder down. A numbness creeps through her, like standing outside in the snow. Here she is, all her possessions in one rucksack, the countryside she knows speeding past her, alone and pregnant.

Take aim
1975

The van is rather like a cheap doll's house; everything is flimsy and in miniature. Moira spends the week with her back curved, and her head dipped. It was Ted's idea in the first place. 'We'll rent a caravan!' as though holidays themselves were his invention. St Audries Bay on the Somerset coast. The first time they came, the children must have been three and five.

Parked in the middle of a line of identical vans, they overlook a wide stretch of lawn. Beyond it are the steps down through the woods to the beach. Moira's favourite features are all the nautical touches. The embroidered life buoy in blue-and-white check, compass on the wall, porthole window low on the side. Andrew and Bea take turns to kneel on the carpet while the other one runs outside, and ten seconds later a face fills the little round of glass. At nine, Andrew is less thrilled by this, but if Bea pokes him in the ribs and shoots out the door, he dutifully hunkers down to greet her. Andrew weathers his sister's turbulence in a way Moira does not. This morning, Bea stared her out over two uneaten Weetabix, while Andrew quietly built his Lego lighthouse. Moira understands Andrew, his caution and vigilance. A little like David but not too much, she tells herself. Not too much.

Grains of sand find their way into everything. The sheets, sandwiches, her book, her toothbrush. On wet days, the van struggles to contain Bea, who whips up a tantrum in the turn of a head, leaving Ted startled and pinned to the scratchy sofa. Clear days like today are easier. Dams, burials, lopsided sandcastles. 'Sand *and* stones,' Ted says every year, rubbing his hands at the endless possibilities of these two materials. They are down there now. Moira should go and join them.

The children will be squealing at the incoming tide. The sea frightens Ted; too cold and too murky. And vast. 'No higher than your knees,' he instructs the children, though Bea always hurls herself in for a dunk.

The sea fills Bea's ears. Her skin burns. Icy, slapping water seals over her head for split seconds, gurgling to silence before she rockets up, then ducks back under, silencing her father's shouts. He says people have drowned here. *Not me!* She lifts her feet off the ground and floats. Flat on her back, with bits of seaweed tapping against her, she lies weightless, staring up into bright, thick cloud. Then she rolls over and splashes hard in front crawl. She learned in the pool, to pull with the arms. Here, there are no classmates' feet in her way. Here, she's got the whole ocean! All to herself. Even if it is brown.

Head down, she opens her eyes and the water hits, cold on her eyeballs, and dark. No one comes in after her. She can just about touch the bottom here. She pivots back. On the beach, her father waves loopy, frantic arms, still shouting. Can't he see she can *swim*? She pivots the other way: only sea and sky. The jutting cliff is away to her left, but if she looks straight out, there's nothing between her and everything.

Ted's in the water up to his shins. Why's Moira taking so long? The clouds are frothy and patchy, with openings of blue now on the horizon. The wind keeps picking up, and then suddenly calms down. It's not swimming weather. Behind him, Andrew's reedy voice calls out 'Dad. She's alright.' But what if she's not?

The sea sloshes and swells. Tangles of kelp stroke his calves and his feet find lumps. Any minute now, something will sink its teeth into his ankles – some deadly breed found only in the Bristol Channel. Don't tread where you can't see, that's Ted's motto. He yells again to Bea. He's close now, water above his knees, but she pretends not to hear him and ducks back under. Inside his head, terror battles fury. His heart pumps away. Up she jumps and slaps her arms on the surface. With a lunge, he grabs her wrist. *Got her*. She yanks it back but he holds firm, managing to keep his balance.

'I can *swim*,' she squeals, 'look!' But Ted holds on and drags her behind him, back through the shallows. She struggles.

'Let me *go*!' She thrashes her legs. It takes all his strength to keep hold of her, a wild, flapping thing. Finally, he pulls her in; a fisherman with a catch. When the water is ankle-deep, she gives in. Her feet find the sand and she stands up and stalks behind him. He holds her wrist until they are clear of the water. When he lets go, she bolts away, off along the pebbles towards the cliff, each footfall a clatter.

Bea runs. *Away. Get away.* Her ankles sink and turn in the stones. They might snap. She'll get to the far end, where the waves crash up the cliff, *Baff!* Right there, a gigantic spray of white. Bea jumps in time with it on the beach. She's a stick of dynamite, an explosion. She's hot and prickly. There's too much breath inside her, like the sea now, at the cliff, rising, rising, *Baff!* Her own waves build inside her. And here comes the roar through her open mouth.

'Beee aaaa triss.' Up to the sky. 'Beee aaaa triss.' Loud, out over the water, her eyes squeezed shut.

It's like being sick – the purge is similar – her insides bursting out before she can settle again.

Ted towels his legs, while Andrew frets beside him. They watch Bea's yellow swimming costume get smaller and smaller down the beach.

'She's heading for the cliff,' Andrew says, fearful. 'D'you think she'll climb it?' Ted only huffs. Surely she won't go in the water again? He starts along the stones but it's too painful on the soles of his feet. How can she *run*? She's shouting something, or singing? He cranes to listen. Three long notes, whisked away by the wind. Her small body is dwarfed by the marly cliff, dark as rust. He takes another few tentative steps, cocks his head. Is she shouting her *own name*?

*

The castle trip is a regular. Ted usually looks forward to it. It's the last day of the holiday, grey and clammy. The turreted castle itself remains almost intact, circled by a jagged outer wall, and surrounded by fields and a wood. At the entrance, on a giant poster, a large, tunicked man points his bow and arrow at the sky above the words 'Medieval Pursuits! Pay at Reception!'

Moira heads off for her circular walk of the grounds. Andrew and Bea head over the back field, towards a small tent and a tethered bird. Ted trails after them.

'It's a hawk,' Andrew says. 'Or it might be a kestrel.'

'Can we stroke it?' Bea asks. The man from the poster appears, his brown dress tied with a rope over his belly. He holds up a large glove.

'You can fly her if you buy a ticket,' he says. 'She'll soar around the castle and come to land right on your arm.' He waggles the glove.

'What if she doesn't come back?' Andrew says, worried. If Ted could only drum a bit of bite into his son. A bit of *man*liness.

'Pet shop's ten miles that way,' the man thumbs over his shoulder. 'Ha! I'm just teasing you, fella. She always comes back.'

'I wouldn't,' Bea says loudly. The man looks surprised. 'I'd fly away and be *free*.' She puts her arms out behind her, ready to go.

'She's a beauty,' Ted says, nodding at the bird.

'She's called Kerris,' he says. 'Pay me.' He shakes the glove again. Then adds, 'Archery tickets from reception.'

Ted gives them a choice, arrows or hawk. Easy for Andrew, but not so easy for Bea who wants desperately to free Kerris *and* fire arrows.

'In medieval times, archery was survival,' shouts the instructor, a barrel of a woman, same brown tunic. Her volume is set for a group, though it's only Ted and Bea. Bea sulked all the way over because Andrew was allowed to fly the bird alone. Now they're at the faded white line in the field, holding their bows, Bea's face is flushed with excitement. A clutch of steel-tipped arrows rattles in a pouch on the instructor's back. The meadow behind the far-off targets is dotted with red poppies.

Ted gives Bea a wink as they practise drawing the bows. He'll win his daughter over with bows and arrows. It's been a long week and Ted's exhausted. She's even feistier than last year. But here they are in a field together. A private lesson. A chance.

The woman demonstrates theatrically. Each time, there's a quiet *thunk* as she hits the target. Bea is led forward to the 'children's line'. She might argue, but then doesn't. Ted hangs back and watches her receive her arrow solemnly, on two flat palms, as though she's balancing a stick of thin glass. Next to the woman, Bea looks tiny, her legs like pipe-cleaners poking out of her shorts. The day is getting muggier. Ted's armpits are damp.

Her first arrow flings up and flops down on the grass halfway to the targets. Ted edges closer.

'That doesn't count,' Bea says. The next two shoot straight and low into the grass, and Bea's face takes on its bulldog look. Her fourth bounces out high, soars over the top of the target, and clatters against the catching panel. Funny sound, some kind of plastic? Plastic is everywhere. Ted's very sceptical.

'Why can't I *do* it,' Bea demands of the targets. Ted senses danger.

'Next year, longer arms, you'll be a demon,' he says. She shoots him a dark look. 'This time lucky,' he says.

'It's not luck,' the woman says unhelpfully, then flaps a brown arm at him. 'Alright Dad, come and help.'

Ted isn't sure he is qualified. He could tell her that his daughter, aged seven, is already completely herself. If you step into the world like that, what use is a father? But the instructor is miming awkwardly how he should wrap himself around her to guide the aim. Ted understands suddenly that this woman doesn't have children, and feels a pang of sorrow for her. She's around his age – people their age should have children. The thought rallies him. Together they'll get a bulls-eye.

Bea's stiff inside his arms, but when he puts the arrow in her hand with his on top, she leans into him. It's the closest he and Bea have been in a long while, her spine pressing against his middle. He should have taken his jacket off. Moira said it was too warm for leather.

As one, they draw the thing back. 'Three, two, one,' he says into her hair.

Thunk.

'Yesss!' Bea says. The arrow spikes out of the second-to-last circle. Ted's itching for his go now, he might be good at this. *Thunk,* the next one hits the target and Bea wriggles out from Ted's arms, smiling. His heart does a little skip.

'Now on my own,' she says.

'Give her one or two of mine,' Ted says, 'then I'll have a shot from further back.' He holds his breath as she takes aim. *Thunk.* Outer white ring. Bea rushes the next one, and it soars and clatters.

'Your turn,' she mumbles and struts off, chin in the air. He's about to offer her all his arrows, but she's gone. He did his best.

From the back line, Ted's arrow flies straight and true.

'Ha!' Right in the middle! If only Moira was watching. He loads the next. *Easy does it.*

Thunk.

'Champion.' He rocks back on his heels. 'Where's Bea?'

'Here,' a small voice comes from behind. Ted turns with an open mouth, ready to crow.

'What the—'

A little way off, Bea is bent backwards, her hair falling towards the grass, her bow curved and straining. The steel-tipped arrow points at the sky.

'Bea?' Ted steps towards her. She swings round and now the arrow's pointing right at him. Ted drops his bow and holds up his hands.

'Jesus, Bea.' She looks surprised, as though she has forgotten what she's holding. But she keeps it trained on him. What was his thought just now? *She is completely herself.* Yet Ted has no idea who this is. A small, thin girl with half his genes and straight dark hair, in shorts and a T-shirt, never staying one thing for long. Full of some grudge against life. Against *him*? Her arm wobbles from the effort of holding taut the thick string. He searches her stare. Hurt? Exhilaration?

The woman makes a high, sharp sound in the back of her throat.

And Bea lets go.

A blow to the arm. Ted stumbles back but stays standing. Bea's mouth falls open.

The woman cries out. Ted's arm throbs. Bea bites her lip and doesn't move. They stare at each other, and Bea's eyes appear to fill her face, the deepest blue. Ted looks down at his arm in bewilderment. The arrow lies limp from a hole in his leather jacket. He puts his fingertips there. It's sticky. His hand is shaking.

He looks up. Bea's stock still. A thin red strand trickles down her chin, and for a second her blood confuses him. Has he harmed *her* in some way?

'Bea, your lip—'

His arm pulses. *She shot me in the arm.* Bea keeps staring.

'It's alright,' he says.

It's not alright. It's not alright at all.

Dusk has almost given way to night. The cliff looms black ahead of them as Ted and Moira walk along the grass in silence, not touching. They usually take a walk earlier, arm in arm, with the cliff a deep red in the last of the daylight. In their cardboard box room, Bea fell into an instant, noiseless sleep. In the narrow bed next to her, Andrew's still reading by torchlight.

Ted's arm aches. *If I hadn't been wearing leather. If the arrow had landed three inches to the right.*

Moira had peeled off his bloody shirt earlier to reveal his tattoo a mess. She wiped the wound, and they both gasped – or maybe it was only Ted who had gasped – staring at the dark gash in the curve of the heart where it dipped towards the M. 'Bulls-eye,' Ted muttered, while Bea sat mute on the caravan steps. She wouldn't let Moira near her bitten lip. 'I've never known her so quiet,' Moira said as she dressed the cut, and Ted flinched. 'Just a surface wound,' she said. Ted wasn't so sure.

The lawn is soft underfoot. They walk slowly, in step.

'She looked right at me,' Ted says. What was that look in her eyes? Could it have been *revenge*? For what? He didn't tell Moira about Bea earlier in the week, screaming her own name into the wind, strange and unsettling.

'She'll grow out of these rages,' Moira says.

'I couldn't speak,' he says, suddenly desperate. 'My own daughter.'

'What had you done?' Moira asks.

'Nothing! I told you,' his voice rising. 'She did her arrows, then I did a couple. Then there she was, pointing one at my heart.' He puts a hand flat on his chest. A faint cheer comes from the bar at the top of the grass slope; the sea shushes on the stones below. The great rock face ahead, jutting out into the water, appears to Ted like the edge of the world. He stops still.

'She meant to hurt me,' he says quietly.

'Oh Ted,' Moira stops too. 'It was an accident. She's seven.'

'You weren't there.'

Hurtling backwards
1976

Wheezing slightly, Dilys leads the party up Bluebell Lane, back to the house and the promise of 'cocktails'.

'Is Willow old?' Bea asks. Andrew almost drags the dog behind him.

'She's a pensioner,' Dilys says. 'Even older than me.'

'She's twelve,' David says. 'It's very old for a cocker spaniel. Her birthday was last month.' Willow has run out of steam and so has Dilys. Her long shadow sways in front of her, twice as tall as she is. The August sun sits low and yolk-orange over Lower Ashton village. They've come the long way round, over the scorched village green, and past the new Catholic church built by one of the villagers. Small and boxy and unchurch-like, it was the talk of the shop for a while. Lured by comfier benches and spicy incense, Dilys has swapped allegiance, not that she goes all that often. Also, it's not up a vertically steep hill. Plus, the priest's Irish accent is toe-curlingly sexy.

At the house, Dilys puffs up the path with the key.

'We could make Willow a birthday cake,' Bea says with a smirk. That *face*. Dilys could eat her up.

'She's a *dog*,' Andrew says.

'She's on a diet,' Dilys winks at Bea.

'She has her own food,' David says patiently. 'If dogs eat—'

'It was a *joke*,' Dilys snaps. Having other people around makes her snippy with David. They highlight his oddness, his tendency to quibble with everything. It's better when Moira's here.

They all go straight through and out the back door. The dog collapses on the square of yellow grass, panting, and the children fling themselves down beside her.

'Is Moira coming?' David asks.

'Later.' Dilys lowers herself into one of the rickety garden deckchairs. David goes back inside. She lights up a ciggy and admires her grandchildren: a picture of summer's end, scuffed and sun-kissed and on the edge of boredom. She's minding them while Moira's at Valentine's.

'I quite fancy a go at Valentine's myself,' Dilys says, idly.

'It's not a funfair,' Andrew says, his pink face serious, 'it's an old people's home.' Dilys chuckles. The name always makes her think of a seedy club, with low ceilings and barmaids in short skirts, not an overheated last-stop-shop.

'Have my dinner cooked, play backgammon, put my feet up,' she says. Though what she would truly like is not to fast forward but to rewind, all the way to her old life. She is eternally young; her marital status is sketchy; there is romance; her children are attentive, whatever their ages. She works as a singer, or radio announcer, or florist, or in Harrods.

On her wobbly chair, Dilys sighs and blows out a slow stream of smoke into the stifling late afternoon air. She watches Bea roll onto her back and loudly count the birds perched in a line on the telephone wire. The girl kicks up her skinny legs and claps her sandals together, causing a flurry of startled sparrows to fly off in a cloud. Bea smiles with satisfaction, the little minx, a strip of dark hair stuck to her forehead. Moira talks about what a handful she is, but Dilys can't get enough of her.

'Tell me about Butlins,' she says. After last year's incident, the family swapped the caravan for a cabin in Minehead theme park.

'There's a monorail and an ice cream parlour,' Bea says.

'Not as good as the caravan,' Andrew says sulkily.

'Better,' Bea says.

'Maybe you'll go to the van again next year,' Dilys says to Andrew.

'We won't,' Andrew says, then quietly, 'because of her.'

'It's *not.*' Bea flings out a fist which Andrew anticipates and rolls deftly away.

Dilys has heard Ted tell the bow and arrow story more

than once. He makes too much of it, to Dilys's mind. He had stripped to his vest, in her living room, only a few months back, to show off the scar. A little red line right next to his love heart with the 'M'. 'My broken heart!' he'd wailed, and clutched his arm, as though receiving the blow all over again. He had reeled about and knocked his shins on the table, pulling agony faces in the death throes before flinging himself into the armchair. He should have been an actor. During the performance, Dilys had watched Bea chewing her lip, and then the girl's face had crumpled up, poor little scrap, and she ran out to the dog. Dilys had gone straight after her. 'I'm not *bad*,' Bea had whispered, fiercely. It practically broke her heart. 'You're the best,' Dilys had told her, hugging her tight, 'The very best, the bee's knees.'

For all his bravado, Ted was clearly rattled. He seemed to think Bea had it in for him! He still nurses his arm and makes Bea out the villain. Well, when he's round here, Dilys won't stand for it.

'"If it had been a few inches to the right—"'. On the grass, Andrew's quoting their father.

'Shut *up* about it.'

'Ow!'

'Who wants a squash with a twist?' Dilys says.

'Me!'

'Me!'

Dilys hums the 'Chattanooga Choo Choo' as she slices oranges. Through the window, on all fours, Andrew shows Willow how to roll over. He likes teaching her tricks, though this one isn't catching on. Over he goes, then gives her a gentle nudge, bless him. Nope, she's not shifting. Dilys reaches forward with the knife to tap the window and pass him the dog biscuits, when a sharp cry comes from upstairs. She holds the blade in mid-air. Another shout comes, with a strangled edge. *David.*

Up she goes, a swooping owl, so swiftly she has to clutch the bannister at the top. David's door is open. Dilys rarely goes into his room, but she goes in now and finds Bea sitting on the floor. Her eyes do a quick sweep and find everything orderly. Books on the single shelf, the old flower press with screws tight, two potted plants on the windowsill, bed neatly made. On the floorboards under the window, Bea sits with a little pile of rubbish between her legs. Dead leaves, bits of paper and whatnot. Has she upturned the waste-paper basket? No, that's in its place in the corner. David prowls around Bea like a hungry fox.

'Come away,' Dilys starts to say, holding out a hand to Bea, who shuffles sideways. And now Dilys sees a slim box on the floor in front of her, scraps of material, a small watch face. David bobs down, darts out a hand and grabs the watch.

A flat, red box. Dilys tilts her head, though she knows the writing on the side.

Fry's.

She might keel over.

David kneels down. His hands hover over tiny newspaper cuttings, multi-coloured squares of cloth, a circle of assorted buttons. He lets out a small keening sound. Bea giggles. Dilys half expects him to open his mouth and wail. She knows he can't just bundle them away; there will be a strict order.

'David,' she says, a warning to them both. She herself is hurtling backwards, she can't stop.

Dilys stands in another bedroom in another house, in Morden, with David, a boy, groaning in anguish. He's set the baby off. 'There there, my poppet.' She knew something like this would happen, she just knew it. She had told them that morning of the evacuation plan, all arranged. They were to go on ahead, and Dilys would follow with the baby. David's causing a ruckus, of course. More and more packets appear, an envelope, a pillowcase, a paper bag full of feathers. *For the love of God.*

'You can't take it all, there are strict rules for luggage.' Moira ducks under Dilys's arm. Where did she come from? She goes to her brother and pleads with Dilys for David to be allowed to take more.

'No, he bloody can't.'

'Why not?'

'Because.'

Dilys gives him a box she's been saving. A long box that once had chocolate creams in. It quietens the noise momentarily.

This box, on these floorboards.

Where's the baby? For a split second Dilys pats her empty shoulder, while David the man pats over the strewn contents on the floor, very slowly, his hands splayed, as though giving it all a blessing.

Dilys comes fully back to the present. Why has he got all this, *still*? Where has it come from?

Damn you. She's seized by a spark of old rage. 'David,' she says, loud and accusing; a voice from another time. 'Get. It. Away.'

Bea rises to a squat and goes to pick up the pile. Before her hand can touch anything, David shoves Bea, hard. She sits back heavily on her bottom, narrowly avoiding the bedstead. Dilys lets out a cry. Un-phased by the shove, Bea's head swivels from David to Dilys, thrilled to see what will happen next.

A huge silence holds the room.

'Granny, you're being a Red Indian,' Bea says finally. Dilys's hand flutters over her mouth. She must calm herself, for her angel. She smooths her skirt and breathes slowly out. Bea creeps back towards the box on hands and knees. David gives his mother a pleading look that squashes her anger. A grown man guarding his treasure like a child. It's pitiful, really. She would put her arms around him if such a thing were possible. She takes two steps into the room and puts a hand on David's shoulder, leaves it there for a second, two, three, and gives it the smallest squeeze. Then she holds it out to Bea.

'We'll let Uncle David alone to tidy up.' Bea springs up and takes her hand. Dilys knows from Moira that hers is the only hand Bea will hold. Dilys holds on tightly.

'Can I play with it another time?' Bea asks on the stairs.

'It's not really for playing, Toots.'

'What *is* it for?'

'It's a life,' Dilys says. Then, more quietly, 'Another life.'

Bea stops with both feet on a stair to consider this. She turns her blue eyes up to Dilys. 'Whose?'

'Ours,' Dilys says. 'Mine.' The dog appears at the bottom of the stairs, wagging her tail.

'But you're here,' Bea says, 'you can't have *another* life.'

'Oh you can, Beetle,' her voice cracks and she swallows hard. 'You can have many.'

Open wound
1979

Ted hefts another bag of soil on his shoulder down the sideway. The air's got the slightest nip, but he's pretending it's still summer. Late September, the kids are back at school. Bea started at the Girls' Grammar a few weeks ago. 'Big school'. Off on the bus like a grown-up. It can bring a lump to Ted's throat to see Bea in a shirt and tie and too-big blazer. Andrew's taller than Ted now, which pleases them both – gives them a running joke. Ted agreed to lug these bags for Moira before going to site. She's on a late shift. From the alley, he can hear the phone ringing inside. He ignores it.

He thumps the bag down on the patio and surveys the 'conservatory' eyesore, as he frequently does. He's got the rest of the house in good shape, complete with extra storage and kitchen skylight, but these flimsy glass panels still let the place down. Perhaps he puts this off to leave himself a job. What will he do when it's all finished? Back up the sideway, and the phone's still ringing. Whoever it is will get bored soon. How many sacks has Ted lugged in his life? It's a little game he plays. Sacks, boards, planks. The maths is getting harder. He dumps it next to the last one, and this time he avoids looking at the panels. From here, the shrill ringing sound is like a bird's danger call: *prrrr prrrr prrrr.* The sun catches Moira's cheek and she appears to glow, kneeling there forking the earth around her flowers, a peaceful half-smile on her lips.

'What?' she says, turning.

'Nothing,' Ted says, smiling. 'You look a picture.'

She smiles back. 'Asters,' she says, then, 'You could answer that, you know. Someone's got a bee in their bonnet.'

Ted lingers in the sun for a moment longer. As soon as he steps into the shade, a chill spreads through him.

On the shelf at the bottom of the stairs, the alarm call rings on from the old-fashioned telephone they brought with them from the flat. The handle seems to rattle, like in a cartoon.

Finally, he lifts the receiver.

'One of the balconies has collapsed,' Alan Turner tells him, his voice deeper than Ted has ever heard it.

Everyone admired them, magically suspended from the side wall. From the street, flashes of colour peeked over the tops, plants existing in mid-air, held by cantilevered concrete beams. Mighty slabs of precast concrete. Ted remembers the day they were delivered to site before he took over as foreman. The scale of this stuff always makes his heart quicken. It's an astounding thing to watch a structure take shape, like a giant man-made skeleton. When the structure is still naked, there are days when the building could almost lift itself up, and start to move on its own limbs. Terrifying, exhilarating.

Alan Turner tells Ted, in the gravelly voice, that Molly Potts, sixty-nine, occupant of the ground floor flat, may not walk again.

Too-short cantilevered concrete beams, as it turns out. Design flaw. How the hell it was approved, Ted will never know.

Thank god it's only the first floor.

'You need to come into the office, Ted.' There's a long pause, full of his boss's laboured breathing. 'Now.'

Newspaper reporters cluster outside the Turner building. Ted elbows past and goes upstairs. From the corridor, he can hear Alan Turner's raised voice from the end office with the opaque panels. On the phone to lawyers? The insurance company? Molly Potts's family? He's not a shouter, by and large. Ted tries not to think about the distraught son or daughter on the other end, *My mother—*

It was built to design, and the drawings were all approved by the time Ted took over. Planning applications already signed off. Ted completed the site inspection with Building Control. Everything to standard, Alan Turner himself said so.

Standing in the corridor, Ted finds he can't swallow. He pushes open the doors. The open-plan office falls silent. One by one the workers turn to look at him.

*

Ted will fix this. He will fix it.

He'll find the drawings. They're kept in a pair of wide grey cabinets at the back of the basement. The drawings are proof the mistake was made before Ted had anything to do with it. He will clear his name. They'll have to take him back. He'd got himself noticed as foreman and was all set to head up the refurb of the Town Council buildings. It's a good promotion.

Ted and Moira had watched the local news. The fractured balcony was made a TV star, resting cock-eyed on the ground, the camera zooming slowly in on the severed concrete edges, like an open wound.

He goes to the office after dark. He no longer has his badge, but the entry codes are the same. He heads along the main corridor through the fire door and down the metal steps into the basement. He flicks on one row of lights, there's a faint hum, and the whole space turns a dull orange. Around the walls, endless shelves overflow with messy rolls of paper in all sizes. He squints towards the back. No filing cabinets. The floor space is a grid of plan chests, more than he remembers. He's only been down here a few times; it's not really for workers. 'Where the ladies look at drawings,' some of the men say. Ted used to picture something like a gallery – pencil drawings of fine buildings on easels, and hung around the walls – until he came down himself to this stuffy, low-ceilinged archive, smelling of sandpaper and feet. If the old cabinets with the recent builds have gone, the drawings must all now be stored in these low chests. He starts pulling out the wide, heavy drawers on runners. They slide out nicely. He pulls out one or two and pushes them back in, just for the action. Then he gets down to the hunt.

He starts at the far corner, noting the dates, and skips to the middle section. Drawer after drawer, his eyes go straight to the top left, date and reference number. After about twenty, he catches a familiar spiral and hunkers down for a closer look. The multi-storey: his first job. His fingers trace over the tiny numbers, the angles. Here, in miniature, is the top deck where he, Ted, stood in his Turner's sweatshirt, for the photo-op on completion. 'A uniform and a *pension*,' he told Moira the day he got the job. The whole workforce had stood at the top in a line, arms around each other's shoulders, for the *Evening Post*. It felt like he'd arrived somewhere. It felt like a family.

He slaps his palm hard on the drawing and the drawer wobbles. He slams it shut, and starts moving faster, yanking out drawers so they crack to a stop. He kicks them back in, making the whole chest shudder. He looks up. He's covered half the room. He must be getting closer. The dates are not strictly in order, but he's getting there, *Oh yes*. He pictures Alan Turner's bowed head, not meeting his eyes: 'We're letting you go.'

You cunt, he slams another home. *You cunt.*

A thud above his head sends his shoulders to his ears, and his stomach into freefall. He steadies himself, then scuttles to the back of the basement and flicks the light off. In the dark, he can hear only his breath whistling in and out of his nose, and then quick steps along the corridor above. Now the creak of the door, feet tapping down the metal stairs. *Tap, tap, tap*. Whoever it is has stopped halfway down. There's a rustle, a faint click, and a dusty torch beam creeps across the plan chests, closer and closer. Ted holds his breath. His teeth clamp together. The shaft of dust motes sparkles and crawls closer still. Until at last the feeble beam of light finds his trembling face.

Not laughing now

Moira treats the reporters who come to the door with a steely firmness. No, her husband will not be giving an interview. Yes, he will be making an appeal. No, he will not be returning to Turner's for the moment. Ted told her not to talk to them, but they kept ringing the bell, and Bea proved herself a loose cannon in Public Relations. 'My dad knows how to embed a concrete bloody beam, and he will *not* be held responsible for someone else's damn negligence.' It was a direct quote. Moira has no idea if anyone printed it.

She scans for warning signs – a flexed neck muscle, a drop in the pitch of his silence – and whisks the children away. She brings tea, offers to get the paper, slips out and then in from work. There is something wholly familiar about this vigilance, tip-toeing, scanning for signs. It is what she did for David throughout her childhood, for David and her mother through her teens.

The letter is on the sideboard. Ted comes in and opens it without acknowledging her. She sees the underlined word at the top, INJUNCTION. Ted stares at it, his face twitching, then his mouth becomes a snarl; someone Moira doesn't know. He tears the letter slowly in half, puts it back on the side, and leaves the room without a word, knocking against her shoulder as he goes.

*

Andrew pushes the last fish finger around his plate with a fork.

'I'll have yours,' Bea whispers.

'Let him finish,' Moira says, from the sink. Andrew seems to have gone off his food.

'Wasn't asking you,' Bea says. Moira turns around to see Andrew sliding the remains of his tea onto his sister's plate and Bea whistling to prove her innocence. Andrew makes a funny squeak which Moira realises is a laugh. For months, his voice has been trying and failing to break. Bea gulps the fish finger and the two of them smirk at each other. Moira finds herself smiling.

'Shall we have lemonade?' she says. Bea and Andrew look confused.

'It's Thursday,' Andrew says. Fizzy drinks are for weekends.

She shrugs. 'Take it or leave it.'

'Take it.' Bea's up, reaching for the tall glasses from the cupboard. She brings three. The bottle hisses open. Bea gulps hers and her eyes water from the fizz.

'Andrew can drink beer soon,' Bea announces, 'and wine.'

Andrew frowns. 'No. It's eighteen.'

'Fourteen,' Bea says, with authority. 'If you're at home. Like in France. Madame McFarlane says everyone drinks wine in France, *actuellement*.' Bea's full of the new sophistication of her French lessons.

'We'll stick to this for the time being,' Moira says, raising her glass, pleased to be included.

'I'll have your wine if you don't want it,' Bea says to Andrew.

'She would,' he says to Moira with a grin.

The front door closes. Andrew's smile disappears. Moira straightens up and puts her glass on the side. Ted comes in in his socks.

'Did I miss someone's birthday?' he asks.

'You're early,' Moira says.

'We finished the job,' Ted says, with a curled lip. He's been doing a roof with Michael. Moira had been praying the job would go on longer.

'Happy Thursday,' Bea says and opens her mouth for a loud belch. Andrew glares at her and gives a small shake of his head. Ted scowls.

'There'll be another one,' Moira says, trying to sound like herself. 'Everyone needs a good roof for the winter.'

'That's it,' Ted says flatly. 'End of the work.' Then his eyebrows rise in an effort to smile, leaving his mouth behind. 'What's the work in school?' he asks, 'No shortage of that.'

'Autumn poems,' Bea says, rolling her eyes. 'The leaves are *dead*, they're falling on my *head*.'

She flings herself down on the table at the tedium.

'Not yet,' Moira says, 'they're just turning yellow.' She tries to hook Bea back in. 'Bellow? Fellow?'

Andrew looks anxiously at Ted. 'Do you want some lemonade?'

'Or beer or wine?' Bea says, from the table.

'Tea,' Moira says. 'Kettle's on.'

'That's it,' Ted says again, as though she hasn't heard him, then louder, to all of them, 'No more work.' He says it like he's throwing out a challenge.

'Alf might have something?' Moira says, tentative.

'You've talked to Alf, have you?'

'No,' Moira says quietly. Bea's sitting up now, watching her parents like a tennis match. Moira pours the water over the teabag and watches it bob around. If only she'd got the meal finished earlier.

'The council buildings are underway,' Ted says. 'I just drove past.' He sniffs hard, his nostrils pull in and spring back out. 'Scaffold's up.' He claps his hands and Andrew jumps. 'Let's hope they don't arrest me for driving past.' He makes his eyes go wide. 'For *looking*.' Moira sets his tea down on the side. Inside her chest, a wing beat flaps and flaps.

'Bea, Andrew, homework,' she says. They don't move. Ted steps towards the counter. He looks at the mug as though it contains poison. Bea points to the cabinet.

'There's a bottle of wine in—'

'No wine, no beer.' Ted looks at Moira with mad eyes. Then his focus wanders, no doubt back to the men working without him. 'Scaffold,' he spits. 'All of them there.' He draws his hand back. Andrew gasps or says something as he breathes in. 'No' or 'Oh'. Ted swipes the mug and the hot liquid flings onto Moira, the side, the floor. The mug just misses her and clatters against the cupboard, somehow unbroken. Ted looks faintly surprised, as though someone else just knocked boiling tea everywhere. He waits for it to stop spinning on the lino. Then he turns and thumps upstairs.

Moira peels the fabric away from her scalded middle. She wipes the sideboard with a sponge. The children watch her in silence. She keeps her eyes down, opens the cupboard under the sink for the floor cloth. Her skin throbs, the floor will have to wait. The wings flap inside her chest; they will take a while to settle down.

'I'm going to cool it in the bathroom,' she says to the sink. And she does.

*

There is a loud knock at the door. Ted throws it open, ready for a scrawny journalist, or a salesman; someone not welcome. Surely not a journalist – it's been a few months now. A young woman in a thick coat stands square on the porch, a shopping bag in each hand. Her hair is yellow at her shoulders, and brown on her head. She's got the wrong house. Then he looks at her face, hatred in her eyes, and takes a sharp breath.

'I'm Tracey Potts,' the woman says, her voice quivering.

Ted's tongue expands inside his mouth. The woman points her chin at him.

'I'm Molly Potts's daughter.' She's barely moving her lips, as though she cannot bear for him to have anything else from her. 'My mum died. On Tuesday.'

The outside cold spreads through Ted's whole body.

'She wasn't herself after what you did to her.' Molly Potts's daughter stops, puts her two bags down, and stands up straight again. 'She had a stroke, went to hospital, and died.' She glares at Ted, her eyes dark and piercing. And now she does open her mouth. 'I thought you should know.' She hurls this at him. Ted puts a hand against the door frame.

'I'm so sorry,' Ted says when he can speak. Should he say that? It wasn't him! Though what else can he say? A small head appears at the woman's side. How did he not notice another person? The woman's hatred is taking up all the space and air. Ted catches pink ties at the end of two plaits, then the head disappears again behind its mother.

'I don't accept your apology,' Tracey Potts says. 'I never will.' She draws herself up. Her elbows fan out at her sides, like wings, her anger about to set her in flight. 'Amy has no Nana,' she pauses. '*Gone*.' She shakes her head, still disbelieving. 'Her roof fell on her.' Then she says more quietly, with menace, 'You built it, and it *crushed* her.'

They stand there. Ted on the doorstep, Tracey Potts on the path, Amy Potts tucked behind her.

It wasn't me, it wasn't me. He cannot think of a single thing to say to her.

Just as the silence becomes unbearable, the woman picks up both bags and turns around. The child glances up at Ted with big, frightened eyes, before following her mother back up the path.

Ted's body sags, watching them walk away. The girl has to trot to keep up, her pigtails swing, like little pink pendulums. Her high-pitched voice rings out in the street.

'Is that the man?'

Bea slams the door. She considers opening it just to slam it again. She stomps into the front room, drops her bag, and flops down on the chair. It's the worst day of her life. She didn't make the County squad. She cried a bit on the way home just now, in the back of the Hinks's old Volvo. Luckily, Nicky Hinks was in the front with his dad. There's a real danger she'll burst into tears again now.

On the sofa, head in the paper, Dad is pretending she's not here. He never used to ignore her. He's probably been sitting here all day, and *still* he can't be bothered to look up. But she'd rather have Dad here than Mum. Mum will tell her not to worry, there'll be another chance. Mum doesn't get *anything*. She probably doesn't even know that Bea was up for medley, and under 13s' relay. She doesn't know what a good swimmer Bea is. *Not good enough*. A little squeak comes out of her throat. How can she not have made the squad when Fiona Moss did? Lack of fifty-metre practice, Bea thinks bitterly. Worst day of her stupid, loser life.

Dad might get it. He's just been laid off, after all. Feeling sorry for himself is what he does every hour of every day. And he used to come to the galas before she banned him for over-bellowing. She practically died of embarrassment. In the car just now, she decided she would tell him, even if she cried. But sitting here, she can't think how.

She has dreamed, in detail, about getting the coach to County Meets. Taking a packed tea with two KitKats (one for each way), wearing the royal blue sweatshirt with her initials, sitting next to Irish Dayna, a *fourth year*. She has felt her double-handed winning touch, her shoulders rising out of the water to wild, echoing cheers. She feels tears on both cheeks and wipes them angrily away, scraping her face. And she didn't tell anyone these dreams, because the girls in her class dream about other stuff, boys mostly. But Bea only wanted to get into County.

Ted jumps when the door slams. The whole house shudders. Bea thuds in, throws her bag on the floor and flings herself down in the armchair. If she notices him on the sofa, she doesn't show it. He mutters 'Hello'. She huffs and puffs. Ted's not in the mood for her histrionics. He turns the page and is faced with a man with a fat grin, holding up keys to a new house. Every bugger getting their council house, without really earning it. It makes Ted's blood boil.

'Fiona Moss got into County,' Bea mumbles after a time, not really to him.

'Swimming?'

'No, *horse* jumping,' she says. '*Obviously* swimming.' She kicks her shoes off, one of them flies up and lands in the middle of the room. 'I got a faster time in freestyle. Fiona's doing medley.'

The front door closes again, more quietly. Andrew.

'She's such a *cow*,' Bea spits. 'It's only cos she gets to do extra training. At Angel Centre.' Ted has heard Bea talk of this place, where membership's an arm and a leg. 'Fifty-metre pool,' Bea says, talking more to the fireplace. Ted can't stand the sound of his children's voices, Bea's especially. Has she always whined like this? In the kitchen, Andrew closes a cupboard and his toast pops up.

'You might get in next time,' Ted mutters. Now Bea looks at him, with an unpleasant, scornful expression.

'I won't,' she says. 'It's twice a year, and next time I'll be even *more* behind.' Ted pulls the paper onto his lap. Ted's mother and Moira's mother, younger versions, look on from above the fireplace. Mary has a quizzical, confused expression. Dilys's smile is mischievous. He would challenge both of them to know what to do with this daughter of his.

'I might as well give up.' Bea's voice peters out. If he didn't know her better, he'd say she was close to tears, but Bea isn't a crier, never has been, unless she's in real physical pain. She'll yell and rail and brood and accuse. But she won't cry. They hear Andrew's faint tread up the stairs. Which is worse – his son's nervous creeping, or his daughter's lack of it?

'If you play that crap album again,' Bea shouts after him, 'use your headphones.'

'Keep your voice down,' Ted warns.

'Pardon *me*,' Bea says and sniffs loudly. 'Today is the worst day of my *life*.' Then she mutters, 'Like you care.' And Ted has a sudden clear image of her, aged six or seven, pointing an arrow at him. For all the wrong he had done, even then. *Is that the man?* The memory usually fills him with self-doubt, but now it sparks a flame of rage. His head starts an odd spinning.

Bea makes a show of getting up, she pantomimes tiptoeing past him lifting her knees high.

'Sorry,' she says, 'I know you're so *busy*.' She gives a nasty little laugh, and something snaps in the back of Ted's skull. He sits forward. A look of uncertainty crosses Bea's face, then she darts out of the room and up the stairs.

She shot him. She actually *shot* him. No one has ever put her in her place. What about the worst days of *his* life? How is it his own daughter shows him so little respect?

He gets to his feet, throat burning, and strides after her, taking the stairs two at a time.

She's lying on the bed, but she sits bolt-upright as he enters the room. Ted closes the door and stands against it, his head still spinning. He presses his shoulder blades hard against the door. Bea inches backwards, not taking her eyes off him until she's almost in the corner. Some soft toys topple to the floor.

'Dad?' Her voice is small, all the sarcasm gone. The room fills with the noise of his breathing. His arms, his fists are trembling.

'You will not. Speak to me. Like that. Again.' His voice too, trembles. Bea stares at him, her blue eyes huge. They've been here before, but this time he's in charge. Now he raises his voice, to a blast, louder than he's ever done. 'DO YOU UNDERSTAND?'

Her face flickers, Ted sees the possibility of a laugh. He lunges suddenly towards the bed.

Bea starts back.

Her head hits the wall with a crack.

She's not laughing now.

Too big a thing to start with

The driveway at the farm has been tarmacked and feels wider. A Land Rover stands, boxy and ugly, where the chicken coop used to be. As a child, Moira took great pride in her brief role as chicken keeper. Silly, endearing creatures all named by her. She searches her head for some. Lightning, Pecker, Lizzie. She'd like a small brood of her own in the garden, when this thing with Ted blows over perhaps.

The farmhouse seems smaller, sunken, framed by the fields behind. The big wooden door takes up most of the front. Moira hasn't visited in years. Standing here, she can't think why she doesn't come more often; the number sixty-eight runs every two hours. David's been doing the four miles on a bicycle since he was fifteen. Today she's come from her mother's, on a whim, because she didn't want to go home. It's half term, and Ted is taking them ice skating. Something to keep him busy. They can do without her for a little while longer.

Birds flit down and duck into the eaves – house martins? The worrisome chatter in Moira's head is replaced by the chirruping all around. Spring is well underway. What will the current task be? Time here is marked only by the work; ploughing, planting. David will be busy, but she might catch a glimpse of him in the fields. She takes a few steps to her right at the top of the drive, to peek around the side of the house at the kitchen garden. Neat rows, high stakes tied with string, splashes of colour at the back; almost exactly as Moira remembers it.

Now what? The wind whips up, then disappears. The sky looks undecided on an April shower or a blast of sun. Moira doesn't have an umbrella or even a coat. She could walk across the top field and get a view out over the land. A glimpse of David at work will steady her. She looks down at her feet: wrong shoes. Next to the entrance, two white, rounded stones offer themselves as seats. Moira perches on one and hugs her knees. It's rare for her not to have a plan.

The previous evening had been loud and quiet in all the wrong places. Ted came back from a small job with Alf and Michael all stirred up again. It's the first work he's had since Christmas, but it's making things worse, not better. Before this, they'd had a month or so of relative calm, though maybe that's her imagination.

'They said I should have kept fighting,' he had growled at the kitchen cabinets. *Isn't that what you're doing?* Moira didn't say. She sat still – stillness being the only way she can manage herself – while the room filled with his livid, quivering despair. She no longer turns out comforts or diversions. She averts her eyes and keeps quiet. On this occasion, her silence was like a red rag. Ted came right up to her, fury throbbing in his neck. He took her by the shoulders, his fingers pushing in a little too hard.

'Do you understand?' his face so close he was out of focus. 'Because I don't think you *do*.' Moira could have listed for him all the things she *does* understand: that asking questions, especially about the past, is dangerous; that watching his decline has caused within her a series of minuscule collapses, and she may slide away at any moment; that she of all people understands his losses, starting when he was orphaned in his teens, but she doesn't know how to steer him back to himself; that his agony is hers too if only he knew it.

She bought him a gift the other week. It sits in its box at the back of the cupboard, reminding Moira of her own stupidity and misjudgment. A mug that says 'Edward, meaning: Prosperous Guardian'.

Huddled on her stone in the driveway with the wind picking up, Moira is about to go back up the lane to the bus stop when the big wooden door swings open and Alice appears with a black sack for the bin. Moira feels a wave of tenderness for her one-time guardian and gets to her feet. Mrs Alice, straight-backed with cropped white hair, takes slow steps over to the big wheelie bin. She pats it with a flat, outstretched hand before she lifts the lid and hauls in the bag. Then she turns around, almost facing Moira now, cocks her head to the sound of the birds, and smiles to herself.

David has told Moira about Alice losing her sight, but Moira had not appreciated how complete her blindness is. She could call out or walk over – the woman is only a short stretch away across the tarmac – but she stays quiet. They could sit at the giant kitchen table and talk about the language of silence. Moira would confess she hides from her own daughter. She could ask Alice why she, Moira, has the notion she will always be a child, when plainly she is a grown woman. And Alice, fairy godmother, would dish out help and protection as she had years ago, when Moira needed it most, from this place of safety.

Moira does not move. She watches Alice take careful steps back inside the farmhouse, and the door swings shut.

Bea's head is like porridge, her eyelids heavy, her stomach hollow from the anaesthetic. She turns over on the stiff hospital pillow and opens her eyes a fraction to check Mum's still here. In her drugged sleep she had dreamed of holding a bow and arrow aimed at her dad. She can't remember if she fired it.

Mum gets her a Twix from the vending machine, strokes her cheek, talks in the soft voice she saves for emergencies. She repositions Bea's leg and turns down the papery sheet. Mum must be a good nurse. It's a strange thought – Mum doing this as her actual job. Bea puts her head at an angle to be stroked again. How long, she wonders, can she stay in this room and ride the electric bed, pull the swishy curtain, and get a little packet of biscuits on her tray that slots under her chin? Usually she finds her mother deeply annoying, but in here it's different.

She raises herself up enough to read the copy of *Jackie* Mum brought. They're keeping an ear out for the bouncy Welsh nurse who promised tea.

'What happened,' Mum asks in the soft voice, 'at the ice rink?' It takes Bea by surprise. This room is too good to waste thinking about outside things. But Mum asks again, and the day leaps into her porridge head: Dad with his popping eyes, practically crushing her. As soon as she pictures it, heat rises in her neck. She bunches the sheet in her fists. She can feel the impact of the side of the rink as she is slammed against it, a pain shooting up from her ankle; Dad lunging towards her, his face all twisted. Her cheeks burn.

'Bea?' her mother's voice is gentle.

If only it was just the three of them: Mum, Andrew and her. *God*, that would be amazing. Like Naomi Miller, who hasn't stopped smiling since her dad moved out. Julie Clarke says it's the police who keep him away.

Police. Here, in this room, asking her questions, before she went to the operating theatre. Was that today? A tall policeman with a big nose, and a policewoman with a thick fringe who kept her hat tucked under her arm and did all the talking in a singsong voice.

More of the ice rink comes swimming into her head. Dad taking a swing at that man who lifted her off the ice after Dad dropped her the second time; a whole crowd staring; impossible stabbing pain in her leg on the wet ice; her own screams; not being able to move. And the relief of finally being carried away. She pushes up on her elbows and looks straight into her mother's green eyes.

'Dad should be in a *mental* home.' Moira puts her hand to her mouth and straight away Bea sees she has misjudged the whole thing. *Except he should.*

'Bea! That's a horrible thing to say.' Her softness has gone, her voice is back to normal. Bea twists round, square on, and pain flares in her ankle. She cries out and flops back on the pillow. Moira puts her hands on Bea's shoulders.

'Try not to move.'

Bea thumps the covers. 'He *is* mental! Why do you have to take *his* side?'

'Shhh. Look, we'll talk about it another time.'

Oh no we won't! 'He talks to himself, Mum. Haven't you heard him? He *hates* me and Andrew. He punched someone at the ice rink. And he *killed* someone at work.'

Her mother looks at her for a long time. 'Are you talking about last year?' She pauses, and her face goes all sad and pathetic. 'Bea, that's not what happened. Is that what you heard at school?'

'He's like a crazy person,' Bea carries on. 'Today he was off the scale. Another one of his fits, and I hadn't done *anything*. Ask Andrew!' She is almost in tears. How can it be her fault? (didn't Mum just say that?) And isn't this what Mum always does – shushes her up? Shushes *everything* up? Bea makes her voice as low, as threatening, as she can.

'You never, ever listen to me.'

The house is dark, with only a dim moon glow from the kitchen, and chilly. Moira closes the front door quietly and heads up the stairs to check on Andrew: asleep. She should stop her checking, he's almost fourteen. But he was so upset when she called from the hospital. Andrew explained, tearfully, how he and Ted had been to the police station. Ted took the phone then and said there had been an altercation, a 'misunderstanding'. She had caught the shame in his voice and her heart sank.

At the bottom of the stairs, she leans on the thick bannister while she musters the energy to move off. In the kitchen, the radio talks away quietly. Moira switches off the ghostly voice of Margaret Thatcher on the news. She thinks of how her mother used to carry the radio around for comfort. Perhaps

Moira should try it, though she can't imagine being comforted by that spooky voice.

It's odd that Ted hasn't waited up for her. What a horrible thing Bea said in the hospital. Moira doesn't know what to make of it. It had not occurred to her that the Turner's incident would have been talked about at school. What else has she missed? As she passes, she puts her head into the front room, out of habit.

She gasps.

For a heartbeat, the hunched-over figure in the chair looks dead. The shock snaps her alert. And now she can see Ted is not dead, only curled over in the dark, his arms resting on his thighs, his head in his hands. The badly drawn curtains leave a straight beam of light from the streetlamp, floor to ceiling.

'Ted?' He doesn't move. 'Did you not hear me come in?' He still doesn't move. His back rises in fractions with his breathing. Has he had a stroke? Even while this thought passes through, Moira is almost numb to it. Whatever this is, she will carry on. She will do whatever is needed, and then do the next thing. Perhaps she has the soul of a robot; she will respond and respond until her battery runs out. She steps into the room, perches on the arm of the sofa, and almost groans, it is so wonderful to sit down. She tells him Bea is fine, and they'll go back in the morning.

'She says you hit someone,' Moira says quietly. Ted remains silent for a long time.

'It was an accident. Not that bit.' His voice is muffled. 'Bea fell on the ice, Andrew came to get me. She was hurt. I tried to lift her off.' He pauses. 'I slipped.' He's barely audible. 'I made it worse, but I was trying to help. Not that she'll ever know it.' After a long silence, he says in a clenched whisper, 'Someone else helped her.' Moira considers several responses. She can't tell him that everything will be alright, because her certainty is gone, and her energy is sapped shepherding them all around conflict and disaster. This day, unbelievably, is still not over, and she must save her last ounce of resolve for what she needs to tell him. She almost puts a hand on his back, but finds she doesn't want to touch him. All she wants to do is lie down on the sofa and she's on the verge of doing this when Ted lifts his head.

'The fella's not pressing charges,' he says. Moira does not ask who or what. 'They think I'm a liability.' His voice is so heavy with self-loathing that it drops down in his throat, almost to a sob. 'I was trying to help. I'm her *father*.' It's enough to pull Moira to her feet.

She kneels in front of him and puts her head against his, her hair falls around them.

Because she is unable to reassure, she asks a quiet question. 'And what do you think?'

He only shakes his head; shakes both their heads.

Ted feels his wife pull away and sit back on the sofa. Why can't she come down, hard, on *his side*? It's all he's wanted, for months, years, since the beginning. Why doesn't she say 'Of course you were helping Bea. No, you're not a liability. You are my husband and I have faith in you.' Why doesn't she say that they can issue him with all the warnings they like, but she, Moira, would bet all of herself on him?

She says nothing. And there's something in her silence that makes him sit up.

'I have two things to tell you.' Moira's voice is steady. The strand of light from outside falls across her lap. Her hands are clasped. 'I should have told you the first thing weeks ago. I don't know why I didn't.' She's got a wounded look about her. 'That's not true,' she adds quietly, 'I do know.' Ted too knows why his wife has been unable to talk to him. *I'm not my own self*. He can't say these words – they are not a man's words. His foot throbs. Earlier, in the alley, he had kicked and kicked at the wall until Andrew cried and begged him to stop.

He waits for her to go on, but she doesn't. She rests her

chin on her chest, and her hands move from her lap onto her stomach, one placed slowly on top of the other. What she is trying to tell him comes over him inch by inch.

'Another?' he says, when he finds his voice. Though he doesn't need to ask it. *Another baby*. She will be a little while gone, maybe two months. He knows this too. His last fit of lustful anger, that she tolerated, as she tolerates everything.

'Yes,' she says, not looking up.

A better man might drop to his knees and ask for forgiveness. They sit in the quiet, with this immense news between them. When Ted feels steady enough, he stands and offers her his hand. She takes it and looks up at him then, expressionless, as she lets herself be pulled upright. He gives her another pull towards him, and without really meaning to, in one deft movement, he puts his arm around her back and scoops her off her feet. She lets out a squeal of surprise. Hobbling slightly, his toes on fire, he carries her out of the living room and up the stairs.

In their bedroom, Ted places Moira on the bed and lies down beside her with his head propped on his arm. She smiles at him weakly. He doesn't want to think it, but she is wary.

'Tell me the other thing,' he says. Moira too props herself up, mirroring him. She speaks in a rush like she might lose her nerve.

'Dilys is getting worse. They say she hasn't got long. Ted, I think she should come and live here.'

Ted takes this in and sinks onto his back. His breath flows in and out. She has told him the two things.

'Of course,' he says and reaches out an arm that finds her middle, more solid than he expects. *Another baby, sweet Jesus.* 'I'll build your mother a room,' he says with as much authority as he can muster. 'I'll start tomorrow.'

Alone in her brilliant hospital bay, Bea's dream comes back to her. She's in a field, aiming an arrow at her father's chest. His hands are up but it's not a game. This happened in real life.

She has a faint memory of an archery lesson, a fat teacher, but she can't remember shooting the arrow, though she knows she did. Which sort of makes it her fault. But why did she do it? *Was* it an accident? Dad used to tell the story with various slants. Slapstick to Pauline, where he staggered around and fell down; all 'woe-is-me' to Granny and Uncle David, 'She *shot* me!' in a tragic voice, both hands on his heart, or clutching the arm with the scar next to the love heart. Then he would turn to her, 'Yes, *you*', sort of jokey, sort of accusing. Bea never knew what to say. To herself, she said *I'm not bad.* She would get breathless like she might cry, and run outside.

Alright, I did it on purpose. This is what she decides, in her hospital bed, picturing the scene. Even back then he must have done something to deserve it. And anyway, now he's done *plenty.*

'Is your dad violent at home?' the policewoman had asked in her sickly voice, like Bea was six. Someone at the rink must have told them Dad dropped her. And then punched her rescuer. 'Does he ever hurt you?' the policewoman asked. Bea can't for the life of her remember what she said. *Yes. He's a nutter,* is what she hopes she said. Lying here with the mint-green curtain around her, Bea makes a decision: her dad will no longer exist. From now on, she will simply pretend he's not there. Hopefully he'll move out, like Naomi's dad. She wants to ask Andrew what he thinks, but of course she can't – she has never asked him anything, and this seems like too big a thing to start with.

She presses the button to sit herself up, down, up, down and closes her eyes ready for sleep. If she dreams it again tonight, she'll aim the arrow properly, and fire it.

PART TWO

Star Keeper
1986

From his bed, Andrew reaches out a long arm and lowers the stylus back at the beginning. The first fourteen seconds is all he wants, before the words kick in. He loves Morrissey's voice, but not today. Today he wants manic guitar and drums. Undiluted. Over and over.

He's cold. Cloud shadows creep across the ceiling. Even in December, Mum never puts the heating on in the day. He might get under the covers.

The song is 'What She Said' from *Meat is Murder*. He's heard this album over a hundred times. He lifts the stylus again – fourteen seconds – and pictures the blurred hand at the strings, the notes running down the stave. Andrew taught himself to read music from the *A Tune a Day* guitar book. His arm starts to ache from the precision lifting; a spasm twitches his finger and thumb. Lift, replace, lift, replace, needle on vinyl. Then he gets an idea.

He yanks open the stiff bottom drawer by his bed, lifts out the old tape recorder and plugs it in next to the record player. With his left hand he presses play and record, and he sets the needle with his right. Fade in: rattle, scraping guitar, three-note melody high to low, then drums, cymbal. The cymbal is his cue. Andrew plucks off the needle, whips it back, and sets it down without stopping the tape. At least twenty times. Now he's got four minutes. He rewinds the tape, lies back, and listens.

The pauses vary. A longer pause builds tension. Twice he gets 'What— ', once 'What she— '. He can't remember who 'she' is. He knows the words to all the songs but doesn't pay them much attention. Unlike most people, especially girls, Andrew's suspicious of song lyrics. None can be trusted. He's more into the music – harmonies, shifts – than the words, which are slapped on top, mostly rehashed from something else. There are only so many lyrics, but there are infinite melodies.

Every four minutes he rewinds and plays it again. He's trying to put himself in a trance. It's working, sort of.

The trouble is, Andrew doesn't have anything to *do*. He's started to dread weekends; alone in the shrunken house, Dad at work, Mum and Lonnie off doing something. Before Granny died, he'd go to the Annexe. Even his basic magic tricks got a squeal, the ones Lonnie was bored with long ago: the coin, the disappearing hanky. Granny remained impressed even when he showed her the extendable thumb hiding the silk.

'Mum doesn't like that one,' he told her. He had found it odd that his mother would leave the room when he did the trick. He assumed it was the plastic severed digit, which Andrew had to admit was pretty lifelike.

'It's not the thumb,' Granny told him, slumping suddenly as she sometimes did. 'Raymond used to do a similar trick.' Andrew knew Raymond was his dead grandpa. He wanted to ask more, but Granny's fallen face had stopped him.

He should have asked more. He should have asked everything.

Granny liked him to describe the office. The people, his review of the draft month-end figures, the pub on a Friday. He'd get a funny, pleased feeling listening to his descriptions. He told her about Ade Cooper's never-ending jokes, two desks down.

'Is he your friend?' Granny asked. She never hurried him. 'Friend' was still a word that gave Andrew a sinking feeling, from all the times during school Mum had asked if he wanted to bring one. Most people at school had mates, but Andrew never had enough conversation for it. You could, of course, be the person who didn't say much, but then no one notices you, and pretty soon you're dropped.

Andrew didn't get bored in the Annexe. Together, they kept watch over the garden and the changing weather. He told her about being a Keeper of the Truth. It's what his boss calls the

Finance Team. 'Because we know everything and nothing gets past us,' Andrew explained. Granny loved the rivalries between Sales and Finance. Especially Andrew finding out about Sales double-counting their figures, and the boss calling him 'Star Keeper'. Granny made him tell secrets too, about people's salaries.

'You,' she said jabbing a finger, 'are very *important*.' And he felt it.

Granny talked about Bea a lot. Andrew told her what he knew (not much) about the student halls where Bea lived now, ten of them along a corridor. Andrew couldn't picture it. He read to her too. Granny said he had a lovely voice and that he was handsome.

Andrew's always blended in. He's tall but not *too* tall, with long legs which won him a cross-country medal. He keeps his thick hair shortish, and his face is thin but luckily nothing sticks out too far (ears, nose). His eyes are a murky green-brown, not piercing blue like Bea's. Everyone says he looks like Mum and Uncle David: straight nose, dark hair. On balance, he'd rather be like Uncle David, tall and dark, than like Dad, stocky and pale. Lonnie looks like Dad, but pretty. Whenever Granny paid Andrew a compliment – like quoting from his mug, calling him manly and brave – he wanted her to shut up, and also to say it again.

In the Annexe he had read to her from *The Incredible Journey*, which he'd had in his room his whole life, no idea where it came from. They both loved that it was a true story, a properly amazing one, about a cat and two dogs who find their way home across thousands of miles. Andrew spent a stupid amount of time thinking about which of the three animals he was. The real hero was Bodger, the old bull terrier, a fighter and a survivor. You had to admire him carrying on with his blind eye, and being so old. But then Luath, the younger dog, was the driving force. If it wasn't for him, they never would have made it. Andrew didn't want to admire the cat, but Tao had a lot going for him – he was a natural hunter, plus he could survive the best on his own. Maybe Andrew was Tao.

Lying on his bed, Andrew punches the music off. It's not working anymore. All he can think about is how he's the only one here. And that he should have visited Granny in the hospice. Mum gave him the choice. She said Granny was turning yellow, and that's what decided him to write her a letter instead. It took him ages. Now he knows he should have gone, like Bea did. Bea came back from university and stayed with her for the last days. Andrew has tried to imagine how Bea sat there for two whole days. Mum said Granny was unconscious. Did she talk to her? Read? *Cry*? Two days is a long time: it's a whole weekend.

He gets up and goes over to the window, his hair brushing the lampshade. Mum has stopped saying she'll get him another one, because he likes the stroke each time he moves around the room. It's like a very gentle pat on the head. He used to duck until he found it was the perfect height.

Outside, there's a strange silver light, like steel. It might snow. Lonnie's been on a loop all week. 'It might snow. Will it snow? Tonight?' She's talking more to fill the space – even Andrew can see that. Mum's talking less, so Lonnie's talking more. Dad's gone silent too, and anyway he's always at work. Andrew should try harder to keep Mum's spirits up, but he can never think what to say, though he did buy her two new Intermediate crossword books, which she hunches over for ages. The Beginner ones were getting too easy. He can't figure it out. He still does pretty much the same things: goes to work, listens to music, helps Dad with the books, takes Lonnie where she needs to go. But there's less *substance* to it. This happened a bit when Bea first left, and now without Granny it's a lot worse.

He wonders if he will ever leave home. It was astounding when Bea did it; the shock lasted for months. Andrew is twenty – a number he can't quite get his head around – and he's saving. Though what will it be like here if he leaves too?

He leans against the window, damp cold on his forehead.

Soon it'll be dark. Soon it'll be Christmas. Mum delivered the blow yesterday that Bea's not coming home. She's got a job and has to stay put, apparently. Andrew couldn't believe what he was hearing. *He's* got a job, and *he'll* be here. Mum has Bea's number – a phone in the corridor of wherever she's living. He might even phone her. He can't be annoyed though, that will keep her away. Should he plead? If it was him, and he was miles away, he'd be like the three in *The Incredible Journey*: he'd set himself a course and, no matter what, he'd come home.

Look and dry your eyes
1987

'Rum and coke, two pints of Carling.'

Bea sloshes the second pint on the bar, takes the money, and rings it up. 'Next.'

A long-haired, fang-toothed man leans on the bar. 'Large Bells, and whatever you're having.'

'I'll have it later, thanks,' Bea says. 'Next.'

'Pint of Best, love. You new?'

'Five months.' She wafts a cloud of smoke away from her face and bumps into Stan at the till who puts out his tongue. Always a solid two hours pulling pints from eight till ten, after that it's dribs and drabs. She and Stan take it in turns to collect glasses. Stan can stack ten high. Bea tried it when she was drunk, after hours, reached twelve and smashed the lot. 'Nobody take your shoes off,' she'd said, only to Stan, almost wetting herself laughing, before she picked up the broom and chased twinkling shards into the dark, slate corners.

Down the steep steps now comes Boyd, a regular, thin as a rake, spiky hair, and a thick accent that might be Irish, or Scottish. He makes a beeline for Bea.

'Tenants,' he says, putting two hands flat on the bar. 'Imagine there's a nuke, you gotta head underground. Now!' He ducks down, pointy elbows sticking out, pops back up, 'What you gonna save?' His beady eyes narrow and fix on Bea as she puts his pint in front of him. 'Gotta think fast. *Essentials*. Walkman, tapes, food, water,' he taps the bar for each. Bea serves the man behind while Boyd keeps talking. '*What* food though, *what* music, eh? S'why you gotta plan ahead.' His nervous energy crackles across the bar.

'Like the desert island,' Stan says at Bea's shoulder, 'I know my eight discs, just in case they call me tomorrow.'

'Yes and no, mate,' Boyd says. 'Desert island you've got some natural resources.' He touches his nose with his forefinger, *see?* The jukebox against the far wall lights up. Bea notices first and barges past Stan to switch off the bar tape.

'One-nil,' she says. The jukebox throws out 'Jumpin' Jack Flash'. Boyd's still on about the bunker. Always a challenge, a dilemma, a fight against an unnamed enemy. Increasingly, Boyd is the person Bea feels the most aligned with. Unlike her insipid classmates, all eager to please, his pent-up rage is something familiar.

When it calms down, Bea looks around the smoky dark for talent, hoping for Ravi. He's not been in this week. It was a month ago he had sat at the end of the bar and stared at her, all evening, lustily. After midnight, Bea drank with him, a lot, and let him carry her up the steep steps. She had found herself in the morning in his flat, in his bed, in slippery purple silk sheets. She had woken up in another world (wasn't that the plan?). *Who has purple silk sheets?* It was her first thought before her headache had crashed in and he rolled on top of her and they had bendy, muscly sex which somehow cured the headache.

If he doesn't come in tonight, she'll find someone else. Or she'll stay on and tango with Stan, though she won't drink before dancing. The last time, she pulled them both over in a spectacular crash, with Stan squashing her. A bruise like a rare fruit is still ripening on her left hip: haemoglobin breakdown – her biochemical processes following the textbook. She should take a photo and send it to Sarah.

She does a quick round of the tables for glasses and steps over feet, bags, a small dog. The bar's full and noisy; the low ceilings trap the booze-raised voices. What *would* she take to the bunker if there was a nuke? What's *essential*? Nothing. She really can't think of anything. The clothes on her back, Eliza's booties.

Bea had taken a box of Granny's things from the loft after the funeral. Mum said to help herself. She was in a rush and grabbed one of the small shoe boxes sealed with brown tape. She had opened it up here in her room. Two pairs of gloves, some cutlery, a few books, and wrapped in a shawl were the baby shoes, just like the ones in the shop on the High Street: two bright pearls. Bea had lifted them out and held the soft fabric against her cheeks before shoving the box under the bed in her square, empty room. No one to show them to. Conversations with her fellow students don't go anywhere; nothing essential.

Bea had made the journey to the hospice as quickly as she could, hurling herself out of the taxi in roadworks, and running the last part in the cold drizzle, terrified of being too late. In the end, they had two whole days in the overheated room that smelled of sweet potpourri and blankets and medicine. Bea and the little mound of Granny in the raised bed, still here, her closed eyes fluttering.

It was sometime during the night that Bea had made her confession. She put her chin on the blankets, closed her eyes and pretended they were in the Annexe. 'I felt it move, I swear, while I was in the waiting room. Can you believe that?' Bea wasn't sure she believed it herself, but while she sat in the crappy clinic waiting room on a creaky folding chair in late September with her pyjamas in a bag, she had been certain. A flutter. Cells, arranging themselves into a foetus: a *baby*. She had not allowed herself to even think the word until it moved inside her. Tiny hands and feet crammed her head then, crumpled faces, little outfits.

'I got rid of the baby,' she said to Granny. 'They hoovered it out of me.' Granny breathed on, in barely-there rises and falls, and it was all Bea could do not to climb under the blankets with her.

In that hot, dimly lit room last November Bea had talked until she was empty. She told Granny about her distracted, not-in-the-world feeling; her boxy bedroom that could be anywhere; pulling pints in the dark; sex with strangers; swimming slow, endless lengths, until exhaustion forced her to stop; the flutter she's sure she felt. And Granny listened. It came over Bea in a great wave of sorrow that they had this in common. If Bea could only rewind to the sitting room – holding Granny in her arms when she first heard Eliza's name – she might know what to say. Though she probably wouldn't.

Mum came to the hospice while Bea was there. She said that Bea had brought Granny back to life in the Annexe, and given her an extra three years.

'It was a miracle,' Mum said, 'I saw it with my own eyes.' A nice thing to say. Bea had almost asked her about Eliza, *Mum's sister*, but she chickened out. It was only while they were there together, over Granny's dying body, that Bea properly realised the baby who died was Mum's sister. And if she's totally honest, it was the first time she really considered that Granny was Mum's *mum;* that they'd had a whole life together before Bea. How dumb was that? Bea did ask about where Moira was born, but she didn't seem to remember much or didn't want to say. In the end, there were too many questions, so Bea gave up asking. Thinking about it since, she's glad. Why had Mum never told her about Eliza? Mum never gives anything away, so neither would Bea.

Bea stepped into the Rhino underworld by accident, on her city wanderings. It was the lure of the steep steps down into the dark, past the rhino head on a plaque. It's what happened to Stan: walked in, had a drink, had another, got a job and stayed. It swallows you in: the cavernous back room that disappears into the shadows; little coloured lanterns in the shape of beer barrels looped around the bar; framed pictures of elk and pheasants. Nothing goes with anything else. Bea likes the all-day darkness, the smoke, the absence of students. At the end of the bar, the fat cream jukebox stands against the wall like a bouncer. Bea listens closely to Joe Jackson, Elvis Costello,

David Bowie. 'Look and dry your eyes,' Joe tells her. 'I would rather be anywhere else,' Elvis says.

No one would tell her why 'Rhino'. 'You'll see,' they said. And after a month of Bea pulling pints and wiping stale beer, down the steep steps he came: a square man with a Neanderthal forehead, hooked nose, and boxy chin. She recognised him instantly as the owner. You wouldn't think it possible for a man to resemble so closely a giant animal. His name's Monty, but no one calls him that. He's got another bar across town; Stan practically runs this one now. Stan's a third-year psychology student and the only other student in Rhino. It feels like their secret. He's tall and chiselled and wears blue nail varnish. He lives upstairs and works for the rent. It was Stan who offered her the job.

It's one in the morning, the main lights are out, and the bar is lit only with the glow of the barrel lanterns. Bea's long legs in black jeans dangle from the bar stool. She wears thick eyeliner, her fringe comes right over her eyes. Someone said she looked like Chrissie Hynde. She'll take that – it brings her out of her teens. 'Androgynous' was how she'd been described once, by Morris Lightfoot. She took it as a compliment before she knew what it meant. And still after. Her line in androgyny, she's coming to find, is coupled with a powerful sex appeal. She can sit at the bar, stretch out her legs and arch her back, just a little, and sooner or later she'll hook one. It's her talent, her skill. Good to be good at something.

Stan puts a cloth and table spray on the bar, then a handful of change.

'Go wipe, Cinderella, make them gleam.' She picks out all the fifties, posts them clunking into the jukebox, and wipes in rhythm to the Boomtown Rats.

'You need to watch yourself,' Stan shouts over the music, and Bea pretends not to hear. She knows he's talking about the night before. At kicking out time, he'd stepped in front of her at the bottom of the stairs and peeled her off a suited man with a belly like a waterbed. (Did Boyd march the suit up the stairs?) She hadn't taken much peeling. Not like the times in the beginning when Stan had to peel her off himself. Waterbelly was pissed off though, while Stan was always amusedly patient.

'Mean old world out there.' Stan's still going, but she's not listening.

Tell me why, I don't like Mondays—

She should go to a lecture in the morning, on plasma, which is most of blood and mainly water. Bea half expects herself to evaporate one of these days. And she gets restless in the lectures. What's the point of learning all this stuff when someone else knows it already? People scribbling all around her. Thinking of which, she should write to Sarah's parents. Eleanor wrote her an annoying, fussing letter. She'll send them a postcard. Now she's away from there, she no longer wants them as her parents. She's done with parents.

'The Lovecats' comes on the jukebox. Did she pick this? Andrew must have been in her subconscious. He phoned her again last week. Someone knocked on her bedroom door, saying 'Your brother.' In the grey corridor that makes Bea think of a prison, she had pressed the phone to her ear. 'Just wondered if you're coming home for Mum's birthday,' Andrew said. It was amazing to hear him, even though he sounded sad and far away. It was definitely Andrew, and he was definitely her brother. She asked about Lonnie, and his voice lifted. 'She got her orange belt,' Andrew said. 'Brilliant,' Bea said.'Tell her I said brilliant.' That was about it.

When the going gets tough/ the tough get going. It bursts from the speakers above the bar, so loud the glasses tremble. A call to arms. Stan sashays out from behind the bar, clapping over his head, and now holding out his arms to her. Billy Ocean duets with The Cure while Bea and Stan strut in a straight line in front of the barrel lights: cheeks, hips, thighs pressed together, arms straight like rifles.

'You can tango to anything,' Stan shouts, his face lit pink

at that moment by a beer barrel lantern. When Bea tangoes with Stan, her sinking, panicky feeling disappears, and for the duration of the dance, she's peachy.

Beginnings of letters pile up on the desk in her room.

Dear Sarah,

Comment ça va? Moi, je ne suis pas splendide, if I'm honest. If university is the best days of your life, mine's an epic tragedy.

Dear Sarah,

Did you go to Edinburgh? Is everyone in a kilt? My room is a tiny box, what's yours like? The girl in the next room skips, like a ticking clock. She's a connasse, doing Sports Management. I'm working in a bar. It's dark all the time. I'm considering being a Goth, or a vampire. My one friend, Sexy Stan, has mortifyingly rejected my advances due to his preference for boys.

Dear Sarah,

I think I left myself on the train, or in the hospice, or in Simon's bed. I don't remember what I was like, can you let me know ASAP? La vie est dure. Simon came to see me in the first week, but he got kicked out of the Halls. He said he didn't think it would work, but he'll keep me in his heart. I don't want to be stuck in his fucking heart.

Dear Sarah,

Do you think we'll ever see each other again? I keep you in my heart.

Dear Sarah,

If you go home at Easter, will you go and see Lonnie and take a picture of her, and send it? I'm working in the bar. Tell her she's a rare gem.

Dear Sarah,

I wake up and I can't believe I have to do it all again. Another whole day.

Stan works less during his exams. Bea pulls pints next to Rhino and forgets that's not his actual name. She asks him one night about Boyd, who hasn't been in for a while.

'Crazy fucker,' Rhino says with a sad smile that tells Bea something bad has happened. At the end of the shift, she repeats the question.

'He got himself sectioned again,' Rhino says. Creases line his jutting forehead and his shoulders slope. Bea thinks of a wounded beast; he loves his regulars. 'He's on the top floor at The Wharf,' Rhino says. Bea has heard of this place – its violence and secrecy – and the news runs her over. It knocks her down and flattens her. If only Boyd had gone to the bunker with his Walkman while he had the chance. If he'd asked her, she would have gone with him.

She sits at the bar after hours. Rhino pours her a whisky from the end of the row: the good stuff. Those hanging-down bottles have always made Bea think of strangled, upside-down swans. Her throat flares. She loves the sensation if not the taste.

On the unsteady walk home, she considers how she might get herself sectioned. If she broke into the bar later, drank along the strangled necks until there was nothing left. If she took off all her clothes, right now, and wandered the streets until someone stopped her.

She stays in bed for two days.

On the third morning, there's a quiet knock at her door.

'It's open.'

Stan puts his head around, then comes inside. He takes in the bare walls, bare floor apart from a pair of shoes, her jacket screwed up in a corner of the desk on the pile of unsent letters.

'Is this a safe house? Are you in witness protection?'

'No protection,' Bea says, peeking out from under the covers.

He pulls the curtains open and sunlight leaps into the room. Bea screws up her eyes and opens them slowly. *Is it summer*? In the bar it's always dark; the real world can be disorientating.

It's the end of May. End of exams.

Stan sits on the bed and claps his hands to get her attention. Grudgingly, she sits up. Reflecting magnolia from the walls, Stan looks like a new person, his brown hair neat, not messy like at work. He's wearing a pair of faded khakis and a baggy blue sweatshirt, on his feet a pair of pumps, like he's off to the beach. He toes these off and curls his legs up under him. He looks like a student.

Bea smiles at him shyly. 'You look different.'

'So do you,' he says. 'You look like Oliver Twist. You need a good meal.' It feels mightily good to have Stan curled up on her bed. No one else comes into her room.

'You know you'll have to move out,' he says after a pause, patting the duvet. Bea has been avoiding all thoughts of what happens next. She goes to work, she comes back here.

'I don't want a lecture,' she says.

'That's the problem,' he says, smirking at his joke. He's been warning for a while that if she doesn't go to the lectures, she'll get kicked out of the accommodation.

He tells her he's going to America in the summer, to see his aunt, then starting a placement there.

'Maybe I could move into your place and run Rhino?' she says in a small voice.

'Is that what you want to do?' he asks, doubtful. Bea pulls the covers around her legs. She's got a heart sinking, backed-into-a-corner feeling.

'No,' she says. He looks relieved. 'I want to stay here, and sleep. *Forever*.' She whips the covers over her head and lies back. He'll appreciate this – Stan loves melodrama. She waits under the covers, feels him stand up, and hears his sigh. She peeks out, and then, like a sulky child, she sits back up. He's got his shoes on, hands in his pockets, looking all *adult*. It comes to

Bea that the bar is not Stan's whole life. It was a stop-gap. *Shit.*

'Look, sleeping beauty, you need a plan.' He sits again, on the chair this time, like a patient parent, and tells her that he knows Professor Nuttall, one of the biology lecturers. Bea could speak to him about doing the year again. Her head spins. Stan looks at her steadily, concern filling his light brown eyes, almost gold around the pupils. She prefers the dark of the bar.

'It's a pile of crap that your Gran died,' he says quietly and checks her face before carrying on the list. 'That Boyd's in the Black Hole, that you won't see my *Vogue*-cover face for a while,' he frames his face with straight hands: top and bottom, sides. 'But you're here—' he's lost his thread. He holds out his arms to the empty magnolia room. 'With all this!'

Bea bites her lip; to laugh would be disrespectful. He stands in the open doorway.

'And maybe stay away from men.' His voice is gentle but firm, he'd make a good teacher. 'If you need to hear how integral you are, call *me*.'

When Stan's gone, Bea pulls the covers back over. She lies there and listens to voices passing the window, presses a pillow over her head to drown them out. She used to snog a pillow, in Sarah's room. It wasn't so long ago, that unreachable world in which Bea knew exactly what she wanted. Before all her certainty slipped away like melting ice.

Dispossessed

From the top deck, Moira stares ahead, only vaguely taking in the passing streets and reddening leaves. Strips of faint gold strain from behind the cloud; the sun is trapped there. When she turns, she is surprised to find Lonnie beside her, cheek pressed to the bus window. For that instant, she had forgotten about her daughter, forgotten where they were going. It happens to her several times each day, and it seems to be getting worse. Of course: Saturday, October, Ted at work, Andrew in his room, her mother almost a year dead. Time looms quietly, everywhere. It's why they are on the bus to Bluebell Lane.

David blinks his surprise at them on the doorstep, the dog at his legs. She should have telephoned. Boy to man – the same readjustment each time – and now, *middle-aged* man, his hair flecked with grey, glasses balanced on his nose. It must be the same for David looking at her.

'It's me,' Moira says, her bag digging into her shoulder.

'I know.'

'Uncle David! Can we play Yahtzee?' Lonnie says, 'Mum always saves her Chance until the end. I use mine straight away.' It's true, Andrew teases Moira about her cautious tactic.

Moira practically shoves her brother into the house, steering them all into the poky living room. The dimensions always surprise her, and she feels the need to duck. It reminds her of the caravan. Yahtzee forgotten, Lonnie heads for the cupboard and hauls out the box of old Lego.

'It's so good to see you, David,' Moira says, and finally he almost smiles.

'It's good to see you too,' he says, then he turns to his niece.

'It's good to see you,' he says to Lonnie, who ignores him and tips out the box with a loud clatter.

'I'll do a suspension bridge,' Lonnie says. It's what they're making at school, a great big one across the classroom, though Moira has been keeping her at home on the pretext of a slight temperature. For the first time in Moira's life, her own company is unappealing.

'The Severn Bridge is closest, then Clifton Suspension Bridge,' David says as he leaves the room. Moira follows him and stands in the kitchen doorway.

'It's so good to see you,' she says again. Moira thumps her bag on the dining room table; she can't think why it's so heavy. She reaches inside, and under Lonnie's coat she finds a large yellow melon which she places in the middle of the empty table. *David's table*. After their mother moved in with her, Moira attached his name to things – David's house, David's kettle – it reminded her he was safe: a man in his own home. He stands next to her in the doorway, and they both stare at the melon on David's table.

'I bought it because it looked like the sun.'

'It's not round.'

'No,' Moira agrees. 'It's like an exotic rugby ball.' She gives a high laugh. David glances at her uncertainly, then takes their two mugs from the hooks in the kitchen. It's always gloomy in this dining room, Moira thinks, and even now Ted has put in radiators the draught still lurks around. She never liked this house. Instantly, the thought pokes at her guilt. Moira nods at the mugs on the sideboard.

'What am I again?'

'Moira, meaning: Bitter, Beloved, Drop of the Sea', David says, ultra-serious.

Moira cringes. 'It's a bit much.'

'And you're not bitter.'

She doesn't answer. David puts a teabag in each mug.

Taped on the fridge is a chart with lots of boxes and numbers.

It resembles Pauline's work rota. Moira steps into the cramped kitchen and reads bird names down the left-hand column. Pinned below it, there's a battered bit of paper that seems vaguely familiar. She can't read the small writing without her glasses.

'We made that list in 1945,' David says. The kettle boils and he fills the mugs. 'Many are in decline, have you noticed?'

'What?' Moira peers closer, and reads the faded words: 'Wren, pigeon, magpie, song thrush (*M), starling, goldfinch.' They had sat by the pond with their paper and pen, waiting for landings. The bright melon on the table catches her eye.

'Endangered birds,' David says. 'They're disappearing. And insects. It's the start of the sixth mass extinction. I'm sending my data to the RSPB.'

'When I was in the shop,' Moira says, distracted, 'I forgot what I was doing there.'

David looks inspired. 'You could join me, counting.'

'I've had enough disappearance,' Moira says, curtly. She sees Song Thrush and Greenfinch are in red. She turns away and steps back into the drab dining room. 'It's like I might float away. Things aren't *real.*' What exactly is she trying to tell him? 'There's a word for it. Dis— dis— located. No. Dis—pos*sessed*!' David's blinking at her. 'Maybe that's it. What does it mean? It's a good word. It could be one across, along the top.' She hasn't talked this much in ages. Though she's not making herself clear.

For the past few months, Moira's been slipping out of the present. She wants to tell David about Bea in the hospice last year, how they had stood over Dilys's deathbed and almost understood each other; about the darkness that has returned to Ted ever since Bea left for university; about her own desire to grab onto him, David, right now, the only person in the world she truly knows.

'They're asking lay people to give data,' David says.

'Can you just *listen*?' she shouts, from nowhere. 'To *me*. For a minute?' David ducks his head away. Moira picks up her cup, flounces out through the dining room, into the lounge and flops down on the sofa. Tea sloshes onto her trousers and scalds her leg. She considers pouring the whole cup over herself. The dog puts its head on her thigh and appraises her with worried eyes. She strokes absently, she can't recall the name, Willow was the first one. Maybe she's losing her marbles. 'All over the shop', Ted would say. Lonnie has abandoned the Clifton Suspension Bridge for Granny Dil's room – it will always be known as this – where Lonnie still likes to dress up. Moira sips her tea and rests a hand on the dog's soft head. *Dispossessed.* Is that what she is? She'll have to look it up. Two single tears roll down her cheeks; the first tears, and not for her mother. What did she think would happen? Did she honestly think David would understand? That he would restore her to herself? It's what usually happens when she's with David.

He brings his tea and sits down next to her. The dog changes allegiance.

'I'm sorry,' Moira says, then after a bit, 'She's not here anymore,' not quite sure who she's talking about.

'No,' David says. 'She died. On November the fifteenth last year.' Sadness hangs around them in the silence that follows. Moira wipes the tears that have stopped before they started; all her tears were used up long ago. David gets up suddenly and the dog startles.

'Sorry Bear,' he says as he leaves the room. *Bear*. Moira hears Lonnie say something to him from Dilys's room, then there's a loud thud above her head, David moving something heavy in his bedroom. The bed? Chest of drawers? He comes back in, holding a thin red box with both his hands underneath, like an altar boy. Goosebumps tingle down Moira's arms.

Fry's. The very first box.

He sets it down on the low table and lifts the lid. Fluff and scraps of paper, seemingly a pile of rubbish. But she gets her eye in and picks out a familiar piece of material, then another. She reaches in a hand.

'Let me,' he says, gently pushing her arm away. He lays out little swatches of material in a line: a square of white shirt, a yellow silk circle, scrap of tea towel, bit of frayed pink cloth, then a watch face without glass, and finishes with a circle of assorted buttons, like punctuation.

'They're in order,' he says.

A weariness comes over Moira and she sinks back on the sofa. 'What order?'

'The order I collected them.' He's too tall to be kneeling, his folded limbs look all wrong. The round piece of yellow silk glows like a new coin.

'Is that from Dad's hanky?' Moira whispers. 'His magic trick?' She gets a sudden clear flash of her father's face, his kindly eyes, creased at the edges. Raymond. Ray. His questioning look, *Can you guess?* accompanying the flourish as he reappears the hanky.

'Yes!' David beams, 'I figured it out, it's like the one Andrew used to—'

'I know,' she whispers.

'Why are you whispering?'

'Oh David,' she says. *This is not what I came for.*

'I thought you'd like to see it.' His expectant face tells her he has been waiting a long time to share all this. But Moira doesn't want to admire the miniature display of their loss. She *won't*.

'Do you know what this is?' David asks.

Please don't make me guess. He holds out an envelope, squeezed open like a mouth. Tucked in the crease is a whorl of gold thread. Or a lock of *hair*?

'Put it away,' she says, sounding like their mother.

David looks up, crestfallen. 'I thought— '

'We're not the *same* David,' Moira interrupts, only seeing the full truth of this as she says it. She has still not been able to tell Ted about their dead sister. She's not sure if she ever will. She doesn't want David's disappearing birds, old buttons, relics from their childhood that bring with them only unbearable sadness. Should she have kept a lock of

Bea's hair, she thinks, in a sudden panic. In case she never comes home again?

Clack-clack-clack, footsteps on the stairs. Lonnie! She stumbles into the room, high heels tripping on the swirling hem of a pink, satiny dress.

'I'm a foxy lady!' Lonnie regains her balance and puts one hand on her hip and one behind her head. It could be a nightie now but was probably an evening dress in the thirties. A black felt hat half covers her face, and when she tips her chin back, Moira can see her lips, swollen with dark pink lipstick. David taps his finger on the frayed pink square. *This dress*? David nods as though pink dresses through the ages are his area of specialism. She braces for a story. Or for David to take the swatch, find the small hole in the folds of Lonnie's dress and replace it; a jigsaw finally complete. But to her relief, he starts packing it all away, satisfied for now the contents have been aired.

'Shall we eat the melon?' Lonnie says through her grotesque mouth.

'Yes,' Moira and David say together, as her brother picks up the last buttons with his finger and thumb, dot dot dot.

To be a hero
1989

David pushes the old bicycle along the lane, with the *flap-flap* of the tyre, and the click of his feet on the tarmac, silvery in places from the light frost. Later there might be rain, though the forecast is not always correct. Potato picking is a bugger of a job in the rain. 'A bugger of a job' is how the others describe all rain-soaked activities. David doesn't mind the rain in the way the others do. It might hinder in some ways, but it benefits the soil, and therefore the crop, and therefore the farm. In the summer months, they complain of the 'bugger of a heat'.

The last puncture he had in the lanes was around 1983, before he got the Austin Metro, which is now in the garage. Mister Jem will comment on the unreliability of new machines, but you could also say that about the bicycle *flap-flap-flap*. He used to carry a puncture repair kit, but today he doesn't have it. In fact, he doesn't know where it is, which is extremely unusual as David knows the whereabouts of almost everything. This whole morning is unusual: he doesn't have the car, he's meeting Mister at the field gate instead of in the yard as he does every other day – Mister doesn't work in the fields anymore – and David is late. He starts up a trot with his teeth clenched and his hands clutching the handlebars. *Flapflapflapflapflap.*

He leans the bicycle against the end shed door and checks his watch: half an hour late. Though he's puffing, and too hot inside his big coat, he keeps up his jog around the barn, along the kitchen garden and across the first field. The sun is just coming through, and even in his agitation David marvels at the gleaming spider webs suspended over the frosty ground. A white veil, like low cloud, stretches across the whole field to the gate in the distance, where Mister Jem should be. But isn't.

David's teeth start to grind. As he jogs, he scours the horizon and scans the fields for the tractor, the harvester. His gaze returns to the gate and he stops jogging. There's a dark lump along the bottom. Mister is lying on the ground, as though he's fallen asleep there. David starts to run.

'Mister!' he calls out, his voice not loud enough to reach across the field. His boots crunch the uneven soil. He sprints the last stretch and crouches, panting, next to Mister's lying body. His coat has flapped open, and David kneels on the soft blue lining. Where the man's collar has been pulled down, there's a white moon of skin after the reddish-brown neck ends. His eyes are closed and his face is a sheen of sweat. He shouldn't be hot – he's lying in the first frost.

'Mister,' David says, then louder, 'Mister Jem!' The old man opens his eyes, blinks, and gasps with great effort.

'Help me.'

David already has his arms underneath the body, and with one great heave, he gathers and lifts Mister upright, banging him against the gate. Without checking his face (David doesn't want to look again) he bends down so the man flops over his back, letting out a quiet groan. With the farmer over his shoulder like a sack, David crunches off towards the farmhouse, small rasps and whimpers audible over his back. His shoulder aches. He repeats a phrase in his head *Go with the flow, go with the flow.*

David had been required to lift his mother on two occasions, just before she went to hospital and then moved in with Moira. She was not heavy, only bony and breakable, and David had not known how to handle her. She had let out high squeaks of pain that had travelled like tiny arrows into David's body. She was a bugger to move. This was the truth. She gave him slow, precise instructions: 'Wrap your arms around my back. Lower. Yes.' And like this, he had lifted her with only minimal squeaks. At each moment he wanted it to end, but he had moved her. In between instructions his mother whispered, to herself and to him, 'Go with the flow. Go with the flow.' She said it helped her. It was one of Bea's expressions. *Cool, man, go with the flow,* with one hand on her hip and the other, palm flat, moving slowly from left to right as though stroking an animal. David's mother said a lot of things that Bea said. She claimed they all helped her.

In the lightening morning in the first frost, with Mister on his shoulder, David repeats his mother's words, which were first Bea's words, and before that, someone else's – everything passed along – *Go with the flow*. They don't help him, how could they? But it is better than thinking about Mister's red face and moon-white neck bumping gently, gently against his back.

'What a hero,' Ted says again as they pull up at Bluebell Lane in the dark. They're dropping David home. Ted claps David on the back when they get out of the van, and Moira pulls him away. She and her brother stand in a huddle on the path while Ted gets the bicycle from the boot, his breath steaming in front of him. If you can't give your brother-in-law a pat on the back when he's saved a life, when can you? After the ambulance took the farmer away, David went out into the fields and did the best part of a full day's work! If Alice hadn't telephoned Moira from the hospital, Ted has no doubt David would have pushed his punctured bike all the way home as well. Two sandwiches short of a picnic, no doubt about that, but strong as an ox. *And a hero*.

All three of them stand on the path in the cold, Ted balancing the punctured bike against his leg. He stares up at the house front, lit dimly by the street lamp, as he did the first time he came here for tea thirty-odd years ago, all eager to please. The speckly grey wall still annoys him. He understands pebbledash – it holds the render together – but whenever he's faced with it, Ted can't help thinking we could all do *better*. On that tea party day, he recalls the feeling of being left out. It's exactly how he feels now. How can things be the same, after all this time?

'It must have been so *frightening*,' Moira says, with a puff of breath, still flushed from the excitement.

'He was quite heavy,' is all David says, his face blank, rolling his shoulders. Ted tries to imagine how he got the old codger all the way across the field.

'If you hadn't got to him,' Ted says, 'he'd be up there with the angels now, not lying in Gloucester Royal.' Moira and David actually *look up* with the same anxious expression, into the dark, starless sky. And then at each other. Both of them are keeping something in their faces, is how it seems to Ted; on the verge of saying something and then *not* saying it. It gets his goat. He was trying to join in.

'Well, you saved his life,' Moira says, beaming again at her brother as they stroll up the path like newlyweds. Ted rolls his eyes – haven't they just been through this?

'Like you saved *my* life,' David says to her, matter of fact.

'Moira saves everyone,' Ted mutters, carrying the bike off to the side alley.

'She *did* save my life,' David says, turning, but Ted doesn't stop. As they open the door, he hears Moira say something about a pond, and they start on another story he doesn't know and doesn't want to hear.

The truth is, Ted would give anything to save a life. Isn't it what everyone wants, deep down: to be a hero? Ted's hero-yearning was born in the conflicted heart of the boy who watched life cling cruelly to his mother. It has grown steadily, and now it sits inside him like an organ; kidney or spleen. In their sparse terraced house in 1947, his mother's suffering smelled of curdled milk, then of talc and disinfectant when his aunt came, then creeping sour again. Ted wanted his mother to live, he really did, but found it increasingly hard to look at her or be in the same room. He stoked the fire and sat close, taking in the scent of burning coal. His aunt barked instructions to Ted and then carried them out herself. He felt useless, which he was. But he had football on the green, a group to loll about with, weekend work on the building sites, and a carefree spirit. The war was over and boys like Ted knew what the world needed of them: to make things, build things, fix things.

His mother's death didn't change very much for Ted on the surface. The aunt moved in for a short time; he stayed out later and worked harder. At home, he harboured a strange feeling there was something he should be doing. His aunt, practical but not unkind, had no interest in him.

There had been a father, but Ted had no memory of him. He didn't come home when the war ended. There was uncertainty around his end: attempted desertion; killed on the battlefield; frozen to death in a drunken stupor. Ted can't remember who he heard these from – mother or aunt – and by the time he wanted to ask, there was no one left.

When Ted found himself in a strange bedroom in a strange house, alone, aged sixteen, his losses hit him with a force. Not only was he family-less, he was house-less. Suddenly, profoundly, he yearned for his own walls, bed, cold tiles, his mother's green army blankets. Mostly, it was the smells of his new lodgings that offended him: wood polish and candle wax. Ted pined for the sour and smoky smells of home. A vague sense followed him like a shadow, that he was to blame for their disappearance. He could have done more. He could have done *something*.

Right now, outside his brother-in-law's pebbledashed house, Ted's brimming with envy for David the hero. He pictures himself carrying a body across a field, or out of a crumbling building. In wartime. The Blitz. Ted the hero, stumbling in through smoke and rubble, his clothes in tatters from the blast. And there in the corner, in her rocker, sits an old woman, heaped in threadbare blankets. He picks his way to her and lifts her, one arm under her legs, one scooped around her back. It's his mother; slight, yet solidly alive in his arms, her face creased and yellowing in the moonlight. 'I've got you,' he says, then louder, certain: 'I've got you.' They make their way back through the splintered house to loud cracks of anti-aircraft fire. An icy raindrop hits his neck in Bluebell Lane. The image falls away.

He would have liked a good look at his mother's face.

A half-hearted spatter of rain peters quickly out. On the path facing the alley, holding the handlebars, Ted looks skyward and wills a downpour. He's an idiot with his Hollywood saviour fantasies. Crumbling buildings? *Christ.* The crushed woman is with him then. Poor Molly Potts. *Not my fault.* And the daughter, livid on his doorstep. And the little girl, *Is that the man?* And the boy Ted dragged away from Bea, to *save her*. He lets out a low moan. It makes his stomach turn to think of Bea in the bedroom – an image he's worked hard to erase. Even if he wanted to patch things up with Bea, he can't. She won't come home. He would do anything to turn back time, though it would need to be a long rewind.

He pushes the bike into the alley and the tyre flaps. His hands are almost numb now. Moira's voice singsongs from the house, the front door left open, 'On the weeping willow, like a monkey!' she says, with a peel of laughter. Even his wife doesn't need him, having as she does her half-baked brother for a hero. And with Andrew, it has become him looking after Ted. With the finances at any rate – spreadsheets, end-of-the-month. Andrew has saved his bacon more than once, and Ted's grateful, of course he is, but it's the *wrong way round*.

Ted grips the thick, cold frame of the bicycle with both hands and brings it right up above his head, like a weightlifter: a show of his own strength, to himself, out here in the dark. The front wheel swings around and he lets go and jumps back, to avoid being clobbered in the face. The bike clatters down on its side, the wheel still spinning. Ted almost boots it.

Easy now.

He needs to get home to Lonnie, the one person at least who adores him. For now. But today it's not enough. What action can he perform to make amends and change the story? The wall of pebbledash stretches high and wide in front of him. Ted searches his mind but draws a blank: he cannot think of a single one.

A different family
1991, 1993

Bea paces the platform underneath the soft, clucking laughter of pigeons in the rafters. She's early; the September air is muggy. She tries to picture the Lonnie who will step off the train, the one who starts 'big school' next week. But she gets the chunky six-year-old in a hideous pink tracksuit: their last station encounter. While Bea speaks to Lonnie on the phone occasionally, she has only seen her sister in the flesh a couple of times since she left, and it's Lonnie's baby face and big cheeks that come to mind. Bea has her reservations about the visit. Her flat is hers alone, and not counting the odd one-night stand, she hasn't had staying guests. Things are going well here, she needs to preserve the status quo.

Lonnie practically falls out of the carriage and into her arms, her strawberry blonde hair smelling of coconut. As Bea buries her face in it, all her misgivings fall away. Lonnie's got on a denim jacket that's too big for her, and purple jodhpur-type leggings. At eleven, she's not all that different from the pink-tracksuited girl, only bigger, with pierced ears. She almost comes up to Bea's shoulder. It's the weirdest, coolest thing: walking out of the train station hand in hand with her own sister. On the phone last month Lonnie said out of the blue, 'I've been to Andrew's, now can I come to yours?'

She pokes and sniffs around the flat like a police dog while Bea phones Moira to confirm the safe arrival. Lonnie opens cupboards in the tiny kitchen, separated from the sitting room by a tall counter. She strokes the blanket on the sofa, spins the little globe by Bea's bed, sifts through her few clothes hanging skinny on the rail in the corner of the bedroom. The inspection doesn't take long.

'Andrew's is bigger,' Lonnie concludes with her hands on her hips, 'but yours is— yours has got more *things*.' Bea is touched by the effort at fairness.

'And his flat is actually *his*,' Bea says. But the achievement of home ownership is lost on Lonnie as she picks up the photo of Bea in her graduation get-up.

'You look good in hats,' Lonnie says. Bea graduated in the summer with First Class Honours. 'How *you* doing?' Stan says when he calls from Minnesota. 'First class,' she replies. 'I've always said it,' Stan says.

She has stayed on to work in the university teaching lab as a general dogsbody, prepping experiments. The first-year students ask her a lot of questions, and Bea gets a kick out of answering all of them. She's even done some tutoring for the third-years. Professor Nuttall, Bea's favourite, and her current fantasy father, is lining her up for a research Masters next year.

Bea takes Lonnie swimming, for old times' sake and because at eleven she's too young for Rhino (still Bea's second home). They float around in the deep end, chlorine strong in their nostrils. Lonnie's body has the first suggestion of curves; little pillows of flesh pushing at the edges of her swimming costume. With her thin, muscly arms Bea gives a push-off, and Lonnie plunges backwards with a great fizzing splash. No one would guess they were siblings. Lonnie dives down and pops back up like a seal. Bea swims a couple of super-fast lengths for her benefit (Lonnie took all of Bea's swim medals for her treasure drawer). Bea doesn't admit to her sister she still grieves for her lost Olympian dreams.

'Tell me about Andrew's place,' Bea asks, back home with damp hair, both smelling of the pool. Bea can't picture Andrew in a flat. Funny how easy it is to halt someone's evolution, and Bea should know better than all of them the incessant nature of change, cell by cell. She tries to place Andrew in the new flat that Lonnie describes, but he doesn't belong there. He belongs in his room, door shut, twanging his guitar, and Bea smouldering in the next room, and Lonnie in her cot. Yet right here in front of her is Lonnie the girl, freckles gathered around her nose, giving Bea every detail.

'It's a *maisonette*,' Lonnie says 'There's steps down.' On the small rug, she walks along Andrew's corridor, bends her knees for the steps into the kitchen, and when she can't get any lower, she walks on her knees on the rug. 'Different levels add interest and texture,' she says. It's as though Bea's father is speaking through this small, red mouth. 'Dad helped with the shelves, coming down the wall like stairs.' She chops her hands one below the other. Her nails are alternate pink and purple. 'When I have my new room, I'm having the same, and Dad says I can put them up myself.'

'What new room?' Bea says, alarmed she has missed a house move. It may not feel like home, but there's no other.

'Dad's knocking through,' Lonnie says proudly, 'mine and Andrew's room.'

Bea takes this in. 'Of course he is.' *A different family* is what she thinks suddenly, looking at damp-haired, purple-legged Lonnie. Her sister has another set of parents entirely from the ones Bea had. It stuns her momentarily. Impossible and possible; obvious, really. And *thank god*, since sweet Lonnie's there alone now.

'Tell me about Andrew,' Bea says, and busies herself with cups on the counter.

Lonnie looks confused. 'What about him?'

What's he like? And what's it like now he's gone – just you and the two of them? 'Has he got a girlfriend?' Bea asks, sure she knows the answer.

Lonnie giggles. 'Nope. Mum says he'll get one when he's good and ready.' She stretches out her arms and flops down, colourful, almost filling the two-seater sofa. 'He's got a band though.'

'A *band*?' Bea almost drops a mug, 'Wha— When did—? What are they called?'

'Chaos something. I'm not allowed to go to the pub show cos it's too late,' Lonnie purses her lips in concentration, then she lights up. 'Chaotica!'

'Chaotica,' Bea repeats, shaking her head. 'Brilliant. Amazing.'

'Dad says they'll be on *Top of the Pops*'. Lonnie cups her hand and says in a stage whisper, 'I don't think they will.'

'Never say never, Lon.'

Lonnie teaches Bea a series of judo moves, in slow motion on the rug. Right arm to opponent's left side, curl around the back, hook right leg inside opponent's left ankle, ground opponent. Lonnie keeps her face trained on Bea's – it's deadly serious this judo, Bea's surprised at her sister's strength.

'Dad's good at this one,' Lonnie says, lowering Bea to the floor, placing her flat. Bea freezes, her neck stiffens. She keeps a tight hold of Lonnie's arm and back, stuck on the image of their father with Lonnie in a headlock.

'Ow!' Lonnie squeals. Bea loosens her grip.

'Sorry, sorry.' She lets go and jumps to her feet, a familiar churning in her belly. She doesn't want to picture her father pinning Lonnie, or anyone, to the floor. What does Lonnie know about Bea's departure from the family home? Does she remember anything about the father Bea had? Should Bea *warn* her?

'Are you cross?' Lonnie says, pulling her hair out of her face.

'Not with you,' Bea says. There's a long silence.

'Why are you always cross with Dad?' Lonnie says sulkily, flouncing back to the sofa.

Fuck. Bea feels hot and cold.

And speechless. The best question of all, one which *everyone* should have been asking her, for years. And she can't speak.

She tries to picture her father out of control; his menace when she and Andrew were young. But what she gets is herself, naked, trying to cover up in her bedroom. The revulsion on his face.

He hit us, Lon. He bullied. Lorded over us his pathetic authority to try and prove he was a man. Why can't she just say this to Lonnie? It's the truth after all. *He made out it was my fault.* The stories her father retold of her as a deranged child; Lonnie must have heard them.

It's one of the truths.

Another one is Bea's numbing humiliation. The shame of being seen, the shame of what she did afterwards. *A flutter.* Did she really feel it? As fast as she can, Bea squeezes her eyes shut and smothers these thoughts with her father coming at her in her bedroom. Here he is, dragging her by the wrist, her skin burning. Now he's knocking her head against Andrew's, twice, three times, until she sees stars.

She unscrews her eyes. Lonnie's lying back, looking up at the ceiling, her hair splayed out. She might be waiting, or she might have forgotten the whole thing.

'It was different for me, Lon,' Bea says.

'What was?'

'Dad. Mum.' Bea should do better than this. And Mum was just a shadow really. 'Home,' she adds lamely. Has their father removed his shirt to show Lonnie the scar next to the heart on his bicep? Does Bea need to defend herself? The rope in her neck tightens, and the one in her gut. Lonnie sits forward, frowns with a new question. And in a heartbeat, Bea's discomfort flicks to indignation. She won't allow anyone else in here. Especially not her father. Here is Lonnie, eleven and a rare gem, innocent of everything. Why shouldn't Bea stick with that?

'Let's make popcorn,' Bea says, and Lonnie's on her feet.

*

The next time Lonnie comes to stay, two years later, Bea's working for Kellars, a start-up company reaching for the big money of clinical trials. It was Prof Nuttall who steered her into it. 'You'll come back for your Masters,' he assured her. After almost a year, Bea still has to pinch herself. She's part of something *big*, even history-making. And she's earning a salary. At Christmas, she took a skiing holiday with a group from work. Finally, Bea owns a car, though not a Spitfire or a Mini Metro. A stuttering navy Ford Cortina, a gift from Stan when he upgraded. It barely gets her to work and back but she loves it. Stan's back from America and working in an NHS clinic north of the city. 'Less psychology, more fire brigade,' is how he describes it. 'Head down, into the burning house, rescue who you can.' Bea's thankful for her Petri dishes; her cells that don't talk back, don't hold up scarred wrists or wounded eyes.

In the Ford Cortina, driving through the dark, Lonnie chooses Nirvana for the tape deck and starts up a sitting version of moshing that flings her hair all over like a mop, her pink lips poking through. It seems impossible that she's a teenager. Bea's taking her to the lab. For weeks, she's been looking forward to showing it off to her sister.

When Lonnie stepped off the train this time, Bea had to play down her surprise at all the curves. But apart from the boobs, thighs, waist, she's still Lonnie.

Hello hello hello hello how low.

'I didn't have you down for a rocker,' Bea says.

'You're the rocker.' Lonnie brushes her hair away and leans over the gearstick to Bea's side. 'The *rebel*.'

'Not these days,' Bea says, ignoring a nudge of discomfort. 'These days I'm a respected scientist. You'll meet my cells. We'll see if they're happy tonight.'

'Can they *feel* things?' Lonnie switches off the tape and changes to the radio.

'Kind of,' Bea says. Lonnie's jigging now to 'I'm too sexy'. Bea flicks the radio off. 'Wait till you see the lab, Lon, it's pretty cool.'

Bea has chosen an evening visit for maximum impact. Lonnie looks doubtful as they park on the empty tarmac in front of the huge grey Kellars building. Inside, she leads Lonnie to the main lab where the fridges and freezers hum in low harmony. Rows of dark benches cross the room; tiny lights blink along the back; boxes are stacked high on the shelves lining the wall.

'It's like the DFS warehouse,' Lonnie mutters, looking around, 'where we picked up Andrew's sofa.'

Bea feels put out. 'That's worth twenty-five thousand,' she says, indicating a boulder of a machine on their left.

Lonnie's eyes widen. '*Pounds?*'

'Pounds,' Bea says, smiling. 'Pricey business, protein receptor research.'

Bea passes her a lab coat. 'Here, you'll need this.' They put on the white coats, Lonnie's too long in the sleeve, then they pull on surgical gloves, and Bea sprays them with ethanol. Lonnie wrinkles her nose at the smell. Bea could put some lights on, but she keeps it dark like a theatre. Bea loves coming here at night to feed her cells, or someone else's, out of hours. She feels like a superhero: a cutting-edge scientist doing something *essential*.

She opens the tissue culture hood, turns keys, presses buttons, and a light glows yellow. A fan whirrs. Then she opens the incubator.

'Thirty-seven degrees in here Lon, like a body.' She lifts out a Petri dish. 'The body keeping these babies alive.' Lonnie's looking around with more interest now, appreciating the seriousness of the place. Bea likes to picture the incubators as bodies. She sees them with limbs, though never heads, just pulsing warm torsos with reaching arms. Lonnie takes in the big, humming freezers behind them.

'Is it all, like, *alive* things inside?' she grimaces and crosses her arms as though something might crawl up her sleeve while she's not looking.

'We freeze the cells until we want to use them,' Bea says. 'Then we wake them up and feed them and study them.'

Lonnie nods slowly. 'Don't you get spooked, here on your own?' Her arms are still straitjacketed around her waist.

'But I'm not alone,' Bea says. 'Come on, we'll check on my cells, we'll give them their dinner.'

With both hands, she removes the red satiny cover from the microscope – a magician un-cloaking a cage with a dove – and she almost says 'Ta daa!' It's the most powerful microscope in the lab. When Bea started here, her heart pounded with each thing she lifted or touched.

'What do they eat?' Lonnie whispers.

'Media,' Bea says, pipetting off the old liquid 'It's their Ready Brek.' The cells sit semi-confluent, covering the bottom of the dish, just as she wants them. 'Nice.' Lonnie watches, stock still, as Bea shoots the red liquid chemical in a quiet whizz from the pipette gun, immersing the cells. Then she sets the dish on the microscope stand. Lonnie steps closer, and Bea guides her to the eyepieces. Lonnie leans over, tentative. Bea flicks on the fluorescent lamp and glowing red shapes emerge.

'Whoa,' Lonnie says, then doesn't say anything for ages. Bea knows exactly what's keeping her attention: complex shapes, endlessly captivating.

'I might split them tomorrow,' Bea says.

'What's that?'

'Divide them into dishes. Then seed them onto cover slips for staining. To work out where the protein is.' She's showing off now, even though Lonnie's not paying attention. 'If I tell you anymore, I'll have to kill you.'

'Why?'

'It's top secret. Look again.' Bea flips the filter wheel and they glow green.

'Cool,' Lonnie breathes, then lifts her head away and asks in a louder voice, 'Where do you *get* the cells?'

'Originally from patients,' Bea says, 'in the hospital.' Lonnie takes this in with furrowed brows. In the gloom, her face so serious, she looks just like their father. She puts her eye back to the magnified dots that Bea has switched again to red. Bea wonders suddenly if 'rebel' was his word.

Still looking, Lonnie lifts her hand slowly. Her fingers find

Bea's sleeve and she tugs gently, the way she used to as a much younger child.

'So this could be Granny Dil.' She says it so softly the words are only just audible.

Bea is stunned. It's as though her breath has been sucked out of her. The freezer hum disappears, overtaken by a rushing in her ears. Then she breathes out and the hum returns. Lonnie still has her sleeve.

'It could be,' Bea says in a whisper, 'but it isn't.'

Lonnie's hair has formed a curtain around the microscope. 'But it's *for* her,' Lonnie says, 'that you're doing this.' And she looks up squarely into Bea's face.

From when she could first walk, Lonnie would waddle into the Annexe, where their frail grandmother did little to interest her. Moira kept her out in her clumsy toddler years, for fear of her being 'too rough', and as their mother told it, 'Granny only has eyes for Bea.' At the funeral, Lonnie had smiled cautiously at everyone, sympathetic and sincere. Death being a sincere event that required comfort but would soon pass over, especially if she smiled and sympathised. Bea remembers holding onto Lonnie's shoulder, propping herself up, undone but also boosted by the smiles.

It's for her. How did Lonnie know this? Bea herself didn't even know this. And while she isn't sure it's exactly right, it's a spectacular thing to say, here in the lab where everything is so important, so *vital*.

'I didn't mean to make you sad,' Lonnie says.

'I'm not,' Bea lies. 'You didn't.' She wipes her face with her sleeve. 'You know what we need in here?' Her sister shakes her head. 'Music!' When she had thought about bringing Lonnie, she planned to fill the lab with tunes and turn the place into a nightclub for two. The tape recorder's in the bottom cupboard, with the tape still in it. She puts it on the bench, she'll clear up in a minute.

There must be an angel playing with my heart oh-oh: Annie

Lennox fills the lab, loud and tinny and glorious. Bea throws her arm around Lonnie's shoulder, and pushing back the too-long sleeve finds her sister's hand. She pulls her in tight and aims their straight, lab-coated arms down the dark corridor between the benches. Lonnie giggles nervously while she's swept along in a tango. *Must be talking to an angel, must be talking to an angel—*

'You can tango to anything,' Bea shouts. They switch direction, straight-armed, back to the microscope. 'Granny loved to dance,' Bea says over the music.

'She's dancing in that dish,' Lonnie says, joining in Bea's craziness. Bea falters for a second before she turns them around. She stamps her feet in big strides, towards the lights winking along the back. But her bravado is gone, and here's the sinking inside her.

Not now.

She squeezes Lonnie tighter, pressing their cheeks together. Lonnie stumbles to the side, and knocks into the bench. Bea's leaning too hard, like she did at the funeral.

This has been my dance, Toots. Granny said this before Bea left for Uni. It might have been the last thing Bea heard her say.

She tries to sing along but finds she can't.

Come on! She's furious with herself. This is exactly what she'd planned – bringing Lonnie here to show her. But the familiar sinking spreads now to her limbs. Even while she leads Lonnie in the dance, her arms and legs become dense, like sandbags, her hands swollen on the ends of her wrists. Her whole body weighs heavy with the ache of her loneliness.

Hand in hand is the only way to land

Onstage at the back of the Golden Lion, right at the spilling, swaying end of the night ('Don't worry, they'll all be too pissed to listen'), Andrew clings to his bass guitar and swallows the acid sick in his throat. Wedged next to him, the guy on drums, Mick? Mike? batters the kit. Andrew can't hear much else. Until Mick falls off his stool, and Dec looks around, still singing. Mick scrambles back up. Andrew keeps going, G, C, A minor, C. He could play this bass part in his sleep. Mick's back on, only tapping now, thank god. Dec screams 'I wanna wanna wanna' into the microphone like he's going to eat it, and the pub shouts it back. It's Chaotica's only original song.

Last time he heard this, Andrew was on the other side, with the shouters. Since then, the regular bass player had broken his collar bone, word got out Andrew had a bass guitar, and here he is, sweat trickling down his neck under his PVC jacket. Now they're almost through the set, he sneaks furtive looks into the pub. A few Sales guys punch the air; a line of girls from Level Two flank the bar, bobbing their shoulders. He sees Susie from Front Desk who Andrew has loved since he started at Gallant Communications almost six years ago. Not a crush – she's too old – a family sort of love. No one else knows this. A sodden beermat flies at the stage, to loud cheers. Dec catches it one-handed and throws it back, to louder cheers. From Andrew's floor, Jez and Cooper raise their pints. They play 'Sweet Child O' Mine' and Dec leans against Andrew while he sings 'Where do we go? Where do we go now?' Andrew plucks the strings with all his might.

At the lock-in afterwards, Dec puts a pint on the bar and punches his arm.

'You rocked, Andrew man.'

Thursday 17th October 1991: the best day of his life.

When Andrew had finally saved enough for a deposit, he bought a small flat a few streets away from the High Street. A 'maisonette' according to the estate agent. He liked the long thin kitchen for the way it funnelled you to the table at the end, everything within reach. He liked the blue DFS sofa, a moving-in present from Mum and Dad, and the angle it faced the telly-and-video, bought by him. He liked his bedroom with the small double bed, also from DFS, 'a present from Granny Dil', as Mum put it. Even the shower curtain with rainbows, chosen by Lonnie. But the flat didn't feel like *his*.

Living was fairly time-consuming when you had to do it all yourself. He found it satisfying in unexpected ways: cooking; buying a lamp, a spatula, tea towels; doing DIY with Dad, and going home on Sundays. He filled his time for almost a year, until Chaotica. And Lisa.

Gigs are every third Thursday, socials last Friday of the month. Dec O'Connell, from Marketing, calls Andrew 'mate'. Around the Gallant offices, people say 'Hey Andrew'. He buys new jeans, black T-shirts, a cap. He gets his hair cut and puts gel in it. He's thinking about getting his ear pierced.

It's the Friday social, end of a nightmare month, and Andrew's drinking faster than usual. Engineering messed up the Excel template he set up. Billing's behind in all departments. Somehow, god knows how, Andrew made it balance. 'What would I do, Mr Starling, Star Keeper, without your know-how?', his boss said at the start of the night, slapping him on the back. It occurred to Andrew halfway through his second pint that without him, his boss might actually be in deep shit. By the end of his third, he discounts this as ridiculous.

The Golden Lion feels much smaller in the actual pub.

Onstage it feels like Wembley; here on the stools, around a table, it's just a normal pub with a raised square in the corner.

Cooper and the others have gone. Jerry rings last orders loudly, and Andrew almost falls off his stool. When he looks up, there's only one person left at the table. A small girl with straight brown hair. Lisa, from the Support Team. Andrew's good with names. She's always here, but on all the other Fridays Andrew has never said more than a few words to her.

'Ding ding, hometime!' Lisa smiles but doesn't move. Her voice sounds American, and she keeps her mouth in a smile even when talking, which must be quite an effort. There's a gap between her front teeth and a lot of dark makeup around her eyes. Andrew wants to say something back and ends up waving at her across the sticky table. A Cure song plays in the background – great bass line. Lisa tilts her head and giggles. She's pretty. They lift their almost empty glasses to their mouths. Then Lisa wobbles her stool around the table so she's beside him. It feels like Robert Smith is singing only to them. *Hand in hand is the only way to land, and always the right way round.*

The alcohol keeps Andrew smiling, right at her. He rounds his shoulders to bring himself nearer her height. He can't think of a single thing to say so he sings quietly along with the song. He can't seem to look away. She's grinning at him with her mouth closed. He wishes she'd open it, he likes the gap between her teeth.

'Almost as good as Chaotica,' Lisa says suddenly.

'The Cure are legends.'

'Drink up, lovebirds,' Jerry shouts, and the bar lights up. They blink in surprise. For a second, she looks frightened, her hands flutter around her face. And then she does an astounding thing. She leans towards him with her hand on his thigh, *almost in his groin.* She smells of soap and sweet alcohol. And before he has time to panic, her mouth is on his.

It's Andrew's first kiss. He's twenty-five.

Lisa spends more time at the flat. They go to the cinema, the steakhouse. She calls him 'Andy' with a twangy American 'A', influenced by endless episodes of Dallas and Dynasty. No one that he can think of has ever called him Andy, and he can't decide if he likes it. There'll be times when his heart pounds it feels so intimate, and other times he isn't sure who she's talking to. Despite the years with his two sisters and his mother, what Andrew knows about women is mostly from song lyrics, none of it much use.

Lisa likes shopping. She looks at herself in mirrors, from different angles, holds things up for approval, and then leads him into the next store where they do it all again. Andrew doesn't mind – left to him he's not sure how they would fill their Saturdays – but it doesn't seem to make her happy.

Sex exceeds all his imaginings. Lisa usually keeps some clothes on. He has a go at peeling off the layers, but she stops him at the T-shirt. He doesn't argue with the clothes; he doesn't argue with anything. There are nights after wine, now and then in the pitch dark, when she gets naked with him. The feel of her skin on his is like a song melody, something deep-toned and throaty. Maybe Janis Joplin. These are the nights he replays in his head when it all stops.

With two of them, the flat starts to feel like a home. It fills with shoes, coats, a pair of tongs resembling a weapon of torture to straighten Lisa's hair, a great many pots and bottles in the bathroom, a curvy vase, and an alarming amount of video tapes for which Andrew will eventually create a grid of extra shelves in the alcove. She knows a lot of them by heart.

Lisa's unlucky with her health; she takes frequent days off for headaches. Andrew learns that migraines can come on fast or slow, last for days or weeks; can cause changes in appetite, floods of tears, even voices in your head. Remedies vary drastically too – hot water bottle or cold compress, darkened rooms, soft music, Andrew reading aloud her horoscope from *Bella*.

Pretty Woman is Lisa's current obsession. Lonnie saw it at the cinema and has a lot to say about Julia Roberts being a prostitute. 'It's outrageous,' Lonnie says. 'Totally sexist.' But Lisa doesn't seem to notice the outrageous sexism. Watching it, she goes into a trance. The bit she replays is Richard Gere going into a bar while Julia Roberts waits with her back to him. He thinks she's not there and is about to leave when Julia Roberts swivels around on her bar stool in a diamond necklace with her hair up and smiles at him. Lisa can't get enough of this scene. Andrew comes back from the weekly Chaotica practice and finds her on the sofa, in a trance. On the screen, Julia turns around, again, with a wide, toothy grin. It gives Andrew the creeps.

He buys her a kitten for her birthday and she allows him to name it Robert, after Robert Smith, though she doesn't like The Cure or any of his music. She calls the cat Bobby, which from her mouth sounds like Barbie.

Alone on the sofa, Lisa upstairs with a cold compress, Andrew sinks his fingers into Robert's soft fur, and quietly sings 'You know that I'd do anything for you.' He thinks of Tao and the dogs on their epic journey. Andrew had always imagined himself one day with a dog, but then none of this is how he imagined it.

*

When neither of them can stall any longer, Andrew takes Lisa to a family lunch on a mild, damp Sunday in February. Lisa changes clothes several times and ends up in her jeans and a pale pink jumper with sequins around the neck and cuffs. He might as well have turned up with a two-headed girlfriend.

'Lisa! Welcome!'

'Come in, come in. About time!'

'Look at you! Here you are!'

'Where did Andrew take you for Valentine's?' Lonnie asks. They're only just inside the door, Lisa wedged to Andrew. Dad bounces around offering drinks, tours and building details. Mum ushers everyone inside as Lonnie launches her questionnaire.

'Do you have any brothers or sisters? Are you in the Band? Where did you get your top? Do you know any judo?'

Christ on a bike. Andrew finds himself wishing Bea were here, with her disinterest and sarcasm. They move as a group across the parquet floor, Dad commentating on the design, then through the kitchen and the Annexe, where Mum takes over with a sketch of Granny Dil, and out onto the wet patio, where the five of them stand in a row, admiring Mum's bedding plants and the apple-less tree.

'Great to have you here Lisa. Champion.' Ted rubs his hands and slaps his son on the back in a new gesture that will be often repeated.

Back inside, Andrew takes Lisa's hand and flees. 'I'll just show her upstairs.'

Because his old room is now part of Lonnie's empire, they go into Bea's room and sit on the bed.

'They'll calm down,' Andrew says.

'They're nice,' Lisa says. She looks around with interest at the coat hangers on the bare wall, the empty desk, the wardrobe with a lone photo still blue-tacked, askew. 'When did your sister move out?'

'Bea? About ten years ago.' Andrew stares at David Bowie's different-coloured eyes on the poster by the bed. Would he see differently out of each?

Lisa counts on her fingers. 'Sixteen? Like me.'

'No,' Andrew says, 'she's not like you.' Lisa looks miffed, but they really are nothing alike. Bea is outspoken, makes herself known, gets what she wants.

'Why did she leave?' Lisa asks. Andrew can see she's looking for similarities with her situation. Lisa doesn't talk much about her parents, but from what he does know they sound like monsters, especially the mum. 'Was she kicked out?' she presses.

'No!' It feels like she's poking a cut. He puts a hand to his head, where his scalp stung when Dad had a hold of him by the hair, and Bea the same. Andrew had met her eyes – was it in this room? – while frozen in terror. But in his sister's eyes, he saw rage alongside the fear. Andrew rubs his scalp now, next to the crown of his head. He almost expects to feel blood. *Was* there blood? He shudders. Lisa is watching him closely but she keeps quiet. Andrew doesn't want to dwell here. It was like living in a nightmare – Dad hit a bad time. Then it was over, finished, and Dad was back to normal.

What was the question? Was Bea kicked out. He remembers his confusion when Bea broke her leg. The police had questioned him. Was Dad a threat? Did Andrew feel afraid? The whole thing bizarre and horrible. Andrew mostly stayed in his room. Except now he thinks of it, Bea didn't move out until much later. One day she was just *gone*, and everyone pretended it was OK. There was a boy, but Andrew never knew him.

'Dad didn't like her boyfriend,' he says finally. In a way, it was better after Bea left – less fighting. Weird though, he barely saw her. Not many people leave home before they leave school. No one he knows, in fact, other than his sister and his girlfriend.

'She left young, same as me,' Lisa says again, pleased. 'What was she like?'

'*Is*,' he says, annoyed. 'She's not *dead*.'

'I mean when you were kids.'

'Restless,' he says, thinking it's an odd word to pick. Unlike Andrew, Bea sat with Granny Dil until she died. 'She's brave,' Andrew says, 'really brave.' And now Lisa smiles, at the compliment that isn't for her.

Andrew would like to see Bea. It would be great if she came home now, for lunch. Except it probably wouldn't – it would be awkward and tense. Andrew used to phone her at university, but she wouldn't come home, so he stopped. Maybe he should have tried harder.

Lisa goes over to the cupboard and peers at the photo. From the bed Andrew can see it's Bea and Granny in the sun at Bluebell Lane; the summer holidays that seemed to last for years. Then he remembers something else.

'There was a thing, one summer,' he's talking to himself. 'Dad still brings it up.' Andrew had heard him telling the story to Lonnie after her PGL holiday with school where she tried archery. 'Bea shot him.'

'*Shot* him?' Lisa's mouth drops open.

'An arrow, not a gun,' Andrew says quickly. 'Though the way Dad tells it, it might as well have been an Uzi. I don't think he was even hurt.' Andrew only has the retellings to go on. He hadn't been there, and he has no memory of the day, only the silent drive home from that holiday. And no return to the caravan. It confuses him still, though he hasn't thought about it in ages. Bea was just a little kid. But Andrew's seen films where small things become bigger and bigger.

'Sounds like they still have *issues*,' Lisa says knowingly. Andrew doesn't want to get into it. Just talking like this he feels vaguely like he's letting someone down. Dad can get an odd look about him when Bea is mentioned. Like the guilty, childish, look he had when Andrew found a whole bunch of expenses without receipts, only sadder. Andrew doesn't want to make his father sad, and he knows to steer clear of the subject of Bea, even though he doesn't fully understand it. It's not so much that Andrew has forgiven his father, it's more that the passage of time has faded everything back to neutral. And he's not one to bear a grudge.

Change the record, he thinks and feels in his pocket for a ten-pence piece. 'See this?' he says, holding it up. Lisa gives a distracted smile. Andrew closes his fist over the coin and opens out both hands: empty. He cups his hand behind his ear and brandishes the coin. Granny Dil loved this one.

Lisa is undeterred. 'What did Bea *do* though?' She runs her finger over the grinning, eight-year-old Bea in the photo. Andrew can't answer the question. Not then, not now. She didn't really *do* anything, she just *was*. Apparently, that was enough to kick things off.

His shoulders sag, he puts the coin away and shakes his head. 'It was all ages ago.'

Lisa comes to sit beside him. 'It always is,' she says with a deep sigh, sounding old in a way she doesn't usually. Then she turns her head up to him with a forlorn smile, and the gap in her teeth makes her herself again. He wants to kiss her.

Mum calls them for lunch. From downstairs their combined voices bounce around, all excited; exaggerations of their usual selves. For the first time in his life, Andrew wants to get out of here. He wants to go home: to *his* flat, with *his* girlfriend. He wants to sit on the sofa and stroke *their* cat. It's a brilliant, heady feeling, like early-stage drunk or the rush from getting up too quickly.

Spidery cracks
1995

A lone book on the desk, *Letts Guide to Les Liaisons Dangereuses*; the faded corduroy beanbag; the ripped poster; the hangers on the wall, are all exactly as Bea left them. Moira stands in the doorway. Outside, the April sky is dark and lumpy and she flicks the light on, but somehow it makes the room even more gloomy. There's a word for it, it's on the tip of Moira's tongue. She and David had it in a crossword just the other week, the long one across the top, they had to look it up.

In the almost decade since she left, Bea has been back once? Twice? And she didn't touch this room, as if it wasn't hers in the first place. The last time was on the way to a conference, and Bea chose to drive on until three in the morning instead of spending the night. Moira called in sick for work the next day, such was her disappointment.

She has never wanted to redecorate. It would feel like painting over Bea. *Anachronism*, that's it. Ted doesn't come in here, he's superstitious about it. *Still*. Well, Moira has a licence to sort it out now, as Bea's bringing a boyfriend home. They're staying the night of Andrew's wedding. Moira was beginning to wonder if Bea would ever come home again, then Lonnie asked her to stay, and just like that, Bea accepted. Moira wasn't expecting her to come at all; a card and a gift at best. She's trying to ignore her mounting anxiety and focus on the task at hand.

Moira doesn't know what to think about Andrew getting married. They barely see Lisa, and when they do she barely talks. But Andrew seems happy enough. Though it's hard to tell. It's all been quite a rush; Moira expects some *news* any day.

She'll need to move the cupboard at the end of the bed,

where one blue-tacked photo still clings on, curled at the edges. Near the ceiling are two empty hangers hooked over nails. Bea hammered them in herself without consulting her father – big mistake. Tiny cracks spider out from the nails. Moira takes the hangers down. It used to alarm her to see a jacket and shirt across the wall, like suspended guests. That was before Bea moved everything to Sarah's. Moira didn't blame her. She understood the pull of that house with all its sophistication, a friend in the next room. But why had Moira allowed it? Why did she give up her daughter so easily? Eleanor Rosefoot had been so kind and reasonable, and so *worldly*, that Moira was unable to compete. She had hated the woman a little, even though she tried not to. And hadn't it been a relief? Moira feels a twinge of guilt. It *had* been a relief. With only the four of them (five while Dilys was still alive) the house was less spiky, less snags to catch yourself on.

'What's going on?' Lonnie appears in the doorway and makes Moira jump. *Caught thinking*. She smiles at Lonnie, all curves. Moira dislikes the new fashion for what's effectively a leotard under jeans. Might as well go around in your bathing suit. It leaves Moira feeling further behind than she already is.

'Gavin prep,' Moira says.

'Ooh *Gavin.*' Lonnie taps her clenched fist against her chest in two fast beats, and again: her sister's beating heart.

'Will I like him?' Moira asks, for at least the third time. Lonnie's already met Bea's boyfriend on one of her visits, which Moira tries not to be envious of.

'Course,' Lonnie says, 'and Dad will.' This is the most important thing. Even Lonnie knows that the thing – *one* of the things – between Bea and Ted, was boy-related.

'What's he like?' Moira can't help herself.

'I *told* you,' Lonnie says, 'he's got a loud voice, he talks a lot. He's funny.'

'Good.' Though a wing-beat has started up inside Moira

and she curses it silently. She can't help but anticipate a scene, a falling out. It's about time Ted and Bea buried the hatchet. Moira is fed up to the teeth of this old panic, and she no longer wants to be the peacekeeper. She feels a sudden annoyance towards Bea, stubborn to her bones. Ted has confessed how much he wants to make things better. He doesn't bring it up often, but when this visit was arranged, he let on to Moira how it needles him that they don't see her; how it is all his fault. His face had fallen practically to his chest while he let himself dwell on it. 'It makes me heartsick,' he said.

Moira gets Lonnie to help pull the bed out, and drags the dusty box that she has hoovered around for almost ten years. Then they move the cupboard, and the photo gets stuck to Lonnie's top. She pulls it off and scrutinises the faces.

'Before my time,' Lonnie says, handing it to Moira, and she moons off.

It's Bea and Dilys, taken in the garden at Bluebell Lane. Bea must be about seven or eight, on the grass with the dog in bright sunshine, her bare legs out straight, next to Dilys in a deckchair with a cigarette. Both of them are laughing.

Moira sits down on the bed and thinks of the three of them in the hospice. The narrow bed, blue walls, stale air smelling of old rose petals. When she thinks of Bea it is often of that day, her mother's last, the two of them standing over the bed, joined for a fleeting, precious moment. The further away it gets, the clearer Moira sees it was a chance missed. She told Bea how good she was for Dilys: *a miracle*. She said that, at least. But Bea had asked her questions, and the truth is, Moira had been frightened to answer them. Her stupid old fear of speaking about her life. Just so much easier *not* to. Keep going forward and don't look over your shoulder. Her own mother may even have said those exact words. And Moira, ever compliant, seeking calm, obeyed.

From Lonnie's room comes a music blast, and *thud-thud* of heavy-footed aerobics. Moira blows the dust off the magazines in the box. Like the rest of the room, Bea has not touched this since she left. Moira long ago stopped asking Ted about that day. She knows only that Bea was in bed with a boy. It's Moira's opinion that Ted overreacted. But it was Bea's decision to leave, not Ted forcing her away.

She plucks a *Jackie* magazine from the box, kicks her legs up onto the bed, and leans back on the pillow. She reads the whole of 'Debbie's Dilemma', a black-and-white photo story with speech bubbles. It follows Debbie's agony over how to make herself noticed by her older brother's friend Phil, with a bloated, deformed-looking chest, and frothy fringe. Debbie might be well advised to seek a better-proportioned boyfriend, though no one points this out. Her friends gather round, put their hands to their cheeks mirroring her pain. But they needn't have worried. Moira turns the page to find big-chested Phil with his arms wide open, and Debbie runs into them. The End. She turns the page. What does it mean The *End*? How ridiculous – it's barely the beginning! She thumps the magazine back in the box and a blue paper corner pokes out. She pulls a wafer-thin airmail letter from under the pile. Without thinking she unfolds it.

Chère Béatrice, It's in French! Moira hums with annoyance. She scans down the page of slanting, loopy writing, and picks out words: *souvenir, lèvres, Clémentine*. She almost scratches the page for it to reveal its meaning.

Je t'embrasse, Laurent.

At the bottom, the writer signs off with a long line on the 't' as though he wants to linger on the page. Moira looks around the room and feels suddenly very small. The beanbag sits in a heap, and the spidery cracks in the wall resemble geriatric stars. The room needs new curtains, a new rug; some *life*.

She gets up and almost stamps her foot. No one will ever write her a letter in French. Or gather round her with hands to their cheeks on her behalf. Why doesn't she know any French? Where is her face-clutching group? And why is she thinking like this, of herself? She must get on. She tucks the letter back in the box.

What must it feel like to know that someone all the way across the sea is thinking of you?

Chère Moira, je t'embrasse.

Happily ever after

They barely fill the front two rows in the pale peach room at Fern Ashton Town Hall. Bea counts twelve of them in suit jackets and bright dresses, coughing and murmuring. She's got Gavin on one side and Lonnie on the other. Cheers and whistles of the last wedding reach them through the high, open windows. Andrew stands tall at the front, in a dark blue suit and pink tie. He keeps turning around for quick glances at the entrance. His dark hair is cut square, like the Lego figures they used to play with. Two spots high on his cheeks match the tie. He is the same brother, only dressed as a man.

'Doesn't he look lovely,' she hears Moira say to Lonnie in a tormented tone.

'Gain a daughter, not lose a son,' Lonnie says, like some wise old crone, squeezing their mother's arm. Bea checks her sister's face: still a freckled teenager. Bea has the feeling they're all being shaken around like the snow globes Lonnie hoards. A smatter of clapping comes from the group outside.

'We're supposed to have Dire Straits 'Romeo and Juliet',' Lonnie whispers to Bea, 'but Cooper brought the wrong tape. He's got the one for the end though,' she taps her nose importantly. Then loud, zigzagging violins announce the bride – lacy, orange-faced, toothy smile – slow-stepping down the gap in the chairs, on the arm of a rigid, unsmiling gentleman. Uncle David! He transfers the bride to Andrew, whose tender smile Bea just catches before David steps back to block her view.

Funny meeting your sister-in-law at her wedding. 'Andrew's very devoted', is all she has got from Mum. And also, a week ago, 'Lisa's pregnant!'. A fact that had blown Bea away. And what surprised her even more was the huge relief she had felt at the news. Bea has tucked this away for another time. Or never. About Lisa, Lonnie had said only, 'She's really pretty'. Though it's hard to tell – the bride's face is literally caked in makeup.

'Does she always wear this much?' Bea asks Lonnie while they sign the register with Tina Turner belting out 'Simply the Best' from Cooper's tinny boom box.

'She might have added a layer for her special day,' Lonnie says, herself looking like a high-class hooker in a skin-tight peacock-blue dress and matching eyeliner.

A shouty, Chaotica version of 'Baby I Love Your Way' propels the beaming couple out of the room. Gavin raises an eyebrow, Bea digs him in the ribs.

Outside, under a milky blue June sky, the steps froth with confetti. Bea stands at the bottom, watching everyone. Gavin's smoking over the other side, and Bea sees Ted stride over to clap him on the back. On the top step, Lisa clings to Andrew next to a small clump of accountants snapping pictures of them. Moira flutters around, like a sage-green moth. From the other side, Gav gives Bea a lascivious wink, which roots her to the spot. She glares at him and shakes her head. Ted looks over. Gavin says something, and Ted laughs loudly. Bea feels a lurch in her stomach. They're staying in her *old room,* on a sofa bed borrowed from Pauline. Maybe they'll go to the Travelodge.

Lonnie pulls Bea over to introduce two lads in grey work suits. 'Bea, this is Jez and Cooper.' They nod formally. Another one swaggers over, shirt open. 'Dec's the lead singer,' Lonnie says, blushing. She lobs another snowy handful in the direction of the bride and groom: 'Your special day!' Bea decides to find Gavin, but a woman in a wide cream hat swerves in front of her.

'Susie, front desk,' the woman introduces herself. 'Lovely day for it. First Gallant wedding,' she gushes, 'I feel like Cilla Black!'

Moira joins them, eyebrows raised in her *Everyone alright?* look.

'Nice suit,' Bea says, and Moira checks her sincerity before smiling, gratefully.

'And you look nice,' Moira says. Bea has paired her tight black trousers with a red silk shirt and her only dressy shoes, a pair of pointy black slingbacks that are cramping her toes.

'I'm not much for dressing up,' Bea says.

'Neither is Ted,' Moira says. 'You know him, "Like being in a cardboard box",' she does her Ted voice. 'He and Gavin are getting on well, aren't they?'

'Gav can talk for England,' Bea says. Andrew calls out to Lonnie to ease off the snowstorm. 'Has Lisa got no parents?' Bea asks, looking around for Lisa's people. The girl looks about fifteen, has anyone verified her age?

'Her mum's in America I think,' Susie says. 'There might be a stepdad.'

Moira looks put out. 'You know more than me,' she says.

'She never sees them,' Susie front desk says. 'It's very sad.'

'That *is* sad,' Moira agrees, with a pointed look at Bea who keeps her eyes on the happy couple. Bea's skin feels hot. She has a sudden urge to peel it off and run. She might take up smoking. When does the booze start?

Bea hasn't been home in over two years. She wouldn't be here today, but Gavin saw the invitation. 'I'll send flowers,' Bea said, and Gavin had looked incredulous. 'Your brother's getting *married*.' Gav, an only child, raised by his mum, would give anything for a family wedding – a family.

'Let's get a group photo,' Susie says, teary-eyed. 'You two front and centre,' she smiles indulgently at Bea. 'Big sister of the groom.' Moira looks suddenly worried, like Bea might sabotage the whole thing. Bea lets out a loud groan and flounces off, heels clicking. *What the fuck*? Her body is acting all on its own; she might be seven years old.

She heads to the lone figure round the back of the steps, arms by his sides in the navy blazer he bought for Granny Dil's funeral.

'Uncle David,' she says. His strained attempt at a smile is oddly calming. She has to stop herself from putting her arms around him. The Gallant lads sing a tuneless 'For he's a jolly good fellow—'

'Special day,' Bea says. 'Think you'll ever get married?'

'Is that a joke?' David asks.

'Sort of,' she says, smiling.

His face relaxes. 'The probability is low,' he says.

Bea nods. 'Overrated.' She looks around. 'Where's the dog?' Bea feels sure there's a dog, even if it's a different one.

'At home. I brought the car. I'll walk him after the pudding.'

'I might join you.'

'I chose the lemon cheesecake,' David says solemnly.

Gavin and Ted stride over. Gavin is a head taller than her father. It might be the only time Bea has seen Ted in a suit. He has the same pink tie as Andrew. His short fair hair, greying at the sides, catches the sun. His square jaw is all grin. Ted pats David on the back.

'Gav, this is Uncle David,' Bea says.

'I can see the family resemblance.' Gavin offers his hand, and when David doesn't offer his, Gavin picks it up where it hangs at David's side, and shakes it. 'You're a local, right?'

'I live in Lower Ashton village,' David says. Ted gives Gavin a look that says *Loop the loop*. Bea's breath swirls around. She might step forward and push her father over. She has the sense that some scientific laws are being tested: something to do with magnetism, repelling forces. From behind, Susie herds them into the photo.

'Bea next to the bride, then Lonnie.' She manhandles them into a line.

'Hello,' Bea says, looking down into Lisa's rictus smile. 'And congratulations.' Close up, the girl looks like a startled deer. The small curve of her belly is visible from here. 'I'm Bea.' Bea puts an arm around her new sister-in-law's narrow, lacy shoulders, to steady them both.

Lisa looks up at her through thick mascara. 'I know.'

Upstairs in the Golden Lion – seven either side of a long table, place names in the shape of guitars – the noise rises, trapped by the sloping roof and spongy carpet. It smells of air freshener, with undertones of old beer.

'Two footy teams,' says Jez or Cooper. Apart from the small dormer window, an azure postage stamp in the roof, the room is lit by ineffectual yellow spots along the beams. The dinginess, coupled with the dark suits, makes Bea think of a gangster movie. She looks along the table for the most likely person to pull out a pistol. Probably her.

The roast is delayed, drinks are sent up from the bar. Bea downs a large glass of red and helps herself to another. She's on the end of the family side, near the stairs, where sweaty young waiters in black appear like magic with trays. Gavin is opposite her, on the Gallant side, his tie loose, talking loudly to Susie's husband about draught beer. On Bea's side, there's Lonnie, Lisa, Andrew, Dad, Mum and a space for Uncle David who's gone to walk the dog.

Dec gets to his feet and all his side cheer. He runs a hand through his floppy hair.

'I first met Andrew onstage, right here,' he points to the floor and raises his pint. Andrew's face is heading towards fuchsia. They all drink to Andrew's first gig. Bea settles back, starting to enjoy herself. Her brother's life is fascinating – so much has happened while she's been away. Gavin toes her calf under the table. She leans forward.

'No speeches from you,' she says, as a tray appears at her right hand.

Her father gets up when Dec sits down. He's saying something to Mum that she can't hear. Ted's suit jacket is on the back of his chair, and Bea sees now the whole outfit matches Andrew's. She tries to picture them together, her brother and her father, in Marks and Spencer. *How do I look?* It almost makes her laugh out loud. Though maybe in this new, snow-globe life they go on shopping trips and double dates to the ice rink. She reaches for her glass and swallows too hard, the wine is bitter in the back of her throat.

Ted's shirt buttons strain against his chest. He might be holding his breath. The room falls quiet. Ted clears his throat. Moira glances up at him and nods. Lonnie gives him a giggly thumbs-up, and this seems to do the trick.

'You took your time coming,' Ted says looking at Andrew, who smiles affectionately back. 'But you were worth the wait.' He's choked up. It's obvious to Bea he's not well prepared for this. Her stomach feels tight. *What might he say*? 'Your talents have been mentioned,' Ted carries on in a louder voice, 'and I'd like to add what a help you've been to me, keeping the Rev off my back,' he holds up a hand. 'Sorry, *Inland Revenue.*' This gets a laugh and a clap from the Gallant side. There's a long pause. 'We don't see much of Lisa,' Ted says stiffly, 'but we hope to see her more. And we look forward to the next generation.' Polite clapping from all. Lisa's face must be hurting now. Does she not have any other expressions? 'So.' Ted reaches for his glass. 'To our firstborn and his bride. May you live happily ever after.' He raises his glass and looks up and down the table. The wedding guests all sip their drinks, then put their glasses down and applaud loudly.

Is that it? Surely Andrew deserves more. And Lisa. The newlyweds clap along, grinning around at everyone. Andrew looks so happy, he really does. He puts an arm around his wife (wife!) and kisses her cheek self-consciously. Gavin drums on the table.

'Why are you cheering?' Bea says.

'Babe, lighten up.' The roast arrives.

Bass beats and voices come through the floor during the cheesecake or profiteroles. After the last mouthfuls, Lonnie leads the crowd down the narrow stairs into the heaving pub below. Andrew and Lisa wait till last, and the place erupts in hoots and whistles as they descend, hand in hand, to 'The Lovecats' blasting from the speakers. Crimson again, ducking his head on the stairs, Andrew nods at the DJ in the corner.

Ted and Gavin prop up the bar; Jerry pulls pints and shakes cocktails; Andrew moves between the work huddles, accepting hugs, backslaps, high fives. The Starling women, Lisa included, cluster around one of the little tables. It feels to Bea more like a work do than a wedding. Where are Lisa's friends? People come up to her in twos and threes, say congratulations, then scarper. Mind you, Bea wouldn't have much of a guest list herself, Gav's the one with all the mates. Bea leans around the dancers tripping off the tiny dance floor, to keep an eye on her father. As best they can over the noise, the women discuss the outfits, the cheesecake, the wedding ring.

Bea waits at the bar to be served; the men don't notice her. Ted's hunched over, his head almost touching Gavin's.

'She's taking Andrew for a ride—' Bea hears, and the rest is cut off by a screech from the dancers. Gavin nods and sips his pint. Bea's gut clenches; the repelling forces are back. She needs some air. And suddenly, urgently, she needs to pee. She elbows her way to the Ladies, a cubicle in the alley outside the pub, helping herself to a bottle of Becks from a passing tray.

Outside, she blinks at the brightness, confused to find it's still daytime. The white loo door is shut. The arched red letters in the silver square say ENGAGED. Bea leans against the brick wall, then looks around, vaguely, for somewhere to lie down. Days go on forever here. Whenever she comes back to Fern Ashton, she wonders if it will be the last time. What was it Dad said just now that was so out of order? The flush sounds from behind the door, then it flies open. The handle cracks against the wall. A young Gallant in a short skirt breezes past in a fug of sweet perfume. Bea shuts the door, puts the bottle on the ground, and steadies herself with a hand on the bricks while she pees.

When she comes back the music is louder, and the pub's darker. Her father, ruddy-faced, stands with Andrew and a thin, balding man with an arm around Andrew's shoulders. Gavin has apparently gone for a smoke.

'Our Star Keeper,' says the man – company director? – and mock-punches Andrew's arm. Bea steps into the group.

'This is my other sister,' Andrew says, giving her a warm smile.

'Superstar, hero,' Bea holds up her bottle to her brother and drinks to him. The boss starts on about month-end, blah blah.

'I'm a research scientist,' Bea says loudly. Her father looks unsure. 'I *am*.'

'I know,' Ted says.

'Cancer research,' Andrew says, sounding proud. Then Jez or Cooper moonwalks through them and the group is cleaved in two, leaving Bea and her dad.

'We're making *history*,' Bea says.

'Fantastic,' Ted says. 'I knew it.' He seems nervous, and fidgety, stepping from foot to foot. The other group have been joined by more Gallants; Bea and Ted are on their own.

'Gavin's a nice fella,' Ted says over the music. 'Where did the two of you meet?'

'In a pub,' Bea says. She wants to lean on something. The wooden curve of the bar is further than it looks and she stumbles against the wood. Dad hovers and flaps his hands. She leans successfully. Then she remembers what pissed her off before she went out.

'Lisa's nice too,' Bea shouts over 'Dancing Queen'. 'Not taking anyone for a ride, s'far as I can see.'

Young and sweet, only seventeen—

'No,' says Ted, looking stricken, quickly shaking his head. 'Not at all. They're having a baby.'

'Firstborn,' Bea says and gives a hollow laugh without meaning to. Ted looks over to where Moira's sitting, then back at Bea.

'So, tell me about your scientific experiments,' Ted says, emphasising the last words like he's taking the mickey.

'We grow human cells, in *dishes*,' Bea says, and Ted nods eagerly. 'Get bacteria to make human protein,' she stifles a belch. 'Stain stuff with antibodies.'

'Sounds complicated.' Ted's expression is fixed.

'Currently considered by a big, drug, company,' she leaves pauses for emphasis and jabs a finger. 'Multinational.' Is he getting it? She throws an arm up to the ceiling. 'Gig*an*tic.'

'Champion.' Ted says with his rigid face, then he breaks into a smile. Gavin's at Bea's side, his arm around her waist. He puts a glass of wine on the bar next to her, leans in and kisses her neck. Bea shoves him off.

'Whoa!' Ted catches Gavin. Bea feels sick. She can't be standing here with Gavin groping her.

'Father-daughter business?' Gav shouts over some clashing, screaming music. The volume just went up again, the whole place trembles with bass.

'Andrew's band,' Ted mouths, pointing at the speaker, then he puts the finger in his ear and winces. 'Not really my cup of tea.'

'The lab,' Bea shouts. 'I was telling Dad.'

'Brains of the family,' Ted says, suddenly relaxed. 'Saving lives.' Ted slaps Gavin on the back like it was him finding the cancer cure. 'Bea's always been ahead.'

'Head? What?' *What's he talking about?*

'Best driver in the family,' Ted beams. 'Only one to pass first time.'

'Andrew would've,' Bea scowls. 'Haddapanicattack.'

'Mixing her drinks,' Gav grins at Ted. He puts a firm arm around Bea's shoulder, ignoring her attempt to get away. 'Good name for a band, Panic Attack, where's Andrew?' Gav looks around. Ted excuses himself for the Gents.

'Fuck are you doing?' Bea says to Gav, at the same time as he says 'Are you alright?'

She lurches back to the women, sits down, and leans back, only just in time remembering it's a stool. Wine sloshes onto the red silk.

'Shit. Oops.'

'It started there,' Lisa's pointing a pearly fingernail at the next table where a group of dishevelled guests line up shot glasses. 'First date,' Lisa smiles, gappily. The lacy butterflies around her neck must be itchy by now. How could this girl take anyone for a ride? She could be at school with Lonnie. *Having a baby*. Bea feels suddenly shaky on the inside, like *she* might be having a panic attack, though it has never happened before. 'It's Raining Men' comes on, and her sister and sister-in-law leap up, Lonnie almost taking Mum out with her Bacardi Breezer.

When they're alone, her mother puts a hand on Bea's arm.

'Maybe slow down?' Moira says, slowly. Why is everyone treating her like she's a disabled child?

'Last one,' Bea shouts, chinking her glass against Moira's empty one. 'Where's Uncle David?'

'Long gone,' Moira says. 'Is Gavin having a nice time?'

'Who cares?'

Moira closes her eyes for a long moment.

'Wakey wakey!' Bea might join the formation dance. She sings along: 'Absolutely soaking wet.' The pub is heaving. 'Who *are* all these people?' she shouts at her mother.

'Andrew and Lisa's friends, from work,' Mum says.

'Really? Or just the whole company.'

'Please Bea,' Mum looks like she might cry. 'Don't spoil it for them.'

Then Bea sees them, over by the door.

'Nooo,' she breathes. And she's up. Moira whips around to see what the problem is. Bea falls into a group of dancers, feels wet in her hair, and more on her shoulder. She's pulled up by Lonnie who looks like she's just met Freddie Krueger.

'Chill out, Lon,' Bea says. 'Go with the flow.' Both of her little toes are stinging like mad. She might take her shoes off.

'Some *air?*' Lonnie says, too close to Bea's face.

Bea breaks free and keeps on course for the back door, the rectangle of light where Ted's leaning against the metal bar that opens it, his shirt sleeve flapping around his middle. The last of the sun shines on his bare shoulder.

Showing Gav his scar. Next to the love heart. Made by the delinquent child.

It seems like a long way to get to them. What's this all down her top? Dad and Gavin are laughing. And now Gav is taking off *his* shirt. *What the fuck*? Bea pushes past Dec and a tall woman with hair to her arse, knocks over a chair. Bottles and glasses smash on the tiles.

She lands in front of them on legs of jelly. Her father and her boyfriend, rubbing bare arms.

'What the *fuck*?'

'Tattoos.' Gav grins. Dad doesn't. 'Ted says I should get one of you. In a heart.'

Bea feels like she's underwater.

'Babe?'

'Bea?' Dad takes a step towards her. She wants to knock him over, but she's going in the wrong direction. From the light, many arms and hands reach for her as she falls backwards.

Changing fortunes
1997

In the pedestrian bit of the city centre, Bea dodges buggies, skateboards, Christmas carollers, though it's not even December. She's almost filled her rucksack and still has half the list to go. It's cold and sunny, her favourite kind of day, but her shopping allergy has broken her out in a sweat. She dumps her bag on the pavement outside Accessorize. Behind the glass, a mannequin leers at her in a Santa hat and red feather boa. She's about to call it quits and head for home when she hears her name, shouted from a little way off, over a feeble line of 'In the Bleak Midwinter'. Did she imagine it? She searches the bags and shoppers for the owner of the voice. There it is again, closer. Bea knows that voice.

Suddenly, from nowhere, like an apparition, or an angel, with frizzy hair and Doc Marten boots, Sarah Rosefoot steps out from the crowd. She stares first at Bea's face and then at her enormous belly. A few metres apart, the two women stand like statues. Two lads wheelie between them, their front bike wheels pointing straight up at the sky. Bea and Sarah might have stood like this for hours, too afraid to move in case the other does turn out to be an apparition, and then Sarah's face crumples. Her hand goes to her mouth, but it fails to contain her loud, heart-wrenching sob.

'No way, no way!' Bea keeps saying. 'Is it really you?' They're in a café, sitting across a round table with blue mosaic tiles. 'Lonnie asked me on the phone about you just the other day.'

'God, how em*bar*rassing,' Sarah says, her hands on her still-flushed cheeks. Her forehead is lined, her frizzy hair grey at the roots, her smile wide and full. She's different, and she's exactly the same.

'I get that reaction a lot,' Bea says. 'No wonder – I look like I've swallowed a whale.'

'Maybe it's twins,' Sarah says. 'Lonnie, wow, how's she? And how are *you*?' Sarah looks like she might burst into tears again.

'Massive,' Bea says, stroking her middle. 'Ups and downs.'

'Tell me more,' Sarah says, then before Bea has the chance, 'Oh god, did you hear about Dani Bush?'

'She's a porn star?'

Sarah shakes her head and whispers, 'Run over by a rugby team,' she grimaces. 'Dead.' She puts her hand over her mouth and a giggle escapes through her fingers.

'Fuck,' Bea says.

'I know, it's not funny. A coach, in a car park.' Another laugh bursts out of her. 'I'm sorry, I don't know what's the matter with me.' She looks genuinely stricken.

'Clinically insane?' Bea suggests.

'I may be,' Sarah says, unable to contain her smile. 'As yet undiagnosed.'

'As yet,' Bea says. And then Sarah holds up a finger and puts on the ultra-serious face. A song lyric! Bea feels a bubble of excitement somewhere in her windpipe.

'The silicon chip inside her head gets switched to overload—'

It's right there: 'And nobody's gonna go to school today,' Bea says, matching the seriousness. They speak the next lines together, then pick up their teaspoons, volume rising, and sing the chorus.

'Tell me why, I don't like Mondays?' They grin at one another madly, deliriously. People on other tables turn and stare, but Bea and Sarah don't look away from each other. Bea has a sense of her whole body gasping: her fifteen-year-old self is *right here*, under her skin. She feels lit from the inside, her soul shining, a grin pushing at her ears. One finishes a sentence, the other picks it up. They might have seen each other last week, not a decade ago.

'Eleven years,' Sarah says. 'We finished school in 86.'

Bea fires questions at Sarah. She moved to Newcastle with her parents right after A levels. Her dad's a professor; Sarah kept falling over; she ended up going to university there instead of Edinburgh.

'Falling over?' Bea interrupts.

'Epilepsy. It's why I'm here,' she says, 'to see a specialist neurologist. *Another* one.'

'Sounds serious,' Bea says, worried. Sarah waves a hand and carries on with her story. She hooked up with a medical student, James, went to New Zealand with him for his elective, had two kids, Zac and Jasper, and now they're back here.

'Two children, wow,' Bea says with genuine awe.

'I was surrounded by sheep,' Sarah says, opening her hands. 'What am I gonna do?'

'God, poor Dani Bush,' Bea says.

'I know, poor Dani. She's in a better place.' Sarah smiles sadly. 'Plenty of French boys.'

'What's James like?' Bea asks.

'Busy.' From her face Bea can see it is not a happy marriage. She could weep for the expression on Sarah's face.

'How about you, are you married?' Sarah raises her eyebrows at Bea's huge bump. 'Is that Simon's?' Bea gets a little jolt; a tiny electric shock. She never told Sarah about the abortion. She told no one but Granny Dil. Who was in a coma. *Are you married?* The question seems ridiculous, inhabiting as they just were their younger selves. She makes a clicking sound with the sides of her tongue, and mimes cocking a rifle.

'Shotgun. Gavin.' Bea can't think why they did get married, the two of them in the lifeless Register Office, Stan and Rhino their witnesses. When she found she was pregnant, Gavin came over all traditional, they had a flurry of great sex, Bea got swept along.

'What's Gavin like?' Sarah puts her chin in her hands.

'Busy,' Bea says. There's too much else to talk about, she wants to know everything.

Sarah teaches Spanish and French, private lessons while the boys are at school. Her older boy plays the viola. They came back to England for James's job, they're buying a house. Bea asks about Sarah's parents.

'"We just want you to fulfil your potential",' Sarah says, impersonating her father. Bea instantly recognises Morris Rosefoot. 'They've turned into "we",' Sarah rolls her eyes. 'What about *your* parents? You and your dad reconcile the differences?'

For a second, Bea considers telling Sarah about Andrew's wedding; about the thick wall of shame and rage that rises up in the presence of her father and cuts her off from herself. But she can't have that downer on this miraculous coffee shop reunion. She sidesteps the question and tells Sarah instead about Lonnie in the sixth form, Andrew having a son, her work in the lab, her indefinitely postponed Masters. She's rattling on about the implications of her cell research, and then she stops.

'Hang on. *You* were supposed to be the career one, remember? United Nations?' As soon as it's out of her mouth she wants to stuff it back in. Sarah's face becomes blank, then her right eye twitches before she gets her smile back.

'Got me two boys instead,' she says, in a southern American twang, then adds quietly, 'Turns out they're my potential.' And just like that, the eleven years morph into a vast sea, and Bea pulled away on the tide. She starts talking fast, laying out her imminent dilemma. She tells Sarah how she plans to have the baby then get right back to work. The cells in their dishes are needy – *worse* than babies so everyone says – and the whispers are getting louder that Kellars will be bought by a big pharmaceutical company. But Gavin's growing business requires regular trips abroad, and if she doesn't complete the research, someone else will get the credit.

'How the hell will I do this with a *baby*?' she says, more combative than she intends.

'You work part-time,' Sarah says. She doesn't get it. Bea

explains, her words tumbling over each other, that lab work is full-time, twenty-four-seven.

'You can't make it in research *half the week.*' Telling it to Sarah brings the problem screaming to life, and she finds herself glowering at the mound on her middle.

'So do something else?' Sarah suggests. Bea feels out of breath. There *is* nothing else. This work has filled all the gaps. She has to keep it.

'*It is a real possession in the changing fortunes of time*,' Bea says, her voice rising.

'What is?' Sarah says, confused.

'My career. It's in the downstairs loo.' Surely her friend too knows 'Desiderata' by heart.

Sarah glances up at the clock on the wall. Bea's heart clubs away. This is some last-chance saloon – sitting in a café with Sarah Rosefoot suddenly seems like a fantasy. When Sarah walks out, she will disappear in a puff of smoke. She just told Bea she should do something else.

'What?' Bea asks loudly. She almost grabs Sarah by the collar. 'What else shall I do?' It's both crazy and perfectly logical to be asking Sarah's advice; the person who knows her the best, who she's not seen or spoken to in over a decade. And because Bea's in a panic, Sarah clutches her hair, like they used to do in a crisis. *Zut alors!* And the sea disappears. They could be in Sarah's bedroom, with the globe and Spandau Ballet and Picasso. Bea feels the warmth again in her chest. Sarah lets her hair go and brushes herself down. Her face lights up with an idea.

'Be a teacher,' Sarah says. 'You'd be bloody good at it.' Bea tries to smile. It's not the answer she hoped for. Then she remembers that Sarah's about to disappear in smoke. She's already up, pulling on her coat.

'Let me know what you have,' Sarah nods again at the bump. They have a quick, awkward hug, then Sarah's at the door.

'Good luck,' Bea says to her back, remembering the neurologist. And she's gone.

A skill not a state
1998

It's in the eyebrows. The angular rise that forms two faint creases in the middle, as the eyes widen into big blue coins of bewilderment and wonder. At two, Tom's expressions are show-stoppers. Andrew can't be sure, but it's his firm belief that his son is the most charming, handsome, intelligent child the world has ever known. If only Granny Dil could see him. Tom is well admired for his widely spaced eyes, deep blue like Bea's, his full lips, his tufty dark hair, the dimple on his chin. But mainly it's the eyebrows. He inspires stares, and sometimes bursts of laughter. These grate on Andrew, who alone knows there's more to his son than his looks. There's his witty conversation and his great taste in music, for starters. Tom collects admiration from, for example, the health visitor who gave his jabs, shop assistants, all Gallant employees especially Susie, and women in parks. Like this one.

Tom trowels sand now in careful measures into a bucket at the corner of the sandpit. It's still misty, and there's a real January bite in the air, though Tom doesn't seem to notice. Andrew's never been able to get gloves on him. The playground is quiet compared to last Saturday. They're earlier than usual. By ten, the place is crammed, even when it's raining. Andrew will have Tom safely back home for his nap before then.

When the bucket is half full Tom stands up, his little limbs unfolding. He climbs the ladder – hand, hand, foot, foot, as Andrew has shown him – up to the platform where he heaves on the rope, and magically the bucket inches up to join him. Elbows out wide, Tom balances it with some effort at the lip of the funnel. This is when he gives Andrew the look: a wide-eyed *Here goes* look that moves Andrew every time. Tom has done this bucket routine over and over, and each time the same readiness, the *willingness* to be surprised, impressed, all over again, is almost heartbreaking.

Tom's entry into the world gave Andrew a sense of purpose so tangible it's like an item of clothing. Every morning, Andrew puts on his suit and his fatherhood, goes to work, comes home, and is a father. All the while, Lisa has retreated. She has moved further and further away, so that although she still lives in the same house, Andrew can hardly see her. In his deep concern, bordering hopelessness, he phoned his sister for advice. It turned out to be the most revealing conversation of his life to date.

Bea had listened carefully. And then asked some questions.

'Does she have friends?' Bea said slowly, probably sitting on her sofa, in her own house that Andrew has never much wondered about. And now she too has a baby.

Andrew said No, Lisa didn't have friends. But then neither did he. The band stopped after Dec got a transfer. Where would he fit it in anyway?

'What does she like?' Bea asked.

'Soap operas,' he said. He had paused to think. 'And clothes?' He was aware his wife wasn't coming across too well.

'What *doesn't* she like?' Bea had asked.

Though it made him sick in the pit of his stomach, Andrew had forced himself to say it. 'Me?'

Bea's silence was endless.

'Or herself?' she said.

Andrew had never thought of that. How could *Bea* know it?

From his park bench, Andrew finds Tom back at stage one with the trowel. Did he just doze off? Behind the low railings that separate the play area from the park, a tall blonde woman in a mac, with bright orange lipstick, struts back and forth. She was here last Saturday now Andrew comes to think of it, without any apparent children. Lisa would envy the woman her figure. Would she? It's hard to tell what Lisa will admire. Anything, it seems that isn't herself. Bea might be onto something.

Lonnie still comes over to the flat, and does her best to 'cheer Lisa up' (their mother's phrase). 'Is she happier?' Lonnie whispers to Andrew anxiously, when Lisa's not in earshot. He finds this hard to answer. Andrew has no useful definition of happiness. He had thought himself happy, deliriously so, when he first met Lisa, and again with Tom. But he's starting to see that happiness is not a state that lands on you. It's more of a skill that requires concentration. Like putting up a shelf bracket or changing a tyre; a knack.

Tom's at the top of the slide. Andrew gives a thumbs up, crosses his long legs out in front of him and shuts his eyes again, just for a minute. Sleep didn't come last night. He lay awake in the early hours, his head full of numbers on a spinning wheel like a game show. Andrew's in debt. He's reached the limit on the Barclaycard, shifted the MoneyMagic loan over to Credit Suisse and the repayments are crippling. Nothing he can do will make these figures balance. They only tip one way, pushing Andrew closer to the edge of despair.

A dog yelps, and Andrew sits up. Tom's on the platform and the blonde woman's right there, leaning her shins against the low rail so her head is next to Tom's. A large object swings from her neck. A camera. Has she been photographing him? She says something, and whatever the boy says in reply sparks a wide orange smile.

'Excuse me,' Andrew's on his feet walking around the rail as his son tilts the bucket. *Here goes!* The woman turns to Andrew, beaming as though he's won a prize.

'He's adorable,' she says in a voice like syrup. 'Is he yours?'

Homesick

Here she is, in the spring, at the daffodil-yellow front door of Bea's small terraced house, invited. It's like a dream.

In the dark hallway, Moira steps over shoes and squeezes around the parked buggy. She follows Bea through the middle room, piled with clothes, papers, letters, a hairbrush bushy with hair, to the kitchen at the back of the house. She clears a space on the counter stacked with dirty plates and arranges her Tupperware.

'Sorry about the mess,' Bea says, the baby balanced on her shoulder.

'Well,' Moira says, overwhelmed, 'you've got your hands full.' She and Ted came for a flying visit when Clem was a few weeks old. Moira has thought of her eldest daughter almost constantly in the intervening months. And then, three days ago, as though she willed it, Bea telephoned. *Can you come? Just you.*

Moira takes in the shadows under Bea's eyes, the blue now dulled; her sunken cheeks, sallow skin.

'Shall I take her?' Moira holds out her arms. On cue, the baby starts fussing.

'Not much point,' Bea sighs, 'she's always hungry.' She fiddles with her shoulder and hoiks up her top. To Moira's horror, she sees Bea plans to feed her right here, *standing up*. She ushers them both into the front room, sits them on the sofa, finds a little stool and brings through a glass of water. The ground floor consists of one open-plan room off the kitchen. 'A work in progress', Ted and Gavin had agreed. There are daubs of colour on the greying walls, and a rug covering the concrete floor at the living-room end. A row of pink cards line the shelf above the fireplace, some fallen over. Moira watches Bea's head loll – she might be dozing – before she goes back to the kitchen to heat the soup.

She's touched to find the bed all made up in the narrow guest room, bare but tidy. One day this will be Clem's room, if they stay here, which of course they probably won't. People move now, they move all the time. She and Ted were talking about this only the other day, in one of their *analysing* chats that Moira enjoys. While there are things in her own life that she might have done differently, the endless choices her children have are enough to make her dizzy.

The following afternoon is bright and blustery. When they finally make it out of the house with Clem in the buggy, Bea feels like she's in a new body, bouncing not dragging. It must be the soup. It's sod's law that Gavin's business would take off now, when they have a three-month-old baby. Sod's effing law. Clem sleeps in little bursts. It's almost worse than her being awake – at least awake it's obvious she's *alive*. She was whimpering in the buggy just now, but minutes from the house she's given up and dozed off. The wind dances crisp packets along the pavement. With Moira pushing, Bea feels oddly unhinged, like a helium balloon that might float away. She walks in stride with her mother and puts a hand on the buggy.

'Ted used to push you around to stop you bellyaching,' Moira says. 'He paced the streets with you at night.' Then she does an odd laugh and adds, 'You came out fighting.' Bea doesn't press for details.

The sun comes out, dazzling them briefly before the clouds smother it. Moira tells her about Lonnie's place at university in the autumn and how excited she is, if she can just get through the exams.

'Lonnie's a superstar, she'll be fine,' Bea says. Though really she can't fathom how her sister has reached the point of facing the world alone. She grips the handle as they skirt the park, and steers them up onto the hilly meadow, where the three-wheeler comes into its own.

'We didn't have prams like this in my day.' Moira says, 'Even when Lonnie was little.' Her face lights up at a magnolia tree laden with fat pink flowers. Bea finds something unsettling, overly childlike, about her mother's expression.

'I love this time of year,' Moira says. 'A good time to become a pensioner.' They're at the path crossing the meadow. Two small boys tear past with a dipping kite, which catches the wind and darts upwards.

'Sixty.' Bea pulls a face. 'I forgot. Sorry.' Bea's never bothered with birthdays, though she tends to remember them in the weeks after, and feels disconsolate.

Moira shakes her head. 'I don't want to dwell on it.'

'Right,' Bea agrees. 'High blood pressure, retirement, beige.' It comes to Bea she has not asked her mum about her work, or her health, or anything at all.

'Alright, alright,' Moira laughs, 'I will never wear beige.' Her hair has blown out of its neat shape and she tucks it behind her ears. Today she's in blue trousers, almost jeans, and a plum polo neck with a thin black scarf under her raincoat. Bea feels self-conscious, *checking out* her mother in this way. She can see that they do look alike, as people used to say – lean and angular, straight nose, thin lips – apart from the eyes. She takes in more. The gnarly knot on Moira's fingers on the buggy; and her shoulders slope, just a little, in the protective way of older people. And when did her mother go grey?

'Andrew came over and cooked chicken fricassée,' Moira says. Bea stops in her tracks. This is getting into the realm of fantasy. The path has petered out, long grass flicks at her legs.

'*Andrew*?'

'Lisa won't come, we've stopped asking.' Moira's going to say more, but Bea has got stuck.

'*Andrew* cooking *dinner*?'

'People do learn things, Bea,' Moira says, annoyed. 'They

change,' she shakes her head a fraction as though to dislodge the next word. 'They evolve.' A pair of joggers huff between them. 'Look at you with Clem,' Moira says, while Bea stands in the grass, unevolved and gawping. She runs to catch up and grabs the handle. Clem kicks her legs and whimpers. Bea's breasts prickle in response. She marvels at her body's responses; half thrill, half disquiet. She still hasn't resolved her return-to-work plan, and time's running out.

They're in position again with the curtains drawn: Bea on the sofa, Clem asleep on her chest, Moira in the chair by the fireplace. The house is draughty, it feels like deep winter, not April. Bea had meant to get someone round to look at the fireplace. She's given up asking Gavin. How nice it would be to have it crackling away now, instead of the clanking, ineffectual radiator. The other half of the room looks unusually tidy: neat piles against the wall, the table cleared of clutter. And there's a good smell coming from the kitchen. Bea sinks into the sofa with a peaceful, almost blissful feeling, entirely new. The baby moves with her and resettles.

Clem is three babies: she is herself, suckling and whining; and she is the baby Bea didn't have, who she secretly named Simone for those four months; and she is Eliza. It isn't pretending, or even fantasising, Clem *is* all of these. She can't say any of this to Moira, though maybe she knows. It occurs to Bea that her mother has been in this exact place in her past, a baby asleep on her.

'What was it like when you had Andrew?' she asks. Moira has a good think, a faint smile pulls at her lips.

'He cured me of my homesickness.'

'Homesickness?' Bea keeps repeating things.

'It was strange for me,' Moira says, 'living away from David.' This is not what Bea expected. It takes her a moment to recall her mother's other life; to place her with Granny Dil and David. And then further back still.

'He went to the library to look up the meaning of her name,' Moira says, a little shy.

'Who's name?' She's just rewound her mother to a girl, sister to a baby with silk shoes.

'Clementine, of course.'

'Oh.' For a moment Bea had forgotten about Clem, right here, warm on her chest – she keeps doing that since her mother arrived.

'It means "Mild and merciful",' Moira says.

Bea scoffs. 'Gav'll be pleased.' Gavin's main objective being not to be disrupted.

'David was,' Moira says, 'he thought it was a good omen.' Bea thinks of her uncle and smiles. She can hear him saying to Moira in his earnest way 'It's a good omen', both of them nodding into their mugs.

'That was really nice of him to look it up,' Bea says. She'll go and see him when she next visits. Going to that house in Bluebell Lane always feels like a kind of pilgrimage, and David's presence a strange and steadying company. Clem does a high sigh in her sleep. Bea gets another pleasant wave of calm and cups the feet in the soft babygrow. Maybe, just maybe, this will be alright after all, and not the catastrophe she anticipates. She squeezes the feet, closes her eyes, listens to the wind. Clem's toes wiggle. A thought unfolds: she could put on the slippers! They're somewhere in the loft. What would her mother make of that? Bea has no idea. She has a feeling it might spoil this new serenity.

'Did Granny Dil make you soup?' she asks instead. Her mother looks surprised.

'I don't think so,' she says. Bea wonders why they never talk about Granny Dil. And then she remembers it's because she never sees her mother.

'I'm worried about Andrew,' Moira says, obviously changing the subject. But Bea doesn't mind, she wants to hear about Andrew.

'Tell me,' she says. And Moira tells her. About Lisa's absence, Andrew's exhaustion, Tom's beauty.

'He has your eyes,' Moira says. Bea finds she is hungry, ravenous, for this family news; this *gossip*. It might be her version of homesickness. She watches her mother choose carefully the words to describe Andrew's situation.

'He's spending a lot of money on Lisa,' she pauses, 'to make her happy,' Moira shakes her head, this isn't what she means. 'To make her *better*.' Bea thinks she gets the picture. She met Lisa just the once, and the girl seemed totally lost. Though to be fair, on that day she herself hadn't been the most stable or clear-thinking. Bea has a flinch of pessimism that Andrew is out of his depth; that presents won't fix it. They had that odd phone call – nice odd – a real brother and sister exchange like they've never had before. Bea had sat with the phone in her lap long afterwards, hoping he would call again. She doesn't mention this to Moira. She'll send Andrew a copy of 'Desiderata'. Everyone should have a copy, standard issue, when they turn eighteen. Or twelve, even better.

'Money on what?' she asks. Her mother looks pained and bites her lip. If it wasn't for Clem, Bea would be on the edge of her seat. 'On what?'

'She goes to a clinic,' Moira says, 'she's had some *adjustments*.'

'Jesus!' Bea shoots forward and has to catch the baby who falls sideways. 'And Andrew *tells* you this?'

Moira shakes her head. 'Lonnie does. She gets it from Lisa. Bits and bobs when she goes round to help with Tom.' Moira wrings her hands. 'I'm not sure Andrew knows I know.'

'What *kind* of adjustments?' Bea asks, and now Moira looks uncomfortable.

'It's hard to say, we hardly see her.' Moira checks right and left, as though for eavesdroppers. 'She's had her ears pinned back I think,' she winces as she says it. 'And some dental work. The gap's gone.' Then she leans forward and Bea can't imagine what's coming next. 'I think she may have clinical depression,'

Moira whispers. 'A lot of people do. It's on the radio.' Bea had forgotten her mother's dedication to *Woman's Hour* and similar. Maybe Lisa listens too – anyone would get clinical depression listening to that bollocks.

'I know people working on clinical trials,' Bea says, rueful. 'Anti-depressants are a boom. Tested on mice. Shedload of money in it.' With both her hands she adjusts Clem's lolling head. 'Have you said this to Andrew? About the depression?'

'No,' Moira looks disappointed, 'I never seem to—'

'And what does Dad think about Andrew's spending?' Bea interrupts.

Moira looks up sharply. 'He doesn't know.'

Something heavy settles in the room, replacing all the earlier lightness.

'The plot thickens,' Bea says drily.

'It's not a story, Bea. It's not *pretend*.'

'Yeah, well.' She stalls. She's not used to her mother's indignation. 'No, sorry.' Bea had been thinking of her brother, but now she thinks of her father, and without meaning to she lets out a snort. 'And he can't know, because?' She raises her eyebrows. When Moira doesn't answer, Bea answers herself. 'Because his judgement will rain down, is that it? *Christ*.'

Moira rises in her seat. 'When's this going to end, Bea?' She's affronted, almost angry. Bea is so taken aback she can't think of a reply. Moira takes a breath. 'Isn't it about time you laid down your— all your grudges, whatever they may be. They're so *old* now. It seems to me your resentment is a habit. And Ted and Gavin get along so well. And Ted wants to get on with his grandpa-ing. He loves it.' It's the most she has ever said on the subject. Bea suspects her mother has made this speech in her head many times. She might have rehearsed it in her train carriage. It's true that Dad and Gavin get along, but some things are fluid and others are fixed. If she's learnt anything in the lab, it is that you respect the things you can't change. She'll leave Dad to Gavin. They're welcome to each other.

Leaving gift

'What we're gonna do here is bring out the metaphor,' Noah says, deeply serious, to his team of actress, ASM, lighting guy, and Jonno. They're on the stage in the miniature studio theatre, for a 'Cast and Crew Meet'. Lonnie tilts her head to signal deep thought and tries to conceal her smile. She's a big fan of metaphor, applying as it does to everything, everywhere, but here she wants to say *metaphor for what?*

'OK, back to stations.' Noah double-claps over his head and flexes his biceps in his black T-shirt. Noah's a third year, which puts him in a whole other world. Lonnie scurries off backstage and out to the workshop.

She stands on the wooden strip of road with her paintbrush. Is it a bit narrow? She hunkers down and measures with her arms: only just enough room for clothes, suitcase and Erica. It'd better be OK because there isn't enough wood for another go. She sits down on the end, where the white stripes have already dried. The road curves away pleasingly to the right, thanks to the jigsaw Noah came in brandishing this morning. On loan from Dr Carl Raw, the lecturer with the weird doormat hair, his subject Commedia dell'arte, whatever that is.

'Wow,' Noah says, striding into the workshop, 'cool road.'

'Thanks,' Lonnie says, swallowing a yelp of joy.

'Seriously.' He squats down and runs his hand over the 'tarmac'. 'I wouldn't have the first clue how to swing that saw.' He stands up straight and gives a slow bow, his palms flat together as though in prayer. 'Pink-haired Goddess of all things practical. Amazing.'

Lonnie grins at him. She almost blurts out about the chair and pepperpot, but Jonno comes in from the far door and slaps the script down on the worktop. They hunch over it, muttering, while she pretends to sand the far edge.

'A horizon backdrop?' Noah turns to her, raising his voice. 'Or skyline?' He draws angles with his hand in a robotic motion. 'Any chance of that, Lorrie?'

Lonnie looks up from her pretend absorption. She's read the script, but to her it seems like a lot of words not quite in the right order. They don't wait for her reply.

'Or get Paddy to do it with lighting?' Noah says to Jonno, who snaps the folder shut.

'Could take it to Edinburgh,' Jonno says as they leave the workshop. What *is* that? What is everyone taking to Edinburgh?

Alone again, Lonnie breathes deeply. Most of her last three weeks have been spent in this long, thin workshop, thinner still due to the sets of previous productions piled against the walls and hung on hooks. She keeps knocking against a large round fish with green and blue gills, teardrops of tissue paper that flutter when a breeze comes in through the high windows set at pavement level. The view from the workshop is feet and ankles. It smells of dust, and paint, and something vaguely citrus. ASM; she even loves the acronym: Assistant Stage Manager. Not something she's earned, all first-years have to do it. Noah is the director, and, she assumes, stage manager since there doesn't appear to be anyone else. The play is *The Road*. Not the famous book, a one-act play written by a German third-year student called Van, or Vin, and starring Noah's sleek, political girlfriend Erica, always dressed in black, with a nose ring thin as a cobweb, and asymmetrical hair. With a few well-placed nods, Lonnie has given Erica to believe they share the same political opinions. Three weeks of opinions flying at her, like wasps, from all directions. Lonnie has observed that her own unusual hair generally substitutes for an opinion. Luckily.

It was the chair. And the pepperpot. People would come into their kitchen at home and say 'Nice chair', running their hand over its high back with the pleasing oval cut out at the top. Either Mum or Dad would invite them to sit on it. Then they would be handed the pepperpot: a slender wooden cylinder with an hourglass curve, smooth to the touch and heavy. The sitter would turn it over, stroke it and mutter a compliment. While in the chair, Joe, Dad's workmate, had smacked the pepperpot on his open palm, like a baseball bat.

'T'riffic Lon,' he said, 'how about you come and work with us?' And Lonnie had watched hope light up her father's face.

Was it after this the world became suddenly flat? She'd be walking home after college, past the chippy, hairdresser, I LOVE MY PC, ('I don't,' Dad always said when they drove past), Boots, A Slice of Cak (the 'e' disappeared again every time it reappeared), and from nowhere, she felt the urge to hurl her backpack through a shop window and watch the glass shatter to pieces.

Bea had gone to Uni, so it could be done. Lonnie would do Theatre Set Design. Why not? She'd been to the theatre once in Cheltenham – a pantomime and a bit crap, but the way the whole stage rotated was the coolest thing she'd ever seen.

'You'll be great at that, Lon,' her friends said. 'Look at your chair!'

The night before she left, she had packed up her belongings into two big boxes, plus a knotted bin bag with her duvet and pillow. Was this enough? Too much? Maybe she should take next to nothing like Bea did.

After waving Bea off at the station, Lonnie's six-year-old self had stared, in Bea's room, with grave concern, at the row of hedgehogs left on the shelf. Her concern, she clearly remembers, was for both Bea and the hedgehogs: the forgetter and the forgotten. She rehoused the hedgehogs in her room. Only years later, when Lonnie went to visit, did she see it was Bea's intention to shed herself; leave herself here and start again. On the eve of her own departure, Lonnie felt sure this must be impossible; the line between past, present and future being more durable than that. At least she hoped so.

Dad had come upstairs and stood in her doorway, eyeing the boxes with dismay. After a long while, he came in and sat down on the bed. He was holding a hammer. The one with the chunky wooden handle Lonnie had used for the shelves, stepping down across the wall, and now almost empty. Maybe that was the advantage of a swift exit: leave everything, leave enough of yourself; keep your options open.

Dad held up the hammer on both palms. It made her think of the harvest festival.

This was a leaving gift.

She wobbled over to the bed and sat down. He gave her a peck in her hair, placed the hammer gently on her lap, and cleared his throat.

'Take it with you,' he said. He may as well have laid himself down there, for all the sorrow in his voice.

She almost said, *Don't put this all on me, Andrew's up the road.* She almost said *I'm sorry for whatever Bea did.* She almost said, *You'll be alright.* I'll *be alright.* She almost said, *Come with me, help me with the set designs.*

It was only a hammer.

'Thanks,' she said.

After he went downstairs, Lonnie gripped the handle and her knuckles turned to gristle. She could not imagine these hands making sets for plays, yet that's what she'd signed up for. She packed the hammer in the box on top of her pyjamas, reached down, and pulled up a snow globe. Barcelona, her favourite and a present from Bea. She shook it hard and watched the tiny flecks of glitter and red starfish swirl around in the blue. It came to her all of a sudden. Snow globes were a metaphor for Bea! Kicking up a storm that sends their father to a dark place, leaving Lonnie responsible for the rescue.

Bea hadn't been home since she got pissed up and passed out at the wedding. Or maybe once, with Gavin. Once in three years. Lonnie always had to go and visit her – everything on Bea's terms. At her last visit, Bea had quizzed her about Andrew and Lisa. Lonnie told her Lisa was better now she's taking pills she got from the doctor. And if Bea was so concerned, why didn't she come and see Andrew herself? They'd almost had a row. As usual, Bea just changed the subject, and Lonnie knew it was pointless to keep going.

In her bedroom, she shook the Barcelona globe again, then shoved the swirling red snowstorm back into the box, and flipped the lids shut.

*

It's Wednesday. The show goes up on Friday. It's what happens to shows, they 'go up', like balloons. Lonnie creeps into the back of the studio theatre and sits in the dark. Onstage, dimly lit, Erica sits cross-legged on the road (the road!) amongst piles of bundled-up towels. Noah's in the second row, chewing a pencil and rubbing his temples.

'It's not that it's long and winding, it's that I can't see an *end*,' Erica says, squinting in the spotlight towards Lonnie, who sinks down to make herself invisible. Erica rifles through the piles and holds up a towel, 'I need actual *clothes*.' She glares at Noah. She's gone off script.

'I know babe, just keep the intensity. You're nailing it, feels like Beckett.'

'My fault,' Lonnie says. Without thinking she grabs a garment from the seat in front, Erica's jumper, animal-soft in her hand. 'Here.' She throws it onto the stage where it lands on the edge and slithers off. Erica leans down and recovers it, blinking out at Lonnie.

'Thanks.'

Lonnie sits forward, 'I'll get the pile from the costume—'

'Later,' Noah waves a hand. 'Go from "end".'

Erica hugs the jumper to her chest, deep mauve with a

dangling arm like an unravelling heart. Lonnie gets a squirm of pleasure and chews her lip in the dark. Erica's deep voice rises, and she looks meaningfully at the signpost (the signpost!) then springs to her feet, making Lonnie jump. Something clicks behind Lonnie's head and Erica turns orange.

'Try an edge of green, Paddy,' Noah says. Now Erica and the rest of the stage look like they've been slimed.

'It's not the fucking *frog* chorus,' Erica snaps. Lonnie claps a hand over her mouth and gets a look from the stage that she can't read.

'Take five!' Noah shouts, though there's no need to shout, they're all about two metres from each other. Erica shoots Lonnie a smirk, sits down and arranges the jumper on the towels. Lonnie waits in case she looks again, and when Erica doesn't, she creeps back to the workshop.

A breeze shimmers the fish's blue-green gills. No feet at the small windows today. No lectures on Wednesday afternoons. Lonnie lines up strips of wood on the workbench for the front-of-house sign. It's her last job. She takes up her own hammer, the ones in the basket are too thick or too thin, and curling her fingers around the smooth wooden handle, she feels a tug in her chest. She bangs in a few half-hearted nails and then sets the hammer down. A whole six weeks has finally caught up with her. What she wants is for someone else to know she is here; someone who *knows* her to be able to picture her in this corridor of a room, old sets propped against the wall. And all the terrifying, gorgeous people. Give her a phone, right now, and she will dial any member of her family, any friend, the guy in the chip shop on the High Street, and give them every detail of this place.

She could call Andrew, only his world bears no resemblance. Mum would listen and be nice, and ask if her bedroom has enough natural light. Dad would get *this* room – the basket of hammers, saws and pliers attached to a magnetic strip – but to Lonnie's knowledge he has never been in a theatre. Her friends are scattered around the country, and too dangerous to call them in case they've found a new place in the world without her. Maybe she'll call Bea. Though she's got the baby, and Mum says she's 'finding it difficult'. Bea would get it, or she'd get it enough. Lonnie could ask *How did you do it?* Or she could make Bea tell her whatever it was that happened with Dad. Or she could ask her sister how long before this floating, adrift feeling will pass. The fish's dull black eye stares from the hook. It occurs to Lonnie that Bea may not have any of the answers; may still be floating herself. The thought makes her shiver.

She picks up the hammer and squeezes its perfect grip, balances its perfect weight.

She won't call anyone. She's not sure she can even describe her new life to herself yet.

A shuffling from the far end makes Lonnie look up. Erica is in the doorway, watching her. How long has she been there?

'I love your hair,' Erica says with a half-smile.

'It's a metaphor,' Lonnie says, quick as a flash. Erica throws back her head and laughs – a rich 'har-har' sound, almost a gargle – and Lonnie catches the tiny point of her neck in profile, delicate as a fish bone.

Four faces

'If I had a house like that,' Billy says 'I'd put a tennis court in the basement.'

'Wouldn't fit,' Joe says.

'Ping-pong then, pool table, darts.' He aims an imaginary dart at the traffic lights. Billy is Ted's new apprentice. It's working out well, except for today now the van's overheated in all this traffic, and they've pulled into a garage forecourt by the T-junction that's causing the problem. Three-way lights for road closure, cars lined up in every direction, engines running. The three of them stand on the grass verge. It's a dank October day, and they've not even made it to site – an oversized house being carved up into flats. Joe's fed up with Ted for insisting they pass by the supplier to pick up the extra wall ties, not required in the building regs. They wouldn't be stuck here if it wasn't for the detour. Ted ignores Joe's mutterings about Ted's 'paranoia', his over-dedication to safety. It's a longstanding grumble. And now there's a turn for the worse, which Ted will have to admit to Joe if it carries on.

'What would you put in the basement, Ted?' Billy asks. The two men look at him, one only a boy really.

'Casino,' Ted says, joining in. Or maybe a hot tub, for all his aches. Though that'd only fix his body, and it's his head that's the problem. Or both.

The lights change, four or five cars speed off, an extra one sneaks through, and the rest grind to a revving halt. The itchy frustration of the drivers is felt by the three on the verge. Petrol fumes billow around them. Ted clocks a big oak tree over the other side, still with all its leaves. It's the one tree he can name, after the arguments on the last site about a protection order.

The new owner wanted it chopped down. Ted was firmly on the side of the mighty oak, solid, heroic, its leathery trunk so obviously a monument to time. He'd been close to tears when the decision came to save it. Did Billy just ask him a question?

'He's taking stock,' Joe explains to Billy. 'He does this, drifts off, since his daughter left last month for university.'

'University.' Billy nods, impressed.

'Hmm?' Ted checks his watch. 'We'll give it another ten minutes.' Gunning cracks rip the air and they all take a step back. A silver hatchback roars past, through the red light. For a horrible moment, it looks set for a head-on collision with the Astra coming through. Astra's breaks screech, the hatchback speeds off, and a long-held horn blares out, followed by a chorus of badly tuned honking like a pack of angry, tone-deaf geese. The horns peter out. Back to the revving and the stink.

'Death wish,' Joe says, shaking his head.

'Nutter,' Billy says.

Ted's thought about offering to teach Billy to drive. He still gets dewy-eyed about the lessons he gave Bea, round and round the carpark, watching the sunset. He had the photo album out again last night while Moira was at one of her classes (she finds his nostalgia irritating). Caravan, beach, spades, ice creams – a life in holidays. If Ted had his way, photo albums would contain cement mixers, stud walls, dinner time, changing the tyre: a proper record. There are pages and pages of Lonnie as a baby, in different arms and laps. Moira then Andrew then Bea. Ted likes to flick to the back of the third album. A picture of him and Bea, on either side of the Fiesta, doors open. Moira must have taken it from the front path with the sun behind their heads. Both of them are in shadow, leaning on their open doors like in a car advert, their teeth shining from their grinning mouths. It's Ted's favourite photo. He hardly ever sees Bea now, and he's only got himself to blame for that.

He had sat there, clutching the album, with the dull pain in the back of his skull moving slowly towards his eyes, *coming to get me*. And there are days when a shadow comes right over, and he can't get himself going. All he wants to do is lie down and hide.

It starts to rain. A fine drizzle, which the men wipe from their faces like a light sweat. There's another round of honking as another driver runs the red. Then the quiet *ffd ffd ffd* of windscreen wipers. Ted taught Lonnie to drive as well, though she hasn't passed her test yet – one failed attempt and she gave up. And now she too is gone. Ted takes deep breaths. He needs to keep a hold of himself.

It all comes down to Before and After. Before and after Moira, his job loss, Lonnie, Bea and the boy. Gain, loss, gain, loss. Not so much balancing out as resettling, like footprints in wet sand. Lonnie, his sweet accident sent to save him. And now when he opens the front door, the absence of her bright smile from her pink head crushes him, almost knocks him over. It can't be right. Ted's beginning to suspect something medical, something *decrepit*. Stomach ulcer, brain tumour, madness. He's distracted, weary, naps at all hours, forgets things.

Moira gave him the once-over – blood pressure, skin test, peak flow – and with a tender kiss on his cheek pronounced him fit as a fiddle, only missing his younger daughter. But Ted fears she's wrong. He's sixty-three and feels a hundred. He'll take his telegram from the Queen, right now, and be done with it. 'Don't dwell,' Moira says, 'Keep moving.' It's what she's doing; it's what she's always done.

What if I can't?

'Hang on,' Joe says, touching Ted on the shoulder. 'Isn't that your lad's little boy?' Ted looks around for Andrew and Tom. The drizzle has stopped, the pavements are bare and shining, and there's only the queue of cars and an old man in a trilby hat tottering past the oak. What would they be doing out here anyway? Joe points at the white van right in front of them, third in the queue for the lights. Four multicoloured faces stare out at Ted from the side panel. He takes it in, and gapes.

'What in the—'

It's Tom.

A different Tom gazes out of each square: pink and green and orange and yellow.

'That guy in the seventies,' Billy taps his forehead.

'Sixties,' Joe says, 'Al something.'

'Andy Warhol,' Billy says with a clap, pleased as punch.

That's it. That's what Ted's looking at. An Andy Warhol version of his grandson. Four larger-than-life Tom's, when he was a toddler, each with a different expression. That face! Such a perfect window into his little soul. Here's Tom on a background of orange, his face all confusion, two small creases between his tilted eyebrows. In only one of the pictures can Ted find the boy's own blue eyes, and to this one Ted says 'Hello Tom,' because even printed on metal, he can't ignore his own grandchild. Ted scans across. 'Blooming Kids!' is written large on a tub in the bottom corner.

Why? How?

Ted, Joe and Billy study one face at a time, and without meaning to they mimic Tom's expressions one by one, in slow motion. From their cars, the drivers – and many of them are looking – watch three men spanning three generations, side by side on the tarmac, pulling faces. Bewildered at first, then screwed up in anger, then wide-eyed in terror, then they all break into beaming smiles, mirroring Tom's face in the last square, pink on purple, his mouth wide, his face lit with elation.

Confusion, fury, fear, joy.

'Well, well,' Joe says, still fixed on the van. 'A poster boy for vitamins.'

'I'd buy 'em,' Billy says. 'He's a smasher.'

Ted shakes his head in disbelief. Maybe he is going doolally. He scrutinises each brightly coloured face and sinks into each emotion. The expressions cover a lot, but there's plenty missing. Sorrow, for example, *hurt*. And scorn, hatred, despair. But here's the fourth Tom, shining out, radiant, gleeful. If only he, Ted, could stick with that last one. He must try harder for it.

The van pulls away, beeping its horn, and Ted waves and leans out, further and further, watching the faces shrink and disappear.

You won't find yourself
2002

'Genetic information from two individuals carried on chromosomes within the nucleus of gametes.' Revision from the last lesson. Bea writes the keywords on the whiteboard and shouts them out over the scraping of stools, low talking, bag thudding, pencil-case shuffling.

'Sex,' she says loudly, to an instant hush. 'What you've all been waiting for.' A murmur from the third row, giggles from the back, a loud snort.

'Robbie's waiting—'

'Shut up, Nabil.'

'Carpels and pistils,' Bea continues. 'Remember these? And stamen, anther, producing pollen.' She loves the words in biology, perfectly balanced between fact and mystery. In the second row, Laura Curd whispers something to Kelly Brooker. Bea lets it go. These two, sparky and irreverent, always together, remind Bea of her and Sarah at that age. Sarah has gone quiet lately. Bea means to get in touch but life keeps getting in the way.

'Strawberries can reproduce sexually,' Bea says to the class. 'Did you know that?' More giggles, nudges, a 'twit-twoo' whistle. The lab teeters on the edge of hysteria. Monica Jordan swings her hair.

'Juicy, Miss.'

It's the last lesson of the day, the last term of the school year, and the whole class, pink and ripe behind their benches, jitters with anticipation. Except for Magnus Chase, always in the front row, always poised and studious.

'Juicy, as Monica says.' Bea looks them over. 'This crazy world might be changing fast, but we're still not so different to plants. We all carry the same DNA. Where?'

'Cells, Miss,' they chorus.

'Where in the cell?'

'The nucleus.'

'Nucleus of the cell,' Bea announces, 'home of genetic information. Chromosomes are a way of organising this information. Sexual reproduction, the combining of pairs of chromosomes.'

Cells. Feeding and nurturing, the watch-and-wait, cutting-edge science. The life Bea could have had and still mourns, some days. Hard to say if it's the science she misses, the not knowing, chasing something just out of reach, or the prestige of a big drug company. The life she glimpsed snatched away, not of her choosing. So easy to imagine a life more sexy, more illustrious than the one she has. Her daydreams of herself alone in a giant laboratory – a loaded pipette gun, great fridges full of genetic information – could be her own inventions, exaggerations, mistaken memories.

The noise in this lab rises.

'Robbie's gonna combine his genetic infor—'

'Enough.' Bea holds up her hand and they fall quiet. She has this down. It surprises her sometimes, how willing the kids are to listen when she calls for their attention. This year, for the first time, she is a form tutor. Her own class, year nine. *On the cusp,* as Bea thinks of them. Lumbering and desperate, sprouting, careful, carefree; knowing nothing and everything. They have taught her a great deal. At their age, Bea was in a frantic rush. They remind her how much she loved school, not that she knew it at the time. She always forgets the good things.

'Page forty-two,' Bea says. The most well-thumbed page, with all the diagrams.

'Sperm and the egg.' It all comes down to this. Clem, in her new school sweatshirt, five years old, bright-eyed. A fusion, an inconvenience, a marvel. Bea can hardly believe her daughter is at school, right now, an exercise book open in front of her, her small hand gripping the pencil, teeth clamped over her lower lip. Clem, at breakfast yesterday, with a plastic red nose covering her face.

'I found it,' she said.

'Will the teacher let you wear it?' Bea asked. Red Nose Day was ages ago.

Clem nodded, 'It's expressing myself. That's good.'

'That *is* good.' Bea's always relieved when they hit agreement. 'When did you do that?' Bea asked, pointing at the messy collage beside Clem's bowl.

'Collaboration.' Bea laughed and Clem looked offended. 'It means you have to let everyone stick things on.'

'I bet you're good at that,' Bea said.

'Not really.'

What should Bea say? *At least you can run fast.*

'Do you like being a teacher?' Clem asked.

'Some days,' Bea said. *When I'm not wishing I was in another life*. How truthful to be? At least Clem didn't ask 'Do you like Daddy?'

Clem stayed with Gavin again last night. Bea had watched his car pull away, the back of Clem's head bobbing left to right on the back seat, the way she does only when she's singing. Probably S Club 7 on the stereo. Long after the car had gone, Bea stared up the empty street, where she and Gavin had lived for seven years. Nothing in it looked familiar. Front doors in bright colours, a neat hedge in between two wild ones, an orange camper van parked at the end of the street, half on the pavement. She couldn't get any breath in. Some horrible trick was being played on her. She almost fell backwards into the house and paced all evening until she was tired enough to sleep.

Her fault, of course, the final straw being Bea's brief, shabby, affair with Nathan at Kellars. Gav has his own confessions that Bea neither wants nor needs to hear. He would have left anyway, they do nothing but fight.

Bea talks the class through the reproductive systems. Sperm cells, egg cells, genes within the cell: astonishingly tiny, astonishingly mighty. She tolerates the 'cock' and 'scrote' mutterings.

'Ever thought about what determines your eye colour? Height? Whether you can roll your 'r's?' Apparently not. 'A combination of alleles.' She writes this up, the pen squeaks on the whiteboard. If only they knew what a colossal word it is. 'Take note,' she raises her volume. 'It's the key to how you turn out.' *How everything turns out.* Clem, on the back seat, head bobbing.

'How many pairs of chromosomes do we have?' she asks the class.

'Twenty-three,' Magnus Chase answers.

'So. Two to the power of twenty-three, *those* are the possibilities!' She says this to everyone, but it only makes an impression on Magnus (it's beyond the GCSE remit). Magnus alone has respect for haploid gametes. Bea wonders what she would have done with a son. A boy might be less mysterious, easier to know. As if anyone is knowable, after nature is messed about by fate and nurture and memory. Bea has a private dread of Clem as a teenager, but she squashes it back down whenever it taunts her.

Of the three science labs, this one is Bea's favourite, still with the old-fashioned wooden benches, under constant threat of a Formica makeover when the money appears. She likes the way the wood keeps the place a bit darker. 'Dingy', her fellow science teachers say, preferring the light bouncing off surfaces in the other labs. This one has the twin skeletons, the Guardians of Death, hanging at the back. One of them does a sudden leg kick now, starting up a can-can.

'Sit down, Jamila,' Bea says firmly and tries not to smile. It is Jamila's favourite trick, and a good one: hook a ruler around the back of the knee joint, and flick. It makes Bea think of dancing in the dark with Lonnie in another lifetime, in between benches not unlike these. And didn't they have some cells under the microscope?

'Does a bigger dick produce more sperm?' Bea sighs. 'No, sperm is produced and stored in the testes. Pay attention.' She unfolds another and reads. 'Is there a limit to how many times humans can have sex?' Bea groans inwardly. 'No.' Should she clarify that? 'Some medical conditions might affect things.'

She has opened it up for questions, end of the lesson. They post them in a box and Bea reads them out. Other teachers don't get this line of questioning, Bea knows this. But for the current topic she likes to foster an atmosphere of play and openness. The questions are both predictable and infinite. She opens another.

'Sex should be only for love. Discuss.' This sets off whispers. The Guardians stare with their hollowed faces. Morality always asserts itself. They're intense, these youngsters, especially the girls. The question puts Bea on edge.

Neither be cynical about love... it is as perennial as the grass. Not in Bea's world.

'Sex should be only for love,' she reads again. At their age, Bea had allowed a randy French boy into her pants, and a year or so older she discovered sex proper. An erotic act of defiance; of independence. A libidinous *talent*. Love, for Bea, has never featured. Not even once. And the wrongness of this, the sadness of it, strikes her now, up in front of the whole class awaiting her advice. Bea feels a need to warn them – to give them the information no one gave her. Bea's own mother, *half of her genome,* gave her nothing.

'Listen,' she says quietly, and they do. 'Having sex is serious. It's the most serious thing two bodies can do.' Behind their benches the class look uneasy, confused at the change of tone. 'Serious, sensual, raucous, wonderful,' she pauses. Some of the faces have changed to amused, some prim. 'But keep it in its place,' she says with more urgency than she means to. This is what she wants to tell them. A tentative hand goes up in the second row. Laura Curd.

'So it *should* be only for love?' Her face says she's sceptical.

It gets the group murmuring.

'I don't mean that, no. Sex is biology, reproduction. It's pleasure, and connection. When you start to have sex, have it for all these things. Especially for pleasure,' she looks around the keen, open faces, 'but don't have it to fill a gap.' She's already gone too far, so she may as well finish. 'You won't find yourselves in it.' The class stare at her in bemused silence for a few seconds. Then the comments start to fly.

'It can be an addiction.'

'Like an eating disorder.'

'Donut or a blow job?'

'You're so gross. Like *you've* ever—'

'Miss is talking about self-esteem, aren't you Miss?'

'Some women and girls feel empowered.'

'On sex lines. My dad's mate got caught—'

'In *Sex and the City*.'

'None of them are *prostitutes*.'

'Have to be a big gap if *I* was filling it.'

'Not talking about the phone, dickhead.'

'Make a load of money, just the noises.' A horrible slurping comes from a group of boys near the back. The whole bench erupts in heavy breathing, falsetto cries, 'Yes! Yes!'. A few of the girls throw things in their direction, screwed-up paper, pens.

What did Bea think she could tell them? They will all do what they will do, just as she did. Dismay creeps over her. She checks the time, scans the whiteboard. And now the whole class is laughing, almost all of them. Robbie Taylor, standing up, smacks his own backside repeatedly. Nabil tries to pull him down, while Kelly and Laura crack up, covering their eyes. Levity, hilarity, have won the day. The whole lab bursts with life: expressing themselves, and that's *good*.

'Clearly not ready for my wisdom,' Bea shouts over the din, and the noise level drops a notch. 'Revise the whole topic. Last test next lesson. You're all experts, so I expect all A's.' Three loud beeps ring out in the lab. Saved by the bell.

The Guardians of Death stare with gaunt severity while the class files out in shoves and shrieks.

'Strawberries and cream—'

'*You* can!'

Bea stares right back at the Guardians as quiet returns. Magnus Chase, precise in his packing up, remains in his place.

'How was that Magnus? Bit noisy?' Bea often gets useful feedback from Magnus. He blinks a lot in the pause before answering. He reminds her of Uncle David: measured, weighing up all the evidence. And there's a lot to be said for facts; for staying with the evidence.

'It wasn't all about biology,' Magnus says.

'No,' she says slowly, unease pressing in. She should stick more closely to the scheme of work.

'But I don't mind,' Magnus says. 'Will the combination of alleles be in the test?'

'Yes,' Bea says without hesitation. If they were in a soap opera, they might do a high five. Instead, Magnus gives a satisfied nod and picks up his bag. Bea almost applauds him walking out. As she watches him leave, the muscles in her jaw, her shoulders, her gut, all relax. In this small moment, she is exactly where she belongs. The outside sun gives the benches a soft shine.

The Guardians continue their stares, and Bea, suddenly sick of their uncompromising, hollowed faces, lifts her middle finger to the back of the lab. Immediately, she knows the action is uncalled for and holds up her hand.

'Sorry,' she says to the skeletons. They're just doing their job. Keeping watch, reminding us what is fixed, what we all have in common in the end.

Too much space
2004

June light blazes in from the big double windows and the dormers up top. It bounces off the white walls, off the three shining pillars holding up the mezzanine floor, off the pale wood under his feet. Ted wants to shade his eyes. The place is unrecognisable from what he and his men took on six months ago; a building with rooms, a kitchen with table and chairs: a *home*. Everything has been ripped out, gutted like a fish, leaving no corner in the shadows. The stairs, suspended in thin air with no bannister or rail, double back at a slim platform against the wall, and land at the edge of the room.

Ted stands with the couple at the bottom of the stairs, facing a long, pale-green sofa, centre-stage, thick plastic bunched around its stocky legs. It reminds Ted of the silly bunched things Bea used to wear on her ankles and wrists years ago. The sofa's a four-seater? Six? It must have been delivered this morning. He wants to push it over into a corner, against a wall. A sofa should be nestled in, not stranded like this. He turns slowly to take in the 'island' with four tall stools, giant lollipops on metal poles, also draped in plastic.

Ten, maybe fifteen years ago, Ted would have been dazzled by this minimalism, this *ambition*. Looking around now he feels bewildered. He would struggle to describe the place. It's not a room or even a house. Ted's all for knocking through, but there are limits. As a builder, he has been ambitious in his way, he's taken on big projects, finished them on time and on budget, give or take. Ted's a homemaker. He extends, widens, partitions. Nowadays, he does the contracts, works with the architect and directs his men without breaking his back. Or his hip. The right one's giving him increasing jip. He'll have to get a new one, Moira says, but even the thought makes him tremble. Over the last few years, Ted's concerns have moved from the general to the specific: from dark, doldrum clouds to a fierce shooting in the joints. On balance, he prefers it this way. Though the clouds still hover.

He's been calling this one his last job. The couple are middle-aged, with a bit of money. No, a *lot* of money. The fella's in computers. They wanted to 'open things up.'

'Bring the light in!' the fella said. He might be religious, though Ted's pretty sure that God would not approve of computer software – any and all of it. Or homes without rooms. They wanted the sort of house you find in a magazine, or on the telly on one of those programmes that gets Ted thumping the arm of the sofa, shouting 'Ponce!' This fella doesn't seem like a ponce. Strangely, Ted feels sorry for him, though he couldn't say why. Nice car, good job, nice wife. Ted can't really tell if wives are nice or not, except his own, who is a wonder.

People like this final meeting, where everything's cleared and swept, and the workers disappeared. Only Ted in his clean shirt, to hand over the keys. A ceremony of sorts. Usually, he finds it deeply satisfying, but today he would have liked it if Joe had stayed. All of them – a few more bodies to fill the place.

The fella pats him on the back several times, the woman gives excited shrug-smiles that say *Aren't we lucky?* The three of them walk around the edges, their footsteps loud on the wood. They take a turn around the island, where the fella lays his hands on the cold marble and nods appreciatively.

'Thank you,' he says. 'You've done wonders.'

Has he? Ted takes the keys from his pocket and places them on the counter. He shakes both their hands and the fella pumps his arm up and down. Ted hurries to the front door and as he closes it, his final image is the two of them, perched on the end of the long sofa, side by side in a sea of light.

'They looked lost,' he says to Moira that evening. 'They've got too much space.' He's changed out of his shirt, and he's back in his sweatshirt and tracksuit bottoms. He pulls out the chair opposite her –Lonnie's homemade chair that's now Ted's chair – and a yellow Post-it note flutters to the floor. He stares at the words LA CHAISE in Moira's careful hand. He picks it up, sticks it on the seat next to him, and the same thing happens. 'I know that one, you can put it away,' Moira says. He puts it in his pocket and sits down. He has told Moira bits about this job, but now he describes it in detail. Moira half-listens, still checking her books, then gives him her full attention when the couple arrive and the three of them walk around the empty space.

'I don't understand people,' Ted says, shaking his head. Moira looks off to the side of him. She might be thinking about the house, or her French words, or something else entirely. Then she meets his eyes, her own green eyes shining.

'That's alright,' she says with tenderness. 'You don't need to understand *people*, you only need to understand yourself.' She floors him sometimes, the things she says.

'Not sure I've even got that licked,' Ted mutters. She puts her hand on his and they exchange a long, comforting look, brewed over a long marriage.

Moira sighs. 'I think for most of us that's a life's work,' she says sadly. Ted turns this over. A life's work to understand yourself. Yep, that's about right. But why's she so sad about it? He's about to question her, but she's too quick.

'Shall we have a drink to celebrate?' Moira says, as though a thought has just come to her. She gets up and reaches for the door labelled LE PLACARD where the glasses are kept.

'Celebrate?' Has he forgotten something important?

Moira raises an eyebrow. 'Your last job?'

'Ah. Well.' Ted should have an answer ready, but he doesn't.

'"Last set of keys," you said this morning. Joe will finally get to be the real boss. New baby, new job, he's waited long enough for both.'

'You've not spoken to Joe, have you?' Ted says, anxious. She tells him she hasn't. 'I just can't imagine it, Moy.' He leans forward, arms on the table. 'Not working. Never pricing up another job.' He sounds wistful, like a boy. That gutted place today was unsettling, but Ted can choose his jobs. He'll keep on with the pricing, planning and closing, and leave the rest to Joe. He doesn't tell Moira about his lurking fear of After. Even though everything is different now, Ted doesn't trust a life without work.

'So keep going then,' Moira says, simply. He can see from her face it's what she was expecting.

'I might,' he says, 'just a few more.'

'*Un peu*,' Moira says, and tuts. 'Nope, that's not it.' She sits down again and searches the pages.

'*Très bon*!' he says. He has the urge to sing. He'll tell her now. 'I'm thinking about a get-together. Soon.' That couple in all that space has made him want to gather his own family around him. 'It's forty years in September,' he says. 'That's Ruby.'

'I told *you* that,' Moira says, smiling.

'Well, I'm taking the reins,' he says, fists on the table. He tells her he's thought about a barbecue, or a dinner out. And then today he decided to scale it up.

'We'll have a weekend away,' he announces.

'A weekend?' Moira says, alarmed.

'I'll find us a nice house to rent,' Ted says, brimming with the thought of it. 'Maybe a swimming pool. The whole family.'

Only one major character

At the splash, they all bundle out onto the deck: Moira, Ted, Bea, Clem, Andrew, Lisa and Lonnie. Tom flaps across the lawn towards them, dripping and shivering. The pool quivers yellow behind him. He's got a big grin on his face from the jump, or somersault, or whatever he's been building up to. He needs his dinner, Moira thinks, looking at Tom's ribcage pushing like a rack against the pale skin.

'Your turn!' Tom says, pointing at Bea. And they all look at Bea as she tries to wriggle out of it. Moira can't blame her, it's getting dark and a bit nippy. Andrew pats Tom's bare shoulder and smiles down at him. Clem jumps up and down on her toes. Moira finds Tom a towel.

'You promised!' Tom's whining now. 'We *shook* on it.' Moira will get him inside for a hot chocolate.

'I'll do it,' Ted says.

Moira wheels around. Ted's jaw is set. Tom starts to protest. A look is exchanged between Ted and Bea, too quick for Moira to interpret.

'I'll do it,' Ted says again and limps off through the vast kitchen. Moira glares at Bea, but she's busy placating Tom. She goes after Ted, knowing that nothing she says will make a blind bit of difference.

As Ted heads outside in his swimmers, with Bea following, the kids make a beeline for the door. Moira puts her arm out to stop them.

'Just let Bea go,' she says, shepherding Tom and Clem from the entrance hall back into the kitchen, where they scramble onto the bench in the bay to watch the show. Over their heads, she catches sight of Ted's silhouette at the diving board. She curses silently. Hadn't she known this trip was a bad idea from the start? This too-big house that none of them feel at home in. She places one hand on her sternum to calm the fluttering underneath – a delicate wingbeat she might yet contain – and the other hand on the great oak table. Moira kicks herself, almost literally, for not taking matters into her own hands and booking a little cottage for just her and Ted. It's their anniversary after all, not everyone's.

'D'you think he'll do it?' Tom says to Clem, their heads side by side.

He will, Moira thinks. In the run-up to the weekend, Ted's had all the photo albums out again, chasing a time that never even existed. Nostalgia used to be a malady, an *illness.* In Victorian times people were known to die of it, there was a whole programme about it on the radio. Inside her ribcage, the wings flutter on. Lonnie appears at her side and strokes her arm. Moira gives her a weak smile. Then Andrew and Lisa join them and they all stand at the window, looking out into the dark.

The whole kitchen holds its breath. Ted's silhouette bounces on the diving board. Bea has her back to them. With a sudden roar, Ted's body flings horribly through the air, his limbs splayed. A huge splash leaps up like a firework, lit by the pool, followed by smaller splashes in the water. At the window, they gape, rooted for an instant, before they all run outside for the second time, across the lawn to the poolside. Andrew jumps in, fully clothed, and hauls Ted, thrashing, to the shallow end, where Bea and Lonnie pull him out. Lonnie yelps when Bea steps on her bare toes.

'Sorry!

Their father is rescued, slumped and coughing on the pool edge.

'Don't be sorry for that,' Moira says, looking at Bea sternly as she drapes a towel around Ted.

Bea is stung. At another time she would sting right back, but she keeps quiet.

Moira, Lisa and the kids head back inside. When Ted gets his breath back, he lets himself be led away by Andrew and Lonnie.

'Easy now,' Andrew says. Has he been this lifesaver, this protector all along and Bea simply hasn't noticed?

She stays on the sandpapery pool edge, contemplating life's sham, drudgery and broken dreams. The sickly yellow water adds to her unease. She closes her eyes and a memory passes through her like a shiver: her father's face, looming and agitated, against a blue-black sky sprinkled with stars. His voice is unsure; he might be afraid. Of *her*? Then it's gone.

Bea hugs her knees, her shirt clings, damp and cold. She feels impossibly weary. Only half an hour ago, before her father jumped, there was the possibility of change; of her being forgiven, or forgiving. But now this seems ridiculous. Everything will stay the same. *People evolve, if you hadn't noticed.* Except Bea, except *her*. Her suspicion, formed at the dinner table when they first arrived at this mansion, is taking shape. It's becoming obvious there's something faulty in her: something *biochemical*, triggered by her family, by her father.

A towel drops into her lap and Andrew sits down beside her.

'Thanks. Nice work saving Dad's life by the way.'

'He put up quite a fight,' Andrew says.

You came out fighting. Her mother's words keep coming for her. And right then, Moira's voice reaches them from the house, the bossy tone audible without the words.

'She's such a control freak,' Bea mutters. Though this isn't really true. How much of what Bea says is just Things She's Always Said?

Bea considers telling Andrew about her own faulty biochemistry and decides against it. Instead, extraordinarily, it's Andrew who starts talking. About Lisa's depression and how, thankfully, she's a lot better now. About perspective, and how hard it is to keep it.

'You were right, sort of, that Lisa didn't like herself. But all her attempts to look different didn't do anything.' The pool light sends ripples across his face. Bea is dying to ask about the surgery. And when did Lisa have her teeth done? Bea could swear there used to be a gap at the front. She can't ask, of course, not when he's blowing her mind with philosophy and lifesaving.

'It's really good she's OK now,' Bea says. And then she tells him how she still misses Granny Dil, especially here, with everyone. It turns out Andrew misses her too. This annoys Bea because she thinks of Granny as *hers.*

'I know what you mean,' Andrew says, and again Bea is moved by his generosity.

'How do you do it?' Bea asks suddenly. Andrew looks puzzled. 'How do you stay so ... *yourself*?' It is precisely, one hundred per cent, the information she needs.

'I don't know,' he says after a time. 'Maybe I just don't try so hard *not* to.' And after another long pause he says, 'D'you think, sometimes you even *like* being angry?'

No! It's not a choice, it's a force within her that she can't control. It's *cellular*. Though this might be hard to prove. She used to like it, but not anymore. Her anger is utterly useless to her.

Bea feels hollowed out, and leaden. She can't think of anything to say.

After a long silence, Andrew gives her a sheepish smile and gets to his feet.

'You coming?'

'In a minute.'

Kneeling up on the kitchen window seat, take two, Tom and Clem press their heads to the thick panes. Cloudy circles of breath balloon and shrink. All eyes are on Bea by the poolside.

'She's looking for a shooting star to wish on,' Clem says.

'S'not clear enough,' Tom says. 'She won't see one.' He still has his towel wrapped around him. In all the excitement he hasn't managed to get dressed. Clem rearranges a plump, peach cushion under each knee. On the grey circle of her breath, with a finger, she draws a five-pointed falling star with a downward smudged arc. She pulls back to look at it, then wipes it away with her sleeve.

'What would she wish?' Tom asks.

Clem shrugs. 'For something good to happen.'

The pair are shooed upstairs. When they're gone, Lonnie, Andrew and Lisa step into the bay. The pool ripples yellowy-green, a gelatinous rectangle. Lonnie flicks the lights off and the scene outside comes into sharp focus: Bea lying in shadow on the pool edge. Opposite her, on the far side, four empty sun loungers line up, semi-reclined. Bea's disappeared audience. The whole image appears unnatural. The wan light has a small reach and gives way quickly to black.

'It's like a theatre set,' Lonnie says.

'It's spooky,' Lisa whispers.

'The lady of the house has finally been banished,' Lonnie says in the low, breathy voice of the narrator. 'All windows and doors are locked,' she pauses. 'It's the final scene.' Upstairs there's thumping, Clem jumping on the bed. From her room, Moira calls a warning.

'I hope your play's better than this,' Andrew says to Lonnie.

'Shh,' Lisa whispers. 'What happens?' On the stage outside, Bea raises an arm and sweeps something from her forehead, then flings it back down.

'She wipes away one final tear,' Lonnie makes her voice a sob, 'for the life she never had.'

'I mean, *that* bit could be true.' Andrew says. Both Lonnie and Lisa turn to him, then back to the window so as not to miss anything.

'How so?' Lonnie says, in her normal voice. Andrew only shrugs, but Lonnie presses him. 'What life she never had?'

'You know. "If only it could have been different." Most people have that a bit.'

'Huh,' Lonnie says. 'I'm not sure I do.'

Andrew smiles down at her. 'Me neither.'

Moira and Ted's voices come from the landing, then their footsteps on the stairs.

'Are the other characters coming back?' Lisa prompts, still glued to the window.

'Only two major characters,' Lonnie says, in her narrator voice.

'Not Bea's story then,' Andrew says. 'She's always been the only major character.'

They all wait for some more movement, but out by the pool, Bea lies completely still.

Stuck somewhere
2005

Bea has only stayed twice in a hospital. Once when she broke her leg as a child, and once to have Clem. She finds them reassuring places: people in uniforms, charts, the smell of chemicals, the beeps of science. Like the labs she used to work in, only better. If she could do it all again, she might be a doctor.

After their chance meeting when she was the size of a walrus, Bea imagined she and Sarah would slip back into each other's lives in exactly the way they left off: schoolgirl error. She hadn't accounted for the enormity of Adulthood: having a baby, toddler, child, retraining, full-time job. Alarmingly, almost another eight years have passed since their epic café reunion. She and Sarah see each other only seldom, but their chats on the phone are regular, and Bea savours them.

She got the text two days ago, it explains why Sarah's not been answering her calls: *I'm in Wilmslow Hospital. Will be here for a few weeks. Any chance of a visit?* This means her seizures have got worse and she finally needs brain surgery.

Bea's later than she intended for evening visiting hours.

'Only twenty minutes,' says a beaky, spectacled receptionist at the front desk.

Sarah's in a small single room at the end of a corridor. Bea steps quietly inside. It smells of disinfectant and unwashed hair. The room is dimly lit, tinted blue from the curtains and floor tiles. The bed is by the window. Sarah's propped up on pillows. Part of her head has been shaved, and clumps of her remaining curls stick up from her scalp in question marks on the pillowcase. A thin tube loops down from a drip and into her wrist. She is a sepia copy of herself, her skin greyish with a hint of blue from the curtain. The whole scene frightens Bea, until her friend's face falls into a relieved smile at the sight of her. A gentle swash of orchestral music comes from somewhere. Bea looks around and finds a speaker embedded in the cabinet.

'It's this or soft rock,' Sarah says. 'It reminds me of the sea.'

Bea pulls a chair close to the bed, shrugs off her puffy coat and makes small talk. The phone call to the sexy-voiced vet about Frisbee, the obese, death-defying guinea pig who Clem's trying to get in the *Guinness Book of Records*; Aliya in year ten who tried to pass off her period for a haemorrhage to get out of the lesson. She makes Sarah laugh – a soft and lovely sound. On top of the cabinet, a thick white candle flickers rhythmically. When Bea looks closer it turns out to be a tiny bulb.

'Zac brought it in,' Sarah says. 'He'll be back at the weekend.'

'How are the boys?' Bea asks, meaning *with you like this*?

'Zac thinks about everyone, everything. Jasper's world is much smaller. It's like he got stuck somewhere.'

'Where?'

'I'm not sure. Where me and James split up?' Sarah grimaces. 'That sounds so self-indulgent. Let's see,' she sighs. 'Puberty? Starting school? In the womb? So many places to get stuck.'

'Right,' Bea says, feeling uneasy about Clem, and about herself. Sarah's children aren't really children, the older one is eighteen. Is that still a child? Eighteen is when Bea left Sarah's house and set out alone. Music swells from the corner; all the strings in a rushing scale.

'When we were at school, I loved your house,' Bea says.

Sarah shrugs her eyebrows wearily. 'Yeah, you loved it more than me.'

'It was so *reassuring*,' Bea says, picturing the grandfather clock, the four of them sitting at the dining table. 'Books, wine,' she stops, and studies Sarah's face which has gained a bit of colour since Bea came in the room. 'What do you mean, "I liked it more than you"?'

'It was just me and them,' Sarah says with a long, slow blink. Perhaps Bea should leave her to sleep. Sarah told her on the phone her parents were here all last week, and have gone for two days to Newcastle, where Morris is delivering a lecture.

'Your parents were *cool*,' she says.

'They were in love,' Sarah says in a flat, sad voice. 'Still are I guess.' She rolls her eyes. 'Puke.'

'Puke,' Bea agrees.

'It was lonely for me,' Sarah says to the ceiling, sounding old. 'Luckily for my kids, I hate James's guts.'

'Amen,' Bea says. 'Viva divorce.' Sarah does a breathy laugh and Bea wants to gather her up. She would embrace her if she wasn't so scared of crushing her. Sarah has halved in size since Bea last saw her, though she can't remember when that was.

The truth is, Bea doesn't hate Gavin. They're well organised now around Clem, and they talk like grown-ups about the divorce. She just can't imagine why either of them thought they might go through life together, or how that's possible for anyone.

'What about your parents?' Sarah asks.

'What about them?' Bea says, not meaning to sound defensive. 'They're OK. Still in the same house. They get along.' She recalls now the look they exchanged when the toast was made at the Ruby weekend last year. Maybe they fell in love more recently. Is that possible? There's a whole lexicon for marriage that fits better in Bea's opinion – more building terminology or cell biology: cement, lime and mortar, unit of life, semipermeable. Though what does she know.

What Bea really wants to run past her friend is her special cell receptor theory. They've not seen each other since Bea formulated this. And Sarah's no scientist, which is a plus, the whole thing not being very scientific. Still, it feels urgent to get Sarah's opinion on Bea's unique biochemistry, activated by her family.

'That funny glass room,' Sarah says, 'was it for your Gran?'

Bea smiles thinking about the Annexe; her whole world for a short time. 'It's not there anymore,' she says. 'Well it is, but it's a proper room with big windows instead of a room made only of windows. Mum's got it full of plants. It's a miniature garden centre.'

'I loved that room,' Sarah says. ''Cept you never invited me to your house.'

'Well yeah. No poetry, no wine,' Bea says. 'Sorry.'

'No problem,' Sarah says with a smile, 'I'm over it.'

Memories. Another thing Bea wants to ask Sarah about. How to interpret them; and how accurate they are. But now she's here, she can't see how she'll bring all this up.

'How are you and your dad?' Sarah asks.

Bea sits forward in her chair. This is her opening, but as usual, she can't put it into words. 'Oh you know. We'll just keep on avoiding each other.' Bea's voice gets quieter as she repeats the thing she always says. 'It's the only reason I miss Gav – he made those visits easier.'

Sarah's giving her a sideways look.

'What?'

'You're the exact same,' Sarah says. Bea wants to squirm, sulk, deny. 'Still trying to avenge yourself,' Sarah says, faintly amused, and with the utmost kindness.

Not you as well, Bea wants to say. *It's the cell receptors!* Though the reason she can't say this to her friend, she sees now, is because it isn't true. And Sarah might be right.

Bea needs to stop this. After all, *she's* not the one in the hospital bed. Sarah's lids are closed; she might be asleep. A memory floats at the edge of Bea's thoughts. Sitting in the fantastic house, in the den, with Sarah quoting someone. The friend she had taken to be the happiest and luckiest of all people. *We choose our parents*. It makes no more sense to her now than it did when she was eighteen. She wonders what Clem would have to say about it. And Andrew, and Lonnie.

Bea goes over to the sink and looks into her face in the mirror. Her blue eyes stare back. Still her best feature. Maybe she'll start wearing makeup again: thick black eyeliner, dark lipstick. In the mirror, she takes on a dejected look. The rogue grey hairs are taking over; she'll have to start dyeing it soon.

'I'm bloody not the same,' she mutters and comes back to the bed. After a while, they're joined by a set of piano chords from the speaker – minor, major, back to minor. Bea recognises it; Sarah may even have played it.

'God, I missed you,' Sarah says, from nowhere, her eyes still closed. Bea leans over and takes her hands, careful not to disturb the tube in her wrist. Her hands are cold and Bea gently rubs the fingers. She had not been brave enough at university to send those letters to her friend. Right now, it feels like her biggest failure, though there's quite a long list. Here is Sarah, fighting for her life. *Everywhere life is full of heroism.*

'I know,' Bea says. 'Me too.' And she means this with all her heart. It actually swells in her chest: love, solid and pulling, perennial as the grass. 'Me too.' She rubs Sarah's hands, then places them on the bed and folds the blanket carefully over them.

'You know what you should try?' Sarah says, and now she opens her eyes.

'Tell me.' Bea will do whatever Sarah advises.

'Go and talk to someone. Give it all to someone else and see what they make of it.' In recent years Sarah's seen various people to help her cope with the uncertainty of her life. Bea knows it has given her friend great consolation. But Sarah has allowed herself to be helped. Could this be possible for Bea?

Sarah's breathing changes, drifting into sleep. How could Bea have got it all wrong? The Sarah she grew up with created her own desires, she didn't follow everyone else's. It turns out even she was not immune to longing and loneliness.

'Tell me again about all of you in that big house,' Sarah whispers, eyes closed. 'Your dad jumping off the diving board.' A smile spreads across her face. 'That story kills me.'

Crucible
2006

Moira spent a long time choosing an outfit. Dressy but warm; something *theatre*-ish. She chose her navy trousers and cream, patterned blouse, and the camel coat that Ted bought her last Christmas. Much too nice to wear, she had thought when she got it. Theatre-ish, most definitely. Lonnie's driving her to see *The Crucible* on a wet evening in August. It's a revival of the show they did two years ago, the second time it's been to Bristol. It won awards. Moira can't help thinking all the troupe must be sick of it, though Lonnie tells her they're not all the same. Moira's quietly delighted with the invite, it seems a mark of Lonnie's respect for her growing interests. She's also a little nervous.

'It's in the round,' Lonnie says approvingly. Moira nods, though she hasn't a clue what Lonnie's talking about. Her daughter's hair is the colour of a new bruise; it makes her look melancholy, older. But then of course she herself is getting older. Moira often has the feeling she's living her life backwards.

The speck of Lonnie's nose stud glints as she reverses into a parking space. A couple walk past under the streetlamp, holding hands, right by her window. Moira catches the faces of two women, and a muscle squeezes in her tummy; a niggle that she can't rid herself of. Only once has Lonnie brought a partner home. Ted has no problem with it, and they don't discuss it. Lonnie opens her car door, smiling with purple lips, and offers her hand like a chauffeur. This daughter has always been easy to love. Tonight, Moira will enjoy herself. Being in the city, in the evening, makes her feel girlish, excited. She takes Lonnie's arm on the cobbles.

'So the audience sits wrapped around the actors,' Lonnie says, 'I'll tell you which bits I made.'

Moira's seat is right next to a bale of hay, on the stage. She can almost touch it! As the lights go down, she gets a wave of unease. Actors in browns and greys troop in, brushing her feet, breathing on her. The atmosphere all around is suspicion. The main one, John Proctor, has a kind, long face, not unlike David's. He and his wife are a bit frosty with each other. Their maid comes back from some court; she has a doll. She's accused of witchcraft. John Proctor's kind face is guarding something. Moira knows about guarding; her unease increases. There's urgency, shouting. The shouts bounce off Moira's clothes.

The stage opens like a mouth and a bench rises from it, by magic.

'That was me,' Lonnie whispers. Moira widens her eyes in the dark at Lonnie. How clever she is! What people do! Lonnie has broken the spell, and Moira glances around the audience at the front, lit up. All these people packed in, watching Lonnie's magic bench appear.

At the interval, Lonnie pops off into the wings to check something. Moira waits for her at the edge of the bar, clutching her bag amid the chatter and clinking glasses. Ted would hate it here. He would describe these interval sounds as 'people holding back from a good time.' Everything Ted doesn't understand he describes as 'people holding back from'.

In the second half, it comes at them from all sides. The play becomes a courtroom, and Moira and Lonnie are in the jury! John Proctor is on trial for committing adultery, which he has, though it's not really his fault. Moira feels a creeping panic she may have to speak up. This ebbs away as she becomes entranced again with the leading man: his big dark eyes, thick hair that kinks out at the edges, full mouth in a slight pout, and his big shoulders, round with his sorrow. He comes close to her, and the urge to touch him, to stroke his back, is almost overwhelming.

Suspicion and judgement whip up like wind, with the truth nowhere to be seen. He confesses the adultery. And now his wife, the cold fish, a slip of a girl compared to him, tells a lie to protect him. Moira could reach out to her, too.

John Proctor will hang. All he has to do is agree to give up his name, and he can go free.

He won't do it.

He's right beside Moira, stock still. She watches his back curve slowly, his stomach pull in as though he might vomit. And out of his mouth comes a sudden cry.

'Because it is my *name*! Because I can never have another all my *life*!'

Such a proud and decent man! She knows exactly how he feels, here, in front of her, a light shining on his anguish, picking out the tiny hairs on his neck. Poor John Proctor! What a terrible dilemma, divorced from his own name: a terrible thing for a man.

He chooses to die. Tears pour down Moira's face. She almost sinks to her knees to pray for him. She doesn't pray often, but here is a man who needs her prayers.

Moira clings to Lonnie on the way out. She needs to get away from the hands pressed to chests, the knowing smiles. What do these people know of John Proctor? It's a relief to be outside on the cobbled street in the dark and the drizzle. She's a little unsteady. The importance of a name – staking your whole self on it.

'What do you think would have happened to him,' she says to Lonnie, 'if he had carried on?' Rain falls in slanting silver needles across the street lights.

Lonnie's face is full of concern. 'It's a good question,' she says, walking Moira slowly. 'Madness?' Then after a few more steps, 'But people get over things. He might have taken another name—'

'I think it would have left him bitter and angry,' Moira cuts in, 'like a deep splinter. And causing a great deal of pain.' She's trembling. Lonnie stops and holds her arm.

'That's very poetic,' she says, gently.

'I don't think John Proctor would have found any poetry in it,' Moira says. A bicycle skids in front of them on the cobbles, Moira stumbles back and Lonnie puts an arm around her back. She would like to go back in there, find the man and hold him to her. She has carried his pain out of the theatre, and it is a dead weight.

*

A week later, Moira still can't shed the feeling of injustice. John Proctor has become Ted. And she herself has a few things in common with the wife, sorry to say. Moira fears at times she may have been a cold fish. The play has got right under her skin. She won't be hurrying back to the theatre anytime soon. Still, she has tucked away a few things for herself, about judgement. Mainly, it has highlighted to her the sadness lodged in her husband: a hovering cloud that comes and goes. It brings her back to the time before Lonnie was born, when Ted lost his job and his way. Moira hadn't paid enough attention then. But she herself had people missing. Life goes on but so does death. In the end, Moira did the best she could. Is it possible that she could have prevented the rift between Ted and Bea? Who knows. No one, that's who! Though she might drive herself loopy thinking about it.

If only John Proctor could have forgiven himself. *Because it is my name. I can never have another all my life.* Ted's suffering was much bigger than his pride. And the cloud that follows him is his guilt – layer upon layer of it – plus a lack of forgiveness.

It has been Moira's lifelong habit to never stir things up. But now she will use up her chance. She will write Bea a letter.

We echo
1944

The kitchen smells of wood smoke, washing hung above the stove, the cold smell of outside when someone opens the back door. It sounds of the hissing kettle, bowls clattered in the sink, next door's dog barking, next door's dad barking. The table is fixed to the wall, and David has the corner seat by the window. Balanced on their mother's chest, the baby's tufty head pokes up over her shoulder while she dollops out porridge. In case the baby slips off, Moira stays close until she takes her bowl and her mother has more hands. David eyes the big clock above the doorway, with its cream face and clear lines for the minutes.

'Minutes change everything, don't they David?' their father says with a wink. 'Handy in wartime, aren't you? Keep a bit of normal in all this chaos.'

One of these porridge-eating mornings in Wilmot Street, Morden, Moira trips into the kitchen to find only his half-finished bowl.

'Where's David?' she asks, accusing, when her dad comes in from the loo. Strangely, he doesn't look at her. That's when she hears the first cry.

David is forced to leave behind most of his life's work. His nine years (it comes clear this morning) have been spent gathering and storing like a squirrel, in piles, envelopes, pillowcases, packets. Moira knows about his collecting, they all do, but not the extent of it. Stashes are excavated from under the bed, the bottom of the wardrobe, behind the coat rack downstairs and under the rug. Given the house itself is the size of a suitcase, the spread and stealth are impressive. Carefully packed feathers, bark, dead woodlice, newspaper words and sentences cut into tiny oblongs, grass, thread, buttons, a pale watch face without glass or hands, leaves, fluff and dust, hair, crusts, and small squares of material: blankets, sheets, coat lining, hankies, socks. It explains the many unexpected holes.

'You can't take it all,' their mother tells him. Which is when he cries out and Moira flies up the stairs. 'You can take one boxful.' And she produces out of nowhere a long, thin, wooden box with red writing on the top and side.

Their mother keeps saying in a loud voice how sorry she is. David groans and sways and the baby starts to wail and their mother, never sorry for long, loses her rag. As she whisks away the surplus, one last sound escapes David: a keening, more animal than human, a fox caught in a trap. After that, Moira doesn't hear his voice again for a very long time.

The farmhouse is full of shadows. The entrance hall has room enough to handstand in, though Moira would not, in her wildest dreams, do a handstand here. A dark chest like a coffin lies under the stairs. Off to the right, there's a sitting room with a sunken sofa and a brick fireplace like a gaping mouth. The kitchen is more like a stable, with a dog wagging around (a dog!) called Buffalo, a gigantic table, and a thick bench instead of chairs. Moira shivers, more from too much space around her than actual cold. The whole of Wilmot Street could come here to avoid the new German rockets, which she imagines as colourful, deadly fireworks in the shape of swastikas. She keeps this all to herself as she stays close to David and sniffs her new home: musty, leafy, damp wool, dog, old fruit, and later something delicious and unfamiliar.

'Casserole,' says the farmer's wife, putting a large bowl in front of each. A thick, honey-coloured stew, nothing like the watery mixtures at home. And bread, soft and hard in the right places.

'Don't get this at home, David Town?' their host asks. David shakes his head but says nothing.

'It's Brown,' Moira corrects bravely.

'But you're from town, so that's what I'm calling you,' the farmer says, with his odd voice, his mouth going all around the vowels. 'I suppose you could call us Mr and Mrs Farm.' He looks like the weather: his face is reddy-brown and tufts of thick, tawny hair flick about his head. The farmer's wife is very straight – her hair, limbs, trousers. To Moira she looks like a man, the women in Moira's life being curlier and curvier, and wearing dresses. Moira follows her to see how things are done: dishes into the great sink, everything *bigger*. Moira thinks of Jack and the Beanstalk.

'We echo,' Moira whispers to her brother as Mrs Farm finally leads them up the wide staircase to their room. David watches his fingers trace the wood all the way to the top of the bannister and round the curly swirl at the top.

Outside, the smells are animals and hay and grass. They're given hard boots that tie up, Moira's too big, and her feet slide about. Hens bob around them on the stony entrance. A giant tractor fills the yard. They peek into battered sheds filled with chains and spikes and long tools; things that might do you harm. Moira can sense David's questions piling up. She wonders if he will ever ask them, and the wondering gets her panicky and hot. They collect new things: jumping crickets, worms, a dead vole, its face so sweet and small and pointy Moira pretends it's still alive.

Moira pods peas, kneads dough, soaks overalls. David sharpens scythes, carries sacks. Things that are on the ration at home are readily available here. Moira gets David to write about the peas and the stew in the letter home – their mother will want to know about the food – though Moira is less and less sure what to say in the letters. In the dark of their room, Moira whispers about the magic trick their father does with a handkerchief, and if the baby has grown another tooth. When she closes her eyes, she can hear her mother's thick morning voice when Moira taps on her door: 'Is that the tea lady?' And her own smiled response: 'It's the tea *girl*.' She aches for her father's wink, the baby's breath. The sky outside their window is sprayed with stars.

Moira's arms sting from picking blackcurrants. She rubs the inky patches on her skirt; everything here leaves marks. She sits at the edge of the kitchen garden picking at the rosemary while Missus digs. Moira likes this area: onions, radishes, lettuce, tomatoes, all in neat lines. The sun appears from behind the cloud and almost blinds her. She buries her head in her blotchy skirt.

'Still all a bit new, Moira?' the woman says, quieter than usual. It feels odd to hear Missus say her name, pleasant and also sad. Missus leans on her spade. 'Can your brother talk?' she asks.

Moira feels breathless even though she's sitting still. 'When he wants to,' she says. Something inside her chest scrabbles to get out. *Please make him talk,* she almost says, *I don't know how*.

Missus nods. 'Close your eyes,' she says, and Moira does. 'Open your mouth.' And Moira opens wide. She feels the woman right by her side, and something is placed on her tongue. 'Now close it.' A softness presses the roof of her mouth, she swallows, and a sweet tangy juice slips down her throat. *Wowee*! It's the sweetest, best thing she has ever tasted. Her eyes flick open. Mrs Farm is smiling at her and Moira notices the dimples in her cheeks. She might be the same age as their mother. Moira wonders suddenly why she doesn't have any children.

'Don't tell anyone,' Missus whispers loudly, pointing at dots of red on spiky straw, under dark green leaves. 'Strawberries. Come and pick one whenever you want.'

School brings all the old perils and some new ones. David's classroom is the larger one, with big oval windows and points at the top like a church. The problem is, Moira's not in the same class. At break time, she ducks through clusters of V-necks, skipping ropes, chants, legs, and finds David in the corner of the playground, alone by the fence. Two boys and then three appear beside him. When David turns away, the boys laugh and shove him between them like a sack. Moira wheels around for help, a wild flapping inside her ribcage. David stumbles and falls to the ground without a sound, crumpled like a leaf. Someone kicks, the bell goes. Another break time, she finds him tied to the railings, his wrists bloody and raw from trying to pull free.

On trembling legs, Moira leads David to Mr Barrow's office. The Headmaster, a towering figure, has extra skin folding over his collar like a turkey, poppy eyes, and a miniature mouth. His chest starts wide and tapers off, his legs are skinny as stilts. He looks like he's made of a kit that got mixed up. His small office is piled with books and smells of pipe smoke.

'At our old school they let David be in my class,' she says, giddy with her own boldness. The Headmaster raises one eyebrow and pulls in his chin, creating many others.

'Your brother will stay in Six, miss, and you will stay in Four.'

In the kitchen that evening, while David holds a lantern in the yard for Mister, Moira sobs out what happened. Her sobs alarm her but she can't stop them.

'Mr Barrow?' Missus says, 'Funny head, funny body, tall as a tree?'

'Yes,' Moira squeaks and Mrs Farm gives her a long look, then pats Moira's leg.

'Leave it to me,' she says. Moira throws her arms around her guardian and clings on. She grips her, she can't help it, and Missus lets her. Missus changes depending on where she is. Digging the garden, she's a sergeant-major, but sitting here now inside Moira's tight hold she is suddenly a fairy godmother.

On Monday, David is allocated a desk at the back of Moira's classroom. Moira sucks in her breath, screws up her eyes, turns back around and opens them. He's still there.

The letter comes in the middle of the potato harvest. The weather's turning cold, the ground hardening, and at school all classes are competing for the longest paper chain. The name is only a guide, anything can be used: hair ribbons, food packets, brown paper bags, strips of old socks, string.

'Your mother has been poorly,' Missus announces at breakfast. 'You two will spend Christmas here.' She winces like she has a pain somewhere. 'I'm sure she'll be well again soon. Perhaps she will come and visit the farm.' Moira can't picture her mother here, and before the news can sink in, Mr Farm gusts into the kitchen, all agitated, his hair a spiky nest.

'Albert has the flu. We're a man down on the harrow,' he says, patting his overalls like he might find another worker in his pockets. After an enormous pause he says, 'David Town, you come with me.' Moira's about to protest, but to her amazement David stands up. He leaves his bowl half full, slips his feet into his boots and follows Mister out the back door, as though he has been waiting all this time to be asked.

That night, David talks! He tells her the whole day: the tractor cab, adjusting the plugs, a paraffin refill, a loose coupling pin. Moira tries hard to follow but gets lost – in his words and her relief. David sounds like normal! And like a proper farmer!

The first half of Christmas Day is the same as any other. The men disappear, while Moira and Missus scrub, peel, chop, stir, baste. At lunchtime, though later than usual, David and Mister return, and four new people appear at the table: two very old, and two like Mister and Missus. Moira and David barely notice the people, they give themselves entirely to the food. Two fat, golden chickens in the middle, a wide slab of beef pink-sliced, pyramids of crispy potatoes, green vegetables of all species, carrots, a thick sauce with lumps that looks like porridge but tastes peppery, a dollop of sweet 'hedge' jelly, and a jug of beefy, salty gravy poured over it all like a lake. Yumsterlicious times a hundred. Moira and David keep going until they can't eat another bite. Then they eat a bowl of Christmas pudding with currants and cream.

Later, after the people leave, two even more unusual things

happen. Mr Farm lights the fire in the sitting room – a room used only by the dog – and both Mister and Missus *sit down* on the concave sofa and drink golden alcohol from glasses like miniature goldfish bowls. Moira and David collapse on the dusty rug with Buffalo.

'Look,' David says suddenly. A small bluish flame flickers at the string end of the 'paper chain'. Moira had hooked it around the bricks, not quite high enough. The four of them follow the flame as it licks around a strip of red card, eats its way along the brick, and flares to a halt at the tied paper bag. Moira is too stuffed to care. Mister stands up suddenly, his cheeks flushed.

'A toast,' he says raising his glass. 'To our young helpers and charges, and to the end of this war, pray to God.' He looks at his wife who gives a serious nod. 'And to an excellent potato harvest.' He gives his quick smile, tips the contents of the glass into his mouth, slumps back onto the sofa and in what seems like seconds, falls fast asleep. Missus reaches behind the sofa and pulls up a pillowcase with something inside.

'For the pair of you,' she says, lowering it onto the rug. Then she too leans back and closes her eyes. Moira and David stare at the lumpy pillowcase in front of them.

'Should we wait until they wake up?' Moira whispers but finds she is unable to. She reaches in and pulls out a wooden hexagon with metal pins spiking up from the edges, then turns it over and around before passing it to David. The fire gives a loud crack like a gunshot and they both jump. Their hosts stir and slide together in their sleep, Missus snuffles like a piglet. David places the contraption flat-side down and starts undoing the screws.

'What is it?' Moira asks, trying not to sound disappointed. As she waits, a sudden sinking feeling takes her, like a magnet pulling at her insides; sinking, sinking. All she wants is to be in the cramped front room at home with her mum and her dad and the baby, their loud aunt, and the neighbours singing 'We Saw Three Ships' tunelessly through the wall. David twiddles each screw while Moira waits to see what this feeling will do next. With the last screw, he lifts off the thick wooden lid and underneath is a pile of cardboard and paper hexagons. A smile spreads slowly across David's face, so wide and so rare that it lifts Moira's sinking, as though her brother himself is a magnet.

'It's a flower press,' he says, fixed on the thing, then pointing his smile at Moira. 'It's brilliant.' He pushes it towards her and says with a serious voice, 'It's to both of us. Merry Christmas, Moira.'

'Merry Christmas, David.'

'Come on,' he says. And they run upstairs to search the box for pressable things.

*

Armed with *Birds of Britain*, they head out across the back field and down the hill. They leave the dog inside because he scares the birds. The July sky is bright blue, the war has ended, and the pair have been at the farm for all the seasons. Moira's pinafores are grass-streaked. Now the ground is dry, she lies flat at the top of the slope, waits for a push-off from David, and spins for a few thrilling light-dark-light-dark seconds. At the bottom, she jumps up, and they carry on to the small pond, nestled in front of a red brick wall. Clumps of dry grass tuft the edges, and a weeping willow dips its fingertips into the water. Despite the smells of mouldy leaves and manure, tucked here by the wall is Moira's favourite spot on the farm.

David takes out *Birds of Britain* and from it the carefully folded list on a sheet pulled from an exercise book. Still as statues, they wait for a bird to land on the wall, or beside the pond, or in the tree. When it flies off, they seize the book and flick through the pages. The current list reads: wren, pigeon, sparrow, starling, great tit, song thrush (*M), robin, sparrow-hawk, goldfinch, bluetit, crow (*D), blackbird, magpie. (Stars for favourites). Sparrowhawk is Moira's least favourite, after the horrid spring murder.

A pair of chubby, fluffy birds had pecked around beside the pond while David and Moira sat poised. 'Baby sparrows,' David had said. 'They're learning how to feed themselves.' From above, like an arrow, a dark catapult hurled in, and in a whirl of squeaking and flapping and feathers, one of the birds disappeared. Two baby sparrows and then only one, terribly, flutteringly alone.

Beside the wall, Moira checks around for predators while David reviews the list on his lap. Out of nowhere, a puff of wind lifts the sheet and carries it sideways. David tries in vain to grab it but it eddies down onto the water's surface. David snorts and gives a funny barking moan that makes Moira's heart quicken. She springs up, grabs a bundle of willow branches and swings out like a monkey, dipping her foot into the pond and lifting the paper. David lunges for it, topples forward like a pillar, and splashes down flat on the water, face first. His cry becomes a terrible gurgle. Moira lets go of the branch and lands waist deep in the middle of the pond, while David splashes, face down, flinging up arcs of muddy water.

'Put your feet down,' she yells, but he only flaps and gargles. Then he is silent. 'DAVID! STAND UP!' she bellows, trying to grip his sleeve. A scream rises inside her. She dives down, dipping her head underneath his body. She wedges her shoulder under his chest, plants her feet on the bottom, and with all her might, pushes up, flipping her brother over. He coughs violently, bends in half and shoots upright, looking surprised to find himself standing up, knee-deep in water. He coughs some more and looks around. Brown slime drips onto his cheeks.

'Where's the paper?' he says when he can talk. He climbs out of the pond.

'What?' At that moment, Moira sees David as others see him. She considers that what people say about her brother could be true: that he is *not the full shilling*.

'The *list*,' he says, impatient. She clambers out, and stuck to her leg is the sodden sheet. David peels it off and scowls. He takes the spare sheet from the book and starts to copy.

Moira glares at him, her chest and shoulders tight. 'You almost *died*,' she says in a piercing voice.

David doesn't raise his head from the page. 'It's unlikely I'll die before I'm sixty, or seventy,' he says. Then looks up and adds, 'Unless I go to war.' The tightness in her gains heat – it's in her throat. She might stamp her feet, or cry out, or push him in the pond all over again.

She wants something *back*.

She stands up straight, her dress clinging to her middle, the sun bright in her face. She shades her eyes with a hand.

'I saved your *life!*,' she shouts.

David peers at her face in shadow. Slowly, he lifts his hand and cups it over his eyes in the same gesture. It takes her a while to understand that he is copying her. He thinks she is doing a salute. He never understands *anything*. Her breath trickles out of her in a shaky sigh, the tightness drains away, and she slumps down, hopeless, on the grass. A sparrow lands on the wall, then another. David holds his salute.

'In war, soldiers salute their lieutenants,' he says. 'Or at a funeral, all the army salutes for the dead person. But I didn't die because you saved my life.' Then he drops his hand, turns back to the paper and carries on with his list.

Moira lies back, looks up into the blue, and feels a single tear roll from the corner of each eye, through her hair and into the grass. She had felt so lonely all that time he wouldn't speak, yet here they are and she feels exactly the same.

On the way back, their clothes are dry and stiff. Moira drags her steps. She has found out something she wishes she hadn't and wants desperately to run backwards in time and un-know it. Perhaps Missus will know what to do. Moira will wait for another fairy godmother moment and ask her.

The dog's bark reaches them in the field. Missus is in the

doorway, holding Buffalo by the scruff. As they approach, Missus opens and closes her mouth without sound. And why is she holding onto the dog?

Standing in the dark entrance hall is a small woman in a blue jacket with a wide straw hat. In a slow, grand gesture she lifts it off her head.

'Ta daa!' she says, keeping the hat in the air. She has on pink lipstick, a string of shiny pearls, a flowery dress.

It is their mother.

The shiny, flowery woman lowers the hat and opens her arms. Moira's knees go wobbly. She stumbles into the open arms and is squeezed against her mother's soft chest. Then her mother pulls them both outside.

'I want to see you properly,' she says, 'I came as soon as I could.'

In the yard, under the glare of the sun, their mother steps back and looks them up and down, up and down.

'What's all this on your face?' she says. David wipes the dried pond slime with his sleeve and Moira brushes her dress. While her head is patted, her cheeks stroked and kissed, Moira feels as though she is watching the scene from somewhere else. Her mother weeps in big gulps. David lets himself be patted and stroked too. Moira feels in a funny way like a chicken or a goat. She giggles, then feels suddenly sick. A fluttering in her chest signals danger: she will have to leave this place.

'I hardly know you,' her mother keeps saying, and Moira tries to smile. 'Come here, come here.' She positions them one either side of her, facing the chicken coop and the field behind. 'I came as soon as I could, really I did.' She pulls them to her, as though they might disappear in the landscape. 'All this space,' she breathes, 'Don't you get *lost*?'

'It's actually easy,' David says and takes a step away. 'We've been here for nearly thirteen months.'

'You're taller than me!' she says to David. 'Almost eleven years old,' and she starts crying again.

I hardly know you, Moira thinks. She had forgotten her mother's voice, so different from everyone here. She has never seen this woman cry before, but she stays in the crook of her arm and wills Missus to stay inside. She makes a silent promise not to show her mother the strawberries. She looks at her brother, her only friend, and the hollow feeling from the pond returns. She is the spared bird; small and flapping and alone.

David stands up taller, going for an extra inch.

He says, 'Where's the baby?'

What to look out for
2006

The letter lies open in Bea's lap. Two full sheets, all four sides filled with her mother's neat, childish handwriting; plump, even letters so unlike her physical self. On the sofa, in her thin socks, her toes are turning slowly numb, but she won't get up for her slippers and disturb the words. Never in her life has she received a letter from her mother. Cards, on birthdays: *Have a lovely day whatever you're up to, love Mum and Dad.* Moira always signs from both. Or postcards. A sandy Devon beach: *Weather good so far, Dad got sunburnt! Cottage nice.* Small, empty sentences. And never a letter. The last thing Bea was expecting on this dismal September Saturday was her mum's life story. It has taken her almost an hour, a paragraph at a time, with long pauses in between.

She feels liquid.

At the end, she goes straight back to the beginning.

Dear Bea,

I don't know where to start. This is not my first try at writing this. I have got a lot of things wrong and I would like to put some right.

She can see Moira very clearly: her watery green eyes lightly mascaraed, powdered cheeks, straight nose the same as her own. Reading the letter is like her mother holding her gaze. Bea smooths the sheets and watches the rain tapping on the bay window. She'll make a coffee before reading it again. She doesn't get up. It's like in films where it starts to rain in the sad bit; Bea finds this intensely annoying. Though, watching the window now, she expects hail, lightning, a great clap of thunder. *When we left the farm, there was only me and David, no Dad and no baby Eliza. It was so terribly sad that we had to pretend she had never lived. Such a bonny, sweet baby.* Tears crowd Bea's throat, but she doesn't cry them. *We loved our father, Raymond, too, he was a good kind man.*

In her child's writing, Moira describes how, in her childhood, she was responsible for everyone: for Dilys who stared into space or snapped, and for David who needed her protection. Moira's job was to defuse all conflict and keep things moving forward. Steady drops keep on at the window, no hail or thunder. She'll get up and put all the lights on, lamps and candles too, light the gas fire. Still, she doesn't move. Her liquid self sloshes back into the shape of her body. Her fingers tremble as she turns the page, even though she's just read it.

For your dad, losing his job was like having his whole self taken from him, and I tried to pretend it wasn't happening.

There's a new quiet in the room. The rain has stopped. It's weirdly dark, like evening in the morning, the day inverted. What would this signify in a film? Dark times ahead? The end of the dark times? Pause for the viewer to decide?

She folds the letter. She thinks *You can't be in anyone's skin but your own.* She thinks *I have never known my mother.*

The tears in her throat sink back down. The deep aubergine wall beside the kitchen, almost black, adds to the darkness. She never got around to whitewashing. So many shades to choose from – chalk white, linen white, cloud white. She'll do it tomorrow. Or maybe right now: she'll redecorate the whole house, cook Clem a roast, organise her books in alphabetical order, write the chapter on Alleles for the new Cambridge University Press syllabus. All the things she claims she'll do and never does.

She slides the pages back into the envelope. It might have been an hour, or a day since she sat down. Maybe it *is* evening. The liquid feeling comes over her again. If she looks in the mirror now, a whole new person will look back at her.

At last, she gets up, stretches her arms high, wiggles her toes and pulls on a fleece. In the small mirror above the fireplace, the face looking back is still her own. She tries to smile and look herself in the eyes. They move shiftily; even her own gaze is hard to hold. Her reflection flinches and she turns away.

Upstairs, she looks for the long rod that opens the loft hatch – never in its place on the landing – and finds it in the corner of Clem's bedroom, last used to dislodge a spider, wisps of the web dangling from the hook.

Bea clambers up the wobbly ladder into the dark and curses herself for not replacing the bulb. She rarely comes up here. Lots of the boxes and piles still belong to Gavin. She cracks her head on a beam, swears, squats down, and finds it's easier to crawl.

On her hands and knees, she moves slowly along the planked edge, where the roof narrows, avoiding the rotten boards in the middle that need replacing. It's freezing up here and there's a musty, mothball smell, home to whole extended spider families that would make Clem squeal and shriek, for the drama more than the fear. Bea smiles to herself. The square of light from the landing doesn't reach far, and as she crawls along she heads into almost total blackness. She should have looked for the torch. What she's after is on this side somewhere. She shoves aside the bigger boxes, a pile of Gavin's junk, and her hand meets a series of squashy carrier bags tied with bows – Clem's first clothes Bea had surprised herself at being unable to part with. Her knees ache. Lumpy outlines appear as her eyes get used to the dark. Baby's knees must get pretty sore in the crawling phase.

Here it is. Her hands alight on a small-ish oblong, the tape cold on her fingers: a shoe box. Bea sits back and the contents give a faint rattle as she pulls it onto her crossed legs. She bends forward to avoid banging her head again. The tape comes away easily.

She lifts out two nests of cutlery wrapped in leather gloves, a few books, and here is the soft shawl. Bea's heart flips; the tears are back in her throat. She unwraps the shawl, peeling away one side and then another. In her lap, pearly, luminous in the gloom, are Eliza's slippers. *We had to pretend she had never lived.* Two miniature, shining ovals for wriggly new toes. For the second time in her life, Bea wishes her mother was here. How strange and how not strange it would be to have Moira ducked down beside her in the dark. *You were such a fierce little thing, full of passion. I didn't know what to make of you, but thank God Granny Dil did.*

The slippers seem to glow.

'Eliza.' Bea speaks her dead aunt's name into the musty cold of the loft. She pinches her fingers together and squeezes them into each little shoe. She strokes them against her cheeks, silky soft, the ribbons tickling her neck, and pictures a chubby baby with bright blue eyes. *Are you me? Am I you?*

If only she could have another go at her own life, a second run, now she knows what to look out for.

Both true

A knock at the door interrupts *Gardeners' World*. Bison cocks his head. David is extremely pleased to see this, as he knows Bison is very deaf. Then he remembers the door and is less pleased. The knock comes again and Bison barks his huffing bark. 'Like a twenty-a-day smoker,' Ted said when they visited at Christmas, and Moira had laughed. It wasn't funny, but it's quite accurate because Bison is hoarse. There might be something wrong with his vocal cords, but he's definitely not in pain or he would stop eating. Bison will never stop eating as long as he lives, which may not be for much longer. David switches off the television and goes to the door with Bison stuck to his shin, due to the dog's hearing and balance. David likes answering the door like this; if it wasn't for Bison he might not answer it at all.

A man with a high-visibility jacket and long sideburns stands on the step holding a package, a red post van parked on the road behind him.

'Parcel for you,' says the man, the sideburns moving as he speaks. Bison flicks his head in a quick jerk, and the man reaches down to stroke him. Bison growls.

'He can't see or hear you very well, but he won't bite you,' David says, then adds, 'Although he might.' The postman stands up again.

'You need to sign for it.' He holds out the parcel.

'Is it for me?' David asks.

'If you're— David Brown,' the postman says, reading the name upside down, 'then yes. Sign on—'

'Is it the analysis software from the RSPB?' David asks. The postman gives him a long look. Bison jerks his head again.

'How would I know?' the postman says.

'You've brought it,' David says. The postman shakes his head and his sideburns look like two ferrets stuck on his cheeks. David takes the package and puts it down inside the door. The dog pushes past his legs to sniff it.

'He can still smell very well,' David says. The man hands him a pen and a clipboard which David takes.

'Sign your name in the empty box there,' the postman says in a slow, loud voice.

'My hearing is intact,' David says, writing his name, careful not to go over the lines.

'Well that's something,' the postman says taking the clipboard. Then he walks back to the van shaking his head as he goes.

Confused about who's going, Bison tries to follow him out the door. David blocks his way. Bison knows it's him by the smell of his trousers, turns back inside and bumps into the parcel.

It's very light and quite big. David puts it on the small table in the lounge, pulls his chair forward, sits back down and gets Bison settled. Alice sent him a dog calendar and a large packet of bulbs in a box for his sixtieth birthday, but that was a long time ago. She died quite soon after and no one has sent him anything since.

He has missed a whole section of the programme now, so he may as well open the package and wait for the start of *Countdown*. He pulls off the parcel tape and flips the top open. Inside, there's a lot of bubble wrap that looks like clear frogspawn, and two smaller boxes, both saying Mendip Mug Co in black swirly writing. These are harder to open. With his nails, he picks at the clear tape and finally uses his teeth. Inside the first one is a cream-coloured mug in pink tissue paper. He lifts it out and reads the green writing, first in his head, and then out loud to Bison.

'Eliza, meaning: Joyful'. Bison cocks his ears. David puts the mug on the table with a small clunk. The dog makes to get up and David puts a hand on his back to keep him in place.

Then he takes out the second box, flicks the tape with his nails and bites it. His heart, he notices as he peels it off, is beating quite fast. This mug is light blue in white tissue paper. He lifts it out. The writing is purple, it says 'Raymond, meaning: Wise Protector'. He says this out loud too. Then he puts it on the table, the two mugs next to each other, and stares at them for a long time. Eliza's green letters have curly tops and bottoms, Raymond's are thick and straight. David looks at his watch: nine minutes until *Countdown*.

He does something now that he has only done once before, when his mother was very ill in 1982. He reaches from his chair over to the windowsill, for the telephone on the stand. He doesn't disturb the dog. And he doesn't need to look up the number because it's stored in the phone, with Moira's writing on the inside of the handle, 'Moira, press 1.' He presses it and listens to the ringing.

'Hello, Moira speaking.' She sounds different over the phone, more breathless. David's heart is still beating fast.

'The mugs are here on the table,' he says.

'I'm sorry? David? Are you alright?' Now she sounds squeaky.

'Yes I'm—'

'Where are you? Oh, you're at home. I can see from the number.' She goes back to normal, though still a bit breathy. 'You never phone me, so I thought—'

'I'm in the lounge. The mugs are on the table.'

'What mugs?'

'The mugs in the box. I just opened them.'

'I don't—'

'Eliza, meaning Joyful. Raymond, meaning Wise Protector.' On the other end, Moira does a high, small sigh, then there is silence.

'Hello?' David says after a long time.

'I'm still here,' Moira says, in a voice like the small sigh but further away.

'They are both true,' David says.

'Yes,' Moira says, and her voice sounds very wobbly and very far away now. 'Yes, they are.'

'I'm going to hang them up,' David says.

'OK,' she says. He puts the phone back on the stand and pats Bison gently on the back to let him know the plan. They both get up slowly, and David picks up the mugs. Bison walks at his shin into the kitchen and waits. David takes down the two plain white ones on the last two hooks, next to 'Lorna, meaning: Fox, and Forsaken', which isn't true but they didn't have Lonnie. And Lonnie likes 'fox' because it's like 'foxy'. He looks at the two empty hooks and can't decide which order to put them in. He checks his watch. He puts Raymond on the second to last one, and Eliza on the last hook. He might swap them all around tomorrow.

'Eight mugs for eight people,' he says. His heart has slowed down again, back to normal. He turns around slowly, for Bison, and they go back to the lounge for *Countdown*.

You have a right to be here

In the cosy loft sitting room, Lonnie and Bea have pulled the two wicker chairs side by side into the dormer alcove, suspended in the night, their heads squeezed together at the window. Below them, the scene stretches out in strips: dark green lawn, tufty dunes, flat sand, black sea, sky. A thinly veiled moon hangs low over the water. Bea opens the window and they inhale the damp, salty air until they shiver and shut it again. Rhythmic long white lines roll in in the moonlight. Clem's just gone to bed with her music.

'She's a honey,' Lonnie says.

'She is tonight,' Bea says, then corrects herself. 'Yeah, she is.' In the car on the way down, they sang the whole of *Shania Twain's Greatest Hits*, both really going for 'Man! I feel like a woman!' It's the most Bea has laughed in years.

A bigger wave throws up uneven sprays of white froth.

'It's going to be freezing in there tomorrow,' Bea says. 'You sure about the surf lesson?'

'Yep,' Lonnie says. Tomorrow is Lonnie's birthday. She has been in this rented cottage in Harlyn Bay all week with friends, recently departed; a rare break from her hectic schedule. She invited her family to join her for the weekend. 'Guardian of the family', Bea is calling her. 'Someone's got to,' Lonnie says. Their parents arrive tomorrow. Cornwall's a long drive for Ted with his hip. A year or so after he finally got one replaced, now the other one's on the blink. Andrew and Lisa can't make it as Tom has a magic show and they always watch him. Bea loves to think of Andrew teaching his son the tricks she used to scorn, the three of them whipping rabbits out of hats. A magical threesome who survived.

She sips her Malbec, it's like velvet. There's a quiet rattle above them and Bea looks up.

'How many times d'you think Dad will mention that?' she nods at the skylight, a dark square in the slopy roof.

'Ten?' Lonnie says, 'twenty?' They smile and turn back to the sea. 'Delicious,' Lonnie says, keeping her eyes on the water.

'It's from Sarah, wine buff, she did a course in New Zealand.'

'How is she?' Lonnie asks.

'Pretty good. Still here.' Bea lifts her glass and Lonnie copies. 'To Sarah,' Bea says, and they clink. 'Did I ever tell you she said she was lonely as a child. Do you know why?' Lonnie shakes her head. 'Her parents were in love. She said that was profoundly unlucky.'

'That's so sad,' Lonnie says and pulls her chair out so they can talk without being head-to-head. Bea does the same. 'I need to think about that one,' Lonnie says, as they readjust to the dim lamplight from the corner of the room, much weaker than the moon.

'Me too,' Bea says.

Following Sarah's advice, Bea did go and talk to someone. A small, round woman with a powdery face in a furry front room – fluffy rugs, downy cushions, everything strokable. She sat on a sofa and the round woman said in a breathy voice 'Tell me a bit about yourself.' And Bea did. She talked about herself and it was so fucking good. Bea couldn't believe how good it was to talk about herself. She talked about restlessness and resentment, about Gavin and Simon and Magnus Chase. She went backwards and forwards. She talked about her cells in Petri dishes, her unborn baby. She talked about Granny Dil and cried a little. The woman tried to interject, but Bea held up her hand: no questions please, no *interpretation.* It was enough to speak out loud; to unravel herself. 'God forbid, Toots', Granny would have said, 'God forbid a *commentary*'. Like the Catholic confession Granny had described, and Bea found so fascinating. 'Why would you *admit* the sins?' she had asked. 'To receive forgiveness,' Granny said. Which seemed convenient when she didn't even believe in God. She only went because she fancied the priest.

On her second visit to the furry room, Bea told the woman about shooting her father with the arrow. An accident, not an act of evil, and anyway it didn't matter, she was a child. Bea felt a softening in her gut; a knot somewhere untied. She had an odd instinct to grab it back. The woman snuck in something profound then, while Bea paused for breath.

'Even things that are finished are rarely over.' Bea might have that on her gravestone.

She voiced the one confusion about parents that Sarah planted years ago. 'I still can't see why I chose them.'

The woman gave a slanted, penetrating reply. 'Or perhaps we choose what we see in people? What we take, and what we leave behind? In this way perhaps we *make* our parents – we make them who we see them as.'

Who's doing the talking? That was quite enough from her. Bea talked about her father walking in on her and Simon. Alarmingly, she described the scene in minute detail: the sudden light around Simon's shoulder at the opening door; her own gasping horror as she pushed him out of her; her father's face in shadow, sneering in disgust; her throat on fire with screams while everything crashed down around her, flattening her in shame. His face might have shown shock or outrage or fear? For her? At sixteen, Bea could only see herself. She couldn't know what it was to be a father, scanning for danger. He was only doing his job, however badly.

She felt mightily unburdened, fluffy like the rug. But by the end of the second hour, she had started to bore herself. She paid and thanked the woman and texted Sarah on her way home: *I did it. Enough for now.* Something had lifted, though that might not be the end of it. Could it be that those who come out fighting fight to the death? Bea hoped not.

In the loft room by the sea, Bea watches Lonnie lean back

in her chair, her hair flame-red in this light. It's easier to tell strangers the big stuff, but she wants to share this with her sister. It's what Lonnie deserves.

'Mum wrote me a letter,' Bea says, taking a gulp of wine.

'A *letter*?'

'She wrote it after your play.'

'Yeah, she had a funny turn after that,' Lonnie says. 'What did it say?'

'The arrow I fired at Dad could equally have been fired at Mum.'

'Really?' Lonnie knows the story, but her frown says she doesn't get it.

'It's what she meant. She said that she bottled things up. She said it kept her apart, and that she missed things at home when Dad lost his job. She likened him to the man in the play.'

If I had understood your dad better, things could have been better between the two of you.

Bea takes in her sister's pretty, trusting face, and considers the many things she should have said to Lonnie when she was younger. She sits up straight.

'*As far as possible, without surrender, be on good terms with all persons*. And also, *You are a child of the universe no less than the trees and the stars; you have a right to be here*.' She drains her glass.

Lonnie nods thoughtfully. 'Yep, that sounds like Mum.' This makes Bea smile.

'Actually, she said "Life goes on but so does death".'

'Wow,' Lonnie says quietly.

Bea quotes more of the letter. '"It goes on and on, especially if you are unable to talk or think about the people who died".' Bea leaves out the part about Granny Dil's role in this because there are two sides to everything. Or three, or four.

'Poor Mum,' Lonnie says. A faint gull cry comes from outside, over the ocean. 'Next time I'll take her to a comedy.'

'It was a sort of testimony,' Bea says. She knows the letter by heart. What had really surprised her was that Moira only told Ted about Eliza long after Dilys died. Bea knew about the dead baby years before her father. It was the wrong way round, and though the letter didn't say so, Bea was sure her mother felt the same.

'And it's lonely if your parents are in love,' Lonnie reminds her.

'Right,' Bea says, 'but we choose them anyway.'

'Do we?'

'Who knows,' Bea's reaching her limit. 'I'm better with biology than philosophy.'

'And did you write back?' Lonnie asks. 'To Mum?'

'I thought about it,' Bea says, in the understatement of the century.

'That's something,' Lonnie says, and Bea loves her then. What Bea had thought about most, dreamed about, was not Mum or Dad, but Granny Dil and Eliza. In her dream, they came to see Bea at university, the baby in a sling, Granny Dil with ballet slippers pirouetting the halls. She had wanted badly to write back to Mum and had started many letters (story of her life), but none of them had the right tone. Or any of the right words.

'I didn't know what to say,' she tells Lonnie. 'In the end, bit random, I sent Uncle David—'

'The mugs!' Lonnie flings out her arms and her empty glass goes flying. It lands with a small thump on the sofa, and they both gasp in surprise. 'The mugs!' Lonnie shrills again, 'Oh my god Bea, that was a stroke of genius! Mum was *literally* over the moon, I'm telling you.' She spreads both hands, for emphasis. 'She took me *round there.*'

'When? Why?'

'I was home for a brief visit. She took me round to Uncle David's, to have a cup of tea, *in the mugs.*' With a lot of hand movement, Lonnie tells her how Uncle David had taken them into the tiny kitchen to view the line of eight mugs, a fact David stated more than once. She describes the long discussion they had at the table about who would have which mug. Lonnie was given Eliza's, David drank out of Raymond's, Moira out of her own, and a second cup out of Granny Dil's. 'Because Uncle David said Mum is genuine, steadfast and true. Mum was a bit teary then,' Lonnie shakes her head, her smile full of warmth and incomprehension. 'They're such a couple of oddballs.' Her lips thin in concentration, recalling the scene for Bea. 'They went quiet for a moment, once the tea was poured, like they needed to leave some space for the others.' Bea leans closer, hanging on her sister's every word.

'Then what?' Bea wants to be there herself. She can see them at the table, and she can feel the joy and the desolation.

'That's it,' Lonnie says, 'we drank the tea.' She giggles and mimes the drinking, and Bea laughs with her, though she could just as easily cry. She looks around the table while it is vivid in her head: her mother, her sister, Uncle David, each cradling their mug. And she saves the memory in all its detail.

They pull their chairs back into the alcove and press their heads against the window. Thin white breakers peel in, one after the other.

It's a gusty afternoon in late October, exactly twenty-six years from the day Lonnie was born. She jumps up on the huge surfboard, knees bent, arms out, her red hair like a flag in the wind.

'Awesome!' says Terry, their surf instructor, in his shortie wetsuit, thighs wide as trunks. Bea's ready for a sit-down, and they're not even in the sea yet. The tide's out. It was a hike to get here, hefting one board between them while the instructor carried two. Wet, corrugated sand stretches like a desert as far as Bea can see. They're zipped into their wetsuits, booted and gloved: upright seals.

The water's alright up to Bea's thighs, then it hits like ice at her groin, and further in, it slices freezing daggers down her back. *Fuck*. Lonnie's next to her, biting hard on her bottom lip.

'A good time,' Lonnie shouts. 'What are we having?'

'A good time,' Bea squeaks, a hand on her board, pushing out into the sloshing, lumpy ocean. More icy daggers slice her back.

With furious arms, they paddle out. Bea's face is burning raw. Along with the pain and effort, there's something brilliantly familiar: freezing cold water, danger, freedom.

Out in the deep, again and again the waves lift and gently drop them. Bea's head is numb with cold, but the rest of her has warmed up.

'This one, THIS ONE!' Terry yells. Bea turns to face a great, rising shoulder of water. She grits her teeth and works her arms. Before she can attempt a jump up onto the board, she is rushed forward. She grips the sides with both hands and clings on, flat to the deck, spray and wind in her face, water up her nose, in her mouth. Hurtling towards the shore, she gets a flash of Lonnie's face, shocked and delighted, through the froth. Then they are pitched into the shallows. They lie there, stunned, coughing, laughing.

'Happy birthday,' Bea pants.

Lonnie's on her feet. 'Hang on. Is that *Dad*?'

'Oh my god.' Loping towards them across the sand is Ted, waving a gloved hand. He's got on a shortie wetsuit and boots. As he gets closer, his limp becomes more obvious, and his pale legs look too skinny under his thick black torso.

'Dad, you're mad,' Lonnie says. 'Here, take my board.' She pulls at the Velcro on her ankle, but he stops her.

'No way,' he says, 'I'm seventy-three. But I'll bloody well swim. They tell me with the salt and the suit it's a piece of cake.' He eyes the murky ocean behind them. 'I'll float. That'll do me.'

Bea watches his expression change. He might turn straight around and walk away. Quickly, she unstraps her board, pushes it onto the sand and takes his wrist in her mittened hand. They lock eyes for a second. A strong feeling of déjà vu ghosts through her: clutched wrists, lumpy sea, endless sky, resistance. Is he thinking the same?

'Come on,' she says and leads her father through the breakers while Lonnie heads back into the deep.

'I saw you two whizzing in,' Ted says, 'like a couple of speedy sharks. Good on you.' He nods nervously. Wisps of his grey hair dance around his head. The wind is getting up.

'Are you sure about this?' Bea says.

'I am.' He pulls away from her to walk, chin first, into the sea, already up to his shins. 'If Lonnie can be twenty-six, I can swim,' he says over his shoulder with perfect logic. 'Or float.'

He lets out a series of yelps as he goes deeper. He stops with the water up to his middle, hands on hips as though it was the Mediterranean, where he will never go. She stands beside him and shivers. The water has gone flat and quiet. The dark cliff over to their right seems closer now the sea is calm. Way out, a mile or three in the distance, a tanker inches its way along the horizon. A single gull flies low in front of them.

'Jeepers creepers,' Ted's arm goes up. 'I thought it was a plane.'

Bea scans his face. His determined stare morphs into doubt, then a shadow of fear. She can't think what to say. Her head, her ears burn with cold.

'It may be too late,' he says, shaking his head. Bea thinks of the letter: *I wonder where forgiveness comes in.*

'Never!' She pulls him two steps further out.

Ted rallies: he puffs out his chest and sets his jaw. 'Should I just lean back?'

'Try this.' She lies back and brings her legs up. Her black toes peek out of the water while she makes small circles with her arms. Her father goes to lean back and jerks upright with a wild flapping splash. He paws his face. They've been here before. Maybe his backflip gift for her wasn't for nothing after all.

'It gets me wondering which way's up,' he says. His teeth are chattering. He looks to the sky; he might be praying. He gives her a long look that says *Can I? Can* we?

'Mass per unit volume, Dad, the water density's got you.' A wave rises almost to Ted's chin and sloshes down. 'Don't close your eyes,' Bea says. 'You're only floating, not swimming to Wales. It's easy.' Again, she shows him. Then she stands in close. The sea slops around them, and she puts her gloved hand in the small of his back in the water and presses there. It could be Bea's imagination, but he seems close to tears. She thinks, When did you get old? A minute ago he was a warrior, then all doubt and fear, and now frail; many versions, all at once. Throughout her life, Bea has fixed on only one. *We make them who we see them as.*

Her hand is still in his back. She takes his arm in a tight grip and pushes him upwards from underneath. His torso rises and he tries to hold his head up. He's rigid and heavy, legs flicking. He shuts his eyes for a long moment and then opens them.

'Keep still, lean back,' she says. 'I've got you.'

Ted feels her hand in his back. In a minute he'll do it. Do what he's told. He lets her take his arm, and she squeezes. Then she half pushes, half pulls him up, and his feet leave the sand. He thrusts his head forward. Why can't he lean back? He'll only flap again – spiral into panic. He scrunches his eyes shut and behind his eyelids, people rush towards him: Moira at the dance in her pale blue dress; Andrew leaving for work in his new suit; joyful Tom in multicolour; Lonnie in his arms just born, with pink hair holding a hammer; Bea pointing an arrow, cowering in her room, hooting with laughter in the Fiesta, waiting for him on the diving board. When he opens his eyes and looks, her blue eyes are on him, willing, certain.

'I've got you,' she says. His daughter, who is so much like him and so much herself. He breathes out and rests his head on the freezing water. And it's the strangest thing: there's her hand underneath, the sea all around him. Then the hand is gone, and he is floating.

Bea takes her hand away. Her father's eyes are closed again. Not screwed shut; he looks peaceful. *See?* she could say, but she doesn't disturb him. She stays with his face for a moment, then leans back on the water next to him. An icy trickle crawls down her back, her ears fill up, her head is numb. She squints up into the bright cloud, then she closes her eyes and they float, side by side, weightless under the sky.

Desiderata

GO PLACIDLY amid the noise and the haste, and remember what peace there may be in silence. As far as possible, without surrender, be on good terms with all persons.

Speak your truth quietly and clearly; and listen to others, even to the dull and the ignorant; they too have their story.

Avoid loud and aggressive persons; they are vexatious to the spirit. If you compare yourself with others, you may become vain or bitter, for always there will be greater and lesser persons than yourself.

Enjoy your achievements as well as your plans. Keep interested in your career, however humble; it is a real possession in the changing fortunes of time.

Exercise caution in your business affairs, for the world is full of trickery. But let this not blind you to what virtue there is; many persons strive for high ideals, and everywhere life is full of heroism.

Be yourself. Especially do not feign affection. Neither be cynical about love; for in the face of all aridity and disenchantment, it is as perennial as the grass.

Take kindly the counsel of the years, gracefully surrendering the things of youth.

Nurture strength of spirit to shield you in sudden misfortune. But do not distress yourself with dark imaginings. Many fears are born of fatigue and loneliness.

Beyond a wholesome discipline, be gentle with yourself. You are a child of the universe no less than the trees and the stars; you have a right to be here.

And whether or not it is clear to you, no doubt the universe is unfolding as it should. Therefore be at peace with God, whatever you conceive Him to be. And whatever your labors and aspirations, in the noisy confusion of life, keep peace in your soul. With all its sham, drudgery and broken dreams, it is still a beautiful world. Be cheerful. Strive to be happy.

Max Ehrmann, 1927

Acknowledgements

Thanks to my mum, Angela, for a lifetime of support in my creative endeavours, and for the sporadic, always available boutique hotel accommodation during the writing of this book.

Thanks to Tricia Wastvedt, editor, advisor and chief cheerleader from the first draft onwards. And to Maeve Henry for all of the same. A pair of rare and generous gems.

Thanks to early readers: Mat Parry, Theo Cresser, Anna Raphael, Lizzie Minnion, Patrice Gladwin, Lucy Cory, Louise Mee, Willow Holland, Victoria Chalmers, Katharine Wilkinson, Eve Bates, Christina Shewell, Juliet Harrison, Ellie Price and Fiona Hamilton who met the Starlings first and gave them such a warm welcome.

Thanks to the authors who so kindly made time to read, and gave generous quotes: Liz Jensen, Jane Shemilt, Ken Elkes, Alice Jolly and Kylie Fitzpatrick.

Thanks to Joe Melia for the insider knowledge and support in the final straight.

Thanks to Kylie and Michael at Archetype for their love of books and care of this one, to Barbara Mellor for her laser eyes, and to Michael Phillips for the beautiful cover.

Thanks to Dr Lucy Cory for teaching me everything I know about cell research, and Willow Holland for the patient tutoring in GCSE biology.

Thanks to Sam and Luke for their humour, perspective and good company.

Thanks to Lizzie Minnion, longtime creative collaborator, whose golden belief, friendship and encouragement are an ongoing inspiration.

Thanks to Mat for pretty much everything else.

About the author

Sophie Holland is an award-winning writer of short stories, plays and youth theatre scripts. Her stories are published in two anthologies, and her plays have been performed in theatres in Bristol, Bath and Neath. She holds an MA in Creative Writing from Oxford Brookes University.

Sophie is also a speech and language therapist specialising in voice disorders, and a climate activist. She lives in Bristol with her family.

Peachy Wonderful is her first novel. It was shortlisted for the Caledonia Novel Award 2024.